STONE FORGED

Born in Derry, Northern Ireland, Peter J Merrigan was first published at the age of 17 in the Simon & Schuster anthology *Children of the Troubles*, edited by Laurel Holliday. His first novel was *The Camel Trail*.

Following a Bachelor of Arts in Writing and English from London, Peter spent nineteen years in England as a marketing and advertising professional before returning to his native town. He lives with his fiancé in Co. Tyrone.

Find Peter online at www.peterjmerrigan.co.uk

ALSO BY PETER J MERRIGAN

THE AILIGHWARS SAGA
Stone Heart

THE RIDER SERIES
Rider
Lynch

STANDALONE NOVELS
The Camel Trail

STONE FORGED

PETER J MERRIGAN

NIGHTSGALE

Nightsgale Books

1 3 5 7 9 10 8 6 4 2

Copyright © Peter J Merrigan, 2020

The right of Peter J Merrigan to be identified as the author of this Work
has been asserted by him in accordance with the Copyright, Designs
and Patents Act 1988

All rights reserved

First published in 2020 by
Nightsgale Books, Co. Tyrone, Northern Ireland

ISBN 978 1 9163838 0 7

Cover by Nightsgale Books

A CIP catalogue record of this book
is available from the British Library and the
Library of Trinity College Dublin

Typeset in Perpetua by Nightsgale Books

In memory of
SUSAN POWELL

Go raibh maith agat

Without you,
this book would not exist.

N

Thúr Rí

Northern Druids
(Doagh)

Grianán Ailigh

Knockdhu

¥ Uí Ultan Stronghold

Giant's Ring

Carrowmore

Emain Macha

Tomb of Maeve

Mac Dalaigh
Stronghold §

Ó Nallon
Stronghold

Cruachan

Castlestrange
Stone

Teamhair
(Hill of Tara)

Clonycavan

Poulnabrone

Baurnadomeeny

Ó Hargon
Stronghold

Ardgroom

Drombeg

¥ Áed's birthplace
§ Rónán's birthplace

ÉIRINN

|— 50 miles —|

Pronunciation Guide

Achall	*ackal*
Áed	*aid*
Aífe	*eefa*
Ailigh	*ay-lick*
Ailbe	*alba*
Cáer	*care*
Cormac	*cormack*
Emer	*eemer*
Ethal Anbuail	*ethal an-bwale*
Fionn	*finn*
Gallen	*gaylen*
Grainne	*grawnya*
Grianán	*greenan*
Mogh Roith	*mog roth*
Mordha	*mora*
Muirgel	*murg-ell*
Orlaith	*orla*
Rían	*reean*
Rónán	*rownan*
Seanach	*shaun-ack*
Senan	*shennon*
Teamhair	*ta-war* (modern day Tara)

Chapter 1

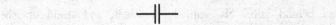

Orlaith screamed.

The snow at her feet was stained with fresh blood. She gripped her stomach with both hands, pressed her back against a cold tree, and closed her eyes to shield the glare of the early morning sun. Her soft leather shoes were soaked and heavy, and the hem of her brightly coloured dress dragged wet in the ice of midwinter.

She was dizzy, her head stuffed full of wool, and when she opened her eyes, her vision spun in disorienting spirals. Her stomach cramped.

Cormac, her sole companion, returned to her side and gripped her arm. 'They are close, I can hear them. We must hurry.'

'Leave me here to stain the earth with my life.'

Cormac spread his fingers over her swollen stomach. 'We have come too far for you to lie down and give yourself to the gods. If you are right, we are close now. One more ridge, maybe two.'

Orlaith shook her head and doubled over in pain. Through clenched teeth she said, 'One ridge; I cannot make it over two.'

In the south, behind them, they heard the soft footfalls of men trying to hide their whereabouts among the trees.

'You will make it,' Cormac whispered, 'or I will drag you across the earth by the ankles.'

With numb fingers, Orlaith slapped his shoulder. 'You have not the strength to snap a twig, let alone drag a pregnant woman behind you.' She smiled, breathed, and stood upright, ignoring the constricting pain in her stomach, ignoring the blood that seeped from her, a flow that had been steady since she woke this morning, high in the boughs of a tree where they had sought shelter from the coldness of the night and the spears of their enemy. For almost a month, they had zigzagged north from their home, aware of the angle of the sun to guide them, avoiding settlements as they journeyed through dense forests and expansive plains. The snow hindered their progress and revealed their journey where fresh snowfall did not hide their tracks. For part of their travels, Cormac had tied a log to his waist and dragged it behind them, churning over their footprints and slowing down the progress of their enemy. But it had slowed their own journey and they were weak with hunger. Their rations had run out two days ago.

Cormac gripped her elbow tighter. 'Come,' he said, and she nodded.

She allowed him to aid her, taking careful steps in the snow, unsure of what was hidden beneath—boggy puddles or tree roots—and they made slow progress until the trees gave way to a steep scarp in the land. It was too sharp to climb down, and in either direction they could see no shallow sections or gentle gradients.

Clinging to Cormac's hand, Orlaith looked over the edge at

the snow-dusted trees, her head still spinning, and she cried.

'We are lost.'

'We are not lost.'

'I do not remember this cliff before.' She looked skyward to seek out the sun. 'We got turned around.'

'We are not lost,' Cormac insisted. 'We're still travelling north. We need to get down there and keep going.'

'Would you care to jump, or shall I push you?' Orlaith said. She gripped her stomach again. She was so numb with the cold that she could not even tell if she continued to bleed. She had no idea if the child within her was alive or lost forever.

Cormac looked east and west along the scarp. 'There has to be a way down. This cliff has been here since the birth of the land, man must have carved steps in her face.'

Orlaith drew her fingers through her thick hair, pinning it back behind one ear, and wiped her tearstained cheek with the back of her hand. Her fingertips were red and tingling from the cold. 'They will find us if we stay here.'

Cormac looked behind them. The trees were dense, and the snow was thick. But their pursuers were close behind; they were always close behind.

The angle of the scarp curved northward in the west, and they could not see a visible indentation of steps or a cragged path to descend, and so Cormac pointed east. 'This way. We'll stick close to the trees and pray to all the gods for a sign.'

'It is not a sign we need,' Orlaith said, 'but a path or a ladder.'

He took her arm again and they turned east, walking along the treeline. They could hear nothing of their pursuers over the wail of the wind that drove along the ridge and sighed among the trees. Orlaith looked behind them. The small specks of blood that fell from the darkness within her dress were covered by the drifting snow as the wind churned in their wake. If they could avoid making any sound to alert the men who chased them, they might still survive.

The pain in her stomach had dulled to a whisper and she was convinced that her bleed was over. But if she no longer bled, she did not know if this was good or bad for the life of the child growing within her. She touched her stomach, fingers tracing the curve, and she prayed that the child should live, even if she herself should perish.

When an arrow penetrated the snow to her left, instinct made her crouch low. Cormac was already drawing his sword. The arrow was a warning shot, for the men that chased them had no intention of killing her. Cormac, however, was fair game.

She drew the dagger from her belt and looked over her shoulder. Seven men ran towards them, spears and swords raised.

Cormac pointed to the trees. 'Hide.'

Orlaith gripped her dagger and clenched her jaw. She did not move. She had killed before and she would do so again; for the sake of her child, she would kill one hundred men if the gods ordered her to.

Cormac raced forward. Had he not already burned his bow as firewood, half of the men would already be dead. As it was, he had his sword, fashioned from strong southern iron, and a small serrated hunting dagger at his waist, but no shield to protect them, nor arrows to volley overhead.

The men staggered towards them over the slick snow and

Orlaith watched as Cormac used his lithe body to his advantage, weaving alongside the closest warrior and cutting through the man's shoulder with his blade.

Cormac fell, rolled, and came back to his feet, dusted white with snow, and he double handed his sword through the leg of a second warrior before jumping upon him and plunging the iron blade into his chest.

Orlaith backed away. While six of the men turned their attention to Cormac, one raced towards her. She was the prize. She was the reason they had journeyed north away from the comforts of their homes.

But she had killed before.

And she would do so again.

She tightened her grip on the leather-wrapped handle of her small dagger, feeling the cross-guard warm against the coldness of her fist, and she raised her other hand in defence. The tall man that bore down on her sheathed his sword as he approached, for he did not fear the girl, and he reached out to grip her hair.

She let him. When he pulled on her and twisted her around, coming to his knees with a cracked smile that broke the stubble of his cheeks, Orlaith gripped the back of his neck and thrust forward with her blade. She was weak, but the blade entered his lower chest by a third of its length. The man held her wrist, stopping her from pushing deeper, and the smile dripped from his face.

'*Bitseach*,' he mouthed.

Orlaith, feeling a fresh wave of blood flooding from beneath her dress, clenched her stomach and smacked her forehead into the man's nose. He fell back from her, the dagger slipping from her grip, and she was quick to lie on top of him, reaching for the blade's handle and forcing it deeper inside him. In her anger, she twisted the small blade, her fingers slick with his blood, and she screamed.

He reached for her face, fingers struggling to take a grip of her hair.

Orlaith pressed harder, twisted further. The man's hand fell away from her and he twitched. And then he lay motionless beneath her weight.

She breathed, rolled off him, and pressed her fingers against the bloodied dress to stem the flow by sheer will. The sky was the same colour as the ground and all around her the trees danced at the edges of her vision.

She turned onto her side, reached for the dagger, and pulled it from the man's chest. She looked for Cormac but could see nothing as her vision blurred. She raised herself onto her hands and knees, but the earth tilted below her and she returned to her side.

Someone said her name, or some whispered approximation of it, and she felt a cold hand on her cheek. She reached out blindly, her dagger flashing bright in the sunlight, and she tried to back away even though she knew she was rooted to the frozen ground, unable to move, unable to see, unable to think.

'Easy,' Cormac said. 'It's me. You're fine.'

Orlaith let him raise her into his arms and she wept against his shoulder until her vision cleared. When the shiver of fear left and her breathing returned to normal, she looked around. He had killed them all.

'Are you hurt?'

Cormac touched his arm. 'A scratch. I'll survive.'

'We should burn them,' she said, though she had not meant it as an offering but as a means of warmth.

'The baby?' he asked.

'It wants to come,' she said. 'But I will not give birth in the snow like the ewe.'

They did not burn the bodies but instead they buried them in the snow in hopes of hiding all trace of their passage. There would be other men.

Cormac gathered some wood from among the trees and cleared a section of snow, lighting a fire at the cliff's edge, and they sheltered there for the afternoon. He rooted through the warriors' packs and found some meagre amounts of bread and cured meats, and Orlaith ate with greed for the first time in two days.

She moved away from Cormac to inspect herself. Blood caked her inner thighs but, for now, it had stopped. She soaked a cloth in the snow to cleanse her skin, and she wrapped a dry section of fabric between her legs. When she returned to the fire, Cormac had spread the warriors' furs on the ground, and he stood to help her sit.

'There is no way down,' Orlaith said, looking out towards the cliff's edge.

'We will find a way.'

'I do not think the child will survive another night.'

Cormac took her hand. 'You said yourself that we are close to Ailigh.'

'But we are lost.'

'We will find a way,' he said again.

Orlaith eased onto her back and Cormac draped a fur over her. 'Wake me when the snow has melted.'

7

'We must keep moving,' Cormac said, 'before another band of Rían's men finds us.'

Orlaith closed her eyes. She would throw herself from the scarp top sooner than allow Rían's men to drag her south to the most violent, angry man she had ever known.

She would throw herself from the scarp top—if she had the energy.

Chapter 2

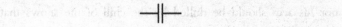

Rónán closed his eyes against the heat of the sweat hut as one of Ailigh's boys poured more water on the heated stones and left, closing the door behind him. He sat on a pile of furs on the floor with his legs crossed and his hands held loosely in his lap. The steam was cleansing, his pores sweating out the toils of a long day. He had been fighting his eastern borders for twelve nights, and only returned to Ailigh to attend to some other duties. No king was satisfied with his lot anymore. Since ascending to the kingseat two years ago, Rónán had spent his days training a new wave of boys at Grianán Ailigh, just as he had been trained some years before, and defending his borders against encroaching clans. It was a vicious cycle—the bigger his training camp grew, the more his neighbours wanted his lands.

The solidarity among clans during the Great Invasion was a distant memory. War brought a nation together, and now, two years later, kinships had drifted, and clans returned to petty squabbling, bickering and border disputes. Land ownership was at the forefront of daily life again, and the man you stood beside in battle two years ago would just as quickly gut you as look at you if it meant he could stretch his borderlines.

Rónán breathed in the hot air, held his breath, and exhaled

slow and deliberate. Sweat beaded on his upper lip and ran the curves of his brow, collecting at the corners of his blond eyelashes. He wiped his face and ladled more water on the stones, steam swelling to fill the dark room. His druid had insisted that he perform this body cleansing once a week, especially during the frozen months of winter when, as king, neither his mind nor his arm should be dulled by the chill of the snows that dragged itself down from the mountains on its annual pilgrimage to the lowlands.

The heated stones were arranged on a bed of herbs, and the smell that filled his nose was pungent and cloying, but it cleared his senses and woke his mind. He was uninjured in this most recent battle, but he had lost some good men, and each death stung him as though he himself had sustained those fatal blows. A clan of warriors was as strong as its numbers and each warrior had a role. To lose one man was to create a hole in his defences that could not easily be filled.

He breathed again, deep, through the nose. He should not be king; he had never wanted to be king. But the invasion came and the Ó Mordha tribesmen had lost three good kings in quick succession. And now here he was, leading an army of warriors and boys when he was little more than a boy himself. He longed for his childhood to return, nights spent on the shore of the lough with Áed and a couple of wineskins, getting drunk and swimming naked under a midnight sky.

He shook his head, sweat-drenched hair whipping his cheeks. Áed was gone. Everyone was gone. But though he had lost so much, he had gained enough that kept him from tethering a horse to a carbad and disappearing into the forests beyond his walls. His druid, strong and loyal, had kept her word to her dying brother and stayed at Rónán's side. Their kinship was solid, and she continued to teach him many things. His army was growing—when they returned from Knockdhu two years ago, he had marched home to Ailigh with less than two hundred men. They set out the year before with over one thousand.

Now, he commanded four hundred men and boys who pledged themselves to his name from neighbouring tribes before the apathy set in. And when Imbolc arrived, marking the first day of spring, more boys would come to Ailigh to train under the great Rónán Ó Mordha, overking of the north, who—legend had it—singlehandedly drove the invading Fir Bolg from their lands. Neighbouring clans sought to impinge his borders, but they knew there was no finer fighting force in the north than the Ó Mordha warriors.

Sweat ran the length of his back and collected on the furs beneath him. He flexed his neck and inhaled the caustic scent that filled the room. He closed his eyes again to allow the silence to envelop him, and in the quiet darkness, he felt a breath of cold air brush his left shoulder.

He leapt forward and rolled to the right, alert, reaching for the sword he had propped against the far wall when he came in, but the man was upon him, hands grasping at his shoulders. Rónán slipped from the man's grip, his skin slick with sweat, and he turned and kicked out with his heel. The man in the shadows blocked the blow and rolled aside.

Rónán scrambled back, hooked his foot under one of the fur rugs and flipped it into the air towards the man. But the weight of his attacker fell on him. Pinned to the ground, Rónán squirmed and freed one arm enough that he could grip the man's hair. He pulled and twisted, brought a knee up to his

11

groin, and his attacker clambered back in pain.

Rónán struggled to his knees but the man was relentless, baring down on him again, his arms wrapping around Rónán's neck. Rónán twisted under his attacker and he pitched the tall man over his shoulder. But he refused to let go and Rónán's body went with him, turning on the ground. He landed with his back on top of his assailant who choked him, the man's breath close to his ear.

'You're dead.'

Rónán slapped Fionn's arm. 'Enough. How long were you hiding in the shadows?'

Fionn released him and they sat apart from one another. 'They were still heating the stones when I came in.'

'And you thought now was a good time to practice, when I am wet with sweat and naked?'

'A real attacker,' Fionn said, 'would not wait to let you dress. Besides, the songs say you are fond of fighting with your pride on display.'

'You promised never to mention those songs in my presence,' Rónán said. He reached for a linen cloth to wipe his face and he stood. 'Come, I need a drink.'

'You need sleep. If I can beat you in a sweat hut, a man half my size would beat you in a barrel hut.'

Fionn had been Rónán's tanist since their return from Knockdhu. When the war was done and he had rebuilt the Ó Mordha tribe back to its glory, Rónán's wife, Achall, insisted that he name their son as tanist, Rónán's heir. But the boy was not truly his and, as much as he loved the child, no baby could be named a tanist. Until he was of age, Fionn would hold the honour of being the king's heir and he would hand off his duties when the child was old enough. Fionn was a few years older than Rónán and he commanded the Ó Mordha army, training the boys daily in the arts of battle, in defensive and offensive tactics. He had grown up with the other boys at Ailigh and was brave and dependable, his impressive height matched by none. When King Áed had died from his wounds at the Battle of Knockdhu and Rónán was appointed ruler of the Ó Mordha, Fionn was the only man he could trust. And for the last two years, his commander had sought to better him in surprise attack, honing both their skills in single combat. 'A king,' Fionn had said, 'must be conscious of attack not just on the field.'

They left the sweat hut and Rónán plunged himself into a cold spring well outside the hut to cool his skin. He dried, dressed, and joined Fionn in the barrel hut for a drink where they discussed the borderland battle and raised a cup to their fallen men. The war continued without him, and in two nights he would return to the frontline. A king, though he is forged in war, is the product of many campaigns. The younger boys who had not accompanied him into battle, boys who would be singing and cheering and fighting among themselves, were sombre and subdued when Rónán returned to Ailigh and informed them that many had died, but the war was not yet won. One boy played a cruit in the corner, and the melancholy notes draped over the room with gentle unease.

There was no singing, no shouting, just the quiet contemplation that followed a day of battle. On the frontline, his men would be sleeping in shifts and with the dawn they would defend their borders from their neighbours again.

Rónán had not seen his wife since his return from the eastern border. He had met with his druid, and then called for the

13

sweat hut to be heated. He would face her questions when he retired to their quarters within the inner wall but would drink himself stupid beforehand.

He lifted his cup and recited the names of the dead.

When the gate bell clanged an urgent call, every man and boy in the barrel hut rose to his feet. Rónán was quick to the door, racing around the second rampart and out to the third.

The guard atop the outer palisade hailed him as Fionn and some of the other men ran towards the gate. 'A man carries another towards us,' the guard shouted.

'Are they alone?' Rónán asked, his hand on the hilt of his sword.

It was dark out and the moon was shrouded in thick, black clouds. Shadows clung to the blackness. 'I can see no others,' the guard said.

Rónán nodded at Fionn, and with the help of several others, they opened the heavy gate.

The man outside shouted for help and fell to his knees.

Vigilant of attack, for the *sidhe* and chieftains alike are wont to trick you, Rónán stepped outside his walls and approached the man.

'She bleeds, my lord.'

'She is injured?'

'It's the baby,' the man said. He leaned forward and lay his companion on the frozen ground.

Rónán saw a dark spread of blood across the front of her dress. He looked at her face, eyelids fluttering, and then at her swollen belly. He stooped, scooped her up in his arms, and carried her inside the walls as Fionn came to the young man's side and helped him to his feet.

Conscious of the amount of blood loss that soaked his arms, Rónán ran through the outer rampart as others came out of their huts. The staggered entrances through each palisade wall was a hindrance not only to would-be attackers but to the life of the woman he now carried.

'Wake the druid,' he shouted. 'Somebody wake my druid.'

By the time he got to the inner wall, the only one built of stone, Grainne was waiting for him by her door. 'She bleeds from the baby,' Rónán said, hurrying through the door and looking around for somewhere to rest her.

Grainne cleared a table and Rónán stretched her out on it. Behind him, the young man who brought her said, 'Save her, please, my lord.'

Rónán stepped back to allow Grainne some room. 'I need hot water and linens. And furs—plenty of furs. How long has she been bleeding?' She turned to her shelf of herbs and when nobody answered her, she asked again, 'How long?'

'Since sunrise,' the young man said. 'Please, Lady, save her.'

The door to Grainne's quarters opened and Achall entered. 'Husband?' she asked.

Rónán looked at her but he had no words.

The woman on the table twitched and convulsed. Grainne came to her side. 'Help me hold her steady,' she said.

Rónán gripped the woman's shoulders and made a soft noise close to her ear.

'Please,' the man said. 'Save her.'

'Husband, what is—'

'Out,' Grainne shouted. 'Everybody out.'

'What is the meaning of this?' Achall asked.

Rónán turned to her and spread his arms. 'Let's give Grainne some space.'

As they were leaving, Grainne muttered, 'No. Rónán, come quick.'

He closed the door, leaving the others outside, and came back to Grainne's side.

Grainne was mixing some herbs and liquids in a bronze bowl. 'Slap her face,' she said.

'What?'

'I need her awake. Slap her.'

Rónán looked at the woman whose eyes continued to twitch even though her body had stopped. Her dark hair hung in strings around her face and fresh blood spread across her dress. Rónán raised a hand. 'How hard?'

'Hard enough to wake her.'

He slapped the woman's face, leaving a red mark on her cheek, but she did not wake.

Grainne finished mixing her concoction and pinched some between a thumb and finger, and she spread the mixture on the woman's upper lip. She moaned.

With a thick iron blade, the druid cut open the woman's dress and exposed her.

Rónán looked away from the mess of blood. 'I shouldn't be here.'

'Stay where you are,' Grainne said. 'I need you to wrap your arms under hers and hold her back. This is not going to be pleasant.' She took off her robe, a sleeveless dress underneath, and she washed her hands and forearms as far as her elbows.

She felt for the form of the child across the woman's stomach. It was not in the position that it should be. She kneaded the skin before washing the blood from the woman's thighs.

'Hold her tight,' Grainne said, 'and whatever happens, don't let go.'

When her fingers disappeared inside the darkness of matted blood, the woman woke and screamed and thrashed. Rónán linked his fingers together around her chest and held her against him.

Grainne returned to the water bowl and cleansed her hands as the woman cried. 'Are you ready to push?'

'I can't.' The woman's voice was weak and gritty.

'You can and you will.'

Rónán closed his eyes. No man should be present at a birthing. It was unheard of and would upset the gods.

The woman gripped her stomach and screamed.

'That's it,' Grainne said. 'You can do it.'

Rónán turned his head. The stench of fresh blood and faeces accosted him.

'Again. Push.'

In the stillness that followed, Rónán opened his eyes. The woman panted with exhaustion, and Grainne was quiet. He looked at the table where a tiny child lay between the woman's legs, unmoving and blue.

Grainne carried the boy to the bowl of warmed water, cleaning his face with her fingers as she moved. She thrust his still body into the water and withdrew him quickly. He made no movement, uttered no cry.

The woman on the table sobbed and Rónán stared at his druid. 'What are you doing?'

'Waking his soul.'

She plunged the small body back into the water and held him up. She was about to do it a third time when the baby gave a

17

faint gurgling cry. 'A fur,' she said.

Rónán released his grip on the woman, easing her down onto the tabletop, and fetched a deerskin fur from the corner of the room. Grainne wrapped the child in it and said, 'He is marked.'

'Marked?'

Grainne handed the child to Rónán so that she could return to the woman's side. Rónán looked down at the boy and, in the candlelight, he could see a red birthmark spread from forehead, over nose and cheek, and down under his neck to his chest. With such a mark, the boy would never hold a position of power or importance beyond farmer.

The afterbirth was quick to come, and Grainne sat it aside for later divination. She cleaned the woman and covered her in furs.

'She is well?' Rónán asked.

'I cannot be certain. I will bathe them both in a brooklime solution, but there is no telling until morning if they will live.'

Rónán cradled the child to keep it warm and he looked at the woman who slept on the table. 'She is familiar to me.'

'You know her?'

'I have seen her, I am sure. But I cannot recall.' He stepped closer as Grainne mixed her brooklime solution at the opposite table. He studied the woman's face, the curve of her lip, the angle of her jaw. And he smiled. 'Orlaith.'

Grainne came to his side and took the child from him. 'You should leave now. When I have bathed them, they will need rest.'

Rónán nodded. 'The boy's mark—will it harm him?'

As she unwrapped the child, he saw that the red mark

stretched across his chest and under his left arm.

'Not physically,' Grainne said. 'But it is an omen, all the same.'

Rónán left her to her healing, and he went back out into the night. He found his wife and the young man sitting on a log seat. She had a comforting hand on his back. They stood when he approached.

'You have a son,' Rónán said. 'My druid is doing everything she can to keep them well.'

The young man smiled and clasped Rónán's arm. 'They are healthy?'

'They are weak, but I pray that they will be fine.'

Achall hugged the young man. 'I congratulate your sister on her birthing.'

'Sister?' Rónán asked.

'Forgive me, Lord,' the man said. 'I am not the child's father. My sister begged that we come to you, for she said you were the only king who would welcome her.'

'You are both welcome,' the king said. 'I am Rónán Ó Mordha.'

'Cormac,' the young man said, and he bowed low.

'You know who she is?' Achall asked her husband. Rónán could hear the venom in her voice.

'I do. And they are welcome as long as they wish to stay.' He watched his wife walk away and then he turned back to Cormac. 'You will forgive my wife; she and Orlaith have a history.'

'When she told me that she knew the overking of the north I did not believe her.'

'She came here many years ago, at the same time as my wife

and many other girls,' Rónán said. 'She had the strongest will I have ever seen.'

'She still does.'

'Come, I will house you for the night and we can talk in the morning. Are you hungry?'

'I think I am too tired to eat, my lord.'

Rónán led him back through the rampart and down to the next level. 'Why would you travel with your sister in such a condition?'

'You have heard of King Rían in the south?'

'The bastard king who took advantage of the aftermath of war to conquer his neighbouring clans and rule the south?'

'He is the father,' Cormac said. 'He has three wives and ten daughters and not a single son. He sleeps with whomever he can to secure an heir, bastard-child or not, but so far the gods do not reward him.'

'Until now,' Rónán said.

'The boy is truly healthy?'

'He is marked from the birth across his face, but otherwise I trust that he is fine. Such a mark would spare him as an heir.'

'If Rían knows of it, he would have him drowned. Orlaith, too.'

'He will not come to my gates or he would leave without his head.'

'I cannot repay your kindness,' Cormac said.

'You have brought Orlaith back to Ailigh. Consider us even.'

'Rían has already sent men after us to drag Orlaith back to the south. Their bodies dot the land of our passage.'

'If I know Orlaith,' Rónán laughed, 'you did not kill them singlehandedly.'

20

'Despite the size of her belly,' Cormac said, 'I am sure she killed more than I did.'

Rónán stopped outside a small *brú*—a simple thatched home—and pushed the door open. The firepit was lit, for fires were always lit, and the warmth that breathed out from inside cured the chill that Rónán did not realise he felt. 'You may stay as long as you please,' he said, 'and tomorrow I will honour your arrival with a feast.' It was customary to celebrate respected guests and, with everyone else from his childhood gone, Rónán was pleased to honour Orlaith and her brother.

'My lord,' Cormac said, 'with King Rían swallowing up the south, we have no home to return to. I would offer my services to your land or to your army if you would have it.'

Rónán appraised him. Cormac was a similar age to him, but tall and strong. 'To survive the winter snows with a pregnant girl and a king's army at your back, you are good with a sword, I imagine.'

'I am better with the bow,' Cormac said, 'though I had to burn it for firewood when we were cold.'

'I am a fletcher by trade. Speak to the bowyer in the morning, he will see you provided with a bow and you can show me your worth. I am always in need of good archers even if the bow is no longer favoured. We are in the midst of a border dispute in the east. When I return to the frontline in two days you can join me.'

Chapter 3

Grainne watched the woman and child through the night and during the following days. She had stemmed the bleeding, and both mother and baby were comfortable. Orlaith would need to rest another day or two, and she would continue to be tender for a time, but Grainne was confident she would recover well. She burnt the placenta and read the omens in its remains, but the boy's future was unclear. He would live, at least.

The child had cried through the night, weak murmurs that strengthened after he suckled from his mother. The red skin that covered half of his face, neck and chest was worrisome only in terms of the omens it foretold. His physical health, Grainne assured Orlaith, would not suffer, though his station in later life would never be a ranking one as the blemish would be seen as a mark of angry spirits. He may not be considered an outcast, but no man would bow to him as a chieftain.

She was loath to leave the woman's side, but her duties as king's druid were demanding. Ruler of the outlying septs and the clans that resided there, Rónán had a responsibility to his people beyond his own walls, and where a sept did not have its own druid—in the two years since the Battle of Knockdhu, few had joined their ranks, preferring instead to train with the sword—Grainne would make regular visits to those septs to administer medicine and justice where it was needed. Hers was the responsibility of both flesh and soul.

She had risen through the organised structure of druidry with a swiftness far beyond any other, graduating from acolyte when she was still a child among her seasoned fellows. But although the archdruid had decreed her fit to assume the role of druid, Grainne knew she had much to learn.

The winter sun was warming itself ever slowly towards spring, and the first signs of the annual thaw were present in the music of the melting snow that trickled from tree branches and swirled in gullies. She turned a carbad westward and journeyed a short distance to one of the outlying clans, a small collection of homes gathered among farming fields, with a forest of tall birch trees bordering its northern and western regions. She brought remedies that would treat the ailments of the elderly, and some of Achall's baked breads, although the winter hardships were coming to an end.

She was greeted by the people with warmth, for her smile was gifted to her by the gods themselves, and she would stay a day or more when she visited, to sit and eat with them and share stories.

The sick and lame would form a queue, under a covered stall erected for her benefit, and she would treat them throughout the afternoon. She had smiles for the children and she drank from the same vials to prove to them that, though her tinctures were foul-smelling, they were not harmful.

One of the clanswomen presented to her a child of no more than two winters. The girl was flushed and crying, her cheeks swollen. Grainne inspected her mouth and throat and assured the mother that it was nothing more than painful teething. She mixed some dried flowers with water and made it into a paste.

'Rub it on her gums at dawn and evening. Two days and the pain will cease.' She tousled the young girl's hair and waved her goodbye.

A young man was next, fifteen winters old. He showed to her his swollen finger. 'It is both numb and painful at once,' he said.

She had treated him before, most recently for a broken rib when he had fallen from a tree last summer. Tarrin, son of Concobhar, who had perished during the Battle of Knockdhu, had been too young to attend war when it came, but at its end he found himself the man of the family.

Grainne turned his hand over to inspect the finger from all angles. It was swollen to twice the width of his other fingers. 'You work with wood?'

'Daily,' Tarrin said.

'You are infected from a splinter. Did you try to remove it?'

'I removed it four nights ago with my teeth.'

'You did not get it all, it seems. See here—this dark spot on the skin?' She drew her dagger and heated it over a flame.

'Do not take my finger, Lady Druid, I beg you.'

'Do not squirm and I shall try not to.' When the blade was heated and sterile, she held his hand on the table and with great care she worked the deep splinter free. His eyes watered but he clenched his jaw and did not moan. She cleansed the finger and wrapped it, then gave him a small vial of cloudy liquid that would help with the swelling.

'I would have you wed me,' he said, and Grainne laughed.

'Present me with your bride and I will wed the pair of you.'

24

His smile was wide and toothy. 'That is not what I meant, Lady.'

'I know it,' she said. 'Be gone before I splinter your arse.' As he left, she heard his laughter echo into the distance.

When the queue of ailments had dwindled, and Grainne was packing up her items, she noticed an elderly man sitting on a rock with his back to the central fire. He was stooped and thin, his silver hair wispy as the winter grasses. She knew him well.

Walking to him and sitting by his side, she said, 'Ruairi, are you well?'

The old man turned his milky eyes towards the sound of her voice. 'I knew you would come to me when you could.' He raised a hand and she took it in comfort.

'May I inspect you?'

'There is no change, Lady,' Ruairi said. His voice was old and cracked like his vision. 'I see blurs and the blurs trip me.'

Grainne held his cheeks in her hands and with her thumbs she extended the loose and wrinkled skin around his eyes. The blue-white spots over his pupils had grown since she last inspected him and none of her salves were working to reduce them. In time, he would be blind.

'My daughter sits me here by the fire in the mornings and leads me to bed in the nights. Before my vision failed me, I was a cowherd; did I tell you that?'

'Tell me again,' she said as she fished a vial from her robes and shook it.

'I would fight any man who would attempt a cattle raid, with a sword in each hand and the cows at my back.'

'Tilt your head back for me, please, Ruairi.'

He talked while she drizzled two drops of yellow liquid into each eye, and when he was done blinking, he smiled. 'Every time you do this, I believe that I will see well in the morning but, when morning comes, I am as blind as before.'

She touched his shoulder. 'All I can do is slow the deterioration, I'm afraid. Are you getting exercise?'

'I cannot walk alone without tripping over rocks and children. And my daughter is too busy to lead me around all day like a goat on the end of a string. She has a husband and a child; I do not blame her for sitting me by the fire. Here, I am out of harm's path.'

Grainne raised a hand before him and held up two fingers. 'What can you see?'

His smile was forlorn, crooked. 'I expect it is your hand, but it is just a blur.'

She stood and reached for his arm. 'Come. I'd like to try something.'

Ruairi brushed her away. 'You do not need to fuss for an old man, Lady Druid. I am happy to warm my back by the fire and wait for the gods to come for me.'

'You are not so old that the gods would want you yet,' she said. 'Come. Stand.'

She helped him to his feet, steadying him as he groaned and straightened his back.

'Tarrin,' she called to the young man whose splinter she had extracted. 'Fetch me a branch the height of a man. Thin but sturdy.' She watched as he ran towards the trees and then she returned her attention to Ruairi. 'Do you see that I am in front of you?' she asked.

'You are as beautiful as my wife was before she died,' he said, and his laughter became a cough.

'You blind yourself by lying.' She took a step back. 'Do you see me still?'

'A blur, but I see you.'

Another step. 'And now?' He nodded. 'Look to the ground. What lies between us? Is it stones or grass?'

'I cannot tell.'

When Tarrin returned with a long branch from a birch tree, Grainne stripped it of stray twigs and put it into the old man's hand.

'Poke the ground with it. Is it grass or stone?'

'If I cannot see, how can I tell?'

'Poke the ground. You will know.'

Ruairi stabbed the earth before his feet.

'Not so hard,' Grainne said. 'Gentle, as if you are testing the waters of a heated bath.' She watched him prod with less force. 'Is it grass or stone?'

'Grass.'

'Step towards me.' His movement was tentative, but when he slid a foot forward and brought the rear foot in line, Grainne took another step backwards. 'Again. Test the ground. Is it obstructed?'

Ruairi poked the earth and took another step. With his third, he was smiling.

'Again,' Grainne said, but this time she put her own foot forward, his branch prodding her boot.

'An obstacle,' Ruairi said. His voice was high and energetic.

'So, you must move around it.'

He poked either side of her foot and selected his path, his steps small and uncertain, but he was no longer sitting idle by the fire. Ruairi laughed. He moved the branch again. 'Another obstacle.'

Grainne looked for the stone that he had touched, but saw a blackbird, dead under his branch. 'Be careful,' she said. A thud from behind drew her attention and she saw another bird fall from the sky.

She looked up. Cloud cover had rolled in from the south though the sky was not full of rain. And from among the clouds, another bird fell to the earth.

Grainne ran to Ruairi and took his arm. 'You can practice later. We must get inside.'

'What happens?' he asked.

A fourth bird fell beside them, followed by a fifth. The people of the sept took to the great hall and huddled by the doorway. Grainne watched the sky as a flock of birds dropped one after another to the ground. She counted almost sixty dead birds by the time they had ceased to fall.

With hesitant steps, she ventured into the open, keeping her eyes on the sky for a second wave. She prodded one of the birds with her boot and as it turned over, its wings flapped wide, loose, lifeless.

The others waited by the hall, clustering under the overhanging thatch, and watched her in silence.

Grainne crouched to examine the bird. There were no wounds, no bleeding. Its glassy eyes stared at her with reproach. She could not fathom how a flock of birds could fall from the sky without cause.

A wind stirred the bird's feathers.

Grainne looked around her. Across the field, the grasses were dotted with dead blackbirds. Two had fallen into the central fire and the smoke rising from it was thick and dark.

The wind moved her hair.

She turned to the northern trees. Between their silver boles, the wind wept like the dead. A whisper of the ancients filled her ear and the hem of her robes trembled at her ankles.

She squinted against the wind.

The weeping of the boughs became a quiet scream, deep from within the forest, wailing through the naked branches.

Grainne turned in a circle. A host of voices cried to her on the wind. It was a battle cry, the flapping of the dead bird's wings at her feet in the gust a drum beat to accompany the warriors' wails.

The hissing of the wind droned on around her, whipping at her robes and stinging her eyes.

The people backed through the entrance of the great hall and into safety.

Tarrin was the only one to run towards her. 'What is happening?' he asked, staring down at the array of dead birds.

'An omen,' she said. 'The second in as many days.'

On the wind, the dead birds rose and fell, the movement terrifying the boy.

'Do you hear that?' she asked him.

'We must get inside,' he shouted, tugging at her sleeve.

She nodded, but as she turned, the wind blew her back. She fell to the ground, a bird at either side of her head, black eyes staring at her.

He helped her to her feet and, as she rose, she picked up one of the birds with the long sleeve of her robe. They ran to safety within the hall, and when the door was closed against the howling winds, she dropped the bird on a table, and she breathed.

'What killed it?' someone asked.

'I cannot say. I need light.' A candle was brought to her and she turned the bird over. There was no outward indication that it had suffered any untoward fate. When they are not preyed upon, blackbirds have a lifespan of three or four years, but it isn't possible for an entire flock to die of natural causes. She could not say if this creature was dead in the air or died on landing, but either way it had no life. She flexed the bird's wings, inspecting its beak and curled feet. 'Whatever occurred, it came from within the birds. There is no external reason for their fall.'

The gathered crowd backed away as if a sickness were emanating from the winged animal.

Outside, the wind had died to a whisper, but she heard it still, sighing through the trees, crying out to her in pain.

She reached for the small leather pouch at her hip and cast the blackened bones from within it onto the table.

Ruairi stepped forward with his walking-branch until the tip touched a stool. 'What keeps you quiet, Lady Druid?'

She looked at him. 'I must leave.' She scooped up the bones and returned them to her pouch, wrapping the bird in the folds of her robes.

The omens were bad. And many would die.

Chapter 4

Rónán hitched a horse to his carbad and kissed his wife and child goodbye. The forty men he had returned to Ailigh with two days before marched behind him. Cormac, Orlaith's brother, rode in Rónán's carbad with him. Their eastern border was a half day's journey.

Alongside the carbad, Fionn rode on horseback. Riding atop a horse did not come naturally to Rónán's people, but the Fir Bolg invasion had shown them its advantages. Until Rónán sought to train his horses to carry the weight of a man, they were used solely for pulling carbads and carts, or carrying packs. It had been a long process getting to the point where his horses were confident with a human on their backs, one that was still being tweaked and perfected. And Fionn, lacking finesse, was one of his most assured riders, though he declared daily that he would rather stand on firm ground than sit atop a wilful mount.

Cormac watched Fionn riding and said to Rónán, 'Is he well up there?'

Rónán laughed. 'Fionn rides our biggest horse, and it wasn't easy to find one for him. He's a head-and-a-half taller than me. On an average gelding, his feet would drag on the ground.'

'And even from this great height,' Fionn said, 'I could still reach out and kick you.'

'He would, too,' Rónán said. 'If there's anyone at Grianán Ailigh you do not want to cross, it's Fearless Fionn.'

Cormac bowed to the rider, steadying himself against the carbad wall. 'I assume calling you Fearless Fionn would award me the swiftest kick imaginable.'

'My lord teases you, Cormac. I am nothing more than a puppy.'

'A puppy in the body of a giant,' Rónán said.

Their journey east was uneventful, and when they arrived at the camp by mid-afternoon, they could see that the battle was apace in the valley far below. The din of war came on the wind.

Rónán maintained his position on the carbad and his driver crouched, ready to ride. 'Join the ranks,' he said to Cormac, 'and when this is won, we will drink to the birth of your nephew.' A cluster of spears were brought to him in the carbad and Rónán looked for the horn blower. He signalled and the boy raised his carnyx, a long, upright horn with a head carved into the shape of a boar, and he blew three piercing notes.

Rónán and his men charged down the hillside into battle.

From the back of his carbad, he hefted a spear and as the driver pulled the horse left, Rónán released and picked up another. He learned that a spear would take its course even if you do not watch it. So long as you follow through with your arm and your aim was good, you do not need to see it hit its mark; throwing another at the enemy is more important than precision.

Arrows could not be used because both of the armies were enmeshed on the field, and his spears were aimed at the closer enemies, those he knew he could hit without harming his own men.

The carbad drove across the field and he threw his missiles until the floor of the carbad was empty. He lifted his shield and drew the sword that Áed gave him years before. Tarnished and cleaned of blood many times during his kingship, it had served him well.

'About,' he shouted, and the driver tugged on the reins, turning the horse rearward. Rónán raised his sword and jumped from the back. He was swinging even as he landed.

By nightfall, when the fighting ceased, Rónán's men had gained ground. He stationed guards along the expanded perimeter and retired to his tent with his advisors. 'Cormac, as my guest, please join me. A fresh pair of eyes may be helpful.'

In the tent, Rónán, Cormac, Fionn and two others sat on furs on the ground; the tent was too small for chairs. His cumal, a young slave girl, poured wine and they raised a cup for their dead. They had lost three men today, a small figure in terms of war, but less than they lost on previous days. Their names were recited, and more wine was poured.

Speaking as if he was a member of Rónán's counsel, Cormac said, 'This king we face—who is he?'

Fionn said, 'A guest should not speak at a king's meeting.' He was stating a fact with no malice in his voice.

Rónán shook his head. 'Inside this tent, we are all equals. Cormac is here at my request. He may speak.'

Cormac bowed. 'Forgive me, my lord, I do not know the ways of kings.'

'We'll say no more about it. As to your question, he is the chieftain-king, Senan Mac Fachtna. He has ruled over the lands in the east for twenty years. He was at the Battle of Knockdhu two years ago. I did not fight alongside him, but his men were there, and they were a strong support against the invaders. Since then, we have had relative peace, But Senan grew bored of his lands and seeks to widen his borders.'

'But we will not let him,' Fionn said.

'What are his weaknesses?'

'You're a tactician?' Fionn asked.

'I am not, but I have seen men negotiate terms enough to know that all men have a price.'

'Fine wines and finer women,' Rónán said. 'But in this instance, Mac Fachtna cannot be bought. In his bid to extend his borders, he will do all he can to win.'

'Then to stop him,' Cormac said, 'there is only one course of action.'

'Yes. Death.'

'Can he be championed against?'

'We have tried that. Many times, in the early days of our campaign, I challenged him to single combat.'

Fionn scoffed. 'But he dares not go up against the Bare-Arsed Warrior for fear that the last vision he sees before his head is cleaved is my lord's little lord.'

The men laughed, but Rónán was quick to hush them.

'That name is banned in my presence. And when I find the bard who bestowed me with such a moniker, I will string him up by his own bare arse.' He raised his cup for the cumal to pour fresh wine. 'We did well today. Tomorrow, we must do better. If we can kill Mac Fachtna and his chief warriors, the others, I would hope, should fall in line.'

'Forgive me, my lord,' Cormac said, 'but as I pointed out, I do not know the ways of kings—you would not kill them all and assume kingship over their lands?'

'It is a fair question. I do not doubt that many other kings would do so, but my borders are ample, and my men are plenty. I do not need the responsibility of additional territories. Mac Fachtna must be removed from the field, but among his ranks I would hope there is one man who can take his role as chieftain and agree to mutual terms that benefits both parties.'

'And if there is not?'

Fionn laughed. 'He asks a lot of questions, my lord. I have decided I like him.'

Rónán looked from one to the other, and then he smiled. 'If Fearless Fionn approves of you, you must be an impressive man indeed.'

Cormac lowered his head in a simple nod. 'I strive every moment to win his approval, my lord.'

Fionn scrunched his face. 'Does he mock me?'

Laughing, Rónán said, 'Yes, Fionn, I believe he does.'

In the morning, the war efforts were renewed. Rónán offered a speech to his men, but he was inexperienced at rousing discourse and, although his men cheered, he felt his words fell short of their intent. They drove onto the field to meet their neighbours in combat.

From the back of his carbad, hurling spears, Rónán kept his gaze across the valley, seeking out his opponent. Senan Mac Fachtna did not fight at the fore of his army as many kings did, preferring instead to pick off those who had broken through his ranks, cleaving them like a coward. If any of his men could replace him, it would be one of these on the frontline—if Rónán's men did not kill them all first.

With his spears depleted, he shouted, 'About,' and his driver turned the carbad. With shield up and sword raised, Rónán took to the frozen ground. As his feet slipped on bloodstained snow, he hoped that Imbolc and the warmer months would come soon. This far north, the colder months often lasted longer than anyone cared for.

He blocked a thrust from one of Mac Fachtna's men and jabbed with his own sword. The man fell at his feet.

The fighting continued for another two days, but they were gaining ground, pushing their neighbours back towards the original borderlines. Disputes over land were common, but most did not require weeks of fighting. Often, they were quarrels between lesser chieftains who had fewer men and smaller land parcels. An agreement between each chieftain's druid was often enough to cease the infraction. But when an angry chieftain-king who commanded five hundred men wants to expand his borders, not even the druids could appease him. He was out for war, and Rónán brought it to him.

He challenged Senan Mac Fachtna again, and the chieftain-king refused him. Rónán did not make the challenge in the hopes of facing his neighbour in combat, but each time he offered, Mac Fachtna's men would see that their chieftain-king was not a man of honour. It was Rónán's hope that, when Mac Fachtna was killed, the fighting would cease and the man's successor could be appointed, and a new alliance established between them.

In the evenings, Rónán retired to his tent with his advisors and with Cormac, and together they planned their advance. Since his time fighting on the hills outside Knockdhu, Rónán's war tactics had changed. Two years ago, he was in a rage; he had lost his love and he could see no option than to charge the field and cut down any man who stood in his way. He killed his old chieftain, Donal, and the man's son, Faolán, who were responsible for the death of Rónán's father. He spared his chieftain's wife, marking her cheek with his blade so that she would remember him forever. He slaughtered as many foreign invaders as he could, seeing nothing more than the blood that clouded his vision.

Now he knew not to storm the field in an embittered rage. In the last two years, he had developed a box-formation technique where his army would split into six units, three in the front, three in the rear, in a staggered formation. As they drove into the enemy, the units separated, and large swathes of the opposing army were engulfed. He had found it a masterful way of killing his rivals in short order and unravelling the opposing army's structure.

Many tribes of Éirinn did not fight with rigid formation, preferring to storm the field and swing their swords at whomever was near. Rónán's tactics were gaining recognition across the land. It was for this reason, in part, that the chieftains under his command would continue to send their boys to Ailigh each Imbolc for training. Unlike King Deaglán who was overking of Ailigh when Rónán came to its walls, Rónán stated that the boys training under his banner would return home to their fathers and their chieftains when their training was complete. When they were adept at the sword and spear and bow, when he could teach them nothing new, they would be sent home as warriors to protect their lands. His only stipulation was that, when he called, they would come.

On the third day of battle, they took to the field again. They had driven the neighbouring army back across the valley and now they were fighting uphill. If Senan Mac Fachtna fought at the front of his army like a normal chieftain-king, he would have been slaughtered by now. Rónán dove into the fray and killed those closest to him. He could feel his thighs and calves burning as he struggled up the hillside in the churned and slushed snow.

He gripped his sword with a firm hand and recalled the words that his lover had often told him—that the sword was not an item in his grip, but an extension of his arm. He could feel Áed's presence beside him as he stormed forward. They had grown up together and, despite his ruler's insistence that he marry the chieftain's niece, Rónán and Áed had formed a kinship that would not be broken, even in death.

Áed, on his deathbed at Knockdhu, had insisted that Rónán end his life in a warrior's death. He was wounded in the gut from their rival and his wounds were too severe to be cured. He would bleed out in the night if Rónán did not give him the warrior's end. He did not want to perform the act—every moment together was precious—but Áed begged him, and Rónán knew it was the right thing to do. No warrior should die a slow and agonising death; with the end inevitable, it was Rónán's honour to send his companion to Tír na nÓg, the Land of the Young, the warrior's paradise.

It did not make the act any easier, but it stilled his conscience in the days that followed.

In the two years since, Rónán had spoken to Áed's spirit almost daily. Grainne, his druid and Áed's sister, assured him that, even though he does not respond, the gods would pass his words on to his fallen companion. She could sense that Áed was at peace in the halls of the gods. And she knew that he watched over them.

Rónán turned and killed another of Mac Fachtna's men, driving his sword deep into the man's chest, holding it for a moment, and then withdrawing it. The man fell.

He was close to Mac Fachtna now; he could smell the man's fear.

He was not the only one of his men to reach the top of the hill. As he reconnoitred the hillside, he could see that two of his units had advanced close enough that they could turn on their heels and fight back down the hill at an advantage, slaughtering those men who were now behind them.

Rónán sought out the wily shape of Senan Mac Fachtna. He found him at the back as if he was ready to flee. Rónán cut down another of his enemy and ran. Though his feet slipped on the snow and ice, he moved with enough force that he was able to maintain his balance. Once, he dropped to his knees and slid between two enemy warriors, his sword outstretched, cutting one man's leg before turning and driving the sword into the second man's side.

He rose to his feet and continued onward.

Mac Fachtna was close.

Rónán ducked low, swung his sword, and cleaved the arm from another of his enemy, then he barrelled into Mac Fachtna and they fell to the ground. The man did not see him coming from the left.

Rónán raised his arm and brought the wooden shield down on the man's chest. He rolled, gripped Mac Fachtna, and wrapped his arm around his face, bringing his blade to the chieftain-king's neck.

'It is over,' Rónán said. He dragged the blade across soft flesh.

A king on the battlefield needs his spotter, a boy who, too young to fight, stands apart from the field and keeps his king in sight. A by-product of his job is to tally the king's kills so that they can be recorded in story and song, but his main purpose is to alert the carnyx-blower when the opposing army's commander has been slaughtered.

Rónán heard the horns blaring from across the field—one long note repeated three times. It signalled to both armies that a chieftain had been killed. The warriors would only know which side won if they could ascertain from which camp the carnyx blew.

The battle was not done, for most armies continue even when their king is dead, but by the time the sun was at its zenith, Rónán's army had established order on the field and the opposing tribe retreated back behind their original borders.

The overking stationed a team of men the length of the eastern border and they drove new stakes into the ground, painted in the blood of the fallen.

He called for his men to retrieve their dead from the field and looked for Fionn to ensure he lived. When he found him, he saw that Cormac was with him. They were splattered in blood, much as he was, but they were unharmed.

Rónán embraced Fionn, as he would after every day of battle, and offered his arm to Cormac. Cormac clasped him and Rónán said, 'I am pleased to see you alive and well. Orlaith would gut me from throat to groin if I had returned without you.'

Cormac said, 'I am strong enough to look after myself, my

lord.'

'And I am glad of it.' Rónán turned to Fionn. 'Count the dead. I would hear their names before we cremate and bury them.'

'What of the army we chased from your hills?' Cormac asked. 'You would not appoint a new chieftain for them?'

'It was my wish to do so, but they have scurried like rats. They will convene their own meetings after they lick their wounds. When they have appointed a new chieftain, I will be informed. Until then, I will leave a contingent of men behind at the border to ensure they do not encroach again. Come; let us prepare for the funeral rites of our fallen.'

'Without a druid?'

'Grainne has instructed me in the rites. It is not ideal, but it will suffice.'

Forty-seven pyres were lit that evening and the names of the dead were recited. Although one torch lit all the pyres, forty-seven torches were then lit, one from each pyre as it burned, and they would be kept alight throughout the night and remained so on their journey home. When they arrived at Ailigh, each torch would be added to the central fire so that the flames of the fallen would smoke the skies above Ailigh's walls and the spirits of the dead would be remembered.

Rónán knelt and bowed his head to the cold ground before each pyre. He said the words that Grainne taught him, and then he added Áed's mantra, the sentiment that he had carved in runes into each of his blades—into the west, the war is won.

Chapter 5

The Fir Bolg slave, Bromaid, son of Gamid, son of Terrid, who could trace his lineage back to Eochaid the Great, blew warm air into his cupped hands and picked up the shovel again. His fingers were red from the winter cold and the thick fur cloak on his back was not enough to keep the chill at bay.

He stomped his feet on the ice. Movement was key; if he kept moving, he could keep warm. He scooped a layer of snow onto the shovel and hefted it towards the bank at the side of the path. To keep his teeth from chattering, he sang a song of his homeland, a dirge of reminiscence. A song for the sun. Éirinn, for more than half of the year, was devoid of sunlight, or at least the warmth that the sun of his homeland would present to the grasses of his fields. Éirinn's gods must hate her hills and her mountaintops.

It was a rugged landscape they had come to, more so than his homeland. If you were to crest the highest crag in view, you would see, beyond it, a taller mountain. But it was a green land. He had not believed the tales of his chieftains and his bards. The grasses, they would say, were so green that you could roll in them and its rich colour would transfer to your skin and never fade.

But that green did not last. In the colder months—which outweighed the warmer months by twice its number—Éirinn was white, first by frost, then by snow, then by fog. Only then would the green return.

Bromaid looked down the hillside on which he stood. There was a lough below him, though you would not see it for the ice that coated it. If he rolled himself down the hillside, gathering enough speed of force, he would break through that ice and drown. Daily, he contemplated throwing himself down the hill. And then he continued about his day.

The colourful words on his frozen lips ceased when he heard the farmer call to him. He cursed the old man, driving the shovel into the snow, and went to him.

'My lord?' he enquired, facing the stout man who stood at the entrance of his home with his daughter beside him. The girl was in tears and cradled her arm.

The farmer spoke with a loud and slow diction. Their languages were similar, and both could understand the other. Bromaid knew it was nothing more than an insult.

'You have set bones before,' the farmer said. 'The girl has slipped on the ice and twisted her wrist. You will fix it.'

Bromaid bowed, as a slave is required to do. 'With your permission, I will fetch a druid.'

'No druid will climb that hillside in all this snow. Set her arm and send her to bed.'

When the old man disappeared inside his home, the girl looked up at Bromaid with frightened eyes. It was not the first time they had been alone, and Bromaid knew she did not like it.

He beckoned her to follow him to his hut. 'I will be gentle

this time.' He heard the crunch of her leather shoes as she gave in to her reluctance.

In his hut, he gathered small twigs that had been drying for firewood, and he drew a length of twine from a reel. He kicked a stool. 'Sit.'

The girl stood by the door.

'Do you want my help or don't you?'

She sat, hiding her wounded wrist under an armpit, her arm tight across her small breasts. When Bromaid reached for her forearm, she shook her head. He grabbed again and she turned from him.

Bromaid gripped her arm and pulled it towards him. When the girl screamed, he spat on the ground and ignored her. The wrist was not broken. When he prodded the bones underneath the skin, she winced but did not faint as girls often do. He had no formal instruction in the healing of bones save what he had learned on the battlefield. A warrior should always know how to patch up his wounds so that he can continue to fight; if you are not fighting, you are not a warrior.

Bromaid, for the last two years, had been fighting his own battle.

He held her hand straight, told her to make a fist, and strapped his makeshift splints to either side, knotting the twine as tightly as he could. When he was done, she tried to stand, but Bromaid drew her back into the stool with a powerful hand.

Ailbe, with her long blonde hair and her slender neck, was fourteen winters old. The farmer's only child, she helped work the fields at certain periods throughout the year—spring and autumn harvests—and the rest of the time she spent with her mother at the hearth or picking fruits and berries and weaving fabrics into clothing.

The first time he took her to his bed, not half a year since being sold to the farmer, he did so not because he wanted her, but because he wanted the mother and could not have her. Ailbe was his consolation.

He was already aroused when he reached his hand under the folds of her dress.

It was always quick, for it was not a common occurrence, and when a man misses something, his excitement outweighs his interest. Bromaid picked her up in his arms, lowered her to his thin, straw-filled mattress, and came down on top of her. He buried his nose in the crook of her neck and inhaled the fresh scent of her skin. When he climaxed, he cried the names of all his gods against her. He lay there, breathing heavy, and then rolled from her, telling her to wipe her face of the tears she had shed.

'Remember our deal,' he told her as she stood and straightened her dress. 'One word to anybody, and I will slit your *mamaí* and your *daidí's* throats,' he said in her dialect.

She ran from his hut and he sighed. He should get back to shovelling the snow from the path that separated the farmer's home from his fields before the old man took it upon himself to offer a beating.

Bromaid was warm in the afterglow of sex. And that warmth would stay with him for the rest of the day. The girl would say nothing. His threat to her was always the same—she valued her parents' lives over her own. That Bromaid was not chained up or tethered had been an unusual concept to him. He was free to run if he so desired. But where would he go? The golden colour of his skin and the murky brown of his eyes would give him away as a foreigner, a member of the invasion, and he would be killed if found without a master.

They came to Éirinn for a better life, to take back what was rightfully theirs. King Eochaid had ruled these wintery lands in the distant past before his peoples were driven from the hills and onto ships that carried them away. They returned to Hellas where the legend of his people began and, two years ago, they set sail for Éirinn once more.

Though Bromaid was just a warrior among warriors, without the ear of his king, he knew the invasion to be a costly affair. They did not count on the indigenous people being brave or united. Their lore told them that Éirinn's tribes squabbled among themselves, and so the invading Fir Bolg anticipated small battles against small clans. That they encountered, instead, a united front both north and south, was their true downfall.

It occurred to Bromaid, the day that he was captured and enslaved, that it would have been preferable to fall on his own sword than spend the rest of his days ploughing frozen grounds and shovelling snow so that his master could walk unhindered.

But the girl kept him warm when he saw fit to take her, and he dreamed of the mother, and of eventual escape.

For the next twelve nights, feigning an interest in the girl's injury, he raped her almost daily. And then he poured wine for the father and the mother as they ate, and he smiled at them and asked them of their health. He was a dutiful slave, strong of back, and when he was not being beaten for breaking tools, they treated him as they would any slave, even of local origin.

'One day,' the mother said, 'when the chill of our night

fades the colour from your skin, you might pass as a normal man.'

Bromaid bowed to her, and that evening he wrapped his fingers around Ailbe's slender throat while he raped her, waiting until her eyes flickered beneath the lids before releasing his grip on her.

By the time the snows had begun to melt and the upcoming Imbolc celebration was all that anyone could talk about, the farmer tasked Bromaid with hitching a horse to his carbad and driving the wife and the daughter down to the sept where they could barter for the religious paraphernalia that was required for their ceremonies.

Such an excursion, without the farmer's presence, was an infrequent occurrence. When leaving the farm on official duties, Bromaid was given a leather collar to wear, into which had been emblazoned the farmer's mark. It was a property tag, in much the same way as farmers tag their cattle. It was locked at the back and tight enough that if he tried to cut the leather, he could cut his own skin.

The late winter sun was pathetic and pale, but the heat of the woman and the girl in the small carbad beside him was enough to ward off the chill.

He sang for them a song of his people. That they did not understand the words of his elder dialect was a blessing. The song spoke of King Eochaid's slaughter at the hands of the Morrígan.

At the tribe's main sept, where the majority of the clansmen lived, those that did not have outlying farms to keep, Bromaid tethered the horse at the entrance and took a seat under a tall oak around which was erected a wooden bench. Here, the Fir Bolg slaves would throw dice and exchange news as they waited

47

for their masters.

The tribe's king, Ailill, was a short man, shorter than most, and compensated for his stature by glazing his red hair high above him. Their tribal lands were close enough to Teamhair, the seat of the high king, that he was often called upon for the Ard Rí's functions, and his druid would take command of local matters in his absence.

It was this same druid, a tall man who walked with a hunch so as to lessen the difference in height between him and his king, that had been heard by one of the slaves to worry for a war brewing in the south.

'How far south?' Bromaid asked his Fir Bolg brother, under the deep shade of the tree.

The man shrugged and tugged at his leather collar as though it had been fastened too tight. 'Close enough to concern the druid.'

'These people fight among themselves more often than they wash their tunics. Why should this battle concern him?'

'It's not the war itself that concerns him,' the slave said. 'It's how it is being fought. A southern king raids tribe-lands and is said to free our peoples. They join his ranks and fight beside him.'

Bromaid spat on the snow at his feet. 'None of our kin would side with a native in war. They'd sooner slit his throat and dump his body for the birds.'

'If he promises freedom, I would polish his sword for him.'

Bromaid shook his head. 'Is it freedom when one master rescues you from another, only to enslave you in his own army?'

'You may think differently when he gets here. The whispers say he marches on the seat of the high king, and in order to get

48

there, he must come through here.'

They shook hands in the way of their kind.

'At the very least,' the man said, 'it would be better to die in somebody else's war than live out our days in a cold and empty bed.'

Bromaid curled his lips in a grin. 'You need a farmer's daughter to warm your loins.'

He drove the carbad home when the farmer's wife and her daughter were finished with their bartering. When he had brushed the horse, he asked the mistress if Ailbe would help him fetch some firewood; the sky was clear and the night was sure to be a cold one, they would need as much firewood as could be carried.

Ailbe followed him into the trees with her head held low and her arms folded across her body like a shield.

Chapter 6

Orlaith inhaled the scent of her baby, her hand supporting the back of his delicate head. His face, pink and smooth, had lost the blue sheen of starvation. He would be healthy, the druid had told her, so long as he suckled often and slept much. It seemed all he did was sleep. She worried about the boy's birthmark, the red blemish that tainted half of his face and all of his future, but the druid assured her that the mark would not interfere with his health. Orlaith had wept for him for the first three nights of his life, but her tears ran dry as she forgot about his future and fell in love with his presence. She did not know she could love something with such wholeness, his father be damned.

She put him to her breast every moment that she could, but her nipples were sore and swollen, and there were times that he would not take from her. She would coax his lips with her fingertip and when he wanted it, he would take to her for long moments in which she enjoyed the stillness of time. When a child drinks from his mother's milk, the world ceases to be relevant. The sun could fall to the earth and she would not care so long as she held him to her breast, and he drank of her spirit.

When he was not feeding, she swaddled him tight and lay

him on the furs of her bed, staring at him and singing gentle songs to him while he slept. She longed to carry him down to the beautiful lough at the bottom of the hill on the west, where Rónán told her that he had erected a stone in Áed's honour, but the insides of her womanhood were tender still and it made walking difficult for extended periods. If she strained herself, she could bleed again, the druid told her.

If he was awake and refused to suckle from her, she walked him the length of the room and back, rocking him in her arms, unwilling to lay him down for she needed the closeness of his touch. As a grown man, she would still hold and rock him and sing to him. And on her death bed, he would pick her up and rock her like she did to him since his birth. This is what she desired. This is what a mother needed.

Her brother came to her often throughout the days since his return from the border war, and he told her of Rónán's offer to retain him in his services. She clasped Cormac's hand, smiling, and told him that perhaps they had at last found a home.

'I had a home until my chieftain-king bedded you,' he laughed, and she punched his chest.

She did not mind that he took so well to life at Ailigh; she knew that he would. Perhaps, in time, she could think of living here herself. For now, she watched her baby and she kissed his head. And that was enough. She held him and she walked the breadth of the small room and she thought of Áed. Rónán told her of his passing and she had closed her eyes against the tears that she knew would fall. That he had been king before Rónán, if only briefly, was a blessing. She could see in Rónán the desire to change the subject, but she could not help questioning him about the boy who had grown to be a ruler and died in battle against a foreign king. She missed him almost as much as did Rónán. They had met when he was still a child, and she was the first to learn his secret—that his love for Rónán was stronger than any love deserved to be. She knew of his passing, of course—the songs that spoke of Áed the Executioner's heroic deeds travelled far—but to hear Rónán speak the words aloud brought with it a sadness that numbed her. She would miss him for the rest of her nights.

A week after her arrival and her difficult childbirth, when her strength was returning to her in small tides, she ate the cheeses that Rónán's wife brought to her and they sat in silence for a time. Achall held the child in one arm and her own son in the other, not far off two winters old, and neither woman was prepared to mention the past that they shared among Ailigh's walls when Orlaith was seventeen and Achall was a churlish girl. The younger was offered as a bride to a boy-warrior who, at the time, had no interest in her or the kingship. And now he suffered both.

'You have named him?' Achall said when the silence grew too long.

'I have not. And your son?'

'His father named him Áed.'

Orlaith closed her eyes and nodded. To Rónán, there would have been no other choice.

Achall stood and handed the unnamed baby back to his mother. 'I would like to visit with you again, to see that the child is well.'

Orlaith nodded. She could not be rude to the king's wife, despite their history. 'You may.' But she would not say she liked the idea or would encourage it.

When Achall was gone, Orlaith stood and tightened the muscles of her stomach to test them. There came a small rumble of pain, but it was not unbearable. She wrapped herself and her baby in a fur, and she opened the door to the outside world. She could smell the end of winter, but it compared nothing to the smell of the child whose face she nuzzled under her cheek.

She passed through the gate of the thick stone wall and stood among the bustle of a stronghold in preparation for the festival of winter's end when the days would brighten, and the air would grow warm, and fat bees would flit from one brightly coloured flower to another. This inner rampart was filled with the homes and stores of King Rónán's closest advisors, the inner stone wall behind her encasing only his family quarters and those of the druid.

In the years before, she had visited these homes, looking for a warm bed for the night when she left Áed's side to find company. She had not wished to leave his shy conversations, but a girl who does not perform the king's orders was not a girl who would remain for long, and King Déaglán, at the time, would not be spoken against.

Orlaith smiled at some of the young men she saw now, recognising none of them, and with a slow and shuffling step, she circled around to the gate, climbing down the side of the slope to the middle rampart, careful of the clumping snow. Here were the kitchens and the great hall where she had first met young Áed. They had shared a cup of wine before he tried to walk away from her, but she followed him, as her king had bidden her.

She kissed her son and smiled at the memory. Áed had no

interest in her as a woman, she learned that first evening under the stars, down by the lough; his heart was owed to another.

Orlaith leaned against a post, her strength wavering, and she inhaled the scent of her son again that it might nourish her.

She had vowed never to tell Áed's story to another soul, and to this day, she kept that promise. She loved him even then, knowing that he would never want her. But she would slap his face and joke with him, and she thought that he, too, had loved her, if only just a little. If only as a sister.

She walked again, the baby asleep in her arms, the furs pinned tight around them.

On the outer rampart, she found the long hut that Áed had shared with ten or twelve other boys. She stood at the doorway and stared into the darkness beyond. She knew where his bed would have been, Rónán's bed beside it, and she smiled.

She had seen in Rónán's eyes that he loved Áed too, both then and now. If they had made each other happy in life, she would be happy. That he was wed to Achall and was with family was fitting for a king, but she could tell he no more desired it than Orlaith would.

She had walked too far, and her stomach cramped. Orlaith tightened her lips and breathed short intakes of air through her nose until the nausea waned. She held the baby in firm arms and stood still while boys ran around her. Mattresses were being carried in and out of huts to accommodate the new boys who would arrive with the Imbolc.

She tested her movement, feet shuffling with little steps, and then she felt a supportive hand on her arm. She looked up, expecting to see Cormac, but was faced with a man she did not recognise.

'It is Orlaith, I am told,' he said. When she smiled at him, he added, 'You do not remember me.'

'Should I?'

The tall man laughed. 'I am Fionn.'

She squinted at him. 'You cannot possibly be Fionn. When last I was here, Fionn was a skinny stoat of a child, hardly taller than a blade of grass.'

'I have grown.'

'I can see.' She embraced him. In those days before the Battle of Knockdhu, Fionn had sought to bed her, but she rejected him. She could remember little else about him other than he was small and slight of frame.

Fionn pulled back from their embrace and he drew the furs away from the baby's face to inspect him. 'Tell me you are nursing another woman's child,' he said. That he did not mention the angry red splotch on the boy's face impressed her.

She laughed. 'I have made this one myself.' And then she gripped her stomach and closed her eyes.

'You are in pain? Let me help you.' He took her elbow.

'I can manage alone,' she said, but she did not shrug his hand away.

When they reached the inner wall, Fionn said, 'Can I sit with you a while?'

'You do not have the king's business to attend to?'

'He worries about the coming celebrations; he will not miss me for a time.'

She allowed him to enter her quarters and she lay the baby on the bed, kissing his soft, warm head. She folded the fur that she had wrapped herself in, and then she eased herself into a chair.

Fionn brought her a cup of water and she drank it with greed. It cooled her stomach. 'You survived the war, then.'

'I am made of stronger stuff than many. And you—you have a brother, it seems. I was not aware.'

'No one ever asked me of my family life when I was here, Fionn. I was little more than a bed mistress to you boys.'

'Never to me.'

'No.'

'Do you—?' he nodded towards the bed.

'I do not,' Orlaith laughed, holding her stomach. 'You can slice it off with a blade and throw it in the ocean for all I care.'

'Ouch.'

'Nothing personal. The last one gave me a surprise,' she said, indicating her child, 'and I am not ready for another.'

Fionn stood. 'You should come to the hall later, see how some of the boys have grown up.'

'And why should I want to see a bunch of ugly faces?'

'There'll be drinking. And dancing. I remember how you loved to dance.'

'I can still move my body when I need to, Fionn. But for now, I must nurse my child.'

'I could stay,' he said, watching her with intent.

She pressed a hand to the neck of her dress. 'You will do no such thing. Be gone. You're not too big for a smack.'

He laughed and left her alone.

She slept well that night, buried under an abundance of furs, the child close in a cot beside her. She stared at his tiny face until sleep took her and, when she woke, she stared at him again, marvelling at his little chest rising and falling with life. He fed from her and then she bathed him with a damp cloth dipped in warmed water. The stump of the life-cord at his belly was blackening and dry. The druid had assured her it would detach itself before long and she would use it in an offering to the gods, giving thanks for new life.

When Achall came to her door that day, she knocked and entered with food for her to eat. Orlaith allowed the king's wife to cradle her child, and she sat opposite, staring at the flames of the fire. It had not been too many years since they last met, and although Orlaith thought that she had not changed at all, she could see that Achall was now a woman.

'Do I differ in appearance?' she asked Achall.

Achall looked up from the baby who had been suckling on her knuckle, and she studied her. 'Thinner, perhaps. Your hair is longer.'

Orlaith brushed her hair behind her ear. 'I do not appear older?'

Achall returned her attention to the baby. 'We are all older, I fear.'

Orlaith smiled. 'Who would have thought, some years back, that you and I would be sitting here now, each with a child?' Achall had come without young Áed today, no doubt in the arms of a cumal who cared for him when his mother was too busy being queen.

Achall rocked the baby and made clucking noises.

'He must look to be nursed,' Orlaith said, standing and smoothing the front of her dress.

Achall swept her nose across the baby's. 'He is fine for a moment, aren't you my little one?'

Orlaith sat. She watched the fire again for a short time, and then she said, 'Why do you sit with me?' When Achall looked at her, she asked again, 'Why have you come?'

'You have just had a child. I would see that you are both well.'

'As girls, you could not stand to look at me. Have you changed your opinion?'

'I have not. But you are a guest and while you reside in my home, I have a duty to ensure you are well.' She stood.

'It is a duty, then,' Orlaith said. She took the baby from the king's wife.

'I am honour-bound to care for my king's people and those whom he is burdened to protect.'

Orlaith laughed, cold and swift. She bowed low, her stomach cramping. 'I do not wish to be a burden on you, Lady.'

Achall straightened her back. 'I will bring food to you later, and some extra furs for the child, if you could stand it.'

'I would be grateful.'

When Achall left, Orlaith rolled her eyes. She could not turn the king's wife away without causing upset but living in such proximity to the childish woman who had delusions of majesty would not be easy.

Chapter 7

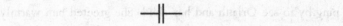

Rónán spent the morning after his return from the border dispute in consultation with his druid, Grainne.

'A flock of birds dropped from the sky just like this one,' she said, pointing at the dead blackbird she had carried home with her from the outlying sept. Its dull eyes no longer shone, and its slick feathers were motionless as it lay on its back on the table.

'And there is no apparent reason for it?'

She shook her head. 'It is not ravaged by disease, but they may have ingested something. I will not know until I cut it open. One or two dead birds could be explained in several ways, but a flock—it is an omen for certain.'

'A second omen,' Rónán said, looking at, but refusing to get too close to, the bird on Grainne's table.

'Yes,' Grainne said. 'First, Orlaith's child is marked. And now this.'

'You think they are linked?'

Grainne wrapped the bird in a length of fabric. 'All omens are linked. One begets another until their meaning becomes clear.'

'Have we angered the gods?'

'I fear it is more complex than that,' Grainne said. 'I will inspect the blackbird's innards. Let us hope they ingested a poison that we can trace. If the gods struck down a flock of birds because we angered them, we will have bigger issues at hand.'

'Keep me informed.' Rónán left her private quarters, stopping by to see Orlaith and her child. She greeted him warmly and when he asked if he could hold the baby, she agreed to it.

Rónán cradled the boy in his arms. 'I forgot how small they are at first.'

'They don't feel so small when they are ripping themselves from your body,' Orlaith laughed.

Rónán shook his head. 'I will never understand a woman who goes through such pains as childbirth, and then willingly has another.'

'You would understand it if the gods had warranted man worthy enough of birthing their own children.'

Letting the child's fingers curl around his thumb, Rónán said, 'Man would never be worthy of such a feat. We care too much about food to offer a part of our stomach up for another.'

'You should ask your druid to instruct you on the intricacies of the female body.'

Rónán laughed. 'You know I have no interest.'

'And yet you have a child. I did not ever imagine it possible.'

Rónán sat on a stool by the hearth and rocked the baby. He had hoped, in the weeks since the child's birth, that the red mark upon his face would fade, but he dared not say it aloud. He stared at the yellow flames. 'You know I have loved only one.'

Orlaith sat beside him and touched his knee with her fingers.

'I know you cannot love your wife the way you ought to, but you must feel that parental bliss from your son.'

He looked at her, a lack of expression on his face, his eyes, blue as ice water, sad and lonely.

'Oh,' she said, understanding the unspoken words in his look. 'Forgive me, I was not aware the child was not yours.'

'No one knows. And that is how it should be.'

'The father?' she asked.

'Died at Knockdhu.'

Orlaith nodded her head and patted his leg. 'He is the son of a king now. Fostering is traditional. And I am sure you love him.'

'I do,' he said. 'I treat him as my own. But sometimes, at night, when I catch him staring at me with wide eyes, I am certain that he knows I am not his father.'

'He is two winters old. He stares because he is intrigued by life, not for any other reason.'

'How long have you been channelling the druids' ways in your speech?' he asked.

Orlaith smiled. 'I am living in a druid's home; I am bound to ingest some knowledge.'

Rónán stood, the fire crackling between them. 'When Grainne tells me that you are well enough, I will have you moved to a home of your own, or if you wish it, you may bunk with Cormac.'

'Cormac needs his space and should not have his sister under foot.' She took the baby back from her king.

'I will arrange it,' he told her. 'Have you named him yet?'

He watched as Orlaith cradled the child and stroked his cheek. 'There is no name worthy,' she said.

'I would suggest that Rónán is a powerful name.'

She slapped his shoulder, as only a close friend could do to a king. 'I forgot how modest you are.'

He bowed to her with a flourish.

That evening, Ailigh feasted in honour of their fallen. The names of those who died on the battlefield in their border dispute were spoken so that the gods would know them, and Grainne sang her songs of fallen warriors.

With a wineskin in hand, Rónán walked down the dark hillside to the lough. He poured a drop of wine against Áed's standing stone and sat facing the gloomy waters. The tide was on its way out and he could see, from the light of the moon, the footprints of boys in a tangled mess from where they had played in the water's edge. Perhaps those footprints had been there for years, Áed's strong feet mingled among them. Perhaps, in spirit, Áed walked the shoreline at dusk when no one could see him.

Rónán tipped his head back and tried to count the uncountable stars. They stretched from horizon to horizon and he knew that Grainne could name each of them. Her instruments would track their alignments and, more than that, she could divine wisdoms from them that no other might.

The ancient stone monuments that shrouded the landscapes as if the earth had grown teeth—planted there by the *sidhe* in centuries past, or so the stories told—were not just gathering points for ceremonies, but they held all the secrets of time. Each one had a purpose, facing sunward on some specific day so that the dawn or the dusk would flood the land among them. Even this solitary stone that was erected in honour of Áed was positioned so that, if you stood just so, the dawn sun would dazzle the top of it on the day that his fallen friend had died. It was his annual reminder, a souvenir of times past. And each year, on that morning, he would stand on the shore, facing the stone with his feet in the water, and when the sun crested the standing stone, he would kneel and bow his head to the earth and smile with his memories intact. And the shadow of Áed the Executioner's standing stone would caress his skin, and Rónán splashed its base with fresh water so that Áed's feet would be cooled in the Otherworld where he dined with the gods and the legends who had gone before him.

As a child, in anger at the death of his father, he had called out the gods as false, and Áed stilled him and begged him not to say it was so. Now he prayed that all the gods were real so that he would know, with certainty, that Áed resided among them.

That Áed's sister served him as druid was a constant reminder of his loss, but he was grateful for her presence in his life so that he could look upon her face and see a strong resemblance of Áed.

She came to him often in those first days after the Battle of Knockdhu. He did not reveal how inconsolable he was, but Grainne could see it in his eyes. She did not speak of her brother unless Rónán mentioned him first, and Rónán was glad for it. Having her there was enough, and they were not just master and druid, but friends ready to lay down their lives for one another. He trusted her more than he trusted himself. And so, when she told him that the omens were bad, he believed her.

He spent two years rebuilding the Ó Mordha army without incident and, now, he was certain that Grainne's omens were directed at him. He had done something, or failed to do something, that angered the gods. There was no other explanation.

He drank from the wineskin and considered it. He was at fault, if only he could determine why. He had observed the religious fire festivals and had given tithe to the gods when he should. If they were angry with him for an action or a deed that he was unaware of, he did not know how to atone.

His army was tough, but it could be better.

In the morning, he would instruct Fionn and the other warriors to recommence training of the boys in advance of the Imbolc celebrations when more trainees would arrive from their chieftains. He knew that the Ó Mordha would never be as strong as it was two years before when they fought against the invasion at Knockdhu. They had suffered a great deal of losses—as did the whole of Éirinn—and the echoes of the dead would be heard for years. There would not be enough men in all the land to repopulate the greatness that the Ó Mordha tribe had been. But Rónán made a promise and his vow could not be broken. Though the influx of boys had been meagre for the last two years by comparison, he would train them well so that one warrior would fight as three.

When he heard a shuffling of feet in the coarse sand behind him, he leaned around the standing stone upon which he rested his back and saw Cormac.

'May I join you, my lord?'

'You fought well,' Rónán said. 'You are a great asset to my army.'

Cormac sat and took the wineskin when it was offered to him. 'You honour me with your words, my lord.'

'Speak plainly, Cormac, please. There is no need to address me so formally.'

Cormac smiled, bright teeth flashing in the moonlight. 'You

are my king and I must respect that.'

'As your king,' Rónán said, snatching the wineskin back with mirth, 'I command you to call me by my given name.'

'And risk the bad graces of all the gods?'

When he had taken a long draw from the wine, Rónán said, 'If the gods know my name, then so should you.'

After a moment, Cormac said, 'This stone—is it truly in honour of Áed the Executioner?'

Rónán leaned his head back against the cold and mossy stone. 'You know his story?'

'Everybody knows his story. He is a legend.'

'It fits him so,' Rónán said. He took another drink to avoid the conversation of his dead lover.

'My lord—Rónán—I have worries that King Rían's army will venture north in search of Orlaith and her child.'

'I have heard the rumours of his army. He frees the Fir Bolg slaves to fight at his back. He was your king in the south. What kind of man is he?'

'Bitter. Though he would never say it aloud, I imagine he fears that the gods have cursed him. Sonless, he beds as many women as he can in search of an heir.'

'If he comes against us,' Rónán said, 'he will not survive. Orlaith is safe.' He changed the subject then. 'After the Imbolc celebrations, I would have need of your strong arm in training the new boys.'

'How many will come?'

Rónán shrugged. A brief parting of the clouds dazzled the lough with broken shards of moonlight. 'I cannot say. With the invasion, there have been too many deaths and far too few births. Will you help me train them?'

Cormac bowed from his seated position. 'It is my honour to serve you.'

In the morning, Rónán met with Grainne for an update on the dead bird. She could find no issue with its innards and spent the evening divining for prophecies. But none had come to her.

When he took to the fields later to train the boys that were already members of his army, he did so with a renewed spirit. It was time to thrust his army back into greatness.

Rónán and Fionn both took up a sling to instruct the boys in the most common method of ranged warfare. Some distance across the field, a target had been erected.

From a pouch at his hip, he drew a stone and seated it at the fatter end of the sling. He began to spin the leather strap. 'You need enough force to keep the ammunition in place, and then—' he continued to twist the sling at his side, elbow in, forearm extended, '—snap to a halt.' He flicked his wrist and the stone shot from the sling towards the target, embedding itself in the leather-covered wood. The boys applauded him. 'Now imagine that target was a man's face.'

One of the boys gripped his head and fell to the ground in mock agony to the amusement of the others.

'Your screams,' Fionn told them, 'would carry you into the Otherworld.'

Rónán dropped his sling to the boy on the ground. 'Your turn.'

'Stand back, boys,' Fionn said. 'If anyone loses an eye, I will beat you to death with the boy who mis-threw the stone.'

As the trainee stood and whipped the sling, Rónán put a hand on his shoulder to stop him. Across the field, one of the cumal girls came towards them, slipping in the slush of melted snow, and she waved her arm with urgency. 'My lord.'

'What is so pressing that you would run through a field of hailing shot?'

She slid on a patch of broken ice and lowered her face from his gaze. 'The winter crops, my lord. They are specked red with rust.'

Chapter 8

The arable fields were ringed with the mud of melting snow. The winter wheat was planted after harvest so their sheaves would grow early before overwintering in dormancy. The crop was still young, short stalks with new leaves that slept through the colder months. It would provide a healthier yield the following year, allowing for an increase in their cereal stores, and mean the winter months would not be so frugal.

Rónán knelt in the sludge beside his druid and inspected the stems of the wheat. They were blistered with spots of tawny-red that clumped together and spread the length of the shoots. He levelled his eyes with the tops of the wheat stalks and scanned the patch around him. When the snow was thick, the young wheat had been buried, but the annual thaw made slush of the ground and revealed the diseased crops.

He came to his feet, staring across the field. 'How much is affected?'

Grainne rose, one of the diseased stalks in her hand, and inspected it in the light of the afternoon. 'This field and the next, my lord. The lower ground is still thick with snow where the sun does not yet reach beyond the hillside; I will have the men dig through them to determine the extent of it.'

'Do not say it.'

'Say what, Lord?'

Rónán turned from her and walked the length of the field between the low wall and the edge of the crop growth. 'A third omen. Do the gods hate me?'

'Wheat rust, while not common,' Grainne said, following behind him, 'does not flow on the breaths of the gods but on the winds of man.'

'Man does not make the winds.' Rónán turned to her, took the small stalk from her hands, and rolled it between his fingers. 'Can we wash the fields? Remove the rust?'

'I'm afraid it will not be so easy, Lord. Wheat rust is airborne. I studied its properties during my training. When all the snows are gone, we will find other farms, other tribes, that are also affected. We should dispatch a runner to the neighbouring chieftains to inform them. It did not originate in our fields and will spread fast if we cannot contain it.'

'Is it salvageable?'

'No, Lord.'

To kill the disease and stop its spread, they would have to cut the crops and burn the infected wheat. Rónán counted in his head how many sacks of grain he was losing and cursed the rust disease for its wanton disregard of life.

He organised a group of men and they came to the field with billhooks. At Grainne's instruction, they cut the sheaves close to the ground. When the lands were dry the wheat stubble would be burned, but until the sun mopped up the melted snow and the stubble was brittle enough to char, they could do nothing more.

Across the field, Grainne oversaw the production line of

wagons. They rolled in from the gateway and eased over the muddied land, pulled by oxen, and as the sheaves were cut, the men tossed the stricken wheat into the bed of the cart before it moved on, circled the rim of the field, and exited from the farthest gate. A second cart laboured over the mire.

Rónán swept his billhook and pulled the stalks from the ground. Beside him, one of the men sang a work song and Rónán joined in. The repetitive melody soon rang across the field in time with the swipes of the cutting tools and the sighing of the stalks as they filled the carts. By late afternoon, they had cleared the field.

The sheared wheat was too wet to burn, and Rónán ordered the failed crops to be dumped in a fallow pasture field away from the sheep and cattle. The bales were covered with pelts and weighed down by stones to stop any further spread of the disease until it was dry enough to light.

The late winter sun cowered behind low clouds and rain threatened from the south. 'We should call it a day,' Rónán said.

Fionn wiped his cutting blade with a cloth and pointed at the neighbouring field. 'If we work fast, we can clear half of it before sundown.'

Rónán looked at the darkening southern horizon. 'We have no time. We'll be soaked before we begin.' He threw his billhook on top of the final cart and nodded to the ploughman who whipped the shorthorn into motion.

He went in search of Grainne in the lower fields and found her knee-deep in snow. On the slope of the hillside, ringed by naked trees, the sun's warmth was not strong enough to penetrate the thick winter deposits. These fields were the last to clear each year, but they yielded the richest crops, their soil fertile despite the late arrival of summer on this side of the hill.

'All four fields,' Grainne called out, wading towards him. 'The wind will have circulated the rust disease in the valley. I pray this is the extent of the damage.'

Rónán cursed. 'How did we fail to spot this before the onset of winter?'

'It is a wily disease, my lord. It will have taken hold in late autumn to hibernate through the cold. Be thankful we caught it now; when the sun wakes the growth in the wheat, and the spring winds pick up strength, we could have lost the entire yield.'

'Clearing these fields of snow will require two days' work before we can cut the stalks. What chance do we have of saving the uninfected fields if it takes so long to clear these?'

'I will make an offering to the gods. If the winds carried it downhill, we should pray they do not blow it back in the other direction.'

Rónán stood at the head of the hill, staring down across the frozen fields that were separated by stone walls. In small patches, he saw pale wheat grasses rise above the cover of snow, but much of the fields were buried in it. Their winter wheat seeds were sown into standing stubble that provided snow-trapping measures, aiding insulation during the colder months for the sleeping stems, but they had no procedures for combating crop failure from disease. Spring sowing would not take place until after Beltaine, and their yield would not be as lucrative.

He returned to Ailigh, looking in on the winter store huts and counting the sacks of grain. When the storm hit, he heard the rain beat the thatching above his head and, with the door open, the wind flickered the tallow candle in his hand. The granary, raised on stilts half a rod above ground to keep rats and waterlogging at bay, was half empty, sacks piled in rows at the rear as high as his waist. Their diet was rich in grains and oats, and his stock was sufficient to last until harvest when the fresh grains were reaped. But without their winter wheat, they will have lost a third of their yield.

He would need to ration it. If he could keep some of the grain to fill out their autumn harvest, the following year may not be so dismal. But rationing crops for an army of four hundred would not be easy.

That evening, in his quarters, he sat on the floor with his son and taught the boy how to jab a block of wood with a dagger. The blade, heavy in Áed's small fist, gleamed in the candlelight as he stabbed it forward, guided by Rónán's hand. The tip of the dagger made minuscule pockmarks in the wood, but Rónán encouraged him. 'You'll be a fine fighting man in no time.'

Fresh from a steaming bath and wrapped in a simple dress that tied in the back, her hair pinned up with bronze combs, Achall brought a cup of wine for her husband. 'Do not teach him such violence. He is too young.'

'He is the son of a king and a warrior,' Rónán said, nudging Áed's shoulder. He held the wooden block closer so that Áed could stab it again. The rain hissed outside.

'He is a baby.' Achall lifted her son from the floor, shook his arm so that he would release the dagger, and it tumbled at Rónán's feet. 'He is too young for battle.'

'And too old to be coddled.' Rónán stretched out on the rugs. The child did not show any early signs of a warrior's spirit and this worried him. If Achall insisted on cossetting Áed, he would never know the joys of a spear throw or the thrill of a deer kill. The boy should be a king's son, an Ó Mordha child, and he should already know the weight of a dagger. It was Rónán's hope that the boys of Ailigh, his son included, would be as great as Mordha the Terrible. They were never too young to learn.

'He has his father's weakness,' he said.

Achall put their son to bed, tucking the furs around him. 'You are his father.'

'I would be if you let me.'

'He is too young to know war. When he is older, then you can train him. Until then, let him be my baby.'

'You smother him in kisses,' Rónán said.

'And you wash them away with your insults. We are even.'

In the morning, he returned to the fields with thirty men. The overnight rain had softened and melted the top layer of snow but, where it remained a rod deep, it was compacted and frozen. The men spread out across the top fields, working downhill, and with shovels they broke the ice sheets underneath and tossed the snow aside. They did not worry about damaging the wheat stalks and, when both fields were cleared, they moved into the lower grounds.

Rónán and a second row of men came behind, scything the damaged stems and pitching them into a waiting cart. The sludge of the land sucked at their boots and their legs and tunics were streaked with mud. No work songs were sung today.

When Cormac slipped in the churned ground and fell to his knees, the others laughed. As he used his hands to break his fall, the mud sparked his face and he blinked grit from his eye.

Laughing, Rónán helped him to his feet. 'You did say you

wanted to remain under my employ. Does this change your mind?'

Cormac wiped his hands on his muddied tunic. 'When harvest comes, send me on a fool's errand. I'd sooner hunt down the Salmon of Knowledge than choke on wheat dust.'

'You'd not have far to look,' Fionn said, already striding ahead of the others with his billhook. 'King Rónán caught the Salmon of Knowledge last year and it swims in the lough.'

'It is true,' Rónán smiled. 'Although there are so many salmon in the lough, I no longer know which is which.' He stooped to scythe the stems and they worked for a short time under the early afternoon sun that warmed their backs and dried the dirt on their clothes. 'I did not ask your profession when you came to me, Cormac.'

'I was trained as a tanner. But I have put my hand to quarrying great southern stone when needed, and to thatching at times—usually when the rains came hard and the thatchers were shorthanded.'

'A man of many skills. I am sure to find you a role that keeps you away from the plough and the field.'

Cormac coughed as dust from the shorn stems clouded before him. 'I would be grateful, my lord.'

They spent two days clearing the fields, and when they were finished, they ran out of pelts to cover the cropped wheat. Rónán stationed a guard on watch over the field to act as shepherd of the cull. Birds would descend for it and wild animals would forage in it, and any disturbance could scatter the rust flecks into the air. It would be days before the stalks were dry enough to burn, and longer for the fields to drain of muddy water so that the stubble could be seared. The fields would be out of action for many months, but the winter and spring crops were never sown in the same areas. If the weather turned with Imbolc as it should, Rónán could still manage a reasonable harvest.

He walked away from the naked fields as the shovelled snow melted into gullies at each end, eddying down the hillside and into the forest beyond. From atop the walls of Ailigh, he could see the distant fields, barren and lifeless. Three days ago, he was rich of crop. Today, he had three winter wheat fields remaining.

And too many mouths to feed.

Chapter 9

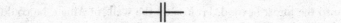

Grainne paced the field and used a measuring rod to count her way. She looked at the dawn sky and knew where the sun would rise two days from now, on the morning of Imbolc, and where the moon would cast its bright glow on the evening before when the fires would be lit. Position was key. For a druid, and her gods, there was order in everything. Chance was not in her vocabulary. From the moment she rose in the mornings, until her head touched the straw mattress after sundown, there was a logical order to her days, a structure that was not easily bent. She would rouse from slumber with the sun's rays and she would whisper a prayer to her personal goddess, the Lady Cáer, swan-daughter of Ethal Anbuail, and then she would bathe and dine on curds. If she was not visiting neighbouring clans, she spent her mornings tending to the sick or wounded boys who were injured in rough play more often than in training, and then her afternoons were spent in her gardens, cultivating herbs and flowers for their medicinal properties. Her evenings, while the men gathered in the barrel hut and the women swept their floors and heated water for the end-of-day bathing, Grainne would lie prostrate on the floor of her quarters, facing the west where the gods resided across the ocean, and she would call to her goddess and talk to her, telling her of the day. That her most gracious Lady Cáer did not answer was of no concern. Grainne knew she listened.

The goddess had not spoken to her in so long, she at first believed that she was no longer worthy of such divine conversation. But after the invasion she realised that, in times of peace, the gods were quiet.

But the omens that were revealed to her in recent days was a worry. She dared to dream that it was enough to warrant her lady's intervention.

While Rónán and the men set to work on the disease-stricken crops, she walked to the highest hill, leading a goat behind her, and she lay upon the wet grasses, facing west, to pray to her gods. She thanked the goat for its offering, and she opened his throat with her ceremonial dagger. She drained his blood onto the earth and when it was spent, Grainne carried the goat back down the hill for cremation, singing praises to it as she walked.

Wheat rust was a devastating disease. She studied its effects during her time at the archdruid's encampment. Airborne, there were no limits to its destruction. The disease was carried on the wind like jellyfish in the ocean, going where the wind bade it, landing where it wished and rooting itself in the crops. If one leaf touched another stem, it was sure to carry the disease with it.

Three days of toil cleared the affected fields, but there was no way of knowing if it had spread until the remaining crop fields showed signs of infection. She would monitor the situation in the coming weeks and pray for a positive outcome.

When the fields were culled, Rónán had come to her. He

worried for the loss of grain and the coming year. Grainne had taken his hands in comfort. 'The Imbolc festival is soon. We will light the fires and Bríg will walk among us. We will suffer no hardships.'

'And if the disease returns?' he asked.

'Do not doubt the gods, my lord. Their will is stronger than yours.'

This morning, she laid her measuring rod on the wet ground, the brown grasses flat from months of heavy snows. At the foot of the western hill, the level of the lough had risen as the snow melted and the rains came heavy. But the thinning clouds told her the rain would hold back for a time. She hoped the grasses would dry.

'Here,' she said, and one of Rónán's boys came to her side, marking the position of the fire that was to be built in advance of the ceremony.

She moved the rod and paced again. Seven fires would be lit—six in a perfect circle, with the seventh, larger fire, erected in the middle. That main fire was to honour the goddess Bríg, giver of life. The lesser fires, too, each had their meaning.

'Here.'

The boy came to her and laid another marker.

Grainne studied the sky before moving again. Nothing would be out of place. There would be no reason for the gods to abhor her as she performed their bidding.

She checked the markings on the length of the measuring rod, filed into the side of the wood. Even the rod, made of yew, was a perfect accompaniment to the presence of her gods. The yew tree was revered by the druids for its green warmth even in the dead of winter. Its branches often stretched towards the earth as if to be eternally at one with the soil. The yew was given to her people by the gods, carried from the Otherworld on Manandán's spectral ship. The dark shadows beneath a yew tree held other life at bay, and not even grasses would grow there, sacred ground on which the gods could rest their fatigued heads if they had a need to.

'Here,' she said, and the final marker was laid. The wood for the fires came from the nearby forests, and each branch would be counted and laid in position for its own specific purpose, in communion with the other logs, in union with the other fires, smoke rising to the moon as the gods had willed it.

She carried the measuring rod back to her quarters within the walls of Ailigh and she greeted Orlaith with a genuine warmth. The woman, just a few years older than Grainne, nursed her child by the fire, still tender from the complicated birth. The child suckled at her in silence.

'Does his redness fade?' Orlaith asked, hopeful.

Grainne inspected the child's face. 'I fear it does not. But he is healthy. You have given him life and you should feel within him the warmth of a god's blessing.'

'I do not worry on his appearance. He is mine.'

In the ways of their people, the child would never eat at king's counsel. But Grainne could see that no disfigurement, however slight, was a curse from the gods. His blemished skin was an omen to her, but he himself was not something to be feared. He smiled as another child would smile and gurgled and cried with no more gusto than any other. Some lesser men might call him a changeling, a child of the *sidhe*, offspring of the fairy folk, sent to this side of the realm as an interloper, but Grainne knew that he was just a child, as she had once been, innocent of crime, free of the shackles of life.

'He is beautiful,' Grainne said.

Orlaith held him back to her breast.

'You have eaten today?'

Orlaith nodded. 'Achall came to me with curds and bread this morning. And extra furs for the boy.'

'You have little love for her, I can see.'

'Who can love a king's wife? Achall and I are known to each other for years. She was a child when she came here, thrust into the arms of a man who had no interest in her.' She paused. 'I did not know Áed was your kin.'

Grainne turned and faced her shelf of herbs. 'It is difficult to speak of.'

'Even for a druid, who speaks with the gods and knows beyond doubt that our dead sit among them?'

'Even for me. His spirit may be at rest, and he makes the gods laugh at his terrible jokes. But he is not here. I cannot see him or embrace him.' She sat on a stool beside the fire, poking the burning logs with an iron. 'I spent my youth in training in the far north. I can recite laws and converse with the gods, and I can mix strong solutions that cure pustules or bleeding of the eyes. But I cannot cure death.'

Orlaith smiled with sincere condolences and she switched the boy from one breast to the other. He had stopped suckling. 'You do not see death as a disease to be cured,' she said.

'No. And to anyone else whose brother—whose whole family—has gone to the gods, I can offer reasoned debate that death is not the end, merely a transition. I can tell you that he walks with the gods and dines at their tables. I can assure you that his suffering is over, and that he is at peace.' She continued to look at the fire, yellow flames pushing shadows into recesses. 'But though his suffering is done, ours is not. And even though his journey has ended, ours must endure alone, with a hole in our heart where once there was a brother, a sister, a parent.'

'Your entire family is gone from us?'

Grainne nodded. 'Yes.' She rose from the stool. 'They are all with the gods. And I blame only myself.'

'The invasion was not your fault.'

'No. And destiny cannot be undone. But that does not stop me from sharing the blame in Áed's death. We are all at fault. Each of us.'

Orlaith had no words.

When the child cried, Grainne was grateful. She gathered some of her vials and mixed them in a wooden bowl. 'I will make him something for sleep,' she said.

Later, when her preparations for Imbolc were complete, and the sun tiptoed low across the south-western mountains, she returned to her quarters and entered her private room. Orlaith was asleep and the child, wide-eyed, stared at the thatched ceiling above him.

Grainne closed the door to her private room and removed her robes and hitched the hem of her full-length, pale blue dress so that she could kneel. When she lay face down on the ground, she inhaled the smell of the earth and closed her eyes.

'My most gracious Lady Cáer,' she whispered. 'I am always your servant, the instrument of your ways, keeper of your love. I call your name in adoration. I am eternally yours, daughter of a prince, swan of swans.' She spread her fingers on the ground. 'I have prepared for Bríg's coming at Imbolc. The fires are ready to be lit and I have chosen a girl to enact Bríg's wonder.

But I am troubled, my dearest Cáer. I have worries in my heart that I cannot shake. Speak to me that you might calm my soul.'

She sealed her lips, for the gods speak in the moments between breaths. But Cáer's words did not come to her.

She felt tears break from her eyes.

'The omens are dark, my lady. And I do not know their meaning. I am lost without your hand to guide me.'

Again, she held her breath and listened.

When she smelled the sweet scent of samphire, she raised her head, but the goddess Cáer was not beside her. The smell faded.

Grainne lowered her forehead to the earth again. 'Take my hand. Show me the way. I am yours always, my most divine Lady Cáer. You have embraced me and cried with me. Let me embrace you once more and cry upon your hair that I may wash you and you may carry away my misery.'

She turned onto her side and curled into a foetal ball. And in the adjoining room, Orlaith's baby cried through his tiredness.

And Grainne cried, too.

Chapter 10

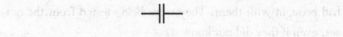

Beyond the outer palisade fence, twenty-six boys huddled together against the evening wind. In the south, a bank of storm clouds was eating up the sky.

From the guard tower, Rónán watched them and recalled his own stay outside the walls, back when he was a child. He came with several boys from his clan, gifted to the northern king by their chieftain. Their journey north took six nights and when they arrived, other clans were already gathering, and yet more came behind him. They were told to wait on the hill and stay vigilant, and on the second day, as the rains came heavy upon them, a boy from another clan was begging for food. His tribe had run dry and they would starve if they were to wait another night outside.

Rónán shared what was left of his bread with the boy. He did not know it at the time, but he would grow to love that boy more than he could ever love his wife. In sharing his bread, he opened his heart to sharing more than food. It took him years to realise it, but he loved Áed the Executioner even then.

He looked at the boys outside his walls. Five of them would be sent home in the morning. Fionn, when they first arrived, instructed them to wait and remain alert, as was said to the new arrivals every year. And any of those who fell asleep were not welcome to train at Ailigh. They would be given food and a bed for the night, but they would be forced to make their journey home without pride or honour.

As was tradition, the boys remained outside the walls for two nights without fire or provisions except for that which they had brought with them. They were being tested from the outset, even if they did not know it.

Tomorrow, Fionn would group the boys into sections and they would begin to train. Tonight, when Rónán deemed it appropriate, they would be let inside to the warmth of hearth and cooked foods.

He looked towards the threatening clouds. They were still some distance away, but they were coming with speed. The hills of his southern border were already blue with rain.

Below him, one of the boys sang a warrior's song and a few others joined him, their voices lulling the winds for a time. They sang of ancient battles and a warrior's love for the goddess Aífe. And, as most songs go, the warrior died in his lover's arms and she took him to the Land of the Young to be her husband.

When the singing concluded, Rónán was chilled by more than the late winter winds. His own lover was also in the spectral lands.

The torch beside him sputtered and shadows spider-webbed on his face.

From within the walls, Fionn called to him and climbed the steps to stand at his side. 'They're a sorry bunch of lads if ever I saw one,' he said.

'Did we not look as sorrowful when we stood out there?'

'We were hardened by lean times. These boys are soft as their mothers' kisses.'

'And it is your responsibility to harden them for war.'

'Should I bring them in before the rains hit, Lord? The fat ones will take days to dry out.'

'No, leave them. Once the rains are heavy enough, then you can let them in. It will do them good. We were drenched like ship rats when we walked through that gate.'

Fionn laughed. 'A man with a streak of evil is what you are, Lord. No mistake.'

He turned back down the steps and left Rónán to watch the clouds. The wind was getting stronger and half the sky had been chewed into darkness. In the days to come, he would keep watch over the new arrivals. He had been through the process himself and knew the signs of who would be the bully, who would be bullied. Every intake had one of each. In his band, Dillon had been the dominant fool, while Áed took the brunt of his abuse. But in time, Áed grew into a legend, a champion for their king. And Dillon met his end at Knockdhu without a sword in his hand.

Dillon—father of Achall's child. Rónán promised to raise the boy as his own, and for the most part he succeeded. Only when young Áed cried and scrunched his face in angry tears did Rónán see the look of Dillon in him. When he was placid and smiling, Rónán could hold him to his chest and cradle his head and forget the truth of it. He begged the gods each night that young Áed would not grow to be the man his real father was, the bully, the tyrant, the smug dictator that Dillon so craved to be. He begged them that his son would be like Áed the Executioner, the man for whom he was named, and that he would

85

grow strong and powerful and peaceful.

A fat drop of rain splashed his face and he blinked. The storm set in.

He retired to his quarters where Achall was feeding their son from a small wooden bowl, candlelight casting warm shadows and the hearth crackling, the sound of yapping hounds echoing from outside. It angered him still that she did not see the necessity in Áed's early training as a warrior. A man is judged by the strength of his sons.

'The boys have entered?' she asked.

'Soon.'

'The rain will soak them through.'

'It will wash away their past.' He cleansed his face and arms in the bowl by the hearth and poured a cup of wine. The bed he shared with her beyond the hearth was a proud monument to the lack of communion between them. He entered it as late as possible and rose before the dawn. The imprint of her body on the straw mattress was warmer than his.

'It excites you, training the new ones.'

'It is good when they are young. They can be shaped into the men they ought to be, not the men they would have become.'

'You mean the men you want them to be.'

'The men they deserve to be. I started life as a fletcher's son; now look at me.'

'They will not all be king one day,' Achall said.

'I will enjoy finding out which ones are fit for it, and which aren't.'

'And your own son when he is old enough—you will consider him for tanist?' She had asked him this many times before.

A king's tanist, his closest confidant and heir, was chosen not

86

entirely by blood, but by means. If a friend can command greater power than your brother or your son, there would be no contest for succession. It was a king's right to choose who should lead his people when he is gone, regardless of who should challenge him at the time.

'Fionn is my tanist until the boy is of age. If Áed should grow to be the warrior I expect him to be, then yes, he will be my tanist. But you must let me train him.'

'When he is older and stronger.' Achall placed the bowl aside and put the child on his pallet. The furs were trimmed so as not to irritate his skin but not so much that they would not provide warmth. Áed yawned and mumbled a few quiet words as she let go of him.

'Can I ask you about Orlaith?' she said.

Rónán kicked his boots off, then drained his cup and poured a second. 'She stays.'

'I have no doubt. But must she sleep so close to us?'

'You fear she will cut your throat in your sleep?' Rónán laughed. 'She sleeps in Grainne's quarters until she is well. Then we will find a more permanent *brú* for her. You are not children any longer, Achall. Put away the past; I'm sure she has already done so.'

'My Lord,' she said, her head bowed. When she called him by a title, he knew that she was angry.

'A few more days,' he said, placating her. 'When she is well, I will personally walk her and her child down to the outer level.'

Achall stroked her son's hair and shushed him to sleep. 'I have nothing against the child. But Orlaith has no respect for me as your wife.'

'I will talk to her.'

'You will not.'

Rónán looked at his wife. He was convinced she contradicted him for sport. There were very few arguments outside of war and farming that he could win against her. 'Then what should I do?'

'I do not want you to do anything. I was telling you that the woman has no respect for your wife.'

'I will not march her from my lands, so you may earn her respect or be silent about it. She is a friend and is in need of our support.'

He fell into bed, his second cup of wine unfinished. She would press him still, through the night, but soon he would be asleep, and her words would fall away from him.

With the dawn, he returned to the guard tower and watched the fields. On the ceremonial hill, Grainne was overseeing the erection of the festival fires, logs and branches piled high in columns. Lighting the fires at dusk would signal the beginning of their festivities in which they were to give thanks for surviving the winter months—wheat rust notwithstanding—and look forward to the fruitful warmth of brighter days. They would sow the spring seeds soon enough and his yield at the harvest, though less than anticipated, must be enough for a new winter, the earth's ever rotating cycle from death to birth.

'My Lord?'

Rónán looked down from the wall to find Cormac below him, bow in hand and with a quiver strapped to his hip. 'Training or hunting?'

'I thought I would get some practice in before the boys take over the fields. Join me?'

'I have matters to attend to in advance of the Imbolc fire lighting. You will be at the ceremony?'

'Will you be giving speeches and handing out drinks?'

'There will definitely be drinking. The speeches I leave for Grainne.'

Cormac waved and, when he was gone, Rónán returned his attention to his lands beyond the palisade wall.

In the northern field, with a clear view of the lough on their right, Fionn gathered the new boys. Minus the five who were sent home at first light, they amounted to twenty-one trainee warriors.

Fionn's voice carried across the field. 'You miserable brats are what your chieftains saw fit to send to Ailigh for training. Your days of crying like whelping pups are over. You came through our gates last night as boys, and you will leave them as men. From now until your last days, you are mine, do you understand? You are no longer the sons of your fathers; you belong to Ailigh now. You belong to the king. You are Ó Mordha. Look at the boy on your left and your right—he is not a friend; he is not an enemy. He is your brother. You will train together, and you will fight together. Ó Mordha men do not quit. Ó Mordha men do not surrender. You will not lose, because you will be mighty. Together you will be strong. And on the day of your death you will face Manandán and he will ask you your name. What will you tell him?'

'Ó Mordha,' the boys said, a mumble that did not reach the skies above them.

'What will you tell him?'

'Ó Mordha,' they shouted.

'You are Ó Mordha and you will be honoured as warriors in

death.'

Rónán watched as Fionn instructed the boys into smaller groups. They would start with fist fighting and there they would learn who was a leader and who was not. The initial fist-strike against your new brother was the hardest. The first boy to throw a punch—he could be a contender for kingship one day.

He did not expect the opening punch to come from the smallest boy, straight in the gut of the tallest in his group. Rónán smiled. Achall was right; training season was under way, and he was excited.

If Grainne's omens were to be believed—and he did not doubt her, for her druid ways were ingrained in her soul—a war was coming. The boys would have to be ready. Trained or not, when the war came, from wherever it came, all boys would be handed a sword and shield and told to march into battle. If such a day arrived, he prayed to all the gods that his army would be strong.

The gate bell rang out and he looked to the east. Marching up the hill were four men, arms stretched wide, away from their swords. Whoever they were, they came in peace.

He took to the ground level and went to his hall where the men would be brought to him. When the hall's door was opened, in view of the king, the four men unhooked their sword belts and laid them on a table, as was customary, indicating no ill intent. They entered and bowed to him.

Rónán greeted them with warmth. 'As guests, you are welcome. A meal will be prepared for you.'

'My Lord,' one of the men said, stepping forward. 'Your hospitality does not go unnoticed by all the gods of Éirinn. We are grateful. I am Cathal, son of Éibhear. I bring words from the great King Rían of Clan Hargon in the south.'

Rónán sat, his mood souring, and the guard who was stationed beside his chair tensed, his grip tightening around his war spear. 'I have heard of your king,' Rónán said, disguising his sudden distrust.

'As he has heard of you, my Lord. The songs of your deeds are plentiful.' Cathal paused and Rónán waited for his next words. 'The mighty King Rían has misplaced some property of his.'

'Misplaced?' Rónán suppressed a smile from the turn of his lips. He expected Rían's men to either attempt to enlist Ailigh in Rían's cause or declare war against him. He had forgotten that Orlaith fled from the brutish king.

'A woman,' Cathal said. 'She was heavy with child.'

Rónán nodded, as though attempting to recall such a sight. 'How does a man as mighty as King Rían misplace a woman? Especially one so round with child?'

'My Lord, the girl stole the child from my king.'

Now Rónán smiled openly. 'She stole a child that was in her belly?'

'It is my king's property. May I ask if you have seen such a woman?'

'You may.'

Cathal looked at him, confusion crossing his face. Rónán had not answered the question and they both knew it.

'I do not believe you expect me to notice every pregnant woman who passes through my hills.'

Cathal, unable to conceal his churlishness, bowed again as though it was an apology. 'You would recognise this one, Lord, for she is a surly thing, slight of body but strong of will.'

'You have just described my wife,' Rónán said, 'and every other woman in the north. Is she a northern woman or a southern girl?'

'My Lord, I do not possibly see how the woman's origins are relevant.'

'If I did know of the girl, and I was to hand her to you, what is to be done with her?'

Cathal smiled. 'We would see her safely back to her king.'

'Safely, is it? I am obliged to offer you a meal and a bed for the night, and you are welcome as my guests. But you will be leaving here empty-handed. No woman is another man's property, king or not.'

'But, my Lord. The child belongs to my king.'

Rónán nodded to the guard who had entered with the four men. 'See that they are fed. There are no pregnant women here. This meeting is over.'

Cathal took a single step forward. 'I must insist, on behalf of my lord.'

Rónán stood. 'Do not forget your manners. You will address me with respect.'

The man, whose skin was now pale and clammy, lowered his head. 'Forgive my ineptitude, my most gracious king. I have come here to perform a task and retrieve the woman. If you harbour her and do not offer her willingly, I must return to my king with the sad news that his request has gone unanswered.'

'I have told you there are no pregnant women here, local or otherwise. If the mighty King Rían begs me for an audience, I might allow him to look around. But until he stands before me, I will hear no more on the subject. Am I understood?'

The four men turned and left, collecting their sword belts as they went.

Rónán paced the hall when he was alone. His skin crawled rich with anger. He must ensure Orlaith's safety. He was confident that Rían's men would not accept the offer of a meal or a bed and they would return south at once. If the southern bastard wanted her, he could come for her himself. And Rónán would slaughter anyone who dared lay a hand on her.

Chapter 11

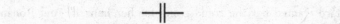

News of King Rían's war spread throughout the southern regions quicker than a virgin wilts on her wedding night. For Bromaid, it was glad tidings. For his owner, and indeed for King Ailill who governed their province, it came as a threat. All Fir Bolg slaves, the king decreed, were to be shackled every evening and put to their duties in daylight under a watchful eye. Any infraction would carry the harshest of penalties.

For nights unending, Bromaid was returned to his small hut and chained to an iron ring that was pegged deep into the ground. The thick chain had ample length to award him movement around the room, and he could open the door and stand a double-step from the threshold to relieve himself, but he could travel no further. He felt like a sacrificial goat tied to a stake and set out for slaughter.

Bromaid tracked the southern king's march by how vocal the farmer became of it. At first, there had been only whispers, and although he was shackled at night, in the day he was left without supervision for the most part. But as the advancing king came ever closer, the Fir Bolg slave was kept under watch and the farmer berated his kind at every opportunity. If Bromaid spoke out of turn, or if the farmer would deem the output of his duties to be less than favourable, he would be beaten and chained up in his *brú* until such times as the farmer needed him again.

Bromaid's one solace was young Ailbe who, despite her fear of him, and even though he was chained like a leper each evening, still came to his side when he called to her.

When he stood at the length of his chain that first night, making his bird call for her, she did not come. In the darkness, he stared across the way at the farmer's home and he cupped his hands over his mouth and hooted to her a second time, but the farmer's door did not open. He did not call to her a third time, for he was not a man to beg. Instead, he returned to his bed and spoke a curse upon the girl's father.

In the morning, when he was freed from his bounds and set to work in the fields among the sheep, he hid among the brambles until she passed, and he leapt upon her. He covered her mouth against her screams, and he waited for her to calm herself. Against her ear, he whispered, 'When I call, you will come to me. I may be shackled at night, but I am still free in the day and if you refuse me, I will murder your father and your mother in the fields where they work. And then I will come for you, too. Do you understand?'

The girl nodded against his hand that covered her mouth, and though her eyes were squinted, they shed no tears.

He did not call for her that second night, but he knew that she would be awake and listening for him; he anticipated her arrival at his door even without his call. When he hooted to her in the darkness of the third night, she came to him with diligence and he said, 'Unchain me so that we can have the freedom of movement.'

'I do not have the key.'

He took her arm and helped her undress. 'Next time, bring the key.'

He lay with her twice that night, and she was silent throughout. When the moon was high above the thatching of their homes, he rose from her, opened his door, and threw her dress into the yard. He stood naked in the entranceway and urinated in the grasses as he watched her scurry home.

In the days that followed, Bromaid was kept under careful watch at turns by the farmer and his wife, but the young girl was never left in charge of him. The farmer sheared his sheep when the sun was warming in the days just before Imbolc, and Bromaid was tasked with rounding them up and holding them still in a small pen designed for the chore. The wife and daughter collected the wool and carried it away with them for spinning and dyeing, and Bromaid walked another of the pregnant ewes into the pen. Pre-lamb shearing, Bromaid had to acknowledge, was a universal practice.

He watched the farmer cut at the wool on the ewe's back and underbelly, but he did not speak to correct him; in his own country, they would use larger secateurs to make the job easier. These farmers knew so little.

Later, when he was mending the farmer's wall on the eastern ridge of the hillside, he looked upon the lough below. The snow and ice had melted, and the water was black and still. The trees between the lough and the low wall at which Bromaid stood were beginning to bud but were naked of leaves or blossom. He could imagine King Rían's Fir Bolg army charging up the hillside among those bare trees to free him and allow him, stripped of his slave's collar, to murder the farmer and his family in retribution for his enslavement.

Like the trees, and the lambs, and the very earth upon which he stood, Imbolc would bring with it a new life for Bromaid also.

He did not trust this King Rían, whose name was on the lips of many, but if he came to free the slaves, he would kneel to him long enough to be set loose, and then he and all the other Fir Bolg men would turn upon their liberator, cleave his head from his shoulders, and one among them would assume the role of high king over Éirinn. But that would only warrant further fighting. Bromaid's people were fiercely independent. Battles for chieftainship were common and a good leader ruled by power and might. Everyone wanted the authority. It is told, in the annals of their histories, that King Manaid's wife gave birth to a son, and that son, on the evening of his birth, crawled from his mother's breast and ate the hands of his father so that the king was no longer fit to rule. The boy was declared chieftain-king by all who witnessed it and he grew tall and powerful overnight.

Their histories were filled with such wondrous tales, but they all pointed to an ever-shifting power of authority. No king was safe from harm, even from his own child.

Bromaid set another stone on top of the wall in the way he had been taught by his father. Each stone was positioned so that it supported the next, and there was a distribution of weight among them. Collapsing walls were not a common occurrence, but the heavy snows of winter, coupled with the strong northerly winds that sliced the rugged hillside, had weakened the structure enough to topple it in one small section. When he rebuilt it, it was stronger than before.

Two days later, the morning before the Imbolc fires would be lit, Bromaid was called upon to help with the birthing of the lambs. Three of the ewes had gone into simultaneous labour, days earlier than had been anticipated, and the farmer's wife and daughter were also present to assist.

Thin but strong strips of twine were coiled into a heated bowl of water, and a jug of plant oils was placed on hand as they waited for the first of the births.

The ewes, separated by hastily erected fences, were alert and bleating, chewing on the loose hay that had been spread for them between contractions. For normal births they would be left alone, and the ewes would do as nature instructed them without intervention, but as was often the case, some lambs do not present themselves at the canal in the correct manner or position.

When the first of the lambs appeared, head and forelegs first, the farmer gave a sigh of relief and turned his attention to the next ewe. The lamb within it was not presenting, even though the ewe was pushing. The farmer eased himself into a position behind her. He cleaned his hands and his wife poured some of the plant oils over his fingers to act as a lubricant. With consideration and gentleness, the farmer inspected the ewe's opening.

Bromaid, who had never witnessed a lambing before, knelt and shuffled closer.

'Its head and forelegs are turned away,' the farmer said, extracting his fingers. 'Ailbe, you have smaller hands. Come. You remember this from last birthing season?'

The young girl nodded. As a farmer's daughter, she assisted in the birthing of the lambs since she was old enough to walk.

The ewe screamed a painful sound and Ailbe cleansed her

hands and held them out for her mother to pour the oils upon them. She rubbed her palms together to ensure the oils were evenly distributed, and then she knelt beside her father.

'Push the lamb back inside,' the farmer told her. 'When you have the space, cup the forelegs and head and bring them forward. Then we can pull when the lamb is presenting right.'

Bromaid watched with awe as she inserted her small fingers into the ewe's birthing passage. 'I can feel it,' she said. Her hands travelled further inside as she pushed the lamb back into the uterus. 'I need more oil.'

Her mother leaned in and poured additional oil at the opening, coating Ailbe's forearms.

Bromaid watched the girl's face. She closed her eyes as if to see better, and she cocked her head in concentration. She worked with speedy diligence. 'It's in position,' she said, extracting her hands. At the opening, the lamb slipped forward with Ailbe's guidance, and the ewe cried a new contraction. She was weak with the invasion, and when the lamb's head and forelegs were visible, the farmer told Bromaid to take the three strips of twine and form a running noose at the ends of them. Each of the forelegs were noosed, and the third was placed over the head, behind the ears and between the jaws at the fore.

The farmer took one of the strands and instructed his slave to hold the remaining two. 'Pull the right foreleg ahead of the left,' he told Bromaid. 'Steady movements; don't be rough with it.'

At the next contraction, Bromaid pulled. The lamb was freed, and the farmer was quick to its head, undoing the noose and forcing his fat fingers into its mouth to clear it of mucus. He raised the lamb by the hindlegs and swung it gently while

Ailbe moved into position again to check for a second lamb. When she found no evidence of one, she slapped the ewe's side with tenderness.

The lamb bleated and the farmer lay it down beside the ewe so that they could smell one another and bond.

While they had been attentive to the lamb, the third ewe gave birth without incident, two infants gulping air beside her. It amazed Bromaid that new-borns know how to breathe when they slip to the hay.

'We must remain alert,' the farmer said. 'When one lamb comes, the rest will follow.' He looked to Bromaid. 'You will watch the pregnant ewes for the remainder of the day and into the night if you have to. Alert me the moment they go into labour.'

'Tonight are the celebrations,' his wife said.

The farmer turned from them. 'A slave has little right to worship the gods.'

Bromaid watched the pregnant ewes, but none deemed it necessary to lie down and push new life from within them. That he was now not tasked with his daily chores was a welcome relief, but boredom came to him as swift as sin to idle hands. The farmer's words stung him, and he contemplated the reasons for it. Slaves were a necessary part of life, one that his own people were adept at employing. When Ailbe, with a quiet coyness, came to check on the ewes at her father's insistence, Bromaid told her of this.

'I am from a nation of slaves. It is my history. For centuries, we worked the fields under the whip, carrying bags of soil from one place to another. But in time, we freed ourselves and we enslaved others in retribution. It was our right to do so.'

She would not come close to him, but she did not flee when he circled her.

'When this king of yours comes for me, I will be free again.'

'He is not my king.'

'You mumble with fear in your throat,' Bromaid said. He looked across the hillside towards the farmer's home, and then he removed his tunic to stand naked before her. She turned her face from him.

Bromaid stepped closer, his shadow spilling over her face. 'If you were a woman of my people, you would have cut me open by now and danced on my entrails. Why have you not?'

Ailbe lowered her head.

'Because you are weak, yes? Because you have not the strength of conviction within your pathetic head.' When he gripped her dress, she raised her arms in compliance so that he could slip it from her. The early spring winds stretched goose bumps across her arms and stomach.

'I am your father's slave,' he said, leaning close to her ear, 'but you are mine.'

He took her waist in his hands and lowered her to the straw among the loud complaining of the ewes.

When he entered her, he was sweating with anticipation, and it cooled on his back as rapid as it formed. He watched her face just as he had done when she was aiding the ewe in giving birth, and now her eyes were closed tight, her lips flattened together, and her head was turned from him.

'When I am freed,' he said, grunting against her cheek, his hands cupping her breasts, 'I will make you my wife to slight your father.'

When a tear rolled from the corner of her eye, he licked it.

And then he buried his face against her pale neck as he bucked between her hips.

Tonight, the Imbolc celebrations would bring with it new life across the land. And Bromaid could already feel his new life descending upon him.

'I will rule over my people,' he said to her when he was finished, pulling his tunic over his head, walking away from her nakedness. 'I will kill this King Rían, and I will rule in his stead. And when I do, I will enslave your entire kind.'

Chapter 12

The Imbolc fires were to be lit at the time of twilight when the sun set on the western shores and the moon was visible in the east. It would mark the start of a new day, a new season in which life returned to the land. This morning, Rónán took up his position on the kingseat in the great hall and awaited the entrance of the new arrivals. They were to swear their loyalty to him both in times of peace and through the ravages of war.

Outside, Ailigh was vibrant with the sounds of a community at work. Doorways were to be thrown open to welcome the goddess Bríg, and floors swept clean. Spent tallow candles would be replaced with new ones and hearth fires put out just before dusk so that they could be relit by the flames of Bríg's fire. All things return to birth. All things are made anew.

Grainne met with him at dawn. She was fearful of the omens and could not yet decipher their meanings, but she was certain that trying times were ahead. She prayed with him before his introduction to the new boys, calling upon her personal goddess for her eminent protection, and she gave offering to her greatest lady Cáer, a tribute to her devotion. A king's druid brought with them the words and favour of all the gods, but each druid had a singular kinship to one deity. While the druid was under the king's employ, he, too, would worship that god above others.

She told him many stories of the goddess Cáer, and with each tale or song, his affinity towards her grew, just as Grainne told him it would.

She sang of Cáer's transformation from swan to woman. Cáer lived for one glorious night as a human, before the curse that was placed upon her would return her to the shape of a splendid swan. Rónán sat in silence, the final notes of her song washing over him.

At length, he said, 'By the grace of your revered lady, I hope that she often embraces Áed in the Otherworld.'

Grainne nodded in solemn thought. 'I believe that he sits at her side and regales her with stories of his life.'

'I can only hope that he depicts me with greatness in his tales to her.'

When the door of his great hall opened and Fionn entered, Rónán sat up in his kingseat to greet the new boys. They filed in behind their commander and fanned out in sheepish innocence. For many, this was their first encounter with a king. Rónán remembered his own meeting with King Déaglán when he first arrived at Ailigh, but he did not know how to inspire such awe in his people in the ways that Déaglán had done or, indeed, the way that Áed would have done if he survived the Battle of Knockdhu.

Perhaps, as Fionn once told him when he was preparing to make a speech soon after their return from the invasion wars, the reverence inspired by a king comes more from the title than the words.

He stood, and the boys quietened to listen. 'Welcome, men

of Ailigh,' he said, promoting them from the boyhood they were leaving behind. 'I am Rónán Ó Mordha, son of Coileán, overking of the Ó Mordha tribesmen. From the moment you walked through my gates, you are now a man of Mordha the Terrible. It is a name to be feared, and rightly so. You will be trained in the ways of Mordha, and you will live each day in service not to your king, but to each other. This is my promise to you—in times of war, I will have your back; in times of peace, I will be your king. Will you honour me?'

An affirmative answer rippled through the rank of twenty-one boys.

'Take a knee,' Fionn commanded them.

They knelt before their king and, in unison, coached by Fionn, they said, 'I kneel to my lord king, Rónán Ó Mordha. It is my honour to serve you.'

Rónán sat and Fionn came to his side. One by one, the boys were named, and they came forward to kiss the gold discs at Rónán's breast, the sign of his kingship.

When they kissed him and bowed to him, he would ask them a question, and their answers were swift and quiet.

To the smallest of the boys, he said, 'What is your name?'

'Darragh Ó Mordha,' the boy said as though he had memorised his new name.

'And who is your father?'

'Diarmuid, my lord.'

'You are from the east?'

The boy nodded.

'You are welcome here. Now is your chance to do your father proud. Tell me, as the smallest among your new brothers, is there someone you look up to?'

The boy twitched his mouth before speaking. 'I will grow, my lord, and soon others will look up to me.'

Rónán laughed. 'I am convinced of it,' he said.

When all the boys had been welcomed, they returned to the floor to kneel at his service. Rónán stood again. 'Your faithfulness to my name has been noted and the gods will look kindly upon you when it is your time to face them.' He pointed to the door behind them. 'These hills that you stand upon, this land, everything that you see—it is yours as it is mine. Look after it well. I will watch your progress in the coming months and in time you will find that I am an honourable king. Mordha the Terrible was a formidable warrior, as is every child of Mordha who has gone before you and will come after. I have faith that you, too, will acquire greatness.'

Fionn commanded them to rise, and he led them out of the hall.

Achall entered from the annex with Áed in her arms. She came to his side and stared at Fionn as he left the room. 'You speak well. The boys will strengthen under your guidance.'

'It is Fionn who guides them. He is the strong arm these boys require.'

'You give him too much power.'

Rónán flicked his finger for a cumal to pour water into his cup. Achall was unrelenting in her grievances.

'He has the power given to him by his position,' Rónán said.

'He stands as your heir and your army's commander. Gods forbid, when you are too old or too weak to rule, he usurps the kingseat from your son.'

Rónán looked at the boy in her arms. 'Fionn would do no such thing. He is loyal.'

'He is a man. And all men wish for more than life has given them.'

'And all women wish for what?'

Achall walked back towards the annex. 'All women wish for their husbands to cherish them. And for their sons to rule one day.'

Vexed, Rónán took to the fields with his sword and shield. Although training was postponed until after Imbolc, so that everyone could prepare, Rónán felt a burning in his limbs to exercise. Today, there were no kingship duties he needed to perform. His outlying septs, if they had need of him, would wait until after the ceremonies. For many, it was a day of reflection. For Rónán, it was a day to avoid painful thoughts.

As he approached the lower training fields, he found Cormac among the log placements, over which he jumped. He watched the young man before coming closer.

'You do well,' he said.

'My lord.'

Rónán raised his shield. 'Spar with me?'

Cormac fetched his shield from the edge of the training field. His sword was in its scabbard at his hip.

They stood rods apart and Cormac bowed to his king. 'I will take it easy on you, my lord.'

Rónán unsheathed his sword and swung it in a swift, calculated strike. Cormac blocked it high, forcing his weight onto his rear leg. 'You will do no such thing.'

Cormac cut his sword in from the right. 'I would not wish to injure my king.'

'Do you pull your blows on the battlefield? Strike me; I can take it.'

As he struck Rónán's shield, Cormac said, 'I thought a king would be busy on the day of Imbolc.'

'My druid sees to the necessary planning.' Rónán bounced back on his feet and lunged for another parry. On the hills behind him, the seven fires of Imbolc had been erected, and boys were stationed on ceremonial guard around the circle.

'I have seen Fionn with the new boys. They look like a hardy bunch of lads.'

'They are wet and green as algae. But we will harden them soon enough.' He gripped the sword. The leather strap encircling his forearm from his shield, and the one at his fist, were taut and slick with sweat.

Cormac sidestepped him and raised his defensive arm against another blow. 'How do you do it? How do you manage to rule an entire province and yet carry yourself so level-headed and calm?'

Rónán blocked, struck, blocked again. 'You have seen a duck on the surface of the lough, yes? Calm above the water but powering frantically underneath.'

'If your feet are webbed,' Cormac said, struggling against another attack, 'I do not wish to see them.'

Rónán came close, shield-arm lifted, and cracked the flat of his blade hard against Cormac's shield.

Cormac stuttered back on the slick grasses and spread his arms. 'Enough,' he said. 'I am defeated.'

'I would have split your neck open sooner had you not distracted me with your incessant questioning.'

Cormac bowed. 'I will remember that on the battlefield when I face the enemy. I will question my opponent to death.'

Rónán looked at him for a moment before speaking. Then he

smiled. 'At least in battle, you do not call me Lord. I see you for what you are and not the polite guest you claim to be.'

'My guard slipped, my lord.'

'See that it remains so loose. It displeases me when I am called anything that is not the name my father gave me.' He made a sign with his fingers at the mention of his father, a man who had passed so long ago that he could scarcely remember his face.

They sat side by side on a log and Rónán inspected the length of his blade to ensure it was not nicked or pocked.

'It is a fine blade,' Cormac said. Then he added, 'You may not like it, but a king commands respect from his people even in times of casual conversation.'

'You are right,' Rónán said. 'It is a fine sword.'

'Have you received an update on the war in the south?'

'King Rían has already sent some men for Orlaith and the baby,' Rónán said. Cormac was quick to his feet, but Rónán touched his leg to still him. 'They have gone, empty-handed. Do not fear, I told you she is safe here. I did not confirm that she was among us. They will return to their king and report nothing.'

'Thank you, Rónán.'

Hearing the man say his given name, Rónán removed his hand from Cormac's leg as though he only now remembered its whereabouts.

He spent the rest of the day in quiet preparations. It had been too long since he felt the desire to know someone. He thought of Áed. And then he thought of Cormac, the young man whose hair was wild around his face, who looked and sounded and acted nothing like the former.

Alone, in his quarters, while his wife and child were being dressed in an annex, he knelt and lowered his forehead to the ground.

And when he closed his eyes, he heard his name whispered in the dark. And he could not be certain if it was Áed's voice he had heard. Or Cormac's.

Chapter 13

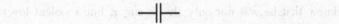

The sunlight revealed dust particles scattering in the air when Orlaith woke and looked at her child. An immediate sense of dread filled her that he did not cry for a feeding with the dawn's first light, but when she touched his chest, she felt him breathe. She did not hear the druid leave her quarters this morning.

Because of her sleep, she felt rested and full of vigour once she was bathed and had eaten. The baby suckled from her for a long while. She had not named him yet, and Grainne did not press her to settle on anything before the naming ceremony when all the tribe would gather to welcome the child as one of their own. Orlaith was not convinced whose tribe the child belonged to. Her parents had succumbed to the war, but she was without doubt unwilling to name him for his father or raise him in his tribe.

Rían was a wicked and cruel man from the moment she arrived to greet her brother. Cormac had warned her, but Orlaith was a strong and self-determined woman who would make her own mistakes. The king was attractive in a plump way, and there was always wine or beer on hand. His bed was comfortable, and his arms were strong around her. And when he gripped her throat as he pushed upon her, she took it as an appetite of playfulness rather than aggressive nature. He soothed her with wine when he was done with her and he whispered words that women love to hear but seldom do. She met with him again the following night.

When he slapped her face and bit the skin of her breast, she knew that he was not only always angry, but a violent lover. She sought to leave his bed, but she had promised a king's command and so she lay obedient while he worked her. His wives were in the adjoining room when she walked from his bed and they gave her flowers as a gift. She was not the first girl to take to his quarters and she would not be the last. That he married no other women, for it was his right to do so as king, was telling. Three wives were plenty for a man who does not care for women as anything other than possession.

When the morning sickness took her and left her feeling broken inside, she knew that she was pregnant. She had known, in fact, even before the sickness. She sensed the life within her not long after taking to Rían's bed. But she did not tell him. He stopped calling for her to join him when he found a younger girl to fold into his bed furs, and Orlaith admitted only to herself that she was stung by his actions. She had slept with many men over the years. She knew what men wanted and her constant companionship was not one of those things. But that King Rían could so carelessly toss her aside after bruising her cheek and breaking her skin, as though she mattered nothing, was a pain that would follow her for months as the seedling grew within her.

When her belly swelled and her dresses were growing tight around her, she tried to hide herself away from view. Rían was not often seen walking the roads of the sept, but his wives and guards were always in the fields. Orlaith unstitched her dresses and added a panel of fabric to give the baby room, and she carried a bundle of furs or kindling or a basket of breads so that she had something with which to hide her belly. The important women of the sept seldom noticed her, and the men only wanted her for their beds. She was in her second trimester when her belly button had pushed forward before even her brother found out.

She did not want to tell him who the father was, but he pulled the information from her. 'No. You know what Rían does to the women who give him a daughter.'

'He has ten daughters,' Orlaith told him.

'Ten that are too old to be drowned in the river.'

Orlaith covered her belly with her hands as if she could protect the child with her fingers. 'And if it's a boy?'

'He will marry you and the boy will be his heir. But it will not be a boy.' He lowered his voice as one of the neighbouring farmers passed by. 'King Rían is cursed. No man is unlucky enough to have ten children and not one of them a boy.'

'Without girls, a man could have no child.'

'But ten of them? In a row?'

'That is not unlucky, that is just nature.'

'It is unlucky for a king,' Cormac said. 'He has been cursed by the Morrígan, and everyone knows it.'

Orlaith remained in her home for longer periods of time, venturing out only after nightfall. If Rían heard of her pregnancy, he did not come for her. Or he assumed the child belonged to another. But she had not gone to bed with another man since she left Rían's side when he made her feel weak and unworthy.

But she was done feeling weak. She discussed with Cormac, as King Rían advanced his army towards the neighbouring tribes and beyond to free the Fir Bolg slaves and strengthen his cause, that she would leave before giving birth.

'And where would you go?' he asked her. 'If you go home, there is nothing there.'

'I'll go north. Far north. In Ailigh, I can have a home.'

'Ailigh?' he scoffed. 'The Overking of the North would care nothing for a pregnant girl running from a southern king he may barely know.'

Her stern look belied the smile in her eyes. 'He will care about me and my child.'

Her preparations took some time, but she knew that if she did not leave soon, she would birth the child and Rían would have them both drowned in the river. She could not wait to cradle the girl in her arms, but she would be damned if she had her daughter in Rían's presence. Before she packed to leave, one of Rían's wives met with her and discovered her condition. 'King Rían will be pleased,' the woman said, but her voice trembled as she spoke. They both knew it would be a girl, as all the others had been girls, and Orlaith's fate would be sealed.

Orlaith pulled herself from her reverie when there was a knock at Grainne's door. She was suckling the child when she called out for the guest to enter.

Fionn opened the door and smiled at her.

'I am busy,' she said, covering her breast with her dress.

'I only come to see how you are.'

'I am alive and so is my child. It is a good day.'

'May I enter?'

'What reason do you have to bother me, Fionn?' She looked

114

away from him, realising that her upper arm was numb under the boy's head, and the child was asleep, a sheen of perspiration behind his ear.

Fionn took this as an invitation. He entered, closing the door behind him and staving off the early spring chill from outside. He wiped the soles of his fur-lined boots at the stoop. 'The Imbolc celebrations are tonight.'

'I am glad you came all this way to tell me, or I might have brushed the hearth for Samhain instead.'

Fionn hooked his foot around the leg of a stool and dragged it close to her. When he sat, he leaned forward. 'You pretend to hate me, but you tease me.'

'Since when did little boy Fionn become so forthright in his words?'

'When I decided what I wanted in life.'

Orlaith looked at the baby so that she would not have to stare into his eyes. 'You were so skinny as a child, you looked like a corpse without flesh.'

'I told you, I have grown. In all areas.'

She looked at him, saw him smiling, his eyes bright in the firelight. 'Do you have a purpose in being here, or do you revel in making women blush?'

'We should be wed.'

Orlaith carried her baby to his cot. When she turned, Fionn had risen and stood behind her, his body close. 'We should not,' she said.

'Why not?' He took her hands in his, but she pulled them away from him.

'Fionn.'

He looked at her.

'We cannot.'

'Why not?'

'Because I am not a woman to be wed. To anybody.'

'You think less of yourself than I do.'

'You think more of yourself than you do of me.' She turned from him, stroked her son's head, and she drew tighter the leather string at the neck of her dress which she had loosened when she was feeding him.

'I think only of you,' Fionn said. 'Since you came back to Ailigh, I have thought of nothing else.'

'That does not bode well for the training of Rónán's boys.'

'Orlaith, it is love.'

'It is nothing of the kind,' she said, finding her resolve. She walked across the room, coming out from under his shadow. 'And love is no reason for marriage. You are too old not to know this.'

'If love means that I would protect you—and your child—from harm, it is every reason for marriage.'

'You have nothing to offer me.'

'What would you like? I will get it for you. Property? I own a third of the cattle in Rónán's fields. I am his tanist.'

Orlaith moved to the door and opened it, standing aside to indicate that he should leave. 'You have no land of your own.'

'As Rónán's heir, all this will be mine one day.'

She shook her head. 'You know that is not true. Rónán has a son. When he is of age, he will assume the role of tanist, and then where will you be? A tall man without a field to piss on.'

'I will buy you a field and we can piss on it together.'

She smiled despite herself. 'And the world would be at rights with the two of us naked and pissing in a sodden field.'

'We can get naked now if this is what you want.'

She flattened her lips to break her smile. 'Go about your business, Little Boy Fionn, before I kick you across every field in a hundred-rod distance.'

Fionn walked to the door, stopped before crossing the threshold into the cold morning, and touched her chin. 'Wed me and you can kick me as far as you like.'

She laughed. 'Go.'

She closed the door behind him and returned to her son's side. She held her breath to calm her heart, and then hurried back to the door.

'Fionn,' she called, and he turned to look at her. 'You may walk me up the hill tonight for the celebrations.'

His smile dimpled his cheeks and stretched his square jaw.

She closed the door again.

To her son, she said, 'When you are old enough to propose marriage to a woman, that is how you should do it.'

The boy twitched in his sleep.

She spent the rest of the day pacing her room. Of the two dresses she had brought with her, neither was suitable for a celebration. But she found some bone needles on Grainne's table and stitched a patch in her green dress.

Grainne did not return home all day, busy with her preparations, and she saw neither Cormac nor Rónán in two days.

By the time the sun was low on the horizon and the Ó Mordha boys were marching up the hill with wineskins and barrels and unlit torches, Orlaith stood by the door and waited for Fionn to arrive.

117

Chapter 14

Tonight, the spirits of the ancestors were watching her. Áed would be there, unseen, among the revellers. As would Bec, her sister, and her parents, all dead at the hands of the Fir Bolg two years prior.

Grainne raised her hood to shield her face from the eyes of the gods, and as she walked the grassy incline towards the unlit fires, she touched her alder staff to the ground with every step, reminding the earth that they were here and eager for the coming sustenance of the warmer season. They were one, the earth and man.

Ahead of her, carried high on a chair, a young girl on the cusp of womanhood wore a long dress dyed the blue of rebirth. A crown of squill flowers circled her head, their buds only just opening—a sure sign of the demise of winter. The four boys that carried her chair sang the song of Bríg, daughter of the Dagda, goddess of fertility and healing.

Behind her, Rónán carried his son in his arms, wrapped in a thick winter fur, while Achall carried Bec, Grainne's niece, named for her mother. Because of her duties as druid, young Bec was fostered to a woman of the Ó Mordha clan, but Grainne visited her and told her tales of the girl's mother, a young woman whom Grainne had not seen since she was a child herself until her final day of life. The two-year-old girl would not meet the same fate as her mother. Grainne would see to it.

At the top of the hill, the boys of Ailigh and the families of the local septs had gathered in a circle around the unlit fires.

The sun was low in the skyline, turning mountains to gold, and when the procession reached the summit, timed with precision, seven boys lit their torches and walked each to one of the fires. The central balefire was ringed by six smaller fires, each one representing a unique element of their culture—the largest being the goddess Bríg, for whom the celebration was honoured; the remaining six were representatives of the other gods of their tribe, the goddesses, the ancestors, the animals, the plants, and for the fortune of futures yet to come.

The girl who was dressed as Bríg, chosen for the timing of her coming womanhood, was raised higher on the shoulders of the boys, and her chair would not be lowered to the ground until the fires were lit and the goddess could walk among them. The gathered clansmen would bow low to her and she would bestow upon them gifts of warm bread from a sack, and a small cutting of an oak tree which would be planted by each family to provide them with shelter and wealth for the year to come.

The procession halted, and Grainne bowed three times to the setting sun as the gold rays dulled to a warm orange glow. Voices were raised in song as they waited for the sun to fall on the final day of winter, and when the last bead of sunlight dazzled the horizon, Grainne beat her staff on the ground, the seven torch-carrying boys raised their arms, and in unison they lowered the torches towards the balefires.

Thick grey smoke swirled around the hilltop, and the people

were silent.

The girl in the chair readied herself, and the boys that carried her struggled to maintain their composure and keep her aloft.

When yellow flames licked over the bales, a cheer erupted from the crowd and Grainne gave thanks to the collective gods. She bowed three times to the memory of the winter sun.

But the crowd grew still and quiet. When Grainne looked, the balefires had not caught, and all of them had gone out.

All seven fires were unlit.

A whispered curse cut through the people.

Grainne tightened her grip on her staff, and she glanced at Rónán. The fear on his face must have matched her own.

In repentance, Grainne lay prostrate on the ground before their representation of Bríg, the girl who looked afraid that her life would be taken from her for the failed fires, and Grainne praised the goddess and sought healing from her wisdom. The boys who carried the chair were two-handing the legs so as not to let Bríg touch the cold ground and destroy their chance of a fruitful summer.

After a moment of silence, Grainne stood, bowed to the goddess, bowed to the sun, and bowed to the central balefire. She touched her staff to the grass and nodded to the torch carriers. The boys made a second attempt to light the fires, and in the stillness that followed, the crackle of damp bales could be heard.

Smoke rose.

And the fires caught.

A joyful cry ruptured from the fearful people, and when Grainne raised her arms in welcome relief, many of the assembly started to laugh, quiet and nervous at first, louder as others joined in. The gods had been toying with them. All was not lost.

Bríg was lowered from her chair and she stood to the applause of everyone. As she weaved her way barefoot through the crowd, handing out warm bread and oak-cuttings, Rónán stepped to Grainne's side.

'An omen?' he whispered.

She nodded. 'A bad one, I fear.'

'But it does not pertain to the coming season.'

'No. The fires are lit and Bríg walks among us; the months will be warm and prosperous. For many weeks, the omens speak of far more sinister tidings. It is with guilt that I say I cannot interpret them alone.'

'What do you propose?'

Grainne looked at her alder staff. It had been cut and carved by her master for the ceremony of her graduation. 'I must seek the advice of the archdruid in the north,' she said. 'He alone will know their meaning or can assist in interpreting these omens.'

The young girl came before them, bowed, and handed their king a small chunk of bread, still ripe with the smells of baking. 'Food for the coming season that the mouths of your home may not go hungry.' She bowed a second time and handed him a cutting from the oak tree. 'A blessing from the earth that you may always have shelter and tools for wealth.'

He accepted the gifts and smiled.

The girl turned to Grainne and repeated the offering. 'Thank you, child.'

Bowing still, the girl said, 'My Lady, the fires?'

Grainne touched her chin and raised her face so that she

would look at her. 'It was not your fault. You are truly a child of Bríg. Go; continue your offerings and then return to your seat for the sacrifice.'

The music, dancing and drinking commenced.

Grainne turned to Rónán. 'I will leave at first light if you will allow it.'

'I would not have my spiritual advisor travel alone in such dark times.'

'I will take a swift carbad and ride only by day. There are enough allied septs between here and the druids that I will have plenty of opportunities for rest and shelter. I can be there in a few days and return with answers.'

Rónán nodded. 'I will have my fastest horses prepared for you. My wife will organise provisions for your journey.'

'Thank you, my Lord.'

'I would still rather send Fionn with you.'

Grainne shook her head. 'He will be needed here to help train the new boys. If war is truly coming, no hand should remain untrained. I will be faster alone; the druids' compound can be unwelcoming to anyone outside of the brehon culture.'

Rónán left her to arrange matters for her journey. Grainne took her position by the central fire, around which the revellers danced, the flickering yellow glow of the flames giving the landscape an ethereal quality, pushing swaying shadows beyond winter's reach.

When the young girl dressed as Bríg returned to her seat, her sacks depleted, a goat was led up the hill towards the fires and was presented to the girl.

She stood, bowed three times to it—three being the sacred number—and praised the animal for its sacrifice. She glanced at

Grainne to ensure she had performed the ritual well, and the druid smiled upon her.

Grainne unsheathed her ceremonial dagger, gave thanks to the bleating goat, and then spilled its blood on the grasses in front of the fire. The goat's spirit would enter the ground as an offering to the goddess Bríg, and the earth would heat with her love for her people.

Grainne stood back and watched the fires. She did not need to cast the bones to see that the omens were being unkind. That the fires did not ignite at first was a disturbing sign, but her prayers had overcome the burdens of evil and winter was truly over.

And yet the omens were unrelenting.

She mouthed a prayer to her personal goddess that the arch-druid would have the answers she needed.

Around her, the festivities continued, though she felt apart from it. In her white robes, she shone like the dawn sun, but her path was twisted with shadows. Her most gracious Lady Cáer had not visited her dreams since before the Battle of Knockdhu, but Grainne longed for one more visitation, a last knowledgeable and peaceful word from the mouth of her god-dess. Without the guidance of Cáer, she was lost and vulnerable. Lacking the goddess' clear path, she would be mired in bramble thorns for the length of her days.

She doubted the words of her own wisdoms. Perhaps she had not been able to interpret the omens because she was not wor-thy to do so. She had overlooked their meaning simply because she had no vision to see them.

The young girl in Bríg's guise bowed to Grainne from her seat. 'You are worthy of the world,' she said, and then she danced away beyond the fires.

Grainne lowered her head and gave thanks to Cáer for her answer. 'But,' she said, shielding her face with her hands, 'next time tell me in person.'

As Grainne left the festivities to return to her quarters and prepare for her travels, she met Orlaith and Fionn coming up the hill. Orlaith carried her infant in her arms and Rónán's chief advisor walked a slow pace beside her.

'We would have come sooner,' Fionn said, 'but my lady was absorbed in preparing herself for the revelries.'

'I am not your lady,' Orlaith said, but Grainne could tell it was in jest.

'May I hold the child?'

Orlaith offered the boy to the druid and she wrapped her cloak closer around her shoulders.

'I must journey north at dawn,' Grainne said, 'but I will return soon.' She cradled the boy for a moment, rocking him in her arms, and she kissed his head and handed him to Fionn. 'May I speak with Orlaith?'

Fionn walked ahead.

'Whenever anyone wants to speak to me in private, I fear it is never good news,' Orlaith said.

'We haven't spoken much since your arrival.'

'You are a druid, worthy of better conversation than I can provide. But I sense you wish to speak about King Rónán.'

Grainne's smile was small. 'You understand people better than many druids.'

'I am gifted by a curse,' Orlaith said. 'May I speak freely?'

Grainne nodded.

'Áed told me about you once—his sister, the great druid.

But mostly he spoke about Rónán. He loved him before he even knew it.'

'I could sense that in his final moments at Knockdhu. I would have liked to have seen them together before the end.'

'They tell me he was king for a short time, before he died.'

'It is true. He fought bravely, and he lived long enough to appoint Rónán as his heir.'

Orlaith laughed. 'With just moments as king, only Áed would do such a thing.'

'You speak of him with fondness.'

'I did not know him long before the war, but I knew that he was good.'

'I can see that you liked him a great deal.'

'I loved him dearly. Not as I would love a husband, but yes, I did. He had a strength in him that I have not seen in anyone else, not even my brother.'

'Rónán has been lost without him,' Grainne said.

'They were two faces of one man, as far as I could see.'

'Will you talk with him, Orlaith? I fear that he worries about things he has no control over. He misses Áed, but he should know that his memories need not be painful while he continues to live his life.'

'I do not see that my words would help, but I will do as you ask.'

As Grainne packed a small travel sack that night, she took her pouch of bones and cast them before sleep.

If the archdruid could not help her, nobody could.

125

Chapter 15

Eight black scars circled the ceremonial hilltop, the remains of seven fires and one spill of goat's blood. The air was redolent with the smell of charred wood and grasses, and the breeze that shifted over the hill stirred Rónán's tunic as it stirred his mind.

Grainne had set off at first light for the northern compound of druids and Rónán watched her carbad run a path towards the distant forest of silver birch until she disappeared under the canopy of naked branches. It would take her several days to arrive at the compound and the gods only knew how long her consultations with the archdruid would last before she returned. The young child's birthmark, the dead birds, the wheat rust, the unlit fires of ceremony—he could not begin to fathom their meanings. Nor would he attempt to do so; his was not to speculate on the divine rulings of the gods.

From his position atop the hill, looking around at the charred dust that circled him, he could forgive himself for thinking that these times of peace would last forever. In the stillness that surrounded him, he could make out the faint birdsong from the distant trees, and the sounds of early morning ablutions and chatter coming from within his walls. There was no training and no thunderous footfalls of approaching armies. He inhaled the smell of burnt wood.

If he had lived, Áed would have called him to his bed on a morning such as today, in the stillness of life, and they would have embraced and coupled together and then lay in quiet intimacy, listening to the sounds of each other's silence and content that life was as it should be.

But he did not live.

Rónán touched the hilt of his sword, the intricately carved work of his deceased companion. And he sighed.

Later today, he would meet with one of his outlying chieftains to discuss property damage that had occurred during the winter months. And then with another to talk about an unusual lapse in tax payments. Following that, he would meet with Fionn to discuss their plans for training the new boys and for rolling them into their daily routines.

'You should be doing this,' he said to the swirling breeze, 'not me. I'm not built for this.'

Soot from the fires settled on his leather boots.

Looking down the hillside towards the lough, he saw two figures standing by the shore and he recognised them. He kicked the dust from his boots and ambled down the hill.

When he was close enough, he could see that Cormac stood on the dark sand holding Orlaith's child, while Orlaith had submerged herself in the cold waters to bathe. They looked like a family at peace, not a displaced brother and sister who had fled from their violent king.

He watched them for a moment, noting how careful Cormac was being with the baby, before he announced his presence.

'It is well that you are well,' Cormac said with a bow to his king.

Orlaith waved from the depths of the dark waters.

'May I hold him?' Rónán asked, reaching his hands out. Cormac offered the child to him and when he was encased in his arms, Rónán said, 'I remember my son at such an age; they do not stay little for long.'

Cormac leaned close to look at the boy's sleeping face. 'Be careful he does not piss in your arms—he has just been fed.'

Stepping naked from the lough, Orlaith said, 'When you two old women are finished, I could do with some privacy.' She swiped excess water from her limbs with her hands, and then used a small linen cloth to dry herself.

Rónán and Cormac turned away to allow her to complete her rituals.

'Women are all the same,' Rónán said. 'We men bathe together and care nothing of it, but women feign a certain coyness that makes men adore them. It is a ploy; I am sure of it.'

'It is a ruse I take no part in advocating.'

'Neither of you,' Orlaith said from behind Áed's standing stone, 'are too big for a smack.'

The men laughed. Rónán said, 'This is why I count your sister among my closest confidantes. She has no problem with calling out the overking on his words.'

With a certain shyness that suggested to Rónán that the young man was testing just how far he could push his familiarity with the king, Cormac said, 'I would push her into a hole and leave her there to rot if I thought she could not find a way to climb out and murder me in my sleep.'

'I would not wait till you slept,' Orlaith said, coming to them now, dressed and with her hair knotted behind her head.

She took her child from Rónán's arms.

'I have no sister,' Rónán said to Cormac, 'but if I did, I would wish it to be Orlaith.'

He turned then, staring at the standing stone, and his features clouded.

Orlaith patted her brother's shoulder. 'Can you give us a moment?'

Looking from his sister to the king, Cormac bowed. 'I think you're in trouble.'

'I don't doubt it.' When Cormac had walked up the hillside towards Ailigh, Rónán turned to the woman and child. 'You may put the boy down before you abuse me.'

She smiled at him, a tender and fleeting response that turned the mood to one of sombre discourse. 'Sit with me,' she said, folding her legs underneath her on the moist sand.

Rónán obliged and they sat in silence.

At length, Orlaith said, 'I know what you are doing.'

He did not look at her.

Orlaith nuzzled her nose against her baby's warm skin. 'I sat here, at this very spot, when I first discovered Áed's love for you. He would not say it aloud, but I could see it in his eyes, could hear it in his voice.'

'And now he is gone,' Rónán said, his voice cracked.

'No. Because you will not let him go.'

He remained silent.

Orlaith shifted so that she faced him, though he continued to look away from her. 'Look at me, Rónán.'

He blinked, looked at her from the corner of his eyes, then looked away again. 'You ask too much of me. I cannot let him go.'

'But you must.'

'How can I forget him?'

'I do not mean to forget him. I would not let you. But look at yourself. You wallow in grief while, all around you, your people need you. You do not give them the attention they deserve.'

'I am overking of many tribes; they get the attention I can afford them.'

'You know they do not. Rónán, you suffer, but you need not suffer alone. I can see him in your face—you carry him around with you like a noose around your neck. You are a king, but you act like a child who longs for his mother's embrace. You try to talk the way he did. You train the boys the way he would have and act as he did. Don't you see? You are not yourself anymore. You are lost and while you look for him, you do not see the world as it is.'

'I died when he died,' Rónán said, looking away from her. The dark waters of the lough lapped against the mossy sand. The sun cast a shadow from Áed's standing stone across his knees.

'Part of you died. Do not let the rest of you be swallowed by your grief.'

Rónán stood and walked away from her, along the sands, and then he turned to her again. 'What would you have me do?' He knew his voice was raised, but he could not lower it even if he wanted to. 'I cannot pretend that my life is normal. When I blink, I see him in the darkness. I killed him; I was the one to pierce him with my blade and end his suffering as he bled out.'

Orlaith stood and nodded. 'You did not wound him. By your own admission, you ended his suffering. It was an act of selfless love, not one of betrayal.' She stepped towards him. 'You pierce your own heart daily because of it. But you need to see it for what it is—you loved him enough to ease his spirit. You gave him passage to Tír na nÓg and life in the Otherworld. You cannot crawl to him now through a fairy mound, as much as I know you want to.' She came closer still, and she softened her voice. 'You have friends to share your burdens. Let us carry them with you. Do not close yourself off from the world when everyone is begging to help you.'

He looked at her and realised that his fist was gripping the hilt of his sword in anger. She was right—every day that he thought of Áed, he stabbed himself against any desire to live. He loosened his grip and flexed his fingers. 'I am grateful for your words,' he said, 'but I have meetings to attend.'

As he turned to leave, Orlaith called his name. He stopped walking but did not turn back to her.

'Love him,' she said. 'Love him always. But now is the time to stop wallowing in self-pity.'

Throughout the day, he could not concentrate on the words the chieftains spoke to him, or the plans that Fionn put before him for the new boys. He thought of Grainne heading north, of what insights her archdruid might offer to her, and of his con- versation with Orlaith.

He respected her and knew that she was right—he was limp- ing through life as only half a man. But that realisation did not make it any easier to overcome.

When his day was complete and he had bathed, alone, in quiet solitude, he retired to his quarters to eat the evening meal with his wife and their child. Their cumal brought a table of meats and fruits, and a warmed jug of wine.

He and his wife sat opposite each other across the table, young Áed on the bench beside her. He was humming a toneless tune while Achall held another segment of fruit before his mouth for him to eat.

'Your meetings with the chieftains went well?'

Rónán drank from his cup and refilled it from the jug. It was a question without merit, and only his wife, unskilled in the arts of casual conversation, would ask him such a thing. 'Very well,' he said. His mind was so troubled that he could not recall the names of those chieftains he had met with.

'Yesterday's ceremonies seemed to go well?'

'Despite the fires unwilling to catch,' Rónán said. It was as though the omen had not even registered in her mind.

'Yes,' she said, pushing a piece of fruit into her son's mouth and then sucking sticky juices from her fingertips.

'You should let him chew before offering him more.'

'I know how to feed my child,' she said. She reached for the jug of wine and filled his cup again, though he had barely drunk from it. 'Did you remember to enquire about the chieftain Ó Ceallaigh's wife and children? They had an illness this time last year.' She gave him no time to answer. 'And the other chieftain—what was his name?—Cabhan Mac Dubhghaill. Did his old sow finally die?'

'I was not aware that his wife was close to death,' Rónán said. Though his voice was flat, the flicker of a smile played at the edges of his mouth.

'I meant his sickly heifer. She had stopped producing milk and calves a long time ago. He told us so on his last visit.'

'I know what you meant.' He consoled himself in the knowledge that Orlaith would have laughed. Anyone but Achall would have laughed.

'You must take these things seriously,' Achall said, holding yet another segment of fruit in front of her child's face. The boy's humming continued, his cheeks puffed with the food already wedged between them. 'An overking should know his chieftains' business. It is your duty to care, and it is only polite to enquire about their wives and their——'

'Cattle?'

'Yes, if needs be. Must I remind you daily in your duties as overking?'

'I can care for my people without needing to know the names of their heifers.' He drained his second cup of wine.

Achall dropped the fruit slice on the table. 'I try to mould you into the king you ought to be, the man that everyone looks up to, and you thank me by being petulant. You are not a child anymore, Rónán.'

'No. I am not a child. I am king.' He pulled the plate of fruit from her. 'And you feed that boy too much.'

She said, 'That boy has a name, one that you suffer me to call him daily.'

'It is a worthy name.'

'It is a dead man's name, a man who stole your heart from me before I could own it.'

'We will not discuss this again,' Rónán said. 'Our marriage was arranged by your sycophant of an uncle. You knew what I was before we wed and that I would never desire you. You are my wife and I respect that, but you cannot force your will upon me.'

'I am more than your wife, Rónán. I am your queen.'

He stood from the table. 'Good night, my queen,' he said,

133

bowing to her. He left his home, walked down through the ramparts, and out through the gates of his domain.

He inhaled the sweet smell of an early spring night and stared up at the stars that circled the fat moon above him. This was not a time of peace, he reminded himself. He faced a daily battle with his wife in his kingly affairs and in his private life. He had made a promise to maintain his marriage and to raise their child together, but that did not mean he would like it. Achall, since the moment they met, had sought to make him into something he was not. It would not work.

Orlaith was right—Rónán shut himself off from everyone to avoid growing too close, to cut relationships with anybody that Achall deemed inappropriate or unsuited to her husband, the king. He was not his own man. But he would take back his own balls before Achall trampled them into the ground.

134

Chapter 16

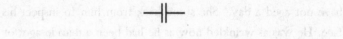

In the quiet stillness of morning, Grainne entered the druid's compound, flanked on the northern shore by a cliff, and to the south, east and west by an impenetrable forest of oak, rowan and alder trees. Not knowing the way, you would be lost among the foliage.

She journeyed through the nights, resting only as long as she needed, and when she arrived in the northern complex, the smell of the Imbolc fires was fresh on the air. She had not been here in so long, she was sure the archdruid would not even recognise her, but as she came to the simple gates—they were not fortified—the old man was waiting for her, his eyes disappearing in the folds of his skin as he smiled. The forest surrounding them was a warren of interconnected treetop lookouts. She knew that the minute she entered the treeline in the south, her master would be alerted to her presence.

'My dear girl,' he said, 'it is so great to see you again.'

She knelt at his feet and touched the earth with her forehead. The first time she saw him she was all of seven winters old, taken from her family because her tribe's druid had seen the earth and sky within her. She had been terrified and cried for the length of the journey north with the druid, Odhran, whom she learned perished during the Great Invasion. But when the archdruid touched her face and smiled at her, she had felt at home in his presence.

'Rise, dear child,' he said, reaching his wrinkled fingers down for her.

When she stood, he embraced her. 'My lord,' she said. 'You have not aged a day.' She stood back from him to inspect his face. He was as wrinkled now as he had been a decade ago, or longer. His silver hair fell about his face and his robes appeared as old as he did.

'And you have become a woman while I blinked.'

'Do not blink so slowly.'

'The omens have brought you here?'

Grainne nodded; of course he would have known about the omens. She long suspected that no bee would buzz its wings without the archdruid willing it.

'Come, dear one,' he said, ushering her further into the compound. 'A meal is being prepared for your arrival. We can talk of darker subjects with a belly full of meats.'

She walked with him to the great hall in the centre of the complex. Further out, the roundhouses and store huts were dotted haphazardly, but in the original heart of the druid's northernmost compound, there was an order to the layout of buildings, a painstaking architectural process that ensured every doorway faced the rising sun on the day of Samhain, so that the new year dawn could be welcomed into every home.

The seven Imbolc fire scars blackened the earth in front of the great hall.

Grainne smiled. She had left her training before the invasion and travelled southeast to take up residency with an eastern tribe in a time when she had known so little. But, as the arch-druid told her, one's training does not cease at the gates of his home, but should continue until the day you lay your head down for the final time and embrace the gods on your journey west.

The door to the great hall was opened as they approached it, and the archdruid bowed before entering. Inside, less than forty druids sat at the long table, waited on by their young initiates. With the archdruid's arrival, everyone stood and fell silent. The old man showed Grainne to an empty seat and then, slow, shuffling, he walked to the head of the table. When he sat, so too did the others.

A boy of thirteen, dressed in the pale grey of an initiate, brought a flattened bronze plate to Grainne and then filled her cup with spring water. 'Blessed are the lips that eat,' he said.

'And blessed the hands that feed,' she replied.

He bowed to her and retreated to the wall with the other initiates. They would eat when the druids were finished and they would swap places, for a druid knows that you are nothing if not for others. To give help and assistance is more important than receiving it, and it is their duty to honour the gods with such service. The initiates, young in their training, were just as important to the order of the earth.

The food was brought to the table and, in a ceremony that was reserved only for special occasions, the young initiates carved the meats for the druids. The lad who served her was quick with the carving knife but lacked the skill at cutting clean slices from the bone. When the first slice broke under the serrated blade, she heard him utter a quiet curse word.

They ate in silence, as is the druid's way, contemplating

their various tasks and offering silent prayer to their personal gods. Grainne gave thanks to her most gracious lady Cáer, grateful that the archdruid was well, but sorrowful that so few druids remained under his service.

When the meal was consumed, the initiates cleared the table and returned, standing behind the chair of the one they had served. Grainne offered the boy her seat. She brought him a fresh bronze plate and filled his cup.

'Blessed are the lips that eat,' she said, bowing to him.

'And blessed the hands that feed,' he mumbled.

She could see a lacklustre sheen in his eyes that reminded her of her brother.

When the initiates had eaten their fill, the druids gathered the plates, and they were taken away for washing.

Grainne returned to the boy's side. 'What is your name?'

'I am Gallen,' he said. That he did not add his father's name was informative. 'And you are Grainne Ní Airic.'

'I am Ní Mordha now,' she said, daughter of Mordha, 'for I have sworn myself to the king, but yes, I am she. How do you know me?'

'Everyone knows you,' he said before walking away.

Grainne came to the archdruid's side and seated herself at his left. She did not wish to interrupt his contemplations, but she knew he would be aware of her presence even with his eyes closed.

'I see you have met young Gallen. He will be a great druid one day, if only he can temper his anger. Come, we should discuss some matters in private.'

He flourished his fingers to honour the gods, and led her to his roundhouse, where they were joined by his three chief advisors. They sat in a circle. Grainne had met Alma many times before, and she greeted her with openness, but she did not recognise the others.

From her pack, Grainne unwrapped her dead blackbird, and the others stared at it as if they could divine the cause of death. Grainne explained, 'A child was born, marked by the stains of birth on his face, and then a flock of birds fell from the sky before me with no discernible reason. And worse,' she said, pausing, composing herself, 'all seven of our Imbolc fires failed to light.'

The gathered druids nodded with grave concern. 'My chieftain,' Alma said, 'had four pregnant sheep—I inspected them myself. Six nights ago, not one of them had any evidence of pregnancy. No stillbirths, no swollen stomachs.'

'How is this possible?' Grainne asked.

Alma shook her head. 'If it was not a spate of false pregnancies among the sheep, then certainly the gods took the lambs from us.'

One of the men spoke. 'I am Seróg,' he said, by way of an introduction to Grainne. 'In the midwinter, thick with snow and rains, our river did not rise despite the rainfall.'

The archdruid stopped them before they could continue to illustrate their omens. 'These are not the only signs that have been brought to me. And it seems the gods are quiet.'

Grainne said, 'There is a king in the south who threatens war.'

The archdruid nodded. 'King Rían marches on the Hill of Teamhair. He amasses a Fir Bolg army as great as that of the invasion, greater even than your Ó Mordha tribesmen have brought together in the times since. If he has not taken the Ard

Rí's seat by now, he soon will.'

'Why would the gods deign to warn us of a war in the south when there is always a war in some dark corner or other?' Alma asked.

The archdruid gripped the shaft of his staff and closed his eyes. 'I am not convinced that this is a war, but an annihilation,' he said. 'Rían Ó Hargon is not a man content with ruling a land but destroying it.'

Seróg said, 'If—or when—he crowns himself as Ard Rí, he will drive his forces north until there is not a man left who is not under his control. But what can we do? Why do the gods tease us with these omens—we are so few and cannot defeat him.'

The archdruid sat back in his chair. 'I will ponder it and give an answer by morning. Perhaps the omens are not for us, but for all of Éirinn.'

The others stood to leave. 'Come,' Alma said to Grainne, 'I will show you to a room for your stay.'

'I don't suppose my old room is available?'

'You wish to sleep with the initiates? So many of the old rooms are empty, I am certain we can accommodate you, but we can give you a home on the east if you wish.'

'My old room will be perfect, thank you.' Grainne bowed to her master and walked with Alma across the yards.

'You have grown,' Alma said.

'You look exactly as I remember. If I did not know better, I would believe that time has no meaning here.'

'You flatter me. I grow old and weary, and my bones clank and creak with every move.'

Grainne smiled and took the woman's arm. 'You must lather

them in oils, then, for I do not hear the music of your bones.'

Alma tapped her temple. 'I hear them here, constantly.'

She led Grainne to the initiates hut, a longhouse divided into many rooms, and when she was settled, Grainne came out of her quarters to take a walk in the sunlight that filtered through the treetops. Outside the doorway of the longhouse, she found the boy who served her during the meal. He sat on a stool, peeling the skins off root vegetables.

'You are not in a lesson?' Grainne asked.

He looked up at her, then returned to his work. 'I am banished from the Lady Niamh's classes.'

'Might I ask why?' Grainne hunkered down beside his pot and inspected one of the peeled roots. He had missed some flecks of skin, but she did not bring it to his attention.

'She does not appreciate spirited debate.'

Grainne suppressed a laugh; the boy did not say it as a joke. 'You must be nearing the end of your initiate training period?'

Gallen dropped a cleaned root into the pot and picked another from the ground. He did not speak at once but considered his answer first. 'Not even the master would take me under his employ. I have yet to conquer my temper, I am told.'

'What is the cause of your temper?'

The boy shrugged in a sullen manner. 'I will tell you when I understand it myself.'

That evening, Grainne slept in her old pallet bed and she felt at peace. The bed was built for a child and her feet protruded from the end of it, but she curled herself tight and slept well and without dreams.

When the morning came, she bathed and dressed, and ate

with the others in the great hall before joining the archdruid and his advisors in his home.

'I have prayed to the gods,' the old man said, his voice thick with worry, 'but they speak no words to me. We must join in silent adoration in the hopes that the purpose of our omens is revealed to us. I am sorry I do not have better comforts to offer you.'

Before she left, Grainne bowed to her master. 'My kindest lord, I must ask you a favour.'

'It is granted. The boy is yours to train if you would have him.'

'You are all-seeing,' she said, with a smile.

'Perhaps the omens have brought you to us for that very reason. The boy is lost here, and I cannot reach him further. I am sure you can temper him and teach him well. Go, now, and ask your gods for their kindness. I fear a great darkness is coming and I have no words to express how anxious this makes me.'

Grainne nodded. That the archdruid, the warmest and bravest man she knew, was scared by the omens that permeated the land, chilled her very soul.

Chapter 17

In the days that followed Imbolc, Bromaid was kept under a tighter watch by the farmer from dawn until dusk. Only in the dark evenings, listening to the braying of the farmer's hounds and the bleating of the new lambs as the sun set, was he alone. The southern warrior-king, Rían Ó Hargon, was drawing closer; that much was clear. No news had come from the sept further down the hillside, and the farmer ceased all dealings with his clansmen. He shut his wife and daughter away and Bromaid had not seen Ailbe in days.

His groin itched for her.

A light burned at the doorway of the farmer's roundhouse, and Bromaid could not be certain that the old man lay in wait for his nightly whistles that begged the girl to his side. The chain at his neck was shortened so that he could travel only as far as the door of his hut but no further. The iron that encased the circle of his neck scratched the skin and bruised his jawline when he slept, uncomfortable, like the dogs that had been chained up outside the farmer's home. That the old man had not killed him yet was a wonder. But when the war was over, if the local tribesmen were successful against the enemy, the farmer's fields would still need to be ploughed, the sheep sheared, the seeds sown.

In the mornings, his collar was removed, and it had become the farmer's ritual to say, 'Move against me and see where your head will fall.'

Bromaid kept his head bowed, plotting as he worked. When King Rían's army came for him, he would tear the old man's heart out with his bare hands and feed it to his wife. And then he would bed Ailbe on their blood, bathing in the sap of her deceased parents.

The farmer, with nothing better to do when he ought to be preparing for war, stood over Bromaid in his daily obligations, his hand on the hilt of his short sword, his feet planted as if ready for battle. Bromaid would find it comical if he had not paused to realise that he, too, would do the same if jeopardised by an unknown entity that threatened to free his slaves.

He carried seed bags from the store hut to the fields for the sheep to feed, and the farmer walked five paces behind him, like a discontented shadow. Even when he dropped the large sack and its seeds spilled across the thin grasses, the farmer stood behind him and waited while he scooped as much of it as he could back into the bag. Had the old man not been preoccupied with fear, Bromaid would have received a beating for his clumsiness.

Several days after the Imbolc fires had ceased smouldering the air with their charred remains, while Bromaid and the farmer were in the fields, a messenger from the tribe's king hurried up the hill towards them.

'King Ailill,' the messenger said, bowing to the farmer, 'has requested all fighting men to attend him.'

'The war has come?'

The messenger, ignoring the question, said, 'All Fir Bolg slaves are to be brought before the king and contained within his walls. You are to assemble for the king by nightfall.'

'What of my wife and daughter? I cannot leave them here unprotected.'

'It is yours to decide. Bring them within the king's walls or hide them safely.' He bowed and hurried away to the next farmstead.

The farmer's wife was frantic, and young Ailbe sobbed against her mother's shoulder. The old man watched the southern horizon as if he could scry signs of attack from the treetops. Beyond the forest that separated their tribe from their neighbours, the sky was black, but Bromaid could not say if it was storm clouds that gathered there, or smoke from a burning sept.

By late afternoon, the farmer locked his wife and daughter in the food store behind his home, and he tethered Bromaid to the back of his cart, wrists bound together and a rope around his neck, walking behind the farmer's wagon. Although the farmer panicked and, on the journey down the hillside, kept checking the sword at his belt as if it would disappear, Bromaid was smiling.

Inside the king's walls, the slaves were forced into a cell built into the side of a small hill. He sat there with thirty-six other Fir Bolg men, vying for the warmer patches of ground near the entrance where the sun filtered in. They were not provided with food or water, and one small latrine had been dug in the corner for their needs. Cramped together as they were, the cell was pungent with body odours and the ground was slick with sweat. It was not designed for so many occupants at once.

When the sun was hidden beyond the distant forest and the moon was not yet visible to them, the Fir Bolg slaves were weary, and conversations halted. They lay together, back to back, and used the warmth of the man beside him to ward off the evening chill that descended around them. Outside the cell, they could hear the crackle of fires and the footfall of guards that marched around the trenches encircling the king's walls. The smell of roasted meat came to them on the wind.

Bromaid could not sleep. In the blue darkness, he listened for sounds of war but heard only the whispers of bored guards and the incessant grating noises of bush-crickets.

'We could overpower the guards,' one man said in the darkness, 'if we could break the cell gate.'

'Hush,' someone responded. 'Why attempt to escape now when we'll be free by morning?'

Bromaid did not realise that he had fallen asleep until the sound of cheering outside the walls woke him at dawn. As a single unit, all thirty-seven Fir Bolg slaves stood and pressed themselves against the narrow gate to see better.

'Have they come?' someone asked.

'Prepare to fight, men,' another said.

At once, the gate was surrounded by guards, their swords drawn. The gate was opened and, too few against the armed warriors, the Fir Bolg slaves were shackled together by thick chains at their necks, their hands bound likewise. Hemmed in on all sides by sword- and spear-carrying guards, the slaves were marched outside of the king's gates, encouraged by a whip, and in two rows were chained to a sturdy oak, the significance of which was not lost on Bromaid—the sacred tree was meant to protect them, not for their own good, but the good of their king.

Bromaid looked across the sloping hillside. King Ailill's men were gathered there, facing south, but beyond that, he could not see the opposing army of ex-slaves, freed by a southern warrior-king, men of his nation who had come to untie their shackles. The slaves at his sides each competed for the finest view of the field, but none could see beyond the local warriors.

King Ailill was easily identifiable when he came through the walls and his army parted for him—a squat man, shorter than most by at least a head, and his bright red hair was combed high in a hollow attempt at increasing his stature. He looked like a child wielding his father's longsword, but Bromaid had heard how vicious the little man could be.

A voice came from across the field, out of Bromaid's view. 'Surrender to me and I will not have you killed.'

The diminutive king with his tall red hair, shouted, 'Your war is folly. You will not have my slaves or my lands.' He pointed behind him to the line of slaves. 'This is the prize you seek. I have brought them forth so that they can witness your death and then they will return to their duties as slaves. Your campaign ends here. You will take nothing of mine.'

'I will take your head, my little friend.' It was the deep voice of a tall man, a man who radiated power. Bromaid would follow that voice for as long as was necessary, until King Rían had taken the seat of the high king, and then he would face the new Ard Rí and would gut him while the rest of his people watched. Bromaid would rule, and lead his men into a new era, a time when the Fir Bolg no longer served any master, where they would be free to do as they wished, so long as they bowed to him.

He could feel the beat of a thousand feet in his chest as the opposing armies charged towards each other, and a tingle itched in his arms. He could see, as King Ailill's men moved down the hillside, the man who had contested their small leader. King Rían was barrel-chested and broad, with a braided moustache that hugged his cheeks as he ran into battle.

'We can count his kills from here,' one of the slaves said, pointing. By the time he had finished the sentence, King Rían had felled two warriors. His was first blood, as any king worth his salt was capable of.

The group of slaves watched him. He was a powerful warrior, full of bluster and bravado, and the men at his back, those Fir Bolg slaves he had already freed, fought side by side with Rían's men as though they were one unit, one tribe. Bromaid could smell the blood that tainted the air.

Rían ran, leather shoes sinking in the mud as the field was churned underfoot. A brave man swung his sword overhead and Rían raised his shield arm. He deflected the blow, but the blade took a slice at his upper arm.

Bromaid could see the blood weeping over his sleeve even from this distance, but Rían cut the man down and moved on.

His quarry was King Ailill, the opposing army mere flies between him and his savagery. The little bastard had disappeared into the fray and, given his size, Rían would be hard pressed to find him among his taller warriors. Being short had its advantages, Bromaid thought; the ability to weave under shields would allow for more kills if your arm was strong.

Rían cut in with a sideswipe of his sword, and the sharpened blade separated one of Ailill's warriors from his forearm.

He saw the tiny man, his hair flapping in the wind despite the thick amounts of oils and resins that had been used to hold it in place.

Rían scooped up a spear that had been broken on the ground and he used the bronze tip to punch through a man's throat, pushing forward with it so that the warrior bounced on the ground.

The tiny king slid in the dirt and came up to hack at one of Rían's men. Rían charged him, taking out two men before he could reach Ailill.

From behind, he gripped the king's long hair and bashed the hilt of his sword against his neck. Ailill stumbled and fell to his knees. Rían reached down and smacked the man's face into the dirt until blood gushed from his broken nose.

Around him, the battle continued. Bromaid held his breath as Rían dragged King Ailill away from the fray, a clump of the man's hair coming loose in his hand, and when he was far enough away, closer to the tethered slaves, he filled his lungs and screamed. Ailill, beaten, knelt at his side. Rían pushed his sword into the man's bent leg, pinning him to the earth, and he removed his shield from his arm.

'Small men have big egos,' Bromaid heard him say, Rían's spittle spraying across Ailill's face. 'Stand your army down.'

Ailill laughed, blood staining his moustache and goatee. 'They do not fight for me. They fight for their lands.'

Rían picked up a stone that weighed heavy in the palm of his hand. 'Their lands are mine now.' He beat Ailill on the head with the stone. 'Tell your men to stand down.'

Dazed, Ailill took a moment before he shook his head. He shouted, 'Fight on. Fight true.'

Rían struck him again. Bromaid heard a crack from within

the man's skull. Ailill's head was bowed, unable or unwilling to move.

Bromaid saw Rían take his dagger from his belt and cut open the smaller king's tunic that was soaked in sweat and blood. He sliced the king's nipples off and still the man did not react. It was the ultimate degradation: a king's loyal subject would kiss his breasts to honour him. Ailill was no longer a king.

Rían smacked the large stone against Ailill's head, and his body fell backwards, pinned at the knee by his sword and twisting in grotesquery. He leaned down and cut open the man's belly, disembowelling him. He pulled forth the guts and raised them aloft. Rían screamed his victory.

But, as Ailill said, his men did not stop fighting.

It was midday by the time the battle was won. The dead were burned and Ailill's body was dumped in the bog waters that flooded his lower fields.

King Rían, bathed black with blood, came before the tethered slaves and he drew his sword again, planting it in the damp ground before him. He said nothing as he appraised them, and when his eyes met theirs, they went to their knee and bowed.

Bromaid, from the middle of the chain, nodded before kneeling. This was a king he could get behind until his own time came. He looked at the tall warrior-king who stood before them, the man's hands red and black from King Ailill's innards.

A druid, taller even than King Rían, came to his side. When he lowered his hood, Bromaid could see that he was Fir Bolg, an ancient, leather-skinned man whose dark eyes spoke of horrors untold. At his hip, obscured by the folds of his cloak, the hilt of his sword, twisted gold, gleamed in the midmorning sunlight.

'You kneel to me,' King Rían said, 'but I am not yet a man deserving of your fealty.' He nodded to his druid. 'Unchain them, Gorid. They are free men now.'

When he was freed, Bromaid stood and rubbed his wrists and his neck. Among the dead that littered the field, he was certain that his farmer had perished. He considered the fate of the farmer's wife and young Ailbe, locked as they were inside the food store in an abandoned farmstead. When King Rían spoke again, Bromaid turned to him.

'I ask nothing of you that you would not willingly give. Refuse my offer and you can leave. I have freed you, and you owe me nothing in return. But hear my offer; if it does not interest you, I will feed and clothe you and you can strike out alone to forge your own path.' He rubbed his hands together, spreading the blood of his enemy, and then he revealed to them his palms. 'When we are done here, I will march east to Teamhair, seat of the high king. I intend to take his seat and rule this land, a land built by invasion. Like your people tried two years ago, my people succeeded many years before. We came here and we took the land from your people who had ruled before us. For centuries, your kind have been enslaved, on these shores and on other coasts. For years you have bowed to one man or another, but I tell you—no more shall you take a knee for a man who does not respect you. You will not carry the weight of another's sins. This I say to you—join my force, not as slaves, not as victims, but as free men. My cause is your cause. When I take the seat of the high king, I will give praise to your gods and to your ancestors, and I will establish a new order over these wondrous hills. Any man who fights for me will be given, in return, a square of land upon which he can build his life. And he will be given my thanks and his weight in gold. Thereafter, I will swear my loyalty to your kind if you swear it in return. We can thrive together, you and me. We can take this land and make it ours. It is your right and your destiny. Together, we will be free. Will you join me?'

Thirty-six Fir Bolg men took to their knees again. Only Bromaid stood, his arms folded across his chest, and his eyes narrowed.

King Rían faced him. 'You are free to leave if you have the desire to do so, my friend. I will not stop you.'

'I have no such desire. But I have a question.'

'Ask it.'

Bromaid looked down at the men on their knees beside him, and then he looked at the tall druid whose left eye twitched with tension. Then he turned to the king. 'In this new world that you seek to establish with our help, you have promised us land and freedom. But when you are high king, when we have won your war for you, how good is your word that you will not round us up and enslave us again? Why should we trust a native who, two years ago, no doubt killed many of our kind?'

King Rían smiled. 'My word is solid. My druid can scry the omens for you, if you seek it, and you will know it to be true. We will slaughter our way across this land and when I am king, you will be safe and free. What use is it to be king if you have no men to join you at your table?'

'My master,' Bromaid said, pointing down the hillside, 'dead at a Fir Bolg's hands I am glad to say, has left his wife and daughter at home.'

King Rían laughed. 'You have no master now. Go; you have my leave. Take some men. Torch your enslaver's home and do what you will with his wife and daughter.' He thrust out his hand in the fashion of the Fir Bolg. 'All I ask is that you return to me and join my cause. Our cause. Do you agree?'

Bromaid looked at the hand for a moment, at the blood that dried there. And then, with a smile, he shook it.

Chapter 18

When Achall came to Orlaith today, she was quieter than usual. 'Walk with me,' she said as she approached. Orlaith had dragged a small wooden chair outside to sit in the early morning sun and feed her baby. A peaceful breeze tousled the ends of her red curls and Ailigh was calm save for the distant ring of sword against sword on the training fields far below.

Orlaith bowed to the queen, wrapping her baby tighter in his fur swaddling, and she fell into step beside the younger woman. Behind them, Achall's own child accompanied his mother on her walk, though he held the hand of a cumal girl. He was a quiet child; Orlaith had yet to hear him scream or cry like most children.

'He will be a broody man, that one,' Orlaith said to Achall.

The queen looked at her son and nodded. 'Men are either broody or violent. There is little in between.'

'Between broody and violent, I would expect to find them loving.'

Achall snorted. 'They are loving only when they want something. Remember that. I have seen you in Fionn's company on occasion.'

'He attends me whether I wish it or not, my lady.'

'Do not encourage him. Fionn seeks one thing from you and one thing only. He is a man, after all.'

Orlaith did not mention that he had asked her to wed him.

'All men think with their poles,' Achall said. 'It is left to us women to slap them when they are deserving of it. Which is often.'

Orlaith had seen Fionn several times in the previous days, but since she rejected his request of marriage, he was reluctant to approach her. She missed his wicked tongue.

They walked in silence for a time, around the inner rampart and down into the second, wider area. A young boy with a bloodied nose, sustained on the training field, bowed to his queen as he ran by, keeping his hand under his nose to catch the dripping blood, and he carried on his way towards the kitchens. With Grainne visiting the druids in the north, the boys sought their care from the women of Ailigh who would nurse them like mothers.

'Are you trained with the sword?' Orlaith asked the queen.

Achall looked at her. 'I am surrounded by warriors and those in training. I would have no need of a sword.'

'What if you are travelling and ambushed?'

Achall picked the colourful head of a weed from the ground. She inspected its petals. 'Even in my own community, I am being watched by Rónán's guards. Were you to assault me, you would have an arrow in your back before your hand would touch me. I cannot think of any circumstance in which I would be ambushed successfully. Besides,' she added, dropping the flower at her feet, 'I do not travel.' She held her hands out. 'May I carry him for a time?'

Orlaith obliged. 'All women should have the knowledge to

at least strike a man should he attack, don't you agree? Especially if they all think with their standing stones.'

Achall touched the baby's nose. 'Slaves and whores may fight in the dirt like wild boars, but a woman of sensible mind must never be seen making a fist.'

'This is how you see me? As a fighting whore?'

'You know my thoughts on the actions you took when we first came to Ailigh.'

'You were a child then,' Orlaith said. 'We all were. You may have come with instruction from your chieftain to be wed to Rónán, but the rest of us, we were sent here for one purpose—to be women. I don't believe any of us liked it much, but we do what our king tells us.'

'You looked as though you enjoyed your time hopping from one bed to another.' Achall kept her gaze on the baby in her arms as she walked. Behind them, young Áed's feet padded with deft skill over a collection of sharp stones and he did not wince.

'There is a difference in liking something and acting as though you do. I would rather have stayed at home with my mother than hike for seven nights across a wet landscape to amuse a bunch of snot-nosed boys who did not bother to learn my name. But when your king calls for you, it is a duty to respond.'

'It is a barbaric practice,' Achall said, 'and one that I am glad my husband has not continued.'

'It was the way of King Déaglán, and the way of all the kings before him, as far back as Mordha the Terrible himself.'

'You accept it as an agreeable term.'

'I do not. We women are more than just flesh to be handled.

But custom or not, when your king commands something of you, you bow to him and obey. This is what we are as a nation.'

Achall scoffed. 'What do you know of our nation?'

'I have travelled far, seen many things that would make an ordinary girl turn blue. From one end of the land to the other, all kings and chieftains command their people to perform tasks that they may not wish to do, but we do it regardless, and most often with a smile on our face.'

'Rónán does not.' They stepped down into the outer rampart and Achall handed the baby back to his mother.

Orlaith smiled. 'If he did, I would not be here. Rónán is the change that the people need. I hope you see that.'

Achall beckoned her child forward, and the cumal hurried him towards her. 'If there is a threat on your tongue, speak it.'

'No threat, my lady. Only that Rónán is as wise as he is kind. For the sake of Ailigh and his people, you should recognise his right to his own choices.'

'I do not force my will upon my husband,' Achall said, picking up her son. 'He has my respect, even if I clearly do not have yours.'

As Achall turned to walk away, Orlaith said, 'The women of Ailigh need to know their own strengths. They should be instructed in combat.'

Without looking back over her shoulder, Achall said, 'The women of Ailigh have our men to protect them. I will hear nothing more of it.'

Orlaith resisted the urge to pick a stone from the ground and throw it at the queen. They would never see eye to eye, and it was getting harder to bite her tongue.

Now that she had come so far, she continued walking. From

the gates of the outer palisade wall, she turned left and circled the hillfort until she could see the lough in the distance. From this height, the waters were dark and still. As she passed the fields of boys in training, she tried not to look for Fionn among them, but her eyes wandered across the grasses in search of him. He was easy to spot—a tall man surrounded by lads of varying ages, like a gate post among the rushes. She could not hear his words, but she could discern their meaning from his gesturing hands. When he saw her, he nodded, and continued his instruction of Rónán's warrior children.

She turned from him and resumed her walk towards the lough.

When she stepped off the grassy dunes onto the dark sand that stretched around the near side of the lough, the sun was already overhead. She thanked Bríg that the snows were melted and that the land was returning to warmth at last.

Dominating the landscape, Áed's standing stone rose above her head. She could not see the flat top where Rónán would climb to contemplate his life. She reached out and touched the sword that had been carved into its side, tracing her fingers along its length from pommel to tip, and she pressed her forehead against the coolness of the stone.

'I am sorry I do not come often.' She adjusted the furs around her baby's face and said, 'I have been a little busy.' She walked around the stone, all four sides smoothed by a sculptor's touch but now chipped with weather and tinged green and brown with moss in small patches. Although the stone had only been erected two years ago, the rock itself was formed from the belly of the gods at the dawn of light, and it would remain long after the tribes of Danu had perished and rotted in the ground.

She sat on the cool sand, facing the side into which had been carved an Áed Branath sword. In his young life as an ironsmith, his blades were known the land over and he marked each of them with his symbol. The sword that Rónán carried with him was one of Áed's.

She looked at the stone. 'Rónán misses you. I can see it in his eyes, in the way his lips curl when he thinks no one is watching him.' She laughed. 'Achall is still a *bitseach*, but don't tell her I told you so.' She looked at her child and traced her fingertip around his tiny ear. 'I have been a fool, Áed. I have fallen in to one bed too many, though I do not regret the outcome. He is beautiful in every way. He came from inside me, formed in my belly as if my body knew what it was doing. I made him. And I will never give him up.' She closed her eyes. 'I need your strength, Áed. I will fight every man who tries to take my son from me, but I do not have the strength to win. I need your power. And I beg you to watch over him.'

Orlaith leaned down and kissed her baby's warm face. 'No one will ever take you from me. With Áed's grace, I will kill anyone who tries.'

She stood, nodded, and touched the stone before turning back towards Ailigh. She imagined him standing behind her, naked and covering himself with his hands while she strode up the hill wearing his tunic. She knew that evening they had met, that she had found a friend. A true friend. And she cried not because he was dead, but that she did not get to hear his laugh or feel the warmth of his shoulder under her cheek. His heart may have belonged to Rónán, but his shoulder was hers.

By the time she walked up the steep hill, the fields around

Ailigh were empty, the boys back within the walls and dining or attending to other duties not included in their training. She ate a small meal and sat with the boys in the hall as their curds were finished and their games were brought out. She never learned to play any of the games with their tiny stone pieces, but she was good with dice. She watched as the stones were thrown and boys yelped and whooped, and she nursed her baby, surrounded by the sounds of excitement. Ailigh, she learned, had two distinct noises—the excitement of war, and the excitement of games. An untrained ear would not be able to distinguish them apart, for a boy cries aloud as much when winning a game as when winning a battle.

She had participated in the rituals of the women of Ailigh, weaving clothes, cooking meals, gathering crops, and cleaning up after hundreds of raucous boys and men, and now she was grateful for the time she had alone with her child. For now, he slept in her arms despite the growing noise, and as the sun set outside and sconces were lit, she was content to listen to the laughter and the name-calling, and watch the games unfold even if she could not tell which boy was winning and which was losing.

When she left the hall to return to Grainne's home, the barrel hut was crowded, and men were spilling out onto the path before it to urinate against the wall or to pick a fight with another man. Men were not content to fight at war and needed always to find some face for his fist.

As she walked past, one of the men, a husky brute with a braided moustache and his hair loose around his face, gestured to his crotch and called to her. 'You can nurse me like you nurse your wain.'

Orlaith kept walking.

'Are you taking me to bed?' he called after her. She heard his footsteps behind her, and she stopped walking, tightening her grip on her child.

'You can go and nurse your own health. I have a child that needs to sleep.'

'We can just have a quick one. We won't wake the wain.'

'I suggest you go back to your wine.'

The man touched her cheek. 'I'd rather drink from you.' She slapped his face, and he gripped her arm. His breath was nauseating. 'Don't be a tease, girl.'

She spat on him and he smiled. 'Let go of me.'

'Don't fight it.'

Orlaith had no time to stop what was coming. She saw Fionn standing behind him at the same time that the drunkard felt his presence. He turned, and Fionn punched him in the face. He staggered back and Fionn followed, punching him again.

The man fell and Fionn knelt along with him. He gripped the man's throat and punched him again. His face, no longer flushed with wine, was red with blood from his broken nose and lip.

'Stop,' Orlaith cried, holding tight to her baby. 'Stop it, Fionn, he's had enough.'

Fionn ignored her. He continued to pummel the man's face until he lay unconscious on the ground.

He stood, kicked the man's side, and then looked at Orlaith. 'The baby is well?'

Orlaith tore her eyes from Fionn's face to check her child. When she looked back, Fionn was walking away.

He disappeared inside the barrel hut. Orlaith looked down

on the unconscious man, spat on him, and went home.

He may think himself a hero for rescuing her, but she could have handled the brute herself. Fionn had no right to interfere.

And when she saw him next, she would tell him so.

Chapter 19

The archdruid clapped his hands and bowed, his forehead touching the earth. He was an old man and Grainne helped him to kneel for the ceremony. They no longer used the sensory isolation hut that she had twice been locked in. During the Fir Bolg invasion, the hut was destroyed. It saddened her; had she not been locked in the darkness when she first came to the druid's compound, she would never have met her personal goddess, the Lady Cáer, daughter of Ethal Anbuail and swan-spirit of prophecy.

Before them, Gallen knelt with his head bowed. This cere-mony was his transition from initiate to druid's acolyte. When the ritual was complete, she would take him to Ailigh for his education to continue under her instruction.

For the last two days, she spent her free time with the boy, learning as much as she could about him. He was angry for the most part and cared little for talking. He was content to listen to her stories and say nothing. She could sense in him the desire to do well in his studies, but his temper got the better of him and his knuckles were red and raw from punching walls or tables. At least, she thought, he was not lashing out at the other initiates.

She understood his frustrations. When she trained here, learning the difference between one taproot and another almost destroyed her. Learning the names of all the gods was nothing compared to remembering the uses of a lesser burdock root.

The archdruid raised his head and drew his ceremonial dagger from its sheath. Into a golden bowl, he cut and measured some oaknut with the petals of the dog rose and the fruit of the cane apple tree, and, with a pestle, he ground them together and mixed them with a measure of water. He raised the bowl to the skies, and he sang a druid's song. Grainne closed her eyes for she could feel the presence of the gods.

The archdruid held the bowl over the ceremonial fire that burned in front of them, and on the other side of the flames, Gallen took it when it was offered to him.

'Drink of its contents,' the archdruid said, 'and when you are done with your task, you will know your personal god just as he has known you since your birth, before you drew your first breath and opened your eyes to see the face of your mother. He has known your countenance and now he will reveal himself to you.'

'It is the will of the gods and I am ready.'

Gallen drank.

When the bowl was empty, he wiped his lips with the back of his hand and curled his mouth at the taste. He licked his teeth to ensure he had consumed it all.

His task was straightforward, if not entirely simple—drink the archdruid's hallucinatory concoction, and then climb the mountain that rose beside them. If he reached the top and knew his personal god, he would be permitted to leave the compound and journey with Grainne to Ailigh.

'Do well,' Grainne said. 'I will see you at the top.'

Although he was tasked with climbing the steep cliff unaided, there was a path carved in the far side of the hill that wound its way skyward. The cliff face was not sheer and there was little risk of him plummeting to his death, but the way was arduous and would entail hand-over-hand climbing rather than walking. The path would take Grainne an afternoon to walk before reaching the summit. Gallen's climb, if he continued at a steady pace, would take him most of the day to ascend.

When Gallen bowed to them and turned towards the cliff face, Grainne picked up the empty bowl. 'I do not know this mixture. You say it is oaknut, dog rose and cane apple?'

'Correct,' the archdruid said, both of his hands folded over the top of his staff. Although it was a ceremonial aid, Grainne knew he relied on it for balance. His feet, when he walked, moved more as a shuffle than a gait.

'I do not understand. What hallucinatory power does this hold?'

The archdruid smiled. 'None,' he said, tapping his temple, 'save for the power of the mind.'

Grainne laughed. 'I may need to ingest some myself.'

She bowed to her master, returned the bowl to its resting place by the fire, and set off for the walk to the top of the cliff. The archdruid, despite having a compound to run, would sit by the fire to ensure it did not extinguish before the boy completed his task. She did not know it at the time, but he sat outside the sensory isolation hut that she was encased in during her own trials. He was invested in the well-being of his people more than any chieftain or king.

Grainne travelled the narrow path that cut into the side of

the mountain and felt the warmth of the spring sun turn colder as she climbed. By the time she reached the summit, she was glad she brought a fur cloak to wrap around her, and another to sit on. She did not bring food; she would not eat until the boy was done with his ritual.

Standing at the edge of the scarp, she steadied herself and looked down. Gallen was a speck on the mountainside, no more than a quarter of its height from the ground. The sun was advancing and before long it would fall behind the mountain and Gallen would disappear in the darkness.

Filled with what he assumed was a hallucinatory drug and tasked with climbing a mountain without rope or tether, Grainne was glad that the sensory isolation hut had been the severest of her suffering. If Gallen reached the top and did not know the image of his personal god, she feared how violent his temper would be.

She found a fallen tree to sit upon and wait for him. It may be his task to perform, but it was in her interest that he do well and she desired the appropriate outcome. The boy fascinated her. He was angry, but he was blunt about it. He was strong, refusing to use his fists against another person. Yesterday, she watched him build a small structure from branches and leaves around an anthill so that it would not be easily stood on. He valued all life, which is the way of the druid, but it was instinctual rather than learned.

Grainne closed her eyes and prayed to Cáer that she helped him on his journey.

By the time the sun was setting, Grainne took from her pack a small torch and lit it with her flint set. She propped it among some stones and peered over the edge. In the darkness, she could not see Gallen on his ascent and hoped he had not fallen or given up in frustration.

Grainne offered a gesture to her goddess with her fingers against her forehead, and then stilled her mind. She was motionless, and in the absence of her thoughts, a vision appeared.

She stood in a large field of drooping snowdrop flowers, their white petals aglow against their bronze-green stems, heads bowed as if in prayer to the gods.

Walking among the flowers that prickled her ankles, the world was serene and quiet. No breeze disturbed the petals and no birdsong or bush-cricket chatter came to her ears. She was alone.

Inhaling the sweet scent of the flowers, she noticed that the white petals were stained red with blood. And the more she looked, the further the blood spread, out across the field, dyeing every flowerhead and blotting every petal.

The field was black with blood.

When she looked to the cloudless sky, it was raining, but the rain did not fall upon the field, it ran laterally above her like a river over her head. She looked back to the ground and saw a swan marching across the bloodied petals, followed by seven cygnets. Their downy feathers were stained with the blood of the land, but they followed behind the white swan.

'My Lady Cáer,' Grainne called to the swan, for she knew that it was she who walked through the field, but the swan did not respond to her calls.

And then she was alone again, in a darkened field, the hem of her robes dragging wet against the stained snowdrops.

She opened her eyes. The torch burned bright beside her, but outside the reach of its flames, all was darkness. She wrapped her furs tighter around her shoulders and considered the vision. Its meaning was not apparent to her, and she had heard no symbology of rain that flows across the sky or blood that appears from nowhere.

She prayed to Cáer for guidance.

It was soon thereafter that she heard the scrabbling of Gallen on the cliff face. In her trancelike vision, she did not know how long she had waited in the evening's darkness for him. Keeping back from the edge, she did not call out to offer him encouragement or support; this was his task to complete.

For some long minutes, she heard him climbing towards her, heard the scrape of his feet and hands on stone, and a grunt or curse when he stumbled. When he appeared over the top of the scarp, crawling on his knees to reach the summit, he looked at Grainne and, despite his appearance, he smiled at her. She came to him and wrapped him in her fur cloak. Gallen was sodden with sweat, his face, hands and feet brown with mud and grime, blue eyes shining in the darkness. His clothing was torn, and he had sustained some bruising to his arms and the flesh of his knuckles was white and raw.

'I do not know his name,' he said, curling into a ball by her legs, 'but I have seen him. I have seen my god—tall and bald and blind.'

Grainne stroked his sweat-dampened hair. 'You have done well. Rest now. We will travel down when you are ready.'

Gallen closed his eyes. 'Push me off the edge, and I will meet you at the bottom.'

Grainne let him rest his head in her lap, and she sang to him an ancient druid's song. Her blood-flower vision plagued her mind, but she was grateful that Gallen had succeeded in his trials. For now, a celebration was due; the omens and her visions could wait.

When they made it down the path, the dawn sun was breaking in the east, brightening the horizon in a red wash of colour. Their stomachs growled in hunger.

At the base of the cliff, they found the archdruid cross-legged on the ground by the fire where they left him. His eyes were closed in meditation, but when they approached, he opened them and smiled. 'You have shown much strength, child. Your god is pleased with you.'

Gallen limped towards him and bowed. 'You do me a kindness,' he said, and he kissed the old druid's hand.

They returned to the compound and Gallen was given time to bathe and dress in his ceremonial robes, the white of the acolyte, and they assembled outside the great hall where the archdruid named him as Grainne's aide. All the druids who gathered cheered for him and kissed him in turn on the cheek, offering gifts of heather for its healing powers, and water from the spring that he may always quench his thirst.

The celebrations continued until midday when they retired for private contemplation. That evening, Grainne visited the boy in his quarters, and sat with him while he rested.

'What is your king like?' he asked her. 'I have heard many stories, but I know tales are often twisted.'

'Believe the tales, for they are true.' Before she left, she told him, 'Your studies are fresh, and your mind is young. You will do well at Ailigh.' He nodded and closed his eyes to sleep. They would leave for Grianán Ailigh in the morning.

Before returning to her room for the night, she sought the company of the archdruid. In his home, he poured her some wine and blessed her with all the power of the gods.

'Your journey is only beginning,' he said. 'I have contemplated the omens and it is clear to me—a great war is coming, and many will perish.'

Grainne drank from the wine and let it warm her chest. 'The southern king will march against the north?'

The old man nodded. 'It is inevitable. You must hurry to your king. It is time to prepare for the worst.'

Chapter 20

It was two days since Bromaid had walked away from the Clonycavan clansmen that had enslaved him for two years and still he was not convinced that he was a free man. King Rían honoured his word and Bromaid was given time to visit his former master's farmstead. He took pleasure in opening the food store where the farmer's wife and daughter were hiding, and for half a day he toyed with them. He chained them up in his old hut, tugged on their leashes so that they were forced to their knees before him, and he raped them both, one after the other, while his fellow Fir Bolg companions cheered him on.

The farmer's wife wept and screamed for mercy, and when her blood was spilled, Bromaid closed her mouth and opened her eyes, propping her against the wall so that in death she could enjoy her daughter's torment. Ailbe was in shock, her face stained by the tracks of fresh tears on her cheeks. When Bromaid came to her, she lay down for him, stripped of her clothes by his companions, and she did not scream or try to beat him away. Even when he wrapped his fingers around her throat, when he punched her face to spark a reaction, she lay in silence, tears slipping from her eyes and running down to the edges of her ears. When he gripped her hair and tugged her head back, she made no noise.

It was not until the life slipped away from her, when he knocked her head against the ground harder than he had intended, did she make a sound—the gasping escape of her soul from her slackened lips.

Even his companions had grown silent.

Bromaid stood, wiped a line of saliva from his cheek with his forearm, and kicked the girl's leg. He hocked from the back of his throat and spat on her face.

'Burn it down.'

Camped on the foothills of Teamhair, surrounded by his Fir Bolg people at a small fire used to cook meats, they swapped stories of their slave days. Bromaid did not involve himself; their discussions of their duties as slaves imprisoned them still. King Rían was right—for centuries, his people had been slaves. Freed of their shackles, they served no master but enslaved themselves. He felt it, too, though he did not speak it aloud. His mind was fettered even if his wrists were free. He expected their new king to renege on his word and collect the Fir Bolg men, slaughtering them until the fields outside Teamhair were black with foreign blood.

He saw little of King Rían in the days since they were freed. He did not come to them and encourage them with speeches, nor did he eat with them. He was ensconced in a large tent at the head of the army and his druid came and went often. Local scouts, men of Rían's tribe, travelled the compass points at intervals and Bromaid was not certain what news they carried or brought with them.

That evening, news spread across the field that they were to attack the Ard Rí at first light.

In the darkness, the lights from atop Teamhair's hills burned bright. They were at a disadvantage, camped on lower ground, and around the compound, the Ard Rí's men and those from other tribes had gathered to protect the high king. Teamhair was not a place in which tribes lived, reserved for ceremony and tribal business. But the high king, when he knew that Rían was marching on the seat, had gathered his tribes there and they reinforced the hill.

It would be a long battle, Bromaid knew. Fighting up hill was arduous at best.

In the morning, they stood in formation, such that only Fir Bolg men could, rank upon rank of warriors with spear and sword. But they did not march on the high king.

A messenger approached from the hilltop, his arms wide to show that he was unarmed and meant only to talk.

Bromaid watched as King Rían strode forward, his hand on the hilt of his sword at his hip. 'I am here for the kingseat,' Rían said to the messenger.

'The Ard Rí is aware of your campaign,' the messenger said, looking at the massive army before him with the stoic hint of defiance on his face that Bromaid could see was false bluster. 'My lord high king requests a parlay that you and he may talk with civility.'

'Before this night is done, I will be your lord high king. When I have pierced the Ard Rí with seven swords, will you bow to me then?'

'I do the bidding of the king I serve.'

'It is the honour of a king to accept a parlay request from another. Tell your lord that I will meet with him and there will be no bloodshed until our talks are done.'

Rían maintained his army's order; it would do no good to let them fall out of line, and if the Ard Rí was not a man of his word, bloodshed would occur before long.

The high king's men erected a tent in the middle of a field edged by heather, and it was filled with furs and cushions to sit upon. The Ard Rí walked down the hill towards the tent, flanked by a guard of ten men, and when he stood outside its entrance, he made a display of unbuckling his sword belt and removing his dagger. He handed these to one of his men, who turned aside with them, and then the high king and his druid entered.

Bromaid folded his arms. A king's parlay could last for days if an agreement could not be reached. Rían pulled his sword from its sheath and planted it in the ground. He unhooked his belt and let it fall. The high king's men were assembled at the top of the hill.

Behind them, Bromaid could see the Stone of Destiny rising tall and majestic. He knew King Rían would touch its surface and be declared Ard Rí of all Éirinn whatever the outcome of these negotiations. He would fight, or the high king would back down.

Bromaid considered the words that would be spoken between the kings. Rían would suggest that High King Cillian was surrounded and had little choice but to give up his kingseat. He would point out the southern tribes that were already slaughtered, and the number of Fir Bolg slaves that Rían had liberated, men that would take a knee for him.

The opposing armies stood top and bottom of the field, with the tent between them, and the sun tracked an arc across the sky, hiding behind infant clouds that wisped across the blue ceiling in unsteady patterns.

Bromaid's armpits were damp and he blotted them with the sleeves of his tunic. Being a slave was not so bad; waiting for war was worse.

Along the side of his rank, four men had taken to their knees to throw dice. He studied their faces. When he took the king-seat from Rían, he would have those men killed. Slavery softened them. Two years ago, they would have had their hands cut off for such disobedience.

Bromaid cleared his throat, but they ignored him.

When the two kings exited the tent, the sun now low in the western skies, Rían looked at his assembled army and raised his hands in victory. A cheer rang across the field. Bromaid was disappointed. The cheer was a mix of relief of winning, and regret that the promised battle was not forthcoming.

The Ard Rí's warriors returned up the hill and out of sight, and King Rían's druid set about his preparations for the crowning of a new high king.

There would still be bloodshed, Bromaid knew. An Ard Rí does not vacate his position without weight on his heart and, when stepping down in favour of his successor, his death would be assured. Bromaid did not know the history of this land, but in Hellas, in the province where his people lived for over one thousand years, kings and high kings were forcibly removed from power with a blood ceremony if they did not die in battle.

When King Rían's people assembled on the hilltop around the Stone of Destiny, with an enormous wood-henge circle behind them, Rían was publicly stripped of his clothes and dressed in finery by his druid. His transition to high king would be visible for all. The incumbent Ard Rí was brought before him, and the man was made to dress in plain colours. His silver torc was removed from his head and the Fir Bolg druid, Gorid, raised it aloft.

In view of the torc crown, King Cillian knelt and Rían came behind him. He carried a ceremonial dagger in his hands.

The people waited.

Bromaid stood on his toes to see over the multitude of men in front of him.

Gorid bowed to the standing stone. 'The gods have spoken. My lord Rían, son of Manus, son of Darroch, son of Hargon will be crowned as high king of all Éirinn. No man alive will fail to bow to him. All worship to your new Ard Rí.'

Rían drew his dagger and, without ceremony, sliced Cillian's neck from ear to ear. The man fell to the dirt and bled at Rían's feet. He stood unopposed and the blood of his predecessor seeped into the ground with his ancestors.

Rían knelt in the blood and faced his people. Gorid, still holding the torc crown, stood behind his king. 'A destiny has been foretold. A new king leads the isles of Éirinn, and it is your duty to serve him.'

He placed the crown on Rían's head, and when Rían stood, all were silent. The ceremony was not complete. Rían walked three times around the standing stone, and on his final pass, he reached out and touched its rough surface. When his fingers connected with it, the assembled men cheered and hollered. According to the legends, when the Stone of Destiny is touched by the rightful king, the stone will sing to his glory. The people's cheer meant that no one could ever say the stone did not croon if it could not be heard above the raucous elation.

A feast followed, as well as a sacrifice in Rían's honour. Each man present would approach their new Ard Rí and they would kiss the discs at his breast as they swore their allegiance to him.

Gorid was first. 'I am forever your servant.'

In the excitement that followed, Bromaid understood that now was not the time to kill the high king and assume his seat. He would wait until the northern tribes fell under Rían's banner and then he would strike. Éirinn would be his.

He took his place in the line of men that knelt before their high king. When he approached the tall man, he leaned in to kiss him. The gold discs that shone in the evening sunlight were as jewels that Bromaid longed to wear.

When the sun gave way to the darkness, Gorid returned from his arrangements for the feast to announce that King Cillian's family were present. The dead king's wife and his children were brought before their new Ard Rí and they bowed to him as instructed.

Rían looked at the woman and her four sons, each unwilling to cry in his presence. It was said, Bromaid learned, that King Rían had ten daughters and no sons. To see his predecessor's family full of men would be a kick to him.

'You are gracious,' the woman said to her husband's replacement. She refused to look at the ground where her husband's body was covered so that his ashen face was not on display in front of the gods. 'We would take our leave at once.'

'I would invite you to stay and be my bed mate, but your sons would not approve. You have gathered one third of your husband's wealth?'

'As was decreed,' Gorid said. 'I counted it myself.'

'Then you have my permission to leave. I am a man of my word. May you find fortune on your travels.'

The woman nudged her children and turned to leave, but the youngest boy was not quick to move. He made fists from his hands and stared at the new Ard Rí.

'Teaghue,' the boy's mother said. 'We are leaving.'

Rían looked down at the lad. 'You wish to oppose me and dishonour the memory of your father?'

Teaghue narrowed his eyes, then loosened his fists and turned from him.

During the feast that honoured him as Éirinn's Ard Rí, Rían walked among his people, shaking hands in the way of the Fir Bolg, talking to them before moving on. It was a spectacle, a show of deference to the people who helped him take the kingseat.

When he spoke to Bromaid, the high king had no recollection of their previous talk two days before. 'We must all look alike to you,' Bromaid said, bowing.

'I will learn your names in time.'

Bromaid did not smile. 'I anticipate that you will keep your word now that you are high king.'

'Each of you is a free man. I am a man of honour. I said as much to the old high king when he begged me to spare the lives of his family and let them walk after his death. And did I not do so? I granted them a third of his wealth and let them leave.'

Bromaid nodded but was unwilling to bow at the waist. 'And what of the northern tribes? Will they kneel before you now, or must we continue to fight?'

'We will feast for two fortnights and then we will strike north. Before midsummer, every king will kneel to me. Or he will die.'

Bromaid took his leave and returned to the warmth of the

fire. He could smell the burning flesh of mutton as the meats were prepared for the feasting. He was one step closer to ascending the role of high king.

Chapter 21

She studied the stars and then cast the bones. The gods were in flux.

When she looked up, Gallen was adding more wood to the fire. They had been on the road for two nights and, although the summer warmth was returning to the land, a chill descended when the sun hid itself from them. Grainne put away her bones and unfurled the pack of food that the druids provided to them for their journey.

Gallen fanned the flames and sat cross-legged beside her, a deer-fur cloak draped over his knees. They ate in silence, boiled root vegetables and mashed grain.

When the meal was done, Grainne took a small cloth-covered parcel from her pack and unfolded it. She broke the honeyed bread in half and gave some to Gallen, then she sucked the sticky honey residue from her fingertips. It was a delicacy of the northern druids, made with emmer wheat which was culti-vated only in certain areas across the north, and soaked with honey from the druids' stores before being rolled in the orange petals of the calendula flower. The dried petals added a pleasant crunch to the otherwise soft dessert.

'Danu,' Grainne said.

'Easy—goddess of all life.' Gallen wiped honey from his lips with a knuckle. 'If you are going to quiz me, you ought to try harder.'

She saw herself in him, if not for the anger that he displayed when he was frustrated and balled his fists or scrunched his face in annoyance. He was inquisitive and asked many questions, but he also argued his point if he did not agree with what she said. The boy's will was strong, and she was grateful for it.

'Lir,' Grainne said.

'The father or the son?'

'Both.'

'Lir, the senior,' Gallen said, 'known as Allód, was the embodiment of the sea and he rivalled Bodb Dearg for the Dannan kingship. His son, Manandán mac Lir, took his father's place as god of the sea. His horse, Aonbharr, could run faster than the wind and could stand on water as easily as on land. His spectral boat carries spirits to Tír na nÓg.'

'And the name of his boat?'

Gallen looked skyward as if for the answer. After a moment, he said, 'Wave-sweeper.'

'Very good.' Grainne finished her honeyed bread and dusted her hands. The fire crackled and thin tendrils of silver smoke rose towards the stars. She watched Gallen as he ate, and when he had only a morsel left, he dug a hole in the ground with his fingers and buried the remaining bread, covering it with the damp soil—a tribute to the gods. She did not ask him whose favour he sought.

'One more before sleep. Finnguala.'

Gallen considered the name. 'I am not familiar with this one.'

'She does not receive much attention in the bardic tales of the gods, but she was a beautiful maiden. She is the daughter of Lir.'

'Stepdaughter of Aoife. Yes, I remember now—cursed to live as a swan for nine hundred years.'

'Correct. She and her brothers were cursed by their stepmother, sister of their mother. For nine hundred years they lived upon the lakes and rivers and they learned all the ancient tales and warrior songs of our lands. They were saved from their curse when Lairgenn and Deoch were wed.'

Gallen adjusted the cloak over his legs so that the chill of the night would not attack him. 'What truth does the story hold? We talk about swans living for nine hundred years, but this is impossible, no?'

'You doubt the gods?'

Gallen lowered his head. 'I do not, for I have heard them call to me. But perhaps I doubt the stories.'

'You are encouraged to doubt. As a druid, it is your duty to question everything. I do not doubt the tales—the gods are powerful, and a curse is not easily broken—but perhaps nine hundred years is a figure meant only to signify an incredibly long period. Unless Finnguala decides to appear before us now and tell us the truth of it, our task is to believe.'

Gallen looked over the top of the fire as if waiting for the swan to appear. 'She was a twin, was she not?'

'She was.' Grainne bowed her head. 'Her twin brother was called Áed, for whom my own brother was named.'

Gallen cocked his head, eyes wide. 'Your brother was Áed the Executioner?'

Grainne made a motion with her fingers to her Lady Cáer.

'You know of him.'

'Everyone knows his name. He is immortalised in song. Perhaps nine hundred years from now, he will return from Tír na nÓg to walk among the living once more.'

Grainne smiled, but there was no mirth in it. 'If he is to be returned to us, I wish it to be sooner than nine hundred years.'

'Forgive me, Lady. I have upset you.'

'It was not intentional. Come, we should sleep now. We will reach Ailigh tomorrow, but I cannot say how long before we must journey south with King Rónán's army.'

'Should we sleep in shifts?'

'There is no need. The fire will keep the animals at bay and the gods will protect us from travelling bandits. And the *sidhe* respect the druids too much to bother us.'

She did not sleep. Áed was not far from her mind and she wished his life had not ended at Knockdhu during the Fir Bolg invasion. But Gallen was correct—he was immortalised in song and tale. Even if he did not return to the living in nine hundred years, his name would be known to them, and that is how legends are made.

In time, when the fire was reduced to embers and the moon was shrouded in clouds, she heard Gallen mumble in his sleep. She sat up and saw that he was twitching, his fingers and his shoulders making miniscule movements, enough to make his furs quiver. His eyes shuddered in dreams.

Grainne poked the embers with a branch and added a few more sticks to the new flames to keep the fire alive. When Gallen sat up, gasping for air, she came to his side. 'What did you see?'

He appeared younger than his thirteen years. 'I saw a field of flowers, their heads bent over towards the earth. I do not know the name of them. And on the flowers, I saw blood. Blood swept across the field like a river.'

Grainne felt her pulse quicken. 'Snowdrops. Small flowers with white petals, their heads drooping?'

He nodded.

'Did you see a swan leading seven cygnets?'

Gallen pulled his head back from her in question. 'No. Does that mean something?'

'What else did you see? Any indication of a god?'

'I saw four tall stones among the field, and they too were covered in thick blood. What does it mean?'

'Four stones? Like standing stones?'

'More like rocks than ceremonial stones. As big as a man.'

'Oftentimes, a vision from the gods is not easy to interpret. If it is their will, its meaning will become clear to you soon.'

'Why must they speak in riddles? If they want us to know something, they should speak it clearly.'

'The gods do not speak as humans speak. They have their own language. They try to convey to us their words, but because we are inferior, we do not always understand them. Sometimes our visions are literal; sometimes they are coded. You will know the meaning of it when the time is right.'

After a moment of silence, Gallen said, 'What if the dreams I had as a child were visions of the future? What if I could have saved my parents from death at the hands of the Fir Bolg but I failed because I did not know the meaning? How can that be fair?'

'Before you were brought to the archdruid, you had no training. You would not have understood the visions and could not have taken any preventative measures.'

'But now they are dead, and I am without family. If the gods would speak plainly, I could have done something. I could have helped.'

'I am sorry that your family perished, and you are left to grieve them. I know how unfair that seems. Those of us who are left behind, even those who do not have the ways of the druids, we seek answers and explanation. "Why have I been spared?" we ask ourselves. "Why am I alive when my mother and my brother died in a senseless war?" And we cannot answer these questions. The gods do not willingly tell us. But, Gallen, you are not alone. As a druid, you are never alone. We are all your family—a sorry replacement for a sister or a mother, I know, but we are here. And you can talk to your loved ones, you can speak to their spirits and they will hear you, even if they do not answer.'

He was angry. 'A consolation of spirit is not what mortal man seeks when he looks at the graves of his family.'

'No. Death is a part of life and we must accept it however difficult it may be. A veil falls between us and the Otherworld and we cannot commune with those on the other side as easily as with our neighbour, but they are there, and they hear us. And one day, with luck, we will see them again. Your family and mine, and many others like them, died so that we may live. That is the ultimate sacrifice to the gods. One life for another.'

'That does not make it easier to bear.'

'No, it does not. And I will not tell you that it gets easier, for I fear it never does. Eventually, we learn to live with the pain.'

In the east, the sky was brightening. 'If we are no longer to sleep, we should break camp.'

Grainne agreed. When they had extinguished the fire, they hitched the carbad to the horses and mounted it. Before taking the reins, she looked at Gallen. His shoulders were raised and knotted in pain or anger—or both.

'You will know the gods' plans for you soon,' she said. 'Until then, we must do what we can to hurry it along.'

'Along the way, you can teach me the prophecies of the stars before they disappear from view.'

She clapped him on the back and then whipped the reins. As the horses jumped forward, she said, 'There is not enough time in all the world to understand the vastness of the skies. But I will do my best.'

Chapter 22

Green shoots were returning to the trees when Grainne's carbad rolled through the outer gates of Ailigh. Rónán, from his position atop the wall, watched as she mounted the hillside, and he came to her when the gates were closed and her horses were led away by a stable hand. The smell of tanning hides was rife, and the boys were on the southern fields practicing their sword skills, the din of metals echoing from all sides. Hawkers walked through the outer rampart, trading their wares, and women splashed water on the ground to sweep their stoops clean. Hounds yapped in the distance.

'I did not miss the commotion,' Grainne said to him as he approached.

'It is the sounds of prosperity.' Rónán embraced her.

'My lord, this is Gallen.' A gangly boy, almost as tall as Grainne, with narrow eyes and a square nose, bowed to the king. 'He is to be my acolyte.'

Rónán said, 'It is good that the sheep are fattening. We will celebrate. What news from the archdruid?'

'We should speak in private.'

Gallen was shown to one of the shared huts; until suitable arrangements could be made, he would bunk with the young warriors.

In his hall, Rónán took conference with his druid. 'The omens stretch to all corners of the land. A great war is coming, the archdruid is convinced of it.'

'King Rían?'

Grainne nodded. 'It is well that you do not have any Fir Bolg slaves.'

'I would sooner they all died during their invasion than have one wash my feet. Do you propose I march my men south to meet them?'

'I have given this some thought on my journey. I assume that the Ard Rí has fallen——have you had word from the south?' When he said no, Grainne continued. 'You have two options. March south now and stumble upon them in unknown territories, fighting at a disadvantage, or strengthen your arm in the north and await their arrival, if they make it this far.'

'There are many strong kings between Teamhair and Ailigh. He cannot possibly defeat them all.'

'That is my hope.'

'If Ard Rí Cillian is dead, Éirinn is doomed.'

Grainne bowed to him. Before she left, she said, 'The north will not kneel for a tyrant. The archdruid calls for a summit of the brehon. If King Rían has not marched on us by Beltaine, all druids are to return to the archdruid's side for instruction.'

'You must wake the gods and rally them to our cause. I have moved Orlaith into a *brú* within the second walls. Where should I have your acolyte housed?'

'He can stay with the boys for a few nights; it will do him good before we delve into his studies. He is a good lad, strong but troubled. He will serve you well, my lord.'

In the coming days, Rónán took to the walls to watch the boys train. In one field, the older lads were throwing spears, in another, impromptu races were occurring. The younger boys, his newest additions, clanged blunted swords together. They were training without shields until they came to know the weight and feel of the blade in their hands. Soon they would be given swords of their own, and the blacksmith had been crafting them since Imbolc, calling each boy to his side to handle the metals. When a man knows a sword, it does not matter the shape of it, but Rónán's hope was that if the boys were involved in the making of their own weapons, they would treat them better.

The neighbouring clans came to him with their tithes, and Rónán greeted each chieftain by name and welcomed them to his hall where they bowed and presented him with their fruit wines or their cattle that were driven up the hills by their cowherds. One chieftain, whose winter had been hard, offered Rónán his eldest daughter in marriage, but Achall, who sat at her husband's side, snorted her derision.

Rónán came from the dais and patted the man's shoulder. 'It is a generous offer, my lord, but I am not a man to have two wives. One is ample. Your daughter is deserving of better. I will waive your tithe for forty nights, and when you return, bring your daughter. I would meet the woman who nearly made my wife bleed from the eye sockets.'

When they were alone, Achall said, 'He assumes you have the working parts of a man that satisfies a woman.'

'Hold your tongue, Achall. I may yet take a second wife and cleave the head of the first.'

'Do not threaten me with a good time.' She marched from

the hall lest the remaining chieftains offer more insulting terms.

As the days warmed towards mid-spring and the Beltaine fires were erected on the ceremonial hilltop, Rónán spent time in the company of Cormac. They sparred often, sharpening their skills against each other, and they ventured into the southern forest to hunt for deer and to slaughter wolves, joined by Fionn and those men who were known for their tracking talents. But Fionn had been absent in more recent days, and Rónán found him alone at home with a growing regularity. Orlaith had rejected his proposal, his tanist told him, but Rónán knew he was not a mawkish character and his absence from the barrel hut was more than a weeping heart.

When Rónán had questioned him, Fionn was adamant that he was well and suffered nothing more than a bout of indigestion. 'I have stomach-ache, not heartache.'

Among the trees, as they stalked through crisp undergrowth, Rónán and Cormac held their throwing spears aloft. A lone doe grazed ahead of them. She would not have strayed too far from her herd, and when they made the kill, they would hear the thunderous beat of their hooves as they fled.

Rónán gave Cormac the prize. He circled around to flush the doe in the opposite direction, and when she darted from him, Cormac hurled his spear. It careened through the trees and struck true. Her warbling cry alerted the herd and birds squawked their annoyance as they took from the treetops when the deer scattered.

In the stillness that followed, Cormac knelt at the doe's head, touched the rapid pulse at her neck, and ended her life with his dagger. Rónán pulled the spear from her side and wiped it clean.

'Your sacrifice will feed many,' Cormac whispered. 'I am grateful to the gods for your sustenance.'

As Rónán turned to retrieve the small cart they would use to wheel her home, he said, 'Do you pray for all your kills?'

'Only those that I would eat.'

They loaded her body onto the cart. 'We should go before the wolves catch a whiff of her blood.' Wolves were a threat to livestock, but they had learned not to approach a human. Only if they were cornered and frightened would they attack a man. But they might try to steal his dinner if they were hungry.

The wolves prowled the dark of night at the outskirts of King Rónán's territory, hopeful of a stray lamb, but the shepherds worked in pairs to patrol the borders with lit torches and chase the hackled beasts away. Only once since Rónán ascended to kingship did they lose any property to the local pack. In one night, three lambs were taken, their corpses emptied and abandoned among the heather when they were picked clean, and their mothers walked aimless around the field for days in search of their young. When a ewe loses her wain, she is not quick to forget.

Rónán joined Cormac that evening, and between them they cut the doe for cooking. Nothing went unused. Cormac would tan the hide—Rónán watched with awe as he pared the skin from her flesh with precision—and the hooves would be ground for Grainne's medicines. The bones could be fashioned into handles for fine combs or brushes, and the druid would make use of the entrails that would not be eaten.

The raw meat was salted and stored for later use.

They joined the other men in the barrel hut, and it was not without interest that Rónán noticed Fionn's absence. He would spend his nights here after training the boys until he could no longer stand and would drag himself home. In the weeks since Imbolc, Rónán saw less of his tanist than he saw of Cormac.

'*Sláinte*,' Cormac said, raising his cup.

'*Táinte*,' Rónán responded.

In the morning, when Rónán took to the walls to watch the boys in their training, he saw that the new recruits milled around their field, flashing their swords, and sparring with each other in jest. Fionn was not present.

'Where is your commander?' he asked when he walked down to them.

'He is late, my lord,' one of the boys said. 'He is late again.'

Rónán instructed them into smaller groups and gave them tasks to perform, then he marched up the hillside to Fionn's home. When he knocked, there was no answer. He hammered on the door with his fist, and Fionn, from behind the hut, called out, 'Leave me alone.'

Rónán expected to find him slumped in a drunken heap, but when he walked around the hut, Fionn was squatting over his latrine, his face pale and clammy.

'Leave me alone.'

Rónán covered his mouth and nose with his hand. 'You smell like eternal death.'

'Kill the cooks, I have eaten something rotten.'

'No one else suffers as you do, Fionn. You were not in the barrel hut last night. Did you pilfer a wineskin or three? You have the beer shits.'

Fionn strained and Rónán backed away. 'I'm as sober as a girl. I've eaten something foul.'

'Do you need the druid?'

'I need privacy, my lord.'

'You need a bath.'

When he was done, Fionn pushed past his king to enter his home. When Rónán followed, he found his tanist stooped over a bowl of water, splashing his face.

'If she does not want you, pull your head from your arse. You are not a man to wilt over the love of a woman.'

'What? Orlaith has nothing to do with me eating bad meat.'

Rónán scanned the room, looking for evidence of discarded wineskins but found none. 'The boys are in the field. Clean yourself up and get down there before they kill each other.'

He returned to the walls and watched as Fionn loped down the hill to instruct the warriors. He would need to keep his eye on the man; if Fionn suffered too much from Orlaith's rejection, he could become a liability. And an unreliable tanist was not a man worthy of his name.

In the ensuing weeks, Rónán prepared for the Beltaine celebrations, the biggest festival of the year aside from Samhain, but he kept a watchful gaze on the trainee warriors. Fionn was losing weight, and his hair was growing lank on his head.

When the fires were lit and Grainne, along with her acolyte, gave their prayers and their thanks, Rónán watched Fionn have a quiet conversation with Orlaith, but he saw no animosity between them. He hoped their differences were resolved.

'We have no differences,' Orlaith told him when he asked her about it. 'Yes, I rejected his proposal—why should I not? You know me well enough to know I am not a woman set to marry.'

'You have not noticed his absence of mind?'

Orlaith looked across the crowd of people on the ceremonial

193

hilltop to find Fionn. 'He grows gaunt. But I cannot be blamed for that.'

Rónán pondered it. Nobody else was sick. If the man were not lovelorn, he could think of no other cause than an illness.

He spoke to Grainne when she finished her sacrifices and was free to enjoy the remainder of the evening. Beltaine, equidistant from the spring and summer solstices, marked the first day of summer, and in two days Rónán's tribe would take to the fields to sow their new crops. The nights still had a chill to them, but the days were long and warm.

'I will inspect him in the morning,' the druid said, 'but I am sure he is well. He works too hard with the boys. A few days rest and he will be fine.'

Rónán was not convinced. For weeks, Fionn's latrine reeked a stench of death. 'Check him for lesions or sores. There have been reports of leprosy in the east.'

'It is not leprosy,' Gallen said as he stood beside his master. 'Others would be infected, too.'

Grainne agreed. 'Do not fear, Rónán. Orlaith turned down his proposal and he drinks too much. He is sick, but only of the mind.'

'I need his mind returned to him. Every day that Rían advances in the south, Fionn is more essential to my army. Without him, we may lose the coming war.'

But it was more than his position as commander that worried Rónán. Fionn was his tanist. He had responsibilities beyond the upkeep of the army. If he lost him to illness, he had no replacement beyond his infant son.

Chapter 23

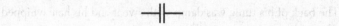

The ards skimmed over the soil, cutting scars through the fields. The early summer morning was thick with midges and the oxen whipped their tails as they hauled the wooden ploughs behind them. Herders thumped the fat rears of the working animals while the ploughmen steered the ard stilts. Orlaith and the women of Ailigh came after them, sowing the crop seeds by hand.

Across the eastern fields, Ailigh was alive with activity. Boys carried pails of water from the well, with cups on straps around their necks. 'Quench your thirst,' they shouted, and the men broke from their work to drink with greed. The shorthorns dumped their faeces as they clomped over the ground, and it was tilled into the soil as fertiliser. In the next field, men were singing.

Orlaith dropped the seeds at intervals. Behind her, a man dragged a coarse harrow to bury her work. When her seed pouch was empty, she returned to the gate for more, and she drank from the water cup that one of the boys handed her. She ruffled his hair and he groaned. Under the shade of an oak tree, a cumal girl entertained Orlaith's child. He had grown so much in the three months since his birth that she was convinced he would soon stand up and perform a stepdance. She cradled him before returning to work.

Achall was missing from the fields and Orlaith expected nothing less. Rónán steered an ard behind Cormac who led, and in the opposite field, Fionn's voice could be heard cursing an ox. She ventured to the low wall but did not approach him. The back of his tunic was damp with sweat and his hair whipped in wet clumps as he shook his head. When one of the boys offered him a cup of water, he poured it on his face. 'Come on, you great bastard of a beast,' he shouted, slapping an ox's rear with a leather strap.

The man who guided the wooden plough laughed. 'He's fatter than most wives, and just as stubborn.'

Since she rejected his proposal, Fionn was avoiding her. Apart from his intervention outside the barrel hut when he beat a man for looking at her, she saw little of him. Their interactions, when they did occur, were brief. Two weeks ago, when she walked past him on the way to breakfast, he had turned to evade her, but she called to him.

'You are well?'

He had nodded. 'The boy is doing fine?'

'We're going to breakfast. Will you join us?'

Fionn had looked at the empty bucket in his hand as though it contained answers. He wiped the rings of sweat from under his eyes with the back of his hand, and he muttered some attempt at sounding busy. She watched him walk away. He did not ask to attend the Beltaine celebrations with her, and he no longer came to her home.

Rónán had moved her into the second rampart to a small *brú* with a bed, a hearth, cooking pots and a trunk for storage. It was more than she needed. The crib from Grainne's quarters was brought down to her and she spent the first day sweeping the floor and repairing the few minor cracks in the wattle walls. She cooked a meal that she enjoyed from the open doorway as the sun faded from view and the vibrant sounds of Ailigh waned into slumber. Cormac's home was on the same level and she could call on him when she wished, and Fionn's home was further around the ringed rampart, out of view but tantalisingly close.

She refilled her seed pouch and watched Fionn work. His head was lowered from the sun and at times he stopped to put a hand to his stomach, taking deep breaths, before shouting at the oxen to drive them on. She was about to return to her sowing when she noticed him marching away from the ox, leaving the ploughman to work alone, and he stepped through the thick berry bushes at the edge of the field. He was gone for a few minutes before returning to his station, his belt unhooked and his face pale under the sheen of perspiration.

'Move it, you hunk of meat,' he said, slapping the ox.

Orlaith returned to her patch as the harrow-man berated her for taking her time. She smiled and blew him a kiss.

By mid-afternoon, she moved onto a new field and the work-songs of crop farming spread across the hillside.

'Put your back into it,' one of the men called.

Orlaith laughed. 'Mind your own soil or I'll break your back.'

She dropped her seeds into the shallow trenches left behind the ards. The women were not scattering them with haphazard attention, but were broadcasting them in neat rows, one palm width between each. Nature would take its course regardless, but centuries of cultivating crops dictated best practice.

When the field was complete, she found a water boy and took two cups to her brother and their king. They were laughing at something and Orlaith was glad to see the men smiling.

'How many more fields to do?'

They took the cups from her and Rónán said, 'Too many for today.' He poured some of the water onto his hand and daubed his neck. 'We'll pick up again after dawn and finish when we finish.'

'I feel like we've been working for a year,' Cormac said.

'Wait until your limbs ache in the morning and your muscles scream with every movement.'

'Fighting a war is less painful.'

When a shout came from the neighbouring field, they ran to the low wall and Rónán leapt over it before the others.

Fionn lay face down in the dirt.

Orlaith was last to his side. When she stood among the men, Rónán had turned Fionn onto his back and was tapping his face for a response. He groaned and Orlaith breathed.

'Alert the druid,' Rónán said. 'Help me pick him up.'

Orlaith came behind them as they carried him down and back up the opposite hill towards Ailigh's gate. His sallow complexion was broken by the flecks of mud on his cheeks. Rónán, Cormac and a third man took him into Grainne's quarters and the door was closed behind them. When they came out a few minutes later, Orlaith rushed to her brother.

'How is he?'

'I cannot say. The druid is inspecting him.'

Rónán touched her arm. 'He has been worsening for months. I should have insisted Grainne examine him before now.'

'He's a stubborn man, Rónán,' she said. 'You know that more than most.'

The three of them sat in vigil outside the druid's room. Twice, Gallen came out with an empty water pail and returned with a fresh one, but he did not acknowledge their presence.

When Achall approached and asked her husband what reason they had for waiting on Grainne, she bowed her head as she heard the news. 'Grainne will cure him of his ills, I am sure.' She left them to their contemplations.

Orlaith put her hand on Rónán's leg to stop it from jittering beside her, and Cormac paced the walkway between them.

'Sit down. You will wear a trench in the ground, and I have no more seeds to fill it.'

The sun was setting when Grainne came from the room. 'He is weak, but I believe he will live.'

'Why did he collapse?' Rónán asked his druid. 'What is wrong with him?'

Grainne motioned that they should step away. 'Let's speak in private.'

Orlaith looked through the open door. Fionn lay on the bed that Orlaith had recently occupied, and the young acolyte sat beside him, patting his forehead and cheeks with a damp cloth. 'Can I see him?'

'For a minute only,' Grainne said. 'Do not rile him.' She and Rónán walked away to speak in confidence, and Orlaith entered the room.

'Is he well?'

'He's resting,' Gallen said.

She brought a stool to his side. Faint traces of colour were returning to him, but his body was wet with sweat and his cheeks were hollow. She had not noticed the extent of his weight loss. She touched the back of his hand and found him burning.

'What sickness disturbs him?'

Gallen dipped the cloth in a bowl of water and wrung it tight. 'My lady discusses it with our king.'

'Will he recover?'

'I am just an acolyte. But I am told he will.'

Grainne returned. She touched his forehead and checked his eyes and tongue. 'You can come back in the morning, Orlaith. Let him sleep the night.'

Orlaith walked home and found the cumal outside the door with her child. 'He cries to be fed, I think,' the girl said.

When she was alone, the fire stoked and the boy asleep, she lay on her bed but could not rest. Her eyes scanned the thatching above her, watching the smoke swirl towards the ceiling. Tarry deposits coated the rafters. A fat moth circled over the flames and settled on the wall. In the distance, Rónán's hounds bayed from their kennels.

Morning was not quick to come, and Orlaith's sleep was broken throughout the night by worry. She bathed herself and her child, ate a small amount, and walked to Grainne's quarters beyond the inner wall.

When she knocked and entered, Fionn was sitting up, drinking from a small bowl of broth. Grainne ushered Gallen out and they were left alone.

'You look better.'

'I'm fine.' He blew on the contents of the bowl to cool it.

Orlaith sat without dragging a stool close to him. She let him drink his broth in silence.

He would not look at her. 'Why have you come?'

'To see that you are well.'

'I am well. You have seen it.'

'You startled half of Ailigh when you collapsed.'

He put the bowl aside and lay back on the bed.

'Did you ever buy that field to piss on?' she asked.

'I have no need of it.'

The heat from the fire stifled her and she nudged her stool away from it. She was caught between the burning of the hearth and the chill of his words. 'I see whatever sickness befell you claimed your sense of humour.'

'What do you want from me, woman?'

'I only seek to comfort you in your sickness. Nobody has told me what ails you or if you will recover.'

'I am flattered by your interest in my welfare.'

'Fionn, have I hurt you so much that you cannot even look at me?'

His feet took the ground, but he did not stand. His nudity was covered by the slip of a woollen blanket. Facing away from her, she could count the bumps of his spine.

'I am sorry,' she said. When he did not respond, she left.

She told herself that she would not cry. But the tears came regardless.

Chapter 24

'Poison,' Grainne told him. He could not believe it. She spent the evening examining Fionn, questioning him when he was alert enough to answer, and prayed over his sweat-dampened body while her acolyte cleansed him with fresh water.

In the morning, when he knew that Fionn would recover, Rónán talked to the cooks who prepared the communal meals, to check every fount of possibility. It was not their fault, they insisted; if their food was tainted, others would be sick, too. Rónán knew it was the case.

He went to Fionn's home with Grainne and they inspected his cooking pots and the smoked meats that hung from hooks on the wall. Rónán picked up a cup that was darkened inside by the stains of wine and he sniffed it. 'I do not know what I am searching for.'

Grainne said, 'Anything that does not belong.' She pulled the furs from his bed. 'It may not be something he ingested. Some plants are poisonous to the touch. Has he been in the forests since Imbolc?'

'We have all been in the forests. Unless he was unlucky enough to sit on the only poison plant in a one hundred rod distance, others would have fallen ill as well.'

Rónán opened his tanist's wooden trunk, cautious not to pry at his belongings but looking for signs of unwanted foliage, and he moved it aside to check behind it. Grainne ran her hand over his mattress, then under it. She prodded the ashes of his hearth and sniffed the pot that hung over it.

'He eats in the hall, does he not?' she asked.

'He looks like he hasn't eaten in weeks.'

'That will be the diarrhoea and the sweats. Whatever he was eating was ejecting from him quicker than he could digest it.' She looked around the room; they found nothing out of place. 'I cannot determine which plant or substance has poisoned him, but so long as he consumes no more of it, I am confident his body will recover. For the next few days, he will eat and drink nothing that I have not prepared myself.'

Rónán opened the door and they stepped into the morning sunlight. 'He was with me when we ate some bad mushrooms. We were children, inept. If it were not for Áed, I am sure we would have died. He sat vigil by my bed for days.' He paused, thinking. 'I do not believe Fionn is naïve enough to eat something he does not know the origins of. It is not a mistake you make twice in life.'

'Then it is something he touched,' Grainne said, 'or has been hidden in his food.'

'He can be surly with the boys, but he is well liked. What use would anyone have of killing him?'

'I am grateful that, whatever it was, it was not a lethal dose.'

Confident in Grainne's abilities, Rónán returned to the crop fields to instruct the men in his absence. He would take to the training grounds to teach the new boys while Fionn recovered. He did not know how long his recuperation period would be, but with the warring in the south unending, the boys needed to be ready when the time came for war.

News came that Ard Rí Cillian had been deposed. The high king was slaughtered in front of the Stone of Destiny and Rían Ó Hargon named himself Ard Rí. It would not be long before his warring Fir Bolg army would march north if they had not already begun their dreaded campaign. In the weeks since hearing the news, Rónán met with Fionn and his advisors to discuss their options. Grainne reiterated that he must train his boys. The crops would need sown and the spring rains would make vast areas of the countryside impassable. He hoped to avoid war until it was necessary.

When he jogged down to the training fields that afternoon, the boys were milling around without purpose. They bowed as Rónán approached, and their chatter ceased.

'Fionn is attending other matters. I hope to see some improvement in you all since your arrival.' He pointed to the rack of throwing spears on the edge of the field. 'Who wants to be the target?'

'I will,' Cormac said. When Rónán turned to him, he bowed. 'I expect none of them will be able to hit me, anyway.'

'Mine are the finest fighters in Éirinn. You would be full of holes when they are through, am I right boys?'

They cheered.

Rónán sent two of the boys to erect a wooden target across the field. 'It'll be safer this way,' he said. When they returned, he selected a spear, twirled it once above his head, and offered it to Cormac. 'Let's see what a southerner can do.'

'I'm a northerner by birth.' Cormac took the spear, balanced it in his hand, and when he threw it, it smacked the base of the target, tearing a chunk from the wood.

Rónán picked another spear and found the smallest boy among them. Darragh, the young boy who had told him he would one day be the biggest among his brothers, eyed the spear but did not take it from him.

'If you can throw this as far as Cormac, you can leave the field and go to the barrel hut,' Rónán said. 'If you do not, everyone else can leave instead. Deal?'

With reluctance, Darragh took the spear, stepped away from the gathered boys, and he looked out across the field towards the target. He hefted the spear shaft in his hand, curved his arm, and took two giant steps before releasing the spear into the air.

It had no lift, and the wind curved its arc. It skidded on the grass when it landed. A cheer bubbled through the boys, and Darragh looked to complain but thought better of it. A blush etched across his cheeks.

Rónán looked at the boy. 'Collect the spears and bring them back to me.'

He and Cormac watched Darragh trot across the field.

'Go then,' Rónán said to the others, 'but don't get too drunk. Training will resume tomorrow.'

Cormac said, 'You mean to keep him out here?' He was watching Darragh forcing the spear free from the target.

'I mean to teach him. He is small but will be mighty.'

'Go easy on the lad. And come to the barrel hut before there's not a drop left.'

As Darragh made his slow way back towards Rónán, the king beckoned him to hurry. When he stood before his king, Rónán said, 'Put them in their rack and pick whichever one you feel will travel the furthest.'

'My lord,' Darragh said, but did not finish his surly sentence.

'Something to say?'

'It isn't fair.'

'Take up a spear.'

The boy turned, picked one without thought, and looked back at the target. His knuckles were white, he gripped the shaft so tight.

'Throw it.'

Darragh looked at him.

'Throw it.'

The boy rolled his eyes. He gave no thought to his form but threw the spear forward. It skipped over the grass.

'Again,' Rónán said.

Darragh looked at him.

Rónán spread his hands. 'It isn't fair?'

'It isn't,' the boy said, shrinking back from the punch he was sure to receive.

Rónán selected a spear and weighted it against another one. 'Why isn't it fair?'

'Cormac is bigger than me.'

'Yes,' Rónán said. 'But why is that unfair?'

'He has a stronger arm. A longer throw.'

'And when you go to war, will your enemy always be smaller than you? Can you pick only the little ones to kill and hope the bigger men do not notice you on the field?'

'My lord,' Darragh said, 'that isn't the same.'

'It's exactly the same. You knew you could not win against Cormac, so you threw your spear without a care or form. What did you do wrong?'

Darragh flattened his lips. Confusion clouded his eyes.

'You acknowledged defeat before you were defeated. That tells me you have no desire to live. "He is bigger than me, so I will lie down and die." This is what you thought before you threw the spear, am I right?'

Darragh turned from him. 'You picked on me because I am the smallest.'

'No, Darragh. I championed you because you are the smallest. What did you do wrong?'

'I defeated myself.'

'Throw the spear,' he said, handing the one he had chosen to the boy.

Darragh took it with hesitancy. He rolled the spear shaft in his hand, weighted it, and took some steps back. Rónán watched as he took a deep breath, flexed his neck the way he had seen Cormac do, and then he leapt forward, his arm rolling over his shoulder, and he released the spear mid-arc.

It sang in the air. It did not travel as far as Cormac's spear had done, but it cut into the grass a great distance from them.

Darragh beamed.

Rónán clapped him on the shoulder. 'Do not lose the battle before you have stepped onto the field. Technique is everything, not size.'

Darragh nodded, his smile wide. He stooped to pick up another spear.

'Leave them,' Rónán said.

'My lord?'

'Go on, get yourself to the barrel hut before they drink all the beer and leave you with none.'

'Let them drink; tomorrow, when they are weakened, I will

show them. And on the battlefield, I will find my opponents' weaknesses in the same manner.'

Rónán laughed. 'What you lack in size, you will make up for in grit.'

In the days that followed, when all the crops were sown and Fionn's health was improving, Rónán continued to instruct the boys in the arts of war. The cause of his tanist's poisoning was not discovered, no plant leaves found, no tainted meats exposed. He was weak and skinny, but he was healing. A week later, the colour returned to his face and he was strong enough to go back to the training fields.

'Be gentle on yourself,' Rónán told him.

'I do not need a mother to fuss over me. Even weakened, I could still pop your head from your shoulders with my fingers.'

Rónán smiled. He was glad Fionn's humour had returned.

He met with Grainne that evening in his hall. He sent his cumal girls away and stationed a guard outside the door so that they could speak freely.

'He eats his own food now,' Grainne said of Fionn. 'Time will tell if somebody means him harm.'

'He is a king's tanist; someone will always mean him harm. Do you fear that if he is being wilfully poisoned, they intend to hurt me? Destroy my tanist so I am forced to choose another, or get close to me in some way?'

'Do you have a replacement in mind? He would be a suspect, for sure.'

'I have never considered it. Fionn is my only choice.'

They turned to other matters. 'News of Rían's war in the south heightens,' Grainne said. 'We cannot be certain how many clans he swallows, but he strengthens his arm at every turn.'

'Those damn Fir Bolg should have been slaughtered instead of captured. You are to return to the archdruid?'

She nodded. 'Now that the Beltaine celebrations are over and the new seeds have been planted, he calls for all brehon to convene for instruction.'

'He cannot mean to put a sword in your hands and force you all to fight.'

'It is an option if it comes to it. But I believe he intends to use our collective influence to end this bloody war without further loss of life.'

'Rían—never mind the Fir Bolg bastards—will not bow to brehon law.'

'Then sharpen your blades, my lord. Either way, with the bogs drying out in the summer warmth, I expect you may be travelling to war before long.'

'Will you take the boy north with you? If I do go to war, I could use the hands of a healer, regardless how small those hands may be.'

'Gallen is good, Lord, and he has learned much since I brought him here. But if you take him to war, he will want to fight. He has little training with weapons, but his temper is solid. If he goes north with me, I can keep his mind in focus.'

'I trust your journey north will be speedy,' Rónán said. 'Return to my side with haste because I will need your counsel.'

She left at dawn with her acolyte. Rónán spent the ensuing days staring at the southern hills for signs of the war braziers alight, and overseeing the training of the boys, not just Fionn's band of young ones, but the older boys whose arms were strong but ought to be stronger. He sent runners south daily in case a messenger rode towards them. And each day, they came back alone.

The braziers were not yet lit.

Chapter 25

Fionn coughed. When Rónán looked up, he could see a thin sheen of sweat under his eyes. 'Are you unwell?'

'I am fine.'

They were sitting in the great hall discussing their options regarding the southern war. His other advisors departed when the meeting was adjourned, but Rónán asked Fionn to stay. For the last three days his concern was growing. 'You are not fine,' Rónán said. 'Somebody was trying to poison you; I think they have started again.'

'Lower your voice, Rónán. Nobody need know of it.'

Rónán came to him and touched his skin. There was a slight fever, and his forehead was clammy. 'I will search everyone in Ailigh if I have to. I will find who this bastard is and have them slaughtered.'

'I eat from the same pots as you; I drink the same water. Nobody has the opportunity to drop anything into my bowls without my seeing it.'

'Then how else do you explain this?'

Fionn coughed again, drank from his cup of water, and sat it down, clenching his fist to stop it from shaking. 'I am either getting old before my time, or the gods have decided they no longer need my services.'

'Do not joke with me, Fionn. You know what Grainne said. All your symptoms point to being poisoned.'

'Would you rather I did not eat?'

Rónán took Fionn's cup and swapped it with his own. 'Drink this. I will put you under guard until I find out who is responsible. You will eat nothing I have not tasted first.'

Fionn placed his large hand over Rónán's on the table. 'Do not put your life in jeopardy to save mine. I am not being poisoned. If somebody means to kill me, they are not doing a good job of it, are they? I will sleep a day and be well again.'

'I need you in full health. I cannot journey to war without you.'

Rónán ordered Fionn to stay in Grainne's quarters for a few days. 'You are not to step outside this door, or I will kill you myself. Do you understand?' He went in search of Cormac and when he found him in the tanner's hut, wet-salting a deer skin to preserve the hide, he said, 'Can I trust you?'

Cormac rinsed his hands, dried them on his apron, and followed Rónán from the hut so that they could speak in private. 'What can I do, my lord?'

'You cannot tell anyone. Swear it.'

'I swear, my lord.'

'Not even Orlaith can know. Stand by Grainne's door. Let no one in but me. And whatever you do, do not let Fionn leave.'

'Have his symptoms returned?'

Rónán lowered his voice. 'He is being poisoned.'

Rónán took to the walls, but he was not staring across the lands. He kept his gaze on Fionn's *brú*. The door was closed, and nobody ambled nearby. He stayed there long into the night, watching the hut. If Fionn was right, that he ate from the same pots as everyone else, the poisoning could not be from his food. When the sky was pocked with stars and torches were lit around the walls of Ailigh, Rónán came down to the kitchens, filled three bowls with stewed vegetables, and took them to Grainne's quarters.

Inside, he ate a mouthful from each of the bowls, then he, Cormac and Fionn ate in silence.

When they were finished, Fionn said, 'The smell of the druid's herbs nauseates me.'

'Better than the taste of poison,' Cormac said.

In the morning, Rónán returned to the walls and Cormac to his station outside Grainne's home.

The boys were in training, the sound of their swords echoing from the fields, and in the distance, beyond sight, he heard the bleating of sheep and the occasional lowing of his cattle. Shouts and calls came from the homes as Ailigh's men were waking and starting their day.

He stood on the walkway of the second parapet, his eyes focused on Fionn's home, but in time his gaze wandered, and his thoughts carried him away. He shook the fog from his mind and returned his attention to the hut. When a guard would pass, he turned in the opposite direction as though searching for the coming war, and twice he saw a man walk close to Fionn's home but did not stop or enter. He had hoped that Grainne would be able to identify the poison, but she found no trace of it. He felt her absence with keen anguish.

Achall and Orlaith walked through the ramparts with their children and Rónán turned to face the south again. At least the two women were getting along. If infants put an end to Achall's bickering, he would have laid with her and given her a second son.

From his position, he could not see Cormac posted outside the druid's home. With Grainne in the north and Fionn out of action, Rónán worried that his circle of confidantes was too small. He counted Cormac among them, despite the short time they had known each other, but the people he trusted could be numbered on one hand. Grainne might say it was wise to keep your advisors few, but holding kingship was a secluded role. The friends he made as a boy within these walls now treated him with utmost respect, but their banter ceased when he approached; he was their king, after all.

Later, as the sun eased westward and a starling murmuration clouded the north, dancing in the late sunlight in perfect accord with each other, Rónán's eyes grew weary and he shouted to one of the guards for a cup of water. As the man dashed away, Rónán noticed a figure outside Fionn's door. They were shrouded in a robe, the hood drawn, and he could make out no identifying details. As twilight took hold of the landscape, colours were muted, and perception was corrupted by evening phantoms.

The man entered Fionn's home, and Rónán bounded down the steps from the wall. His sword was drawn before he approached. With the door ajar, he listened but heard nothing. He steeled himself for the truth and threw the door open.

'Reveal yourself.'

When the figure kneeling beside Fionn's empty bed turned, Rónán cursed.

Achall lowered her hood. 'I was checking Fionn was well.'

He came to her and raised her hand. Gripped in her fist was a small cloth pouch. The smell of it was caustic.

'I found it.'

'You lie.' He hauled Achall to her feet. 'Why? What do you gain from killing him?'

'Let go of me.'

'Answer me!'

Achall said nothing. She released her fist and the pouch fell to the floor.

Rónán gripped the back of her hair and held the tip of his sword to her neck. 'I knew you were a bitch, but I did not know you were deranged, you whore of a necrotic boar.'

'Scar me like you did Muirgel,' she said, naming her aunt, the woman who Rónán let live at the battle of Knockdhu. He had learned that Muirgel's husband, his chieftain, was responsible for his father's death. He gave the woman a permanent reminder of him by cutting her cheek with his blade.

'I will have your head.' He sheathed his sword and gripped her face. 'Raise your hood; I would not have anyone look upon your vile face.'

He dragged her from Fionn's home and through the open gate in the inner wall. When he approached Cormac, he said, 'Open the door.'

Inside, he threw her against the wall, and she fell to her knees.

Fionn looked down at the hooded figure.

'Here is your poisoner. Cormac, go to Fionn's home. Bring me the small pouch that lies on the floor.' When Cormac was gone, Rónán pulled Achall's hood back to reveal her face to her quarry.

215

'My queen?'

Achall spat at Fionn's feet.

Rónán drew his sword.

'Wait,' Fionn said. He crouched before the queen. He did not touch her, and she would not look at him. 'I have protected you for years. As the king's tanist, I have done my best to keep you safe—you, Rónán, and your child.'

Achall was silent.

'Answer him,' Rónán said.

She wiped spit from her lips. 'He did not ask me a question.'

Rónán raised his sword but Fionn held a hand up to still him. 'For months I have been worried that the gods were taking me before I could wed Orlaith. I distanced myself from her to spare her. So, here is my question—why?'

Achall smiled.

'Answer him.'

'Because,' she said, looking over her shoulder at her husband, 'you have a son. An heir. He should be your tanist.'

Rónán laughed. Had he not seen her face he would think she joked with him. 'He is a wain.'

'He is your heir.'

'But too young to serve as tanist.' He circled her.

'Then let me serve as tanist until he is ready,' she said. 'I can act as well as Fionn. No one has his interests more than I do.'

Rónán smacked her cheek with the back of his hand. 'You deceive yourself. It is not his interests you serve but your own. Are you not content with being queen you would kill anyone to put your son on the kingseat? If Fionn had died, who was next? Me?'

'You would have been first if I thought I could have evaded

the accusers.'

When Cormac returned with the cloth pouch, Rónán took it from him. The smell was revolting. 'What is in it?' She did not speak. Rónán crouched before her and took her chin. 'What is in it?' She refused to answer him, so he pressed her cheeks together to force her mouth open. He pushed the pouch between her lips and held his hand there. 'You will tell me, or you will die.'

'Rónán.'

He did not look up.

'Rónán, stop it,' Fionn said. His tanist gripped his arm.

Rónán fell back from her and she spat the pouch to the ground. 'My own wife destroys me. What is in the damn bag?'

'A mix of plants,' she said, wiping her lips with her sleeve. 'Something Muirgel told me of many years ago. Sleep with the smell of it and it weakens you. It is not designed to kill a man. Murder was not my intention.'

'But murder is my intention,' Rónán said.

'My lord, I was doing it for our son. If Fionn was weakened, you would look to your son to replace him.'

He smacked her again. 'He is your son, not mine. I have kept my promise and you have thrown everything I gave you back in my face.' He raised his sword, the tip against her throat.

She cowered from him. 'My lord, please.'

Rónán pulled back his arm to swing, but Fionn caught him.

'Spare her.'

'Spare her? For what reason?'

'Because a mother will do anything for her child, even something as disturbed as this. Do not punish your son by killing his mother.'

'You would have me return to my bed with the woman who tried to kill you?'

Achall said, 'I did not—'

'Silence.' Rónán pulled his arm free from Fionn's grip. He sheathed his sword and withdrew his dagger, slashing a mark across her cheek. Blood poured from it. 'You wanted me to scar you? You have your wish. It is the mark of your vengeful family, now. You have shown yourself for who you are. A spiteful whore who thinks only of herself.' To Cormac, he said, 'Fetch two guards. Put her in an empty *brú* on the inner rampart and they are to be stationed outside her door until I say otherwise. Instruct them they are not to speak to anybody about this.'

Achall covered her cheek with her hand, but she did not wince. 'Cormac, fetch me a poultice from Grainne's quarters.'

Rónán said, 'Rot and fester, woman.'

'What will you do with her?' Fionn asked.

'When Grainne returns from the north, I will have our marriage divorced in front of Ailigh and the gods.' He crouched before her. 'You thought to raise yourself above all others. And now you are a slug without a hovel to hide in. Get her out of my sight.'

Cormac brought two guards and Achall was placed under their watch. When he and Fionn were alone, Rónán said, 'You can stay here; recuperate.'

'The stench of Grainne's herbs and mixtures annoys me. My own bed is fine.'

'I will have men search your home for any more signs of Achall's poison. You should not have stopped me from taking her head.'

Fionn patted his shoulder. 'You would have regretted your actions the second you took them. Now, you can watch her. And the child does not go motherless.'

Rónán picked up the discarded pouch and threw it into Grainne's fire. It sputtered and spat before the flames engulfed it.

He married her to spare Áed. He would divorce her to spare the tribe.

Chapter 26

In the days that followed, no word came of Grainne's return from the druids, and Rónán spent his time on the palisade walls interminably staring both north for signs of his druid friend, and south for signs of the brazier fires in the hillsides that dotted the landscape between septs and tribal lands. The fires were still not lit, and in the fading light of evening, the cloudless sky shone dark blue against a black countryside. The southern usurper, Rían, a man Rónán would never regard as legal Ard Rí, would have marched on the north by now.

He did not visit Achall since she was locked in an empty *brú*, but he did have a cumal collect the boy to visit him. Áed did not speak, but he sat on the floor and played with a small bronze statue of a cat that Rónán once found at the back of the smithy. He could not be certain, but he was convinced it was Áed's namesake who crafted it in years gone by.

Rónán ensured that news of Achall's wrongdoing and her subsequent incarceration behind a locked door was not common knowledge. Only he, Fionn, Cormac and the two guards who watched her knew the truth.

Nobody questioned him about her absence from his side, for she was seldom in attendance at his tribal meetings, and each man had his own worries to contend with. King Rían was stomping through the south and moving closer.

Rónán turned and stared north. Grainne would be a fool to travel the twisted path-routes at night, especially under the cover of trees, for fear of getting lost or ambushed by a band of *fiann* or the *sidhe*, but he wished to see her horse-drawn carbad pull into view even if the night was fogged and black as pitch.

He crossed his arms against the chill of a clear night and felt a breeze stir the fabric of his clothes. He did not know until he drew blood that he had been worrying his thumb- and fingernail together in an incessant nervous twitch. He brought his thumb to his mouth and sucked the edge of his nail where the skin was torn.

When he turned to climb down the ladder from the platform's edge, he noticed an orange glow in the distance. The light vanished from sight when he looked for it across the dark hills, but he saw it again after a moment. It was not the war braziers—a fire was lit by the lough, close to Áed's standing stone.

He could not see who was down there when most of the world should be asleep. Likely, it was some boys who pilfered a wineskin from the kitchens. It did not make him angry, for he did the same in his younger days. A flood of memories came to him, but he forced them down.

He was not a king to remain detached and so he came down from the wall, grabbed a wineskin from the store behind the barrel hut, and walked towards the lough to join the boys. They would be wary of him at first, seeing him outside of the training fields, but they would learn that he could be fun, even if the nature of his daily duties did not allow for good humour. Fun was in short supply in recent times.

When he was close enough to the sandy shore, he saw, instead of a group of boys, one solitary adult—Cormac. The man sat with his back against the standing stone, a torch blazing nearby, and he was staring across the water. When he heard Rónán's soft footfalls approach, he stood and bowed.

'My lord. I'm sorry.' He looked at Áed's marker, then at the king.

Rónán was quick to shake his head. 'Sorry for what? It's a fine spot for contemplating the intricacies of life.'

'I did not mean to disrespect his memory. I spent the day stripping fresh hides from bucks. My back ached and I needed somewhere to rest it.'

'Do not defend your actions to me. I have climbed to the top many times to sit and think.' He touched the stone and looked up along its height, four palm-lengths above his head.

He remembered the wineskin in his other hand and held it out. Cormac took it with a nod, uncorked it, and sipped from it.

When he handed it back to his king, Rónán said, 'You do not strike me as a man to worry about future events. Therefore, I assume you must recall the past, or fear the present. Which is it?'

'Nothing fearful.'

Rónán drank from the skin and walked around Áed's stone. It had been some time since he visited Áed and he felt contrite. At the side facing the lough, he sat and pressed his back against the roughness of the stone. He indicated the mossy sand for Cormac to join him and he took another drink before speaking.

'I should not be king.' He leaned his head against the stone.

'Áed should be Ailigh's ruler. I am here only because he is not.'

Cormac sat beside him. 'I have heard the songs, and the bards' tales. Áed the Executioner appointed you his heir in his dying breath.'

'It was not so simple, but yes, the guts of the truth are there.' He paused, drank some more, and then passed the wineskin to Cormac. 'Áed was trained to be Oisín's tanist, just as Fionn is mine. Despite Achall's recent actions, he lives, and his strength returns to him. Áed was apprenticed to the king's chief advisor and when Oisín was killed, Áed took up the mantle he was meant to bear.' The corners of his lips curled into what could have passed for a smile. 'Me, I was nobody. I should never have been crowned.'

'You are not nobody. Not to all the people who are still alive because a dying king pinned the golden tribute to your breast, and you walked out onto the battlefield to slaughter a foreign army in less than a day.'

'Again, it was not so simple. But yes, I became king and I helped thwart the invaders. I did not do it alone. The bards always leave out the details.'

Cormac took another drink from the warming wine. 'All due respect, but the details don't matter. You are looking at it all wrong; if someone else became king and put an end to the invasion, you would be singing those songs along with the rest of us. You don't see that because you are living inside your own dilemma.'

Rónán looked at him, their shoulders touching as they sat together against Áed's stone. 'If I ever had any doubt that you were Orlaith's brother, you have proved me wrong.' He snatched the wineskin from Cormac's hand, smiling, and drank.

'Rónán.'

'You have proved your point. Let me drink in peace.'

Cormac said, 'Rónán. Look!'

Rónán was on his feet, the wineskin discarded in the sand, its dark red contents soaking into the ground. In the distance, over Cormac's shoulder, the hillside braziers were lit.

'It's the south,' Rónán said.

They hurried up the hill towards Ailigh. Outside the gates, Rónán shouted to the night's watchman and they were let in.

'Ring the bells,' he called. 'The hills are alight.'

'My lord?' Cormac ran through the outer rampart beside his king. 'What can I do?'

'Wake Fionn. Wake everyone. I need my council in the hall at once.'

Cormac nodded and hurried away, but he turned again when Rónán called to him.

'I need you there, too. Gather my advisors and hurry.'

When he got to the hall, his council members, minus Grainne but with the addition of Cormac, were already assembled around the table. Cormac had refused to take a seat—it was not his right—but when Rónán entered, he slapped the man on the back and pointed to a stool.

'I assume Cormac has told you why the bells are ringing.'

His council members nodded. Fionn, bleary-eyed but with colour back in his cheeks and weight returning to his bones, said, 'If Rían is on the march, the hills will be ablaze from here to the southern shores.'

'If the closest brazier has just been lit, we can expect a king's messenger before dawn. But we need to discuss strategies for any eventuality. With the Ard Rí dead and this bastard in his place, we will have no choice but to fight.'

Fionn said, 'Cormac, this mad king—what more can you tell us about him?'

'Not much beyond what I have already disclosed. He is foolhardy and headstrong. His chief druid is a Fir Bolg slave elevated to Rían's employ soon after the invasion. Likely, he's the real mastermind behind this campaign to free the Fir Bolg and unite them in war.'

'Kill the foreign druid, disable the king?' one of the advisors asked.

Rónán shook his head. 'It can't be that easy. He has started on this path; he will not stop even if his druid is not standing at his side. And I can only imagine that the Fir Bolg will not cease just because we take out their native leader. Fionn, the new boys—are they ready?'

'No, my lord. We have trained them hard since their arrival but most of them don't yet know a sword from an axe.'

'How many trained men do we have?'

'We lost forty-seven in the Yule border fights. But we should still have over four hundred men and lads ready to march.' Fionn shook his head. 'When Déaglán opened this place as a training base, I never expected it to last. Four hundred men may not be enough against Rían's bastard army, but as we march south, we can enlist every capable farmer along the path.'

'It will have to be enough. Rouse the men. We march at dawn whether the messenger has arrived or not.'

The men left, leaving Rónán deep in thought. On his way out, Cormac said, 'My lord?'

Rónán looked up.

'It will be an honour to fight at your side.'

'The honour will be mine.'

As Rónán knew he would, a king's messenger arrived before dawn, running in from the tribe to their south. Rónán had not gone to sleep. He sat in his hall, mulling over strategies in his mind while, outside, four hundred men and boys prepared to leave by first light.

The relay was a simple one—a runner would travel to the next sept or tribal lands, offer his news, the hilltop fires would be lit, and he would be given comforts for the night while a fresh messenger from that sept would journey north to the next tribe. One man could not make the journey alone and, though many tribes were at war with one another, a threat as great as this would mean setting aside local differences for the good of the land. The messenger who came to Rónán's gates would have been the eighth or tenth man to carry the news north of Teamhair.

Before the runner spoke, Rónán gathered his council again.

The messenger looked at each face, then at the king. 'No druid, my lord?'

'She is abroad on king's business. Speak your news.'

The messenger bowed. 'My lord, it is with great sadness that I inform you the usurper, King Rían, has marched north of Teamhair and aims for Ailigh. If he can take the overking, he will control all of Éirinn.'

'Damn it,' Fionn said.

The messenger glanced at him before returning his attention to the king. 'My lord, he knows the northern tribes will not bow to him without a fight. Because you are keeper of the north, his plan is to conquer your seat and unite our lands under one banner.'

Rónán said, 'Your chieftain has already departed for war in the south?'

'He was preparing to drive for battle as I left, my lord.'

Rónán stood and clasped the man's arm. 'Rest as long as you need. I will have the cooks prepare a meal for you and you can bathe and drink as much as you care to. The news you bring is distressing, but you are welcome among my people.'

The man bowed. 'My lord. All I request is to bathe and eat. I must return south as soon as I can. You will send a runner north and light your braziers?'

'I have sent a man to light them already. The only tribe north-west of us is the Ó Neill clan and they are under my domain. I will have a messenger sent to inform them, though their fighting boys are here within my walls. Beyond that, in the north, are the druids. If they are not aware, they soon will be.'

The messenger was shown to the kitchens to eat, and Rónán discussed their march south with his council.

Fionn said, 'We could use the choke point south of the Ó Nallon tribe where the path narrows at the base of the mountains. If we journey further south, we'll likely be caught in open ground or slaughtered amid the forests.'

'We can travel beyond the Ó Nallons if we hurry.'

'The messenger relay has travelled nine nights to get to us,' Fionn said. 'If we go beyond the Ó Nallons, we'll be slaughtered in the forests south of the mountains. We cannot say how close the mad king has journeyed.'

Rónán closed his eyes. He nodded. 'Then we shall set camp at the southern Ó Nallon mountains. Are you sure you're up to this?'

Fionn stood. 'I am at full health. Put a sword in my hand and no man will dare to stand in my path. The men are packing their bags and saying goodbye to whichever slave girl or servant they currently have an itch for. I will assemble them on the southern fields before the sun has woken.'

Rónán thanked each of his council members for their service and their time. And as they left, he asked Cormac to remain behind.

'My lord?'

Rónán turned to the table along the back wall and poured two cups of wine from the jug that sat there. He handed one to Cormac. 'You helped to fight our neighbours in the east when they raided our borders, and you have been a friend since your arrival. You have become one of my closest allies. But Rían is your king. I free you from any dishonourable action against him. You do not need to fight alongside me if you choose not to.'

'My lord, Rían has not been my king since Orlaith got with child. I am here, and I am yours to command.' He drank his wine and sat the empty cup down, holding out his arm for Rónán to clasp. 'I do not mean to reiterate what I have already said, but you look through eyes that are inside your own problems. Let me help you see—you are king. You are my king. Whichever way you wish to use my services, I am here. And I am yours.'

Chapter 27

Orlaith paced her room. Everybody was awake and Ailigh was a hub of activity, but no one had come to tell her what was happening. She threw open the door and looked into the night. Dawn was still some time away, but the hillside was aglow with torch and sconce.

Her child woke when the bells rang, but had since fallen asleep, cradled in her arms, and was oblivious to the hustle outside.

There was no sign of imminent attack, so the alarm was raised because of the south, she was convinced. It meant the men would march to war. And it was her fault. She fled from King Rían, taking his son, and Rían now tore Éirinn apart until either he found her, or replaced the child with another boy. She kissed her baby's forehead. She had angered an evil man, and he brought destruction upon them. He would not stop until there was nothing left.

A knock came to her open door and she turned. Fionn blocked the doorway with his large form. When she saw his face, she ran to him and he embraced her, the child between them in her arms.

Against his shoulder, she said, 'When do you march?'

'At dawn,' he said, his lips against her temple. 'I have been a fool. I pushed you away when I should have taken you in my arms and never released you. Be my wife, Orlaith. Let me wed you before I go.'

She did not speak.

Fionn stood back from her and held her upper arms. He looked at the baby, at the birthmark that covered the side of his face. And then he looked at Orlaith. 'Be my wife.'

Orlaith shook her head, but words did not form in her mouth.

'Be my wife.'

'You would wed me for love alone,' she said, her throat coming unstuck at last.

'Be my wife,' Fionn said again. He stepped closer and she moved back from him.

'I cannot.'

'Be my wife.'

'Fionn, you march to battle at dawn's light.'

He was smiling. 'Be my wife.'

'Repeating yourself will not——'

'Be my wife.'

'Yes. If only to make you stop talking. Yes.'

Fionn came to her and kissed her. She felt the heat of his breath, the warmth of his body against her. With his lips still pressed to hers, she said, 'You are crushing the baby.'

He released her. 'We should consummate.'

She slapped his chest. 'You will find a druid to perform the wedding ceremony first.'

Fionn's smile faded. 'The druid. She is not here. Meet me on the field at dawn's light. We will be wed one way or another.'

'I do not have a dress to wear.'

'Then be naked. I do not care. Just promise me you will be there.'

She nodded.

'You will be my wife.'

She laughed. 'Go, before I change my mind.'

When he left, Orlaith looked down at her baby and smiled. She nuzzled her face into the crook of his neck and kissed his warm skin. 'You weren't expecting that, were you, baby? I wasn't expecting that.'

She went to the door to look at the position of the moon, and as she stood there, she saw Fionn walking through the rampart.

'She's going to be my wife,' she heard him tell the people whose paths he crossed.

Soon, with the door closed, and Orlaith staring at the three dresses she owned, undecided on which to wear, the door to her quarters opened and one of the cooks, Aoibhinn entered. Behind her came four girls.

'Take your clothes off,' Aoibhinn said.

'What is going on?'

'Did you not hear the news? You are to be wed.'

Orlaith watched as the girls fanned out across the room, two of them filling a tub with heated water so that she could bathe, one laying a selection of dresses on her bed, and the last unpacking a bag of perfumes and bone-combs.

Aoibhinn snapped her fingers and one of the girl's came to Orlaith's side to help her remove her clothes.

When she was bathed and Aoibhinn had picked a dress for the occasion, Orlaith looked at her. 'Why do you help me? We have hardly spoken since I came here.'

Aoibhinn put a pin between her teeth while she pushed another one through the back of the dress to tighten its waist. 'Why should I not? Show me a woman who does not love a wedding. Besides, it will make Fionn happy, and when Fionn is happy, the boys are happy. And one of those boys is my own. But mostly, weddings are fun. We can get drunk and the men won't mind.'

Orlaith laughed and her ribs hurt from the tightness of the dress. 'The truth at last. Wine is the cause of many weddings.'

'And the ruin of many others.'

When dawn's light broke over the eastern forest, Aoibhinn led Orlaith to the gathering field. Four hundred men and boys were assembled in their warrior's garb, complete with sword and shield, spear and carnyx horn. A drummer beat a pattern as she approached, her green dress trailing in the grasses behind her, a ring of flowers knotted over her head, and the finest silver arm torc adorning her arm. It was loose, for Aoibhinn was a larger woman, but they had bent it into shape around her.

The warriors stepped back from one another, creating a path through the field, at the head of which she saw Fionn, spear in hand, sword at his hip. Beside him stood King Rónán Ó Mordha, whose smile was bigger even than Fionn's. She did not know where Achall was; perhaps the *bitseach* had no interest in weddings, or at least in Orlaith's wedding.

The servant girls spread flower petals on the flattened grass so that Orlaith's bare feet would be scented by their fragrance, and the drummer's slow beat continued until she walked to the fore of the field.

Rónán smiled at her. 'I have the honour of officiating in the absence of Grainne. It will be a soldier's wedding, nothing extravagant, but it will be binding. Will you accept?'

Orlaith looked at Fionn. She did not know how it had happened, how she had fallen in love with this giant man. Months ago, she watched him beat a man for daring to speak to her, and then he avoided her as his health deteriorated. But Grainne cured him, and he stood tall now, broad as he used to be, brighter in the eye than before. Their words were always careless and jovial. She did not intend for it to happen and had no interest in love. A person in love is a person indebted to another, and she did not want to be indebted to anybody. But here she was, smitten—more than smitten. She was entranced. Perhaps she had been from the moment she arrived at Ailigh after the Yule when the snows were thick, and she was close to death. The moment he first approached her—maybe he had taken her heart then.

'Say something,' Aoibhinn whispered.

'Yes. I accept.'

Rónán nodded and Fionn took Orlaith's hands. From a table that was brought for the ceremony, Rónán picked up a length of cloth and wrapped it around their hands, binding them. 'Grainne,' he said, 'will bless this union on her return from the druids. Until then, with all the gods as witness and all the people of Ailigh, I bind you as husband and wife. What is yours alone is now united, just as your bodies are united.'

In the custom of a soldier's wedding, Rónán took a cup from the table and filled it with wine. He held the cup to Fionn's lips and Fionn drank from it, then returned the wine from his mouth to the cup. Rónán raised the cup to Orlaith's mouth and she drank and swallowed.

'As the wine flows from one to another,' Rónán said, 'so too does new life flow between you. You are one, tied together in spirit.' He unwrapped the cloth from around their hands and their fingers remained entwined. He lifted a bowl of blue dye and dipped his thumb in it, then he placed a mark on the back of Fionn's hand, and another on Orlaith's.

'The mark of your union. Let all men see it and bless you.'

Fionn and Orlaith raised their joined hands aloft and the gathered men cheered.

When the noise had quietened, Rónán said, 'It is done,' and again a cheer filled the hillside.

Orlaith's stomach ached, but it was not from the tightness of Aoibhinn's dress. It was a nervous energy that consumed her. Fionn embraced her and she felt his lips on the corner of her mouth. She breathed the scent of him.

Rónán said, 'You have until the sun has fully cleared the eastern forest.' He nudged Fionn. 'You should hurry if you want to make the wedding official.'

Fionn laughed and picked his wife up in his arms, running up the hill towards Ailigh.

'Put me down. I am capable of walking.'

'Not fast enough,' Fionn said. He carried her to his home, and he backed in through the door, laying her down on the pallet bed.

When he took her, it was with love. He was slow, unhurried, and when they were finished, he kissed the hollow of her neck and he traced the contour of her breast with his finger. 'Do you feel it?' he asked her.

'Feel what?' She could feel nothing but the touch of his hand, the brush of his lips against her skin.

'The future. I feel it in the very air.'

Orlaith closed her eyes. Yes, she could feel it. 'Win the war and hurry back to me. I will miss your touch while you are gone.'

'You will not be far from my mind always.'

Orlaith slapped his shoulder. 'Why does sex reduce a man to the emotions of a bard?'

'Let's do it again and see if we can find out.'

Later, when the sun was clear of the forest, Orlaith and the women of Ailigh, along with the younger boys who were not capable of attending the war, stood on the hillside and watched the men march south.

Orlaith stood there long after the fields had emptied, and she could no longer see her husband or their king.

At length, she returned to Ailigh and to Fionn's home which would now be hers. She lay with the baby on Fionn's bed in a stream of afternoon sunlight from the open door, and she inhaled the smell of him that lingered on the mattress. She smiled. She would be smiling for days.

Chapter 28

Rónán nudged the horses at the head of his carbad over the brambles. The road south wound through thick forests and under the canopy of dense leaves, and they were forever in darkness, cut off from the sunlight by the choking foliage.

Before leaving Ailigh, while Fionn and Orlaith were cementing their marriage, Rónán went to the home that Achall was imprisoned in. He opened the door and threw the key at her feet. 'I am leaving sentries to man the walls, but there is not the manpower to guard your door. I trust your madness has passed.'

'You lock me away like a leper for a fortnight and only now do you deign to visit me? When are you leaving for war?' The wound on her cheek was violent and red.

'Be grateful I did not leave you locked in here to rot. The inner walls are forbidden to you.'

'My things are in our quarters.'

'Everything you need is here. If my walls are not standing when I return, it is you I will blame.'

'At least say goodbye to your son.'

The boy sat in the corner, turning a block over in his hands as he inspected the wood grain. Rónán picked him up. '*Daidí*,'

Áed mumbled.

'I hope you do not develop your mother's lunacy.' Rónán kissed the boy's cheek and closed the door behind him when he left.

At his rear, a column of men, three abreast, stretched into the forest and beyond sight. He loved the march, a thousand feet kicking up dirt, the flap of wings as birds scattered from the trees at their approach, the creak of carbad wheels rolling over uneven terrain. To a bystander or an opposing force, Rónán's army was a terrifying sight. They did not march in unison; rather, they stomped and undulated like many limbs of one beast. They were a herd, travelling in the same direction, and any man to fall under their feet would suffer.

Fionn cantered at Rónán's side, unsteady on top of the horse, but he cared more about the blue dye on the back of his hand than where his horse was treading. He had been grinning since they left Ailigh yesterday morning.

'When you look away from your wedding mark,' Rónán said, 'is the world as blue as I assume it to be?'

'My lord?' Confusion scowled across Fionn's forehead.

'You will get us killed in battle if all you can see in your head is your wife.'

'Better dead than lonely, eh?'

From behind them, Cormac said, 'Speak for yourself. I intend to live at all costs.' He nudged his horse up from the centre of the column. 'My lord,' he said to Rónán, 'forgive me for approaching.'

To Fionn, Rónán said, 'If the enemy approaches as stealthily, we are doomed indeed.'

'Pish!' Fionn said. He kissed the mark on his hand. 'Jealousy

237

is not a fair colour on you, my lord.' He slacked his horse off and fell back in feigned anger.

Laughing, Rónán said, 'How are you enjoying the ride, Cormac?'

'You did not tell me that sitting on a horse for so long would make my arse numb and my back nip.'

'It builds character.'

'Some of the younger lads are getting sluggish at the back. In the valley, it's still black as night from the tree cover.'

'We'll stop when the road widens out. A cross-path runs through the forest up ahead; we should have enough space to set camp for a while and eat.'

'Thank you, my lord.' Cormac nudged his horse to turn around but Rónán stopped him.

'Ride with me.'

They journeyed in silence for a time.

As the trees parted and the roadway widened, wet puddles splashed beneath hooves and shards of afternoon sunlight speared from above, Rónán caught Cormac staring at him from the corner of his eye. He looked away, embarrassed.

'You are not like any king I have ever known,' Cormac said.

'Being king is new to me. Perhaps I do not act as I should.'

'This business with Fionn and your wife.'

'I would not speak of it.'

'Forgive me.'

Rónán whipped the reins when his horses slowed, and they picked up their pace. 'I have released her from captivity while we are gone. But my mind is clear. When Grainne decrees it, we will be unwed.'

He raised his hand for silence, and he reined in his carbad. A call moved through the stream of men to cease. Ahead, where the road turned east and the cross-path was on the other side of the hill, Rónán heard the march of many feet. Whomever they were, they were not being discreet.

He pointed to two of his scouts and directed them forward with stealth.

Cormac's hand was raised with his sling ready, but Rónán shook his head. They had to be careful in such tight quarters.

A short time passed in silence before Rónán's scouts returned from the treeline. 'It's Mac Fachtna's army,' one of the men said.

Rónán relaxed. Although he fought them over the Yule at his borders, and he had killed Mac Fachtna himself, he suspected the men were not marching against them but were heeding the call to arms in the south.

'Fionn, Cormac—both of you with me. Wits up.'

They marched ahead while his army waited. When they crested the hill, one of the men came forward with his hands aloft, free of weapon.

'Lord Rónán Ó Mordha,' he said, bowing.

'Who leads you now?'

'I do. I am Seanach, son of Cas. I bear no ill intent, Lord.'

'You are marching south?'

'We take the same direction, it would appear. The bastard Rían will not know what hits him. My lord, your dispute with Senan Mac Fachtna is not a dispute you hold with me. May his bones rot.' He spat on the ground.

'How many are you?'

'We are almost three hundred—a fly on the tail of an elk, by normal standards. If you will allow it, we would march with you in peace.'

'What guarantee do you offer that your men will fight along-side us and not against us?'

Seanach said, 'Mac Fachtna was a scourge, my lord. We are better off without him. My men elected me their chieftain without hesitation. They will do as I say. I will have respect of your borderlines if you respect ours. But more pressing is that if we do not stand together in Rían's path, we may have no borders left to dispute. I have seen you fight, my lord. Trust me, I have no intention of standing against you.'

Rónán stepped forward and offered his arm. 'Your word is enough.'

'May your days be long and full of wealth.'

'And yours. We will rest and eat before we journey on. When my tent is erected, seek me out. We should talk.'

Seanach bowed and moved back to his men.

'You trust him?' Fionn asked.

'He appeared sincere,' Cormac said.

'We could use the extra men. And if he seeks to rise against us, he will lose honour and we would crush his army. I will sound him out before we march further. Instruct the men to make camp.'

When their camp was established at the meeting point of two roads, Seanach's men did not mix well with Rónán's. His army sat apart, eastward along the road they were travelling, while Rónán's army sat in rows along the north-south passage, tucked under the trees at either side so that the road remained clear for the food carts.

Feeding an army of seven hundred was not an easy task and a hierarchy of seniority prevailed; the older or more established you were under Ó Mordha's banner, the sooner you were fed. Younger stomachs growled in hunger until the carts reached them, and by then the curds were running thin and the bread was mostly gone. Empty honey pots were discarded along the roadside to be picked up later.

Rónán's tent, a small affair given the available space, was erected and floored with furs and heather-filled cushions. Wine was brought so that he could drink to peace with Seanach, and he instructed Fionn and Cormac to sit with him.

When Seanach came, he brought two of his own advisors, and the six men sat on the cushions, their swords and weapons left outside, and a cup was passed among them so that they could share a pact.

'You are a most generous host, my lord,' Seanach said. 'When next we stop to eat, I would have you attend as my guest that I may return the favour.'

Rónán nodded. Diplomacy was not his strongest suit, but Grainne instructed him in the art of political discourse, and he was improving. 'It would be my honour.'

When the food was eaten and their hands had been washed, Rónán said, 'I do not recognise you from our border disputes.'

'I was there, my lord. I do not believe any of us had the chance to watch idly when an opponent was swinging a sword in our faces, but I do recall hearing your powerful cries on the field and seeing the arc of blood you left in your wake.'

'You flatter me.'

'As any lesser man should. If you'll permit me to speak freely?'

'I expect it.'

'Since the Fir Bolg invasion, there is not a man in all of

Éirinn that does not know your name, my lord. They call you many things—most of which are whispered in great fear. Mac Fachtna should have known better than to stand against you. In war, when you die, you die because you made a mistake. Mac Fachtna's mistake was forgetting who his neighbour was; I will make no such blunder. My hope is that when we return from war, we may live in peace—yours and ours are the dominance of the north. I would give you a tribute when we march home as victors. One hundred head of cattle, my lord. They will be gifted to you when this southern business is done.'

'I accept your tribute. I believe you to be an honourable man, Seanach. May your children's children be healthy.'

When Seanach and his men left the tent, Fionn said, 'He knows all the words to say, but can we trust that he means them?'

'He would do well to mean them,' Rónán said. 'If his men make no attempt against us through the night, he will keep to his word. When we continue south in the morning, we will have swelled our ranks by more than half. This is a good sign.'

As the sun set that evening, those men among them who fancied themselves as bards, brought out their stringed cruits and their drums and whistles, and songs were sung as wines and beers were consumed. Some men danced with drunken limbs while others huddled in small groups playing dice or other games. Rónán encouraged the two armies to unite in acts of strength—a friendly fistfight was being cheered by a number of men and a rival game of fidhcheall was being watched with interest—and before long the men were integrating with relative ease.

Rónán found Cormac sitting alone by a campfire, a cup of

wine in hand but still untouched. 'May I sit?'

Cormac nodded. 'I have seen you command an army, train a horse to carry you, and now unite two tribes that, a few months ago, were at war with each other. Is there anything you cannot do?'

'Not that I know of. I hope never to find out.'

Cormac raised his cup. '*Sláinte.*'

'Twice I have found you sitting alone in contemplation. Do you have druidic visions, or does something trouble you?'

Cormac drank from his wooden cup before speaking. 'I do not know where I belong anymore. When I was fostered to Rían's tribe as a child, I was put to work in the tannery. Hides are what I know. But here I am, in the middle of nowhere, marching to war against the man who accepted me from my father when I was eight winters old, the man who has managed to overthrow the high king and take the south. I fear that if I were to meet him on the battlefield, I will lie down before him and beg for my life.'

'I would not condemn you for returning to his side. He has been a staple of your childhood and your youth. I would not stand against you on the battlefield.'

'I count you among the bravest people I know, aside from my sister who, trust me, would wrap her hands around Rían's neck and squeeze the life from him if she thought she could. But Rían's Fir Bolg army must surely grow with every clan that he swallows. Are we enough to defeat him?'

'Alone, no. But all the tribes of Éirinn united two years ago against the invasion. And the north will unite again to wipe out his army and destroy his reign. We will win this; I do not fear it.'

'And when the war is done?'

'What of it?'

'My foster tribe—should any of them remain—would not have me back. And my parents died during the Fir Bolg invasion. I have no place to call my own.'

Rónán put his hand on Cormac's shoulder. 'You honestly think that when we return home, I would ask you to leave?'

'No, Lord. And I appreciate your kindness.'

'It is not the kindness of a host to a stranger,' Rónán said, his hand still lingering on Cormac's shoulder. 'You are a friend. Ailigh is your home, and I would not see you go anywhere else. Besides, Orlaith would gut me if I let you walk away.'

'Now that she has Fionn, she may not even remember me.'

Rónán removed his hand. 'Who could forget such a smile?' He stood. Around them, men were retiring to bed among the grasses. 'Come. One more drink before bed.'

As they walked towards the wine barrels, Rónán sensed the tightness in his throat and the flush of his cheeks. He had not felt these sensations since before Áed's passing.

And he liked it.

Chapter 29

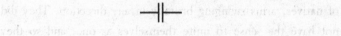

When the dawn broke, Bromaid could no longer discern the glowing fires of the enemy camp across the blood-darkened field save for the black smoke that stirred towards the gods. He had seen no lightning bugs since he left Hellas so long ago, but the glowing sparks from their fires reminded him of them as they danced in the air above the heat.

A solitary bird, too high to tell what species, circled above the empty battlefield between the two armies.

Bromaid flexed the muscles in his neck. The leather vest that was gifted to him by King Rían's men stretched tight around his ribs. He had approached the night's watchman just before the sun brightened the eastern horizon and said that he would take over. But he spent more time watching the north than he did the languid, early-morning activities of the opposing army in the east. Word that Rían had assumed the position of Ard Rí would have reached the northern tribes by now and they would unify against the usurper. It would not be long before they marched to war and Bromaid knew that it would do them no good to be facing away from the north when the time came.

The hostile army that they were in confrontation with—he did not know or care their tribal affiliations or the names of their bastard kings—had been weakened in recent days, but they were a formidable rival. They fought, much like all the armies Bromaid faced since first arriving on these pitiful shores, without unity or clarity. No one called orders to them or commanded them. If they had kings, the kings looked and fought like their serfs. The battlefield was a disarrayed mangle of natives, arms swinging brutally in any direction. They did not have the sense to unite themselves as one, and so they scurried like beetles when you lift the rock under which they were hiding. But the lack of formation among them meant that it was harder for a tactician to plan suitable attacks that would harm them. Although a native man could kill his brother with an accidental swing of the axe or sword, so too could the Fir Bolg army wipe out his comrades as he tried to counter and assault his enemy.

Bromaid could not tell if the lack of order among the enemy was premeditated to cause maximum disorientation among the opposing side, or if it was a fortuitous advantage. When you try to step on a flitting colony of beetles, you will miss many of them. Against a walled unit of warriors, you have a single target; against the scampering natives, a salvo of slingshot or arrows would have little effect.

In the days since marching north from Teamhair, Bromaid had instilled himself among Rían's chief advisors. He proved himself on the field as both a notable warrior and a valid strategist despite the enemy's apparent dislike of structured warfare. It was his idea to use a rounding technique on the field, semi-circling the enemy to box them in. They could not get behind enemy lines to form a complete circle around them, but it was only a matter of time.

He looked around the camp as tent flaps whispered in the morning breeze. They were nine hundred strong. It was a marvel that so many Fir Bolg men were enslaved two years ago instead of slaughtered on the field. But it was to their advantage. They did not get close to the tribal lands behind their enemy to know how many more Fir Bolg slaves would join their ranks, but based on the number of Éirinn's warriors they now faced, he expected there would be more than forty slaves to be freed.

When King Rían stands before the slaves and announces that they are free to leave or fight in his army, not one man turns to depart. The Fir Bolg tribes were proud men; when faced with a fight, they will revel in it. It was their way.

When the fighting began in earnest that day, Bromaid lost count of his kill-number long before the sun was above the field. When the challenge horn blew and both armies retreated to their respective sides, he was drenched in sweat and blood, and the whites of his eyes shone bright against the grime of his face.

The Fir Bolg challenger, a gargantuan man known as Eolid, who stood two heads taller than Bromaid and was as broad as three men, walked onto the field with his leather vest strained taut across his chest and a small leather cap atop his head— more for protection from the sun on his shaved head than defence against an enemy sword, for no man could reach the top of his height without first driving him to his knees. His sword and dagger were sheathed at the hip and he carried only a spear in one hand and his massive shield in the other.

'Who will fight me?' he shouted to the opposing side. 'I will kill two of you at once and send you to your gods.' It was his usual call, and, in twos, they came to him each day.

There was some reluctance from the opposite side to send forth their men, but when Eolid made the call again, they faced him. Were they to stand on top of each other, they would only reach his breast.

The challenge was over as swift as it began. They ran to him, their swords raised, and Eolid butted against them both, knocking them to their faces on the sodden ground. They rolled in opposite directions and Eolid swung but missed them. They redoubled in unison, one from either side, but Eolid pierced one man with his spear, picked him up off his feet, and turned to lance the second man while the former was still attached. When he let go of the spear, they fell to their knees. Eolid unsheathed his sword, flicked it with ceremony, and separated the two men from their heads in one slice.

The Fir Bolg army cheered, and a hiss slithered through the opposing tribe.

Eolid roared into the air and picked up first one head and then the other and kicked them towards the far army.

When the dead were retrieved by their warriors, the battle was renewed. Bolstered by Eolid's continual wins, the Fir Bolg army fought with a strength and vigour that the other army lacked.

As the sun trod its way across the clouded sky, and fires were lit against the coming darkness, the battle wound to a halt for the night. The stench of blood soured the air as Bromaid and his warrior companions walked the field, searching for anyone still alive before the daylight failed them, and retrieving swords and spears from the dead. Those lesser ranked warriors would then scavenge the bodies for jewellery or trinkets or the small bronze idols that most fighters wore around their necks.

After he scraped the dried blood from his skin with the furred underside of broad dock leaves, Rían called a meeting of his advisors. Bromaid attended the king's tent and they sat around on wooden stumps as wine was poured and plans were discussed.

'Have my men returned from the north yet in search of my bastard child?'

The druid, Gorid, said, 'They have come back empty-handed. The girl has disappeared or has been hidden by a northern tribe.'

'You assured me I would have the bitch.'

'I assure it still.'

'How many men did we lose today?'

It was Bromaid who responded. 'I counted fewer than fifty, Lord. Half that of our enemy.'

'It is still fifty too many. You slaves are supposed to be good at this.'

'Ex-slaves,' Bromaid said with defiance. 'And we are the best.'

'If you are the best, how were you defeated in your initial invasion?'

Gorid interrupted them before the argument became too heated. 'My lord, I will make a blood sacrifice of one of the girl slaves you call a cumal. This will please the gods—yours and ours—and we will surely win this battle with morning's light.'

'Be sure not to pick one who is already pregnant.' Rían drank his wine and then threw the empty cup on the ground. 'Gather the men; we will all witness this blood sacrifice of yours.'

Thirty men lifted the broken slab of a nearby dolmen, upsetting the ancestors of Rían's people, and it was carried to the edge of the camp to act as an altar. The men gathered around it with torches, and they waited in silence for the druid to approach with his sacrifice.

The girl who walked towards the stone altar was barely a child, perhaps sixteen winters old. Gorid would have checked to ensure that she was not on her cycle, for blood loss prior to the sacrifice would displease the gods. His inspection was thorough, and she was picked for her comeliness. She was bathed and perfumed, and flower petals were crushed and rubbed into the soles of her feet. The dress she wore was of a yellow dye and its length stretched to her toes.

She cried and struggled against the men who tied her to the stone, and her wailing quietened the opposing army in their distant chatter across the field.

Even the wind stopped to listen.

Gorid sharpened his sacrificial dagger with a whetstone and he sang a song to the gods in the ancient language of his kind. He danced and jerked his body in circles around the stone, breathing his words upon her skin. When he turned around the stone three times, he held the short blade inward and cut her dress open from neck to foot. When the wind refused to peel the fabric away from her body, the druid nudged it aside with his knuckles to reveal her nakedness to the gods. He lay the dagger upon her pale stomach so that it would not touch the ground, and he bathed his hands in the water from a golden bowl decorated with runic inscriptions. As he took the dagger in his fist, the girl screamed in terror.

When he cut her open from her clavicle to her navel, her

screams intensified. And then they abated to a gurning wheeze. Dark blood coated her skin and ran to the stone beneath her. The tall druid licked the flat of the blade so that he would ingest her essence and dropped the dagger into the bowl.

With his hands, he reached inside her to crack her ribs. When he could not do so, he used the butt of the dagger to break them.

Bromaid raised his torch to see better. His men knew not to interrupt the proceedings, but some of them gagged and hurled. Few men ever witnessed a blood sacrifice from such close quarters, but Bromaid had seen it performed on two previous occasions. He came away both times feeling closer to the gods. The sacrifice was a necessity.

Gorid withdrew his hands, a squelching, tearing sound the only noise for miles. And then he raised his prize to the sky as he lifted his voice in renewed song.

The heart did not beat as Bromaid assumed it might when he had first witnessed the spectacle. It simply leaked.

Bromaid looked at his companions. The druid's next action would be certain to have the lesser men among them retching up their earlier meal and crying for their mothers.

Gorid knelt on the wet ground, his hands still raised, and he opened his mouth as he squeezed the heart so that more of the girl's blood would enter him. He did not swallow. He swilled it behind his lips and then he sprayed it on the ground before him.

The girl's body had stopped twitching. For her, it was over.

Gorid bowed so that his forehead touched the bloodstained ground, and then he dug with the fingers of one hand, holding the empty organ aloft in his other, until he had made a hole large enough to bury it. The gods would walk above his offering and bless the land in their favour.

But Gorid's ritual was not complete.

He took up the dagger and returned to the girl's side. He cut her open from shoulders to wrists, from groin to ankle, and sliced her neck so that no blood remained within her. And then he peeled her open for the carrion birds that would descend and take his offering to the gods, piece by fleshy piece.

In the morning, only her bones would remain.

Gorid turned to his king, raising the golden bowl before him, and instructed him to drink the stained water so that the essence of the sacrifice enter him and reinforce his talent on the battlefield. When it was empty, the bowl was upturned, and the ritual was complete.

Bromaid slept little that night—not from any sickening emotions in his gut, but because he sat in the darkness on the edge of the field, watching as a murder of crows descended upon the sacrifice, tearing at the flesh and carrying it away to the gods. He heard them squabble as they fought over the choicest cuts, and the wet sound of it offered him the sense that the gods were near.

When he retired for the night, it was not long before the eastern skies glowed red from the rising sun.

That day, their war was won, as Gorid assured them it would be. They encircled the enemy long before Eolid had his chance at single combat, and at the appointed time for the challenge horns to blow, they did not. The fighting continued until not one enemy warrior was left alive.

Before evening, forty-nine Fir Bolg slaves had been freed to join Rían's army.

By the next morning, as a misty rain fell upon them, Rían ordered his troops to pack up camp and march northward. The hills were slick with summer rain, and booted feet slipped as they walked, but their spirits were high. The sacrifice had pleased the gods, and the Fir Bolg nation was returning to strength.

Chapter 30

Orlaith gazed at the blue dye on the back of her hand until it faded two days after her wedding. When bathing, she was careful not to disturb it, but it disappeared from her like her husband had.

Husband. It was such a surreal word. She was bound to someone now in a way she never thought possible. And she missed him as a drunkard misses ale. But she occupied her time with her child, letting him suckle from her as much as he wanted, and singing to him with the dawn and the dusk.

When the men left for war, Orlaith found Achall sitting in the sun outside a *brú* on the inner rampart beyond the stone wall of her quarters. She wore a simple dress, and the customary circlet on her head was missing. An enraged mark puckered her left cheek. In the doorway beside her, Áed lay on his stomach, drawing swirls in the dry dirt.

The hillfort was quiet, the walkway between huts wider without the press of boys in chaotic play.

'I have not seen you in a fortnight,' Orlaith said. 'You do not journey south with your husband?'

In her lap, Achall was sewing a pattern into a length of fabric intended for the hem of a dress. 'A queen is needed in her husband's home while he attends war.'

Orlaith could not take her eyes from the scar on the queen's cheek. 'You missed the ceremony this morning.' She showed Achall the blue mark on the back of her hand.

'I'm afraid I've been unwell and confined to bed, but I am better now. Am I to congratulate you?'

She did not expect it. She peered through the door of the hut, appraising its simple furnishings. 'Who lives here? Are we expecting a guest?'

'With my husband away, I feel more comfortable sleeping here, closer to the girls.' She put away her sewing. 'I suppose we ought to have a celebration in honour of your union.'

'It is unnecessary.'

'As your queen, it is my duty.'

That evening, Achall gathered the women together in the great hall, along with the guards who remained to watch them and the younger boys who were incapable of fighting, and she sat in Rónán's kingseat while instruments were played and the ladies danced until their feet hurt. She touched the scar on her face at times, but no one dared ask her how she received it. Wine was passed among them and the young boys, who did not care much for dancing with women old enough to be their mothers, were twirled from one hand to another through the night. As the heat of the room increased, and sconce torches were replaced when they burned out, many of the boys and the older women retreated to their beds. With the men at war, the women's duties would not cease, and they would carry out additional tasks to maintain the hillfort. The grain stores were depleted from the winter months, but the wheat rust had not returned. Achall would order rationing for the duration of the summer until harvest. But tonight, they ate and drank without worry.

Orlaith, tired of dancing, found a bench to sit on with her child. The cook, Aoibhinn, came to her and sat at the opposite end of the table. Her words were slurred. 'We don't drink half as much as we ought to.'

'Sounds to me like you've drunk enough for one night.'

Aoibhinn slapped the table with her hand. 'Then I should drink some more.' She stood, unsteady, and leaned her hand on a boy's shoulder. 'You, boy. Lead me to the wine.'

As Achall approached, she said, 'Her head will hurt tomorrow, but for now, let her drink. This is a celebration. You are not drinking?'

Orlaith did not stand to greet her. 'If I drank, my baby would be intoxicated from my milk.'

Achall waved and a cup of wine was brought to her. 'You should name him now.' she looked at the child in Orlaith's arms.

'I have considered names, but none yet speaks to me. I will withhold a naming ceremony until my husband returns.'

Achall, after a moment of silence in which to drink from her cup, said, 'It changes you, you know, having a husband.'

At the far side of the hall, the musicians had stopped playing and were discussing their next tune. Orlaith waited for Achall to continue.

'You and I are in a similar position—a husband and a child who is not his own.'

'Rónán loves your son, does he not?'

'He does. The concern is not with the husband, but with knowing that the son does not originate from the father. You will look at Fionn and you will not see your son in him. And you will look at your son and see somebody else.'

'All I see when I look at either is love.'

'A sickening response. When he starts to walk and talk, you will see that he is not Fionn's.'

'With respect, I do not believe that will matter, my lady. I do not mean to speak out of turn, but your Áed, though a quiet child, is equally as pleasant as your husband. His parentage does not worry you, surely?'

Orlaith could not be certain if the queen had wished young Áed to be Rónán's or wished that she had married the boy's father instead.

When the music started again, Achall stood. 'I will leave you now.' She nodded and Orlaith tipped her chin.

She could see how Achall tried to be polite around her, but she knew her temperament was veiled. And whatever befell her cheek seemed to soften her words. She got what she wanted since she first arrived at Ailigh—to be queen. Orlaith pitied Rónán's personal life, though she knew that being king kept him busy. A king's wife was surrounded more often by her ladies than by her husband.

She sat for a while longer and then, bidding good night to some of the girls, she returned to Fionn's home and stoked the fire for what was left of the night. With the help of some of the boys, the baby's cot-bed and her few belongings had been carried from her *brú* across the rampart and into Fionn's. She placed the child in his bed and touched the alder mobile that hung above him, so that it twisted in the candle glow to lull him to sleep.

Orlaith stretched out on Fionn's pallet and inhaled the scent of him.

In the morning, she went to the cook's hut to offer her help, but the morning meal was already prepared. 'They're out in the southern forest,' Aoibhinn told her, holding her head against the soreness of wine, 'cutting wood for drying.'

As Orlaith came through the gates, her baby in a sling around her waist, she saw Achall organising the women at the foot of the hill. The men would perform the task of cutting and chopping wood for their fires seven times a year so that there was a continual supply of air-drying logs, but while they were away at war, Achall grouped the women into teams to restock their resources. Two large roundhouses in the middle rampart—too far from burning arrows if they were under attack—were used to store and dry the wood.

'Can I help?' Orlaith asked. When she looked up into the trees, some of the smaller, more agile, women were sitting among the leaves, axe in hand as they hacked until branches splintered and crashed to the forest floor.

Without a word, Achall pointed at the chopping stumps where the brawnier women split the logs into manageable pieces. Towards the tree, she shouted, 'That one's too thin, Róisín. I want this one.'

Orlaith curtsied behind Achall's back. At the chopping stumps, she unhooked her baby from her waist and placed him out of harm's way. She spat on her hands the way men do, and she lifted a thin-bladed splitting axe. When she was given a large log to cut, she made a show of standing like a man, feet apart, and she snorted, wiped her nose with her arm, and flexed her shoulders. The women laughed. She swung the axe and it wedged in the neck of the log, her arms buzzing from the vibrations of the strike.

When the log was split into sections, they were thrown into a cart, and a new piece of wood was given to her. Soon, she was stabbing the axe into the ground at her feet and blowing on her burning hands to cool them before splitting the next log. The other women were faster than Orlaith, and she studied their form for guidance before continuing.

It took all morning to fill the cart and, while it trundled up the hill behind a horse, an empty cart took its place. The men would have chopped the trees down and made the most of one bole from trunk to tip, but Achall ordered only the sturdy branches be cut. She stood among the trees and pointed at the branches she wanted while everyone else broke a sweat.

'Not too high, Róisín,' she shouted. 'If you fall and break your neck it will be your own fault.'

By early evening, they had filled three carts with logs, and they were taken up the hillside to be stored for drying. Achall rode in the back of the final cart and the other women followed on foot.

Orlaith approached the queen when she dismounted at the gate. Her hands were blistered, and her arms were weak. 'My lady.'

'Orlaith. The boy is well?'

'He sleeps as though he were the one to chop trees all day.'

'We all performed admirably.'

'These women,' Orlaith said, choosing her words with care, 'they are strong and powerful. I suspect not even the men could have chopped such an amount in one day.'

'They are strong, even if you do have an ulterior motive in saying so.'

'My lady?'

'The women do not need to learn fist fighting.'

'I would consider sword fighting a better fit.'

'I have told you before, this is not a good use of our time, especially now that the men are at war.'

'It is the best time. With the men away, trained swords are few around here. What if Mac Fachtna's men decide to penetrate the borders again in Rónán's absence?'

'We have guards enough to compensate for it. We are not completely without protection.'

'Not completely, no, but if the women knew how to fight, the guards would have help in defending you.'

'You have said enough. I would have hoped that you could hold your tongue in front of your queen, but I see that I was wrong. I forbid any more talk of fighting women. Raise this subject to me again and I will be forced to evict you from our walls.' She turned on her heels and marched away.

Orlaith sat on a stump inside the gates. She adjusted the baby in its sling. '*Bitseach.* I'd put a spear in her back and likely Rónán would thank me for it.' She lifted the child from the sling and pressed her lips against his cheek. 'Or I'll hold her down and you can stab her in the arse.'

When she returned to the food hall, most of the women were finished with their communal meal and had returned to their daily chores. Aoibhinn was scraping off the clay bowls before cleaning them.

'Aoibhinn, have you ever used a sword or spear?' She looked around to ensure they were not overheard.

Stacking a bowl on top of the others, the girl said, 'Many a night I have wanted to spear my husband in the face but, no, I have not.'

'Do you seek to learn?'

'The lady wouldn't like it.'

'She does not need to know.'

'You can teach me?'

'I can teach enough that it matters. Spread the word. But be discreet about it. We shall train while her lady is weaving. We start tomorrow.'

Aoibhinn wiped her hands on a cloth and nodded. She ducked out of the food hall to inform the girls.

The next day, when she knew Achall would be in her home, weaving on a loom, Orlaith walked down to the training fields with a collection of broom handles and found Aoibhinn with three other young women. 'This is everyone?'

'Everyone I could gather at short notice.'

'No matter.' She dropped the broom handles on the grass. 'Pick one and feel the weight of it in your hands.'

The girls looked at the wooden poles. 'Where are the swords?' Aoibhinn asked.

'Or the spears?' another girl said.

'One step at a time, girls. Let's make sure we don't kill each other first.'

Because there were four of them, she arranged them into pairs and showed them how best to hold their weapons. 'Grip one end and imagine the other end is the pointy side. You want to jab and thrust, but you do not want to get too close to your opponent. If you are standing within striking range, you need to be thrusting. The key is to swing often and swing hard, allowing your opponent no chance to parry you.'

She guided them, walking around the pairs as they attacked

one another with humour. She would allow them today to play their games and get the novelty out of the way. Tomorrow, she would enforce some order and structure to their training.

She looked up at Ailigh's walls. She hoped Achall would not catch them.

Chapter 31

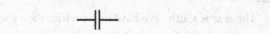

Rónán's army, and the men of Mac Fachtna's tribe, spilled out of the treeline and looked down at the hillfort enclosure of the Ó Nallon clan at the other side of the valley. Only a few fires smoked the sky above the settlement, and it looked deserted. The men would have journeyed south to stand against Rían's Fir Bolg army.

'The women and elderly will let us camp here for the night,' Fionn said, dismounting from his horse and standing beside Rónán's carbad.

'Do we have an offering for them?' Rónán asked. It was customary to bring gifts when visiting a tribe's chieftain or his family.

Fionn looked behind him at the men that stumbled from the underbrush. 'I'm sure many of the boys will have a gift of their own for the girls left within the walls.'

'No doubt, but we are not here for sport. Make sure that if they take to anyone's bed, they can still stand in the morning.' He turned to Seanach and asked, 'Do you know the Ó Nallon chieftain?'

'By reputation only. He was a fearsome warrior in his younger days, by all accounts. He will have travelled south with his men. His wife I am unsure about. From what I can tell, they normally trade west of their settlement and seldom venture north. But she will know your name, I am sure.'

When they reached the settlement walls, they were greeted by two guards atop the rampart, standing to attention above the gate.

'The war is south. We have no provisions for you.'

Rónán nudged his carbad a little closer. 'We have our own provisions. I am Rónán Ó Mordha, overking at Ailigh.'

'The Keeper of the North has no jurisdiction this far south.'

'You protect your lady well. We indeed march south to face the Fir Bolg rising. I ask for nothing but permission to camp at your walls for the night.'

'Our gate is barred to all but our own. Chieftain's order.'

A woman's voice, warm but stern, said from behind the wall, 'My husband is not here, Conn.' She appeared between the two guards and looked down at Rónán. 'I have heard of you, Rónán of the Ó Mordha. You are smaller than I imagined.'

He bowed to her. 'And you are more beautiful than I was told, my lady.'

'You lie well, little one. As my man told you, we have no provisions for you. But we can house twenty of your senior men. Forty if they do not mind bunking together. The rest will have to make camp outside.' Her guard, Conn, looked at her as though she had lost her mind, and she said, 'Open the gates.'

He hesitated, but then shouted down to the gatekeeper. 'Open the gates.'

Rónán, Fionn, Cormac and ten of his best men, along with an equal amount of Seanach's army, entered through the gates and waited while the chieftain's wife came from the walls. As the gate was closed, he heard his men making camp outside.

'I am Emer,' she said as she approached. 'Come, I will house you in my son's quarters while he is in the south with his father. I'm afraid we are a simple tribe with simple lodgings.'

'I would sleep with the dogs if it meant no longer freezing under the stars.'

'My bitch has recently pupped; I fear you would not have a decent sleep.'

She led him to her son's *brú* and left him to wash and change from his travel clothes, and then all the men gathered in the barrel hut for wine and sweet beer. Emer joined them after a time and, despite protesting a lack of provisions, arranged for meats, cheeses and breads to be distributed among those inside her walls. 'I do not have enough for all your army, I am afraid.'

'They have food enough to last them. I am grateful for your kindness to us.' Rónán raised his cup. 'May your son's line remain always healthy.'

'And yours.' When she drank from her cup, she asked, 'You will continue south with the dawn?'

'We will. How long ago did your husband and his men leave for war?'

'Five nights. I expect your men will be the last to pass through this way, given how far north you were.'

'The Ó Neills will be a night or two behind us.'

'My fear is that you meet the bastard king coming north before you reach any southern battlefields, wherever that may be. If that is the case, my husband—' She stopped, unwilling to complete the sentence.

'Worry not, my lady. I am sure your husband's men are strong of arm and heart.'

'You really do not know my kin. We are so few and so old. My wrinkles extend to my knees and my husband is no pup. Not like you, Lord.'

'I protest your youthful image of me.'

'Hush, child. Your eyes are old, but your body is not. I will retire to bed before my bones start to scream like rusted iron. In the morning, I pray that you strike out and win this forsaken war. And when you see my husband, carry him home on your shoulders for I do not think his legs would successfully navigate the forests on his return.'

Rónán stood. 'I will bring him back the victor.'

'See that you do,' she said, and she left.

When his table had been vacated, Fionn and Cormac sat with him, topping up their cups with wine from the jug that sat between them.

'We cannot risk journeying much beyond the mountains south of here,' Fionn said.

'I know. But the lady's husband and his clan, all the other clans south of us, may need our help.'

'If they stop Rían,' Cormac said, 'Rónán's army will not see a fight.'

'And if they do not stop the bastard king,' Fionn said, 'we will be overrun ourselves if we get lost in a forest. We have a plan. We should stick to it.'

Rónán considered it. 'I will make a decision in the morning. It will anger the men if they do not get to fight. But Fionn is right—beyond the mountains and we may be set upon without warning.'

'The Fir Bolg warriors are fierce. If they are not stopped before they reach us, we will need every advantage we can find.

And they are keen to hide in trees. You know this, Lord, from the invasion wars.'

'I will make my decision by dawn.' He looked at Fionn. 'You know the choke point at the mountain pass?'

'Not well.'

'I know it,' Cormac said. 'Orlaith and I came through here after the Yule. It was thick with snow, but I would recognise it. There is a valley beyond it and plenty of vantage points. The pass narrows at times so that no more than eight or ten men could come through abreast. If we can keep them to the path, it should be an easy win.'

'And if they fan out?'

'At least we will have taken a few of them before they get the chance, my lord.'

'The plan will work,' Fionn said. He drained the last of his wine. 'I will go to bed before I get too drunk.' He slapped Cormac on the back. 'I have every intention of dreaming about my beautiful bride.'

Cormac made a show of gagging. 'That's my sister.'

'I will tell you all about my dreams in the morning.'

When they were alone, Rónán said, 'You really think this plan will work?'

'It has to, Lord. As Fionn points out, if we get trapped in the forests beyond the mountains and we come across Rían's army, we will not have the space to fight well. We'll be rats in a barrel.'

'But if we wait at the pass, we could be failing this tribe by not strengthening their side.'

'They are five nights ahead of us. If we get to the battlefield, I fear we may find them already perished.'

'That is my worry.' Rónán poured them each another cup of wine, and he drank in one swift gulp. 'I need some air. Will you walk with me?'

Cormac followed him onto the walls, and they walked with feigned leisure around the rampart, passing the guards who were stationed there at intervals. The men neither looked at nor acknowledged them, such was the way of warriors to kings and noblemen.

Rónán traced a line from the top of the crescent moon to the bottom of it, and down to the horizon, and he faced that point in the darkness, knowing it to be south. 'Two years is a long time to soften.'

'You are not soft, Lord. If anything, I expect the Fir Bolg to be softer. You have trained; fought border wars. They have done nothing but work the fields.'

'Working the fields will strengthen their muscles.'

'But they will have forgotten the feel of a sword in their hands.'

'How is it that you know the words to appease me?'

Cormac snorted. 'I have been appeasing Orlaith since I could talk. It is a gift.'

Above them, in the midnight blue, a star flashed across the sky and it drew their attention as a thing imagined more than seen.

'I wish Grainne were at my side. She would know if that falling star was a good omen or bad.'

'In her absence, let us say that it is good.'

'I do not think the omens work that way.'

'We can only hope.'

Rónán searched the sky for additional omens but found

268

none. 'You never married?'

Cormac's face twitched in confusion. 'I have never been so unfortunate, my lord.'

After a moment's silence, Rónán laughed. When Cormac looked at him, Rónán tried to temper his chuckles, but the squint-eyed expression on Cormac's face only served to strengthen Rónán's laughter.

Contagious, Cormac also laughed.

'We have much in common,' Rónán said when his amusement receded.

'I do not know what I said to break your solid exterior, but I am glad of it. May I always make you laugh with such vigour.'

'I was not laughing at you, Cormac; merely at our situation.'

'We have a situation?'

Rónán looked across the darkness to the distant south. 'Am I mistaken?'

Cormac's answer was slow to come. He rested his hands against the wall and followed Rónán's gaze towards the horizon. He said, 'You are not mistaken.'

They refused to look at each other. The silence between them grew.

Troubled by the quiet, Rónán said, 'I should be making considerations for our battle plans.'

'Yes.'

'But I cannot.'

'I am sorry.'

'You are not at fault.'

'I am sorry all the same.'

'We have a war to fight.'

'Yes,' Cormac said.

'And I have—'

'A queen.'

At last Rónán turned to him. 'That is not what I was going to say.'

'But it is true.'

Rónán knew that Cormac's heart had quickened as much as his own; he could see it in his eyes, in his flushed cheeks that were lit by a nearby torch. 'She has hurt me more than any other. She is not my queen. But I have loved before, Cormac. And lost.'

Cormac was quick to nod. 'Say no more of it. There is a war to fight.'

'Yes.'

'So.'

'We stand here like imbeciles. It is late.' He offered his arm to show no animosity, and Cormac clasped it. 'Sleep well,' the king said.

'I do not think I will.'

As Rónán turned to walk away, he said, 'That falling star—I believe you were right.'

'Lord?'

'It was a good omen.'

Chapter 32

'It looks empty,' Gallen said as they rode out from among the trees at the foothills of Grianán Ailigh.

'They will have gone to war already.' Grainne flicked the reins to encourage the horses forward, the wheels of the carbad creaking over stones and uneven ground.

At their gathering in the northern druid's compound, they made sacrifice for a favourable outcome, and they lay prostrate on the earth for three nights. Each druid of their order kissed the master's hand and he prayed with them. He spent his days studying the omens and receiving reports from his network of scouts on the advances of Rían's army. He had hoped to get a message to King Rían's druid, to enter a dialogue with the man, but Rían's chief advisor was a Fir Bolg druid from a foreign order.

'The warring slaves will not be appeased by words,' the archdruid told his people. 'The time for diplomacy has passed. I would not ask you to involve yourselves in the war, though I know you are capable. Return to your chieftains. Your advice in these times is simple—there is no option but to fight.' He raised his hands to still the murmurs that swept among the gathering. 'Your tribes, at times, do not get along. Your kings squabble and fight among themselves. But this is the will of the gods. King Rían must be stopped. The Fir Bolg invaders will be terminated. Beseech your kings and your leaders. They must join the fight. All northern tribes should come together as one, just as they did during the Great Invasion. Take my blessings and go.'

As Grainne's carbad approached, the gate was thrown open for them and, once inside, one of the guards took control of the horses. Grainne lifted her pack and hurried around the outer rampart towards the central areas of Ailigh, Gallen scurrying behind her.

When she entered the great hall, Rónán's wife was in quiet discussion with one of the cooks. 'My lady.'

The cook left them.

'It is well that you have returned,' Achall said.

'When did they leave for war?'

'Six nights ago. You must hurry to my husband's side, Grainne. He will have need of his healer. What news from the druids?'

'Bad omens abound. The gods are fearful for us.'

'The daylight will leave us soon. Eat, and prepare yourselves for your travels in the morning.'

'My lady, your cheek. How did this happen?'

'An unfortunate accident. I tended it as best I could.'

Grainne inspected the red slash on her face. 'It is a wonder it was not infected. It should have been stitched. What caused it?'

Achall covered her cheek as though in shame. 'A mishap with the broken end of a bronze mirror. I should have had it mended months ago. It was my own fault.'

'I will have an ointment brought to you, Lady.'

The druid and her acolyte bowed and retreated from the hall. When they were outside, Gallen said, 'Is she always so warm and inviting?'

'Hold your tongue,' she said, though she was smiling. 'She worries for her husband and his warriors. Come; we will eat first. We will leave to join King Rónán at dawn.'

As they came around the rampart, Orlaith walked towards them, her baby in a sling around her upper body, carrying some broom handles in her hands. They embraced. 'You look well,' Grainne said.

Orlaith kissed the druid's cheek. 'I am wed.'

'It is a good match; I am happy for you. Fionn is a good man.'

'You knew?'

'It was plain to see how much he adored you. We are going to eat before retiring to bed. Will you join us?'

Orlaith raised the broom handles and said, 'I have some things to attend to.'

'Dare I ask?'

'If you do not wish to get into trouble with her ladyship, you will forget you saw me.'

'Tread carefully while your husband and hers are away. If I come back from the frontline and she has murdered you, I will believe it to be your own fault.'

'Better to die at fault than by accident.'

Grainne and Gallen ate in silence in the corner of the dining hut, the leftovers of Ailigh's early evening meal. She watched as he ate with slow deliberation. The wood of the table between them had been carved through the years with marks and spi-ralled patterns, scratched there by boredom or by wicked delight. Gallen ran his fingertips over the indentations.

'You look, but you do not see,' Grainne said.

He raised his eyes to her. 'Lady?'

'You study the table, but your thoughts are elsewhere.'

He lifted a shoulder in a shrug and chewed some more honeyed bread, casting his eyes back down to the food before him.

Grainne let the silence grow until he was ready to speak.

'My dream plagues me,' he said.

'Which dream?'

'The field of snowdrops. And the blood. So much blood.' He chewed, though now it appeared he was doing so to stop himself from speaking further.

Grainne had not told him that she shared his dream, the expansive field of flowers, the blood that marked them. She had seen her goddess appear as a swan, leading seven cygnets across the field, whereas the young acolyte saw four large stones as tall as men, and no apparent apparition from his chosen god. But she was convinced they had both been revealed the same omen. Shared visions were uncommon among the druids as each man dreamt in his own symbolism, so when they did occur, they brought grave prophecies.

She took from her hip her pouch of bones and placed it in front of him. 'Have you been taught the art of casting, yet?'

'The representations escape me,' Gallen said, dusting his fingers together before reaching for the leather pouch. He untied the strap around its neck, looked inside, and scattered the bones on the table.

They studied them together.

Grainne said, 'Here, the way these bones form a wide cross? Coupled with these three aligned side by side?'

'I see it, but I do not understand it.'

'Death is close, but life fights back.'

He looked up at her. 'It's all vagaries.'

'The simplest things always are.' She picked up one blackened bone that had skittered across the table on its own. 'And this one signifies that it is time for bed. We have an early start.'

When they left Ailigh in the morning, under a cloudless sky, it was with a speed their carbad was not designed for. Grainne had no notion how far south the frontline would be, but with a seven-night head start, Rónán and his men were no doubt already engaged in battle, or at least close to it.

'They killed my parents,' Gallen said, as though she asked him a question. Their carbad, led by two of Ailigh's strongest horses, was bouncing over a narrowing of the southern path, and the slick mud did little to grease the wheels.

'They killed many parents,' Grainne said. 'My own included.' Her niece, the daughter of Bec, for whom she was named, was a bastard child of the Fir Bolg. Every day, when she looked at her, she saw the men who came and slaughtered her people. But she could not hate the girl for it. She was a pleasant child, strong-willed even at two winters old. And she was not to blame for her father's sins.

Grainne journeyed with the Fir Bolg during the time of the invasion. They occupied the tribe lands at which she was stationed, and the chieftain, Rónán's surrogate father, had bargained with them—his life for the northern kingship. As she rode with the foreign king, she learned a great deal about their histories and their cultures. And it seemed to her that the warriors who fought for their leaders did so out of loyalty to their kin, more so than any inherent, violent tendencies. She had consoled many of them after the loss of their brothers and fathers in battle.

All men fight for what they believe is true. But convictions do not make a man correct.

When a slingshot pellet chipped the corner of the carbad, Grainne reached for Gallen's sleeve and tugged him to the base of the vehicle, hunkering low so that she could still control the horses. A second shot tore the wooden floor behind her.

'Two of them,' Gallen said, his arm raised to protect his face. 'No, three.'

Grainne whipped the reins. The wheels of the carbad groaned.

'We need to get off the path.' She kept her head above the walls of their carbad but ducked low every time another slingshot found purchase in the wood that enclosed them.

Gallen yelped.

'Are you hit?'

'My shin. I am fine.'

Where the path widened, Grainne steered the horses right. The carbad rolled into a ditch and she grabbed the boy, hauling him from the back and jumping with him into the field beyond the path.

They could not outrun the *fiann* who hunted them.

She pushed him down onto the grasses at the edge of the field to hide among the yellow gorse, but it did not give enough cover.

Grainne drew her dagger. It was all she had.

Gallen balled his fists.

When the riders came into view, they saw four men carried on three horses. They were nothing more than opportunistic brigands, their clothing made up of the colours of various tribes. Even the tunics on their backs had been stolen. The *fianna* were a band of landless men who sought the spoils of robbery from roadside victims. They dismounted beside the ditched carbad, drew their swords, and hopped down towards the field.

Grainne, with her dagger in one hand, gripped Gallen's travel robe in her other fist to keep him low. The field beyond them was filled with small white flowers.

Snowdrops.

One of the men was close, scouring the verge near them. Gallen shifted his feet and looked at Grainne.

Grainne shook her head.

He tugged his robe clear from her hand, put his finger to his lips, and then he leapt.

The thief was knocked from his feet, falling sideways, and the three remaining men were alerted to their presence.

Grainne could not let him walk out there alone. She stood, readjusted her grip on the hilt of the dagger, a short blade that seldom saw use, but one which she sharpened with a regularity that impressed even Rónán. She stepped forward just as Gallen rolled over the nearest thief and bounced to his feet.

She watched the boy kick the man's face, then fall on him, giving the *fiann* no time to raise his sword. He pummelled the bastard's nose with his fists.

Grainne pulled away from the sweep of the thief's sword as he came at her. She flashed the dagger, and he laughed.

'Wasn't aiming to kill a brehon,' he said, calling the druid by their collective noun, 'but I will if you don't drop your pathetic knife.'

She was trained by Rónán, daily for over a year, in the use of weapons and defensive techniques. When he came at her again, his sword swinging a wide arc towards her head, she ducked, twisted, and came up under his arm, forcing her shoulder into his chest. In the same moment, she pivoted to face him, her dagger coming up under his chin. She screamed as the short blade penetrated his fleshy neck, and she was still screaming when she pulled the dagger free. She did not realise how much force it required to extract a blade from a man's throat.

He fell, and she crouched, scanning the area. She could no longer see Gallen, but another of the men was running towards her.

If she had the time, she could flint the gorse bushes and cloud the area in smoke to make escape an option. But she did not.

The man barrelled towards her and Grainne jumped aside. His sword caught the length of her robe and tore it. The force made her twist and fall. He lunged and she rolled away, but he jumped upon her, his sword lost in the folds of her clothing, and his fist found her hair.

Grainne sideswiped her dagger, but the angle at which he knelt over her back meant that she could not get a clear path to him.

He pulled her hair, and when her head lifted from the earth, her eyes muddied and wet, she thought the field of snowdrops was the last thing she would see.

The man punched the back of her head with his free hand and then released her hair to scrabble among her robes for his short sword.

Grainne closed her eyes. Her most gracious lady Cáer led

278

her here, to her resting place. And she was at peace with that.

But the man's weight was no longer on top of her. She heard grunting, a thud.

She twisted her head and opened her eyes.

Gallen stood over the man, a rock clasped between his hands. He swung.

Grainne pushed herself up from the ground, the man's sword falling from her robes. Gallen brought the rock down on his head.

She saw that the other men were dead. She knew the boy was quick to anger but did not know that he could rage so fiercely.

'Gallen,' she said.

He was panting from his exertions as he came to his knees and smacked the rock against the man's face.

The thief no longer twitched when he was struck.

'Gallen, he is gone. You can stop.'

He brought the rock down again and he held it there this time. She could feel the strength ebbing from his limbs. The boy's cheeks were flushed, a line of spittle stringing from the corner of his mouth, his hands, face, robe, all splashed with dark blood. His eyes were wide and filled with tears.

He wheezed.

'He is gone, Gallen.'

He sat back from the body and ran his sleeve across his mouth. 'I thought you were dead.'

'I am not.'

'I thought you were gone.'

'Are you hurt? Are you injured?'

'No.'

She came to his side and held him. The tears on his lashes did not spill. He was not crying; it was energy that clouded his face.

When his breathing returned to a normal rhythm and they had remained in silence for some time, four dead bodies around them, Grainne said, 'Look around. Do you notice it?'

'I saw it when I felled the first man.' They sat among the blood-speckled snowdrops as the sun skittered overhead. In time, he said, 'Four rocks as big as men.'

'Four men,' Grainne said.

'You told me the gods speak in symbols.'

'They do. Usually.' She patted his back and then stood. 'We should find a stream and get clean, change our robes. But we must bury them first.'

She looked around.

'Why?' He wiped his bloodied hands on his robe. 'They tried to murder us.'

'All life is precious.'

'But they tried to kill us. Our lives were not precious to them.'

'No. But to the gods, all lives are important. We will bury them and move on. One day you will understand. Without a burial, they will not stand to face the judges of fate.'

They spent the rest of the afternoon digging holes with the few simple tools that were in their packs, and when each man was buried—there was no time to cremate them—Grainne placed a large rock atop each grave, the symbol from Gallen's dream. They were not huge rocks, but they did each house a man.

They struggled to retrieve their carbad from the ditch and

appease the horses that had been tethered there. But as they rode away, she could not help thinking about the expansive field of bloodied flowers. Gallen was right—there was no symbolism; it was an outright prophecy of events.

The gods were switching things up.

Chapter 33

Orlaith trained her female warriors each day. She took care never to speak of it within earshot of Achall, and the women knew better than to call it to anyone's attention. The four women that joined her training band on the first day had doubled by the third. And this morning, not long after eating honeyed fruits and completing chores, twelve women and girls assembled on the lower training field, furthest from Ailigh's walls.

Orlaith had convinced one of the guards to let her into the armoury. Though the warriors who marched south took their swords and spears with them, the armoury was stocked with older, blunt blades that were kept for training purposes. The guard did not ask for favours of a sexual nature; he laughed when she told him her reason for it and was still laughing when he opened the armoury door.

'Not a word to her ladyship,' Orlaith told him.

'I value my head too much.'

She wrapped the old blades in a length of cloth and carried them to the training field. When she unfurled her bundle to reveal the swords to the women, they cheered.

She had begged one of the cumal girls to care for her baby in her absence and said she would not be long. She spent the morning bouncing him on her knee and nursing him until he was full just before leaving him with the young girl. 'He will sleep well.'

She arranged the women into pairs and gave them one sword between them. 'You have trained well so far. These blades may be blunt, but they will still do damage, so beware.' The other woman from each team was given a broom handle and they would switch after a time.

Before long, the wooden poles were splintered and dissected into pieces.

'No,' Orlaith said to one girl. 'Like this.' She nudged the girl's elbow in, straightened her forearm. 'Swing slowly; you're just getting a feel for it. You're not swatting flies.'

Beside them, Aoibhinn and another of the girls were clashing two swords together after pilfering one from their neighbouring team, and their form was one of casual sport more than violent attack.

'Girls, girls,' Orlaith said. 'It is not a game. You are here to learn. I cannot teach you if you refuse to listen.'

'We should hunt for boar in the woods,' Aoibhinn said. 'We won't learn anything until we start sticking things.'

'I'll stick the sword in your arse. Enough. Practice like I showed you.'

The girls groaned, but they returned to their exercise. She watched them, feeling like an imposter. She had used a sword on many occasions, but her training was not perfect. She observed her brother when he was a child, under instruction from their father before he was fostered away to the south. And in more recent times she watched King Rían's men spar against

283

each other, and Rónán's men fight likewise. And through her observations, she was able to discern patterns of movement, the placement of feet, the fact that a sword was swung not just from the shoulder but from the hip. Legs are bent for maximum control, and feet are always moving.

Achall may be under watchful guard, but the women of Ailigh deserved to know how to hold a sword if nothing else.

When the men returned from war, she would tell her husband so. In days to come, these women may train in fields alongside their men.

Female warriors were not unheard of. Women growing up in households full of men were often far more vicious than her brothers, because she learned to be, because she had a need to be heard among those gruff male voices. Queen Clodagh of the Ó Rannons once led her husband's warriors into battle following his death, and her victory was swift. The bards favoured her in their tales.

Songs may never cry out Orlaith's name, but she was happy with that. She had everything she needed, and everything she thought she did not need.

She missed Fionn, his face a constant mirage before her eyes, and she dreamt of him each night as she lay in his bed, awaiting his return. But she busied herself in the days and kept her longings at bay. In the early summer warmth, she helped the cooks prepare their meals, and she took walks along the shoreline of the lough, resting under Áed's standing stone before returning to Rónán's walls. If she kept busy, she did not miss him as much.

'Again,' Orlaith said, clapping her hands at the girls. 'Strike, dodge, strike. Fiadh, widen your stance or you'll be knocked from your feet.'

The girls complied. Although her exercises were routine and laborious, they enjoyed the time together, learning something new, away from their chores. They did not mind that their manoeuvres were repeated until Orlaith deemed them passable; they knew that, should they have a need of it, they could help defend their homes or their children.

Grianán Ailigh was well defended and, even without most of the men there to protect it, its walls were secure, and the gates were heavy. But in the event of a breach, Orlaith was safe in the knowledge that she would not stand alone against any attacker.

'That's it, Aoibhinn, feet apart, elbows in. Good work.'

She walked the length of the line, watching the women as they parried and thrust against each other, and she clapped her hands and they swapped blades and poles to parry anew.

She felt a moment of pride when one of the younger girls stopped to instruct another in her position and movement.

From behind her, Achall cleared her throat.

Orlaith turned. Rónán's wife had come down from the walls, unseen, carrying Orlaith's child in her arms, the childminding cumal trailing behind her.

She held the baby out. 'I believe this belongs to you and not my servant girl.'

Orlaith took the baby. The women who stood behind her dropped their weapons and lowered their heads in collective apprehension.

They would not raise their eyes to meet the queen's gaze.

'You will join me in the king's hall at once.' Achall marched back up the hillside, her servant girl flashing a pitiful expression at Orlaith before following her queen.

When she was far enough to be out of earshot, Aoibhinn muttered something to the girl beside her and they giggled.

'Keep practicing,' Orlaith said. 'Mind not to cut anyone. I won't be long.'

She strode up the hill towards Achall.

When she entered the hall, the door was closed behind her. Achall sat upon Rónán's kingseat as though she owned it.

Orlaith handed her baby to the servant girl who stood by the door and she came forward to the queen. When she opened her mouth to speak, Achall raised her hand for silence.

'You have said enough.'

'I have said nothing yet.'

'I do not take kindly to your blatant disregard for my authority. You were instructed not to indoctrinate the women of Ailigh into your wild ways of sword-fighting.'

'They have a right to defend themselves, Lady.'

'They have duties that are imperative to the vital running of our community.'

'They work their duties, and they train with me outside of any responsibilities. It is their free time.'

'It interferes with the order of things,' Achall said.

'Are you so blinded by your ways that you do not recognise a good idea when it is presented to you?'

Achall stood, extending her queenly reign to the air around her. 'You were given an order and you disobeyed it. And my servant girls are not here for your whim and fancy. Your baby needs a mother, not a nursemaid.'

'My baby thrives at my side.' Orlaith could feel her cheeks burning red with fury. 'I have trained with him in my arms, and today, for one moment, I leave him with another woman. And now you question me as a mother?'

'You speak to me as if I am a slave to you. You have no respect for my authority.' She came down from the single step upon which the kingseat was mounted. 'I am your queen, sole wife of your king. You will respect my directions and you will carry them out without fault.'

'You take my actions personally because you despise me,' Orlaith said.

'This is not a revelation. You are uncouth and vulgar, parading your body around for all to witness. But you broke my rules. My distaste for you has nothing to do with my decision.'

'Your decision?'

'If you cannot follow orders, you will be removed from these walls.'

'Those girls are strong. They need training. They should know how to defend themselves against threat.'

'You continue to defy me.'

'To protect the women that you are supposed to care for? You're damn right I defy you.'

Achall came forward.

She raised her hand and slapped Orlaith's cheek.

Stunned, Orlaith looked at her. She refused to rub her reddened face even though its sting brought water to her eyes. Instead, she spat at the ground before Achall's feet, an insult without violence.

'Guard. Remove her from my sight. Put her outside the walls.'

'You cannot do this. I am duty-bound to remain here and await the return of my husband.'

'You can wait outside until he returns.'

'And my child? I will not leave him in your care.'

Achall smoothed the front of her dress. 'I will have food and furs brought to you so that your baby does not suffer greatly. He will not see in me that all women are whores and fighters.'

Orlaith clenched her fist. But she eased her fingers apart and slackened her shoulders to release the tension that had amassed in her body.

She turned, retrieved her child from the servant girl, and walked to the door.

'You brought this about by your own actions,' Achall said.

'You abuse your position as king's wife. I feel sorrow for you that you cannot wake with a smile on your scarred face and a heat in your heart.'

The guards followed her to the gates at the outer rampart. They did not speak, but as they ushered her through the exit, she could see in their eyes that they pitied her.

She faced away from the walls. In the lower training field, the girls were gone, too afraid of their queen to continue their training.

A breeze stirred her hair. She did not know where to go. Her husband would one day return for her, when the war was won, and she would not be there to receive him.

She came down the hillside towards the lough.

In the shadow of Áed's standing stone, her bare toes burrowing into the wet sand, she pressed her forehead against the stone.

'She has got her way at last,' she said to Áed's memory. 'Achall will drive anyone away from her that does not bow to her will. No doubt Rónán will be next.'

She slumped down behind the stone, facing the lough, and the baby gurgled.

'I still have you, my little one. You and me, we'll wait for Fionn. He will find us here and then we will leave. Just the three of us.'

When the tide rose, she retreated up the hill and, later, when it receded, she returned to Áed's stone to wait.

Chapter 34

By morning's light, Rónán assembled his warriors outside the Ó Nallon walls and prepared them for a renewed march south. Before they set out, he returned within the settlement and bowed to Emer, who had hosted them with grace.

'Remember your pledge,' she said. 'When you find my husband at war, return him to me the victor.'

'It will be my honour, Lady.'

'I pray you are not too late to the fight.'

'We will end this war. You have my word.'

Emer raised her hand and one of her guards came forward, walking a pup on a leash, a shaggy mess of blue-grey fur.

'A gift to you,' Emer said. 'Our *Cú Faol* are strong and loyal. In time, may he fight alongside you in battle.' The *Cú Faol*, or wolfhound, was two months old and already stood six palms in height. His dark eyes never rested as he looked around him.

Rónán took the strap that was attached to its neck and bowed in acceptance. When he mounted his carbad, the dog curled up at his feet and whined for his brothers and sisters. The Ó Nallon gate was closed, and he gave the call for his men to march. When the dog settled down to sleep, his paws twitched.

Rónán saw Cormac that morning for only a brief glimpse as the army broke camp and formed ranks of men ready for the march. He had slept little, a shooting star exploding in his head, and when he did fall under the spell of sleep, he saw Áed and Cormac standing side by side in battle, bloodthirsty and screaming in the face of their mutual enemy.

He flicked the reins and the two powerful horses that led him pushed into a canter.

The morning was dreary, but as the sun tore holes in the cloud cover, the day brightened, and the westerly wind eased. Summer blossom, pink and white, dusted the wide road ahead. Birdsong led their march, and the sound of lambs retreated behind them.

Fionn brought news that they were approaching their destination, the narrowing of the path at the foothills of the mountain. 'Have you made a decision?' he asked. 'Do we wait or journey further?'

'Have the scouts returned yet?'

'No, Lord.'

The afternoon had toiled into early evening. Rónán said, 'We will make camp and then I will decide.' The hound at his feet yapped at some unseen animal beyond the roadside.

As they came down the steep hillside and reached the plateau before the narrowing of the road, Rónán reined in the horses and stepped from the carbad. The young hound followed him, and Seanach approached. Beyond the foothills, the forest was thick and expansive. Rocky outcroppings rose at either side of the path, not impossible to scale, but if most of the Fir Bolg army came through the path first, Rónán's men would have little need to spread out in defence.

He looked towards the distant south. On the horizon, a tall mountain range rose blue into the sky. Before it was choking forests, cut north-west to south-east by the dark scar of a river.

Mac Fachtna's leader said, 'If we continue, we will need to leave the wagons and horses behind. They would slow us down when trying to navigate a path through the trees.'

'Agreed,' Rónán said.

'So, we journey on?'

'If we do not, we may be condemning many other tribes to their deaths.'

'If we are hit among those trees, we will have no opportunity for defence. That would condemn our own men.'

'We have little choice. We go where the war is. There is no point in waiting for it to come to us.' He surveyed the men that still assembled in their ranks, those at the front of the army who looked at him for answers, and those at the rear who were still clambering down the hillside. 'We will pause here to eat and continue on before nightfall.'

As far back from the road as viable, a temporary camp was established, but tents and sleeping areas were not erected. When the food was distributed and each man had eaten enough, they would travel further south, through the thick forests. A lean-to was set up for Rónán and Seanach to sit under while they ate, and the young pup watched him as he tore chunks from a loaf. He threw it a morsel.

He looked around in search of Cormac but did not see him. He worried he had been too rash the night before. War was not the time for a declaration of feelings, no matter the symptoms that plagued him. Though they did not outright say the words, Rónán knew that Cormac felt the same emotions. He wished that Grainne were with him. The druid would know how to still his heart; she always had the words that would appease his soul.

Fionn was nearby, laughing with a few of the men, drawing lines in the dirt with his fingers in a game of skill. Rónán swore that Fionn was the only man he knew who would smile even in death. He hated marching his men to war the same day Fionn was wed to his bride. But the big man donned his warrior's garb and, save for a few mentions of her on the first day of the march, he assumed his role with adherence to protocol. No man thinks of his wife in battle; they do so afterwards, when the war is won or lost. In the peace that followed the bloodshed, they have time to reflect on what is waiting for them at home. In battle, Áed once told him, the only thing you know for a certainty is that the man before you must fall—or you will. Any other thought will have you killed.

A whistle from further down the road alerted them, and one of the men shouted, 'The scouts have returned.'

Rónán put his foot on the dog's leash to stop him from wandering off, and he waited with Seanach and Fionn. When the scouts crested the rise, their tunics were muddied, and their faces flushed from running.

'My lord,' one of them said, drawing a breath. Fionn handed him a wineskin and, when he had supped enough, he passed the skin to the second scout. 'The enemy marches through the forests. Their head has just crossed the river and the rest are following.'

'Damn it,' Rónán said. 'How soon before they are on us?'

'If they continue through the night, I believe they will be here by sunrise. If not, mid-afternoon at best.'

'Pitch the tents at the rear. Every man must remove himself from the path. I want three men positioned either side of the road, hidden among the rocks. Their scouts will be on us before the bulk of their army and we do not want them getting word back to their king.'

The two armies worked as one to clear the path, and before the sun was low in the western sky, Rónán walked the length of the road to ensure no signs of their armies were visible. He stood on the outcropping rocks on the east of the road with the guards that were stationed there, and he watched the mouth of the forest. If the Fir Bolg army was less than a day away, their advance scouts would be close.

His heart was heavy. The Ó Nallon chieftain must have perished for the enemy to have marched beyond them. He could no longer keep his pledge to Emer, who had been so kind to him. But he was resolute in his demeanour—he would not let King Rían and his bastard Fir Bolg army pass them. Emer would not suffer the same fate as her husband.

When the sun was low and shadows were long, a stirring at the treeline drew the guards' attention. They hunkered and Rónán readied his bow. The ranged weapon had fallen out of favour with most, but he was a child of a fletcher; it would always be his tool.

A single scout emerged from the trees and Rónán raised the flat of his hand to steady the guards. They waited. When a second man stepped from the cover, Rónán expected them to be Fir Bolg, olive-skinned and brown-eyed, but the two men were natives.

'I do not recognise their colours,' Rónán whispered.

'Rían's men, for sure,' the nearest guard said. 'Who else

could they be?'

The two scouts carried spears, and short swords were belted at their hips. They moved with caution, crouching, trying not to attract attention, and stepped with care over the underbrush at the edge of the forest.

Rónán nodded, and he stood, drawing the taut string of his bow and releasing an arrow. It struck the farthest man in the centre of the chest. A slingshot pellet blinded the second scout, and as he fell, one of the guards followed the slingshot with a spear.

Both men were dead.

Rónán motioned. The guards came from their elevated positions towards the road. The bodies would be dragged clear and all evidence of their fall would be erased. The two bodies were dumped without ceremony off a crag in the west of the foothills. The guards returned to their stations.

Fires were not lit—the light they cast or the smoke they shed would give away their advantage—and so the men huddled together with furs as the night's chill set in, their swords and spears at the ready.

The guards remained on watch through the night; if Rían had employed a relay, more scouts would arrive in advance of the army.

Rónán tried to settle but could not. He thought of King Rían, of the Fir Bolg legion that the native king had amassed at his back, and he thought of Cormac and Áed, Orlaith and all the women that were left at Ailigh. Rónán wondered how many tribes were left in Rían's wake. He will have cut a path north-west from Teamhair after he was named Ard Rí, following the road as it wound through the land. Rónán hoped that the tribes not directly in his path were spared. There must be someone left in the south to rebuild society when this was done.

He could not allow himself to believe that Éirinn had become a vacant wasteland behind Rían's feet.

Rían could not possibly know that Orlaith and his child were stationed at Ailigh under Rónán's watch, but when he got the chance to slice the bastard king's head from his shoulders, he would revel in telling him so, that his boy heir was safe and well and would never know who his real father was.

Rónán rose in the darkness. Sleep would not come to him.

Securing his sword belt around his waist, and slinging his bow over his shoulder, he skirted the path south and mounted the rocks higher up from the guards. He stared into the distance, the dark sky black against a silhouette of the hazy mountains on the horizon. Somewhere out there, a massive army was stalking towards them, or perhaps sleeping uneasy among the trees. Either way, it would not be long before his men were at war.

The border dispute he faced against Mac Fachtna's men just after the Yule had been nothing more than a spat if his calculations of the size of Rían's foreign army was correct. After the invasion, all Fir Bolg men who were not slaughtered were rounded up, shackled, and distributed among the tribes without charge or barter. There had been many hundreds in the north, and many more in the south. He refused to take any of the Fir Bolg slaves to Ailigh. He could not bear the sight of them, a constant reminder of Áed's death. And now, with news of Rían freeing the slaves in the south, Rónán feared that if he did take the Fir Bolg men as his labourers, he would have gathered them together and slit their throats before the opportunity of escape came to them.

He heard a scraping behind him, and he spun on his heels, his hand on the hilt of his sword.

A shadow said, 'Forgive me, Lord.'

Rónán released his fingers from the sword and said, 'Now is not the time to sneak up on a man.'

'I did not intend to startle you,' Cormac said. Though he was still some distance away, Rónán could make out his silhouette, strong and broad. 'Anyone could fall from these heights and kill himself if he were not careful.'

'It would be unlucky to fall to your death the night before a battle.'

'It would be a cruel joke, indeed,' Cormac said, picking his way over the dark landscape.

When he stood at Rónán's side, the king said, 'I looked for you today but did not see you.'

'There are too many men to notice us all, Lord.'

'I thought you may be avoiding me.'

'I could never.'

After a pause, Rónán said, 'Are you ready for battle?'

'No more than any other man.'

Rónán's words were useless at the back of his throat. After a brief silence, he stepped into Cormac's warmth. In the darkness, he touched the man's face, cupping his cheek. He leaned close, and when his lips met Cormac's, soft but ringed by the stubble of a day's march, he felt Cormac's breath escape him.

Cormac parted his lips for him and Rónán felt the man's arms embrace him.

When their kiss was done, Cormac pressed his forehead

against Rónán's and said his name.

'Hush. We do not want the enemy to hear us.'

He fumbled in the darkness to lie down, and Cormac joined him there, hidden from the night by the ancient rocks that protected them, naked only to the stars that marked the passage of night as they slipped with quiet longing across the sky.

And when they were joined as one, the moon cast its silver light around them.

And Rónán's body burned with the craving of desire.

Chapter 35

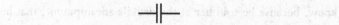

They were on the road for four nights in an endless trek south. Grainne pushed the horses until it was too dark to see the dirt road beneath them, and they tucked the carbad off the path and slept among the trees that lined the area. She roused Gallen before first light and they ate a small amount, hitched the horses to the carbad, and continued their journey.

Unencumbered by the paraphernalia of war, or a massive army to slow them, they made good progress, but for every waking moment, they were still too far from the battlefront. They took turns at the reins and when Gallen was in charge of the trotting horses, Grainne crouched in the bed of the carbad, alternating between praying to Cáer, and sorting through the contents of her pack to ensure no medicinal herb was left behind—dried agrimony petals, a bilberry paste, the black berries of the wild madder, bitter vetch leaves, and the root of the mugwort. The pack included a stoppered jar of the healing waters of the druid's northern spring, as well as runestones and poultices that would heal mind and body.

They did not speak of the four men they buried two days prior, or of the snowdrops in the field that were splashed with their blood. Nor did she ask Gallen about his rage. She had not seen the deaths of the first two men that he killed, which proved how quick to violence he was, but she balked at the memory of the young boy smashing a man's head with a rock. She watched him as he steered the carbad and wondered at how calm he was on the surface. She worried that, underneath the tranquil exterior, his mind was a mess of violence and pain. She knew, because he told her at the druid's encampment, that his angry outbursts were not uncommon, but she witnessed his complete and unconditional love for all living things.

He was a warrior in the body of a druid.

With his hood pulled back, his pale ginger hair licked the air around him as the wind touched him. His eyes squinted against the early afternoon sunlight in a sky burdened by the rising birch trees on either side of the road. Grainne could not imagine him capable of any aggression, but the madness in his eyes as he brought the rock down on the thief's head was all too real.

Gallen eased the reins back and slowed the horses, the carbad's wheels grumbling over the rocky ground until it came to a halt. 'Listen.'

Grainne leaned against the curved carbad wall beside her. 'Men.' She heard a multitude of feet marching over compacted earth. 'Hundreds of them, by the sound of it.'

'Your king's army?'

'They were too far ahead for us to catch up so easily.'

'The enemy?' Gallen puffed his chest to increase his stature.

'The sound is retreating. It is an army marching south, not north.'

Gallen cocked his head to listen. 'How can you tell? The noise is everywhere.'

'Listen for the source, not the echoes. When this is over, I will have King Rónán instruct you in the art of tracking. Quick; we should catch up to them.'

'Is that wise?'

'Road-thieves are one thing,' Grainne said, 'but no army would attack a lonely druid and her acolyte. And if they march south, they are on our side against King Rían.'

'And if they are not, I will kill them all.'

'I have no doubt.' Grainne touched his shoulder and he flicked the reins. The horses jolted forward.

The noise of the marching army made them seem close, but some time had passed before they caught up to the rear guard. As they came into view, the sound of their horses and the creak of their carbad made the warriors turn and raise their spears. Grainne had anticipated this. She waved a length of fabric, the unravelled cloth of a poultice, above her head, indicating no ill intent.

'We travel alone,' she called out as they drew closer. 'I am the overking's druid. We hurry to join King Rónán's army who are days ahead of us.'

The rear-most warrior said, 'I hope you've brought the gods with you, Lady.'

'They fly to our aid, I am promised. Who do you belong to?'

'We are the Ó Neill warriors, Lady. Our lord is up front.' He nudged the butt of his spear against the arm of the man in front. 'Clear a path; the Ó Mordha druid passes.'

The call went up the line, resounding into the distance, and Gallen whipped the reins and clicked his tongue. When they had ridden past half the army, Grainne had lost count of their numbers.

Torin Ó Neill, a young man who led his clan for all but ten years, was an ally of the Ó Mordha, and each year at Imbolc he sent his boys to Ailigh for training. Grainne had met him on several occasions, but they did not have any lengthy discussions or the chance to acquaint themselves fully.

When their carbad reached the front, she called his name in greeting and he told his driver to rein in the horses. 'It is well to see you,' he said, bowing to the druid.

She bowed likewise and dismounted. 'Midir's blessings upon you,' she said, naming his tribal god.

'Join me for a time. Your boy can rein in with the men behind.' Torin held out his hand to help her into his carbad and nodded to the driver to continue. 'You are not with your king?'

She gripped the support rail beside her as the carbad moved out. 'I was in the north attending the archdruid. We've made good ground, but King Rónán will likely be a few days ahead of us.'

'With my boys under his guide, and my men behind me, we will stop this southern bastard before long.'

'War pleases you,' she said.

'War pleases all chieftains. There is little fun in forcing back a border dispute, and you know we have had our share, but war—that is something else. You get a buzz behind your eyes that will not stop until it is over.'

'I understand its necessity, but when you've patched up the wounds of five hundred men in one day, you'll think differently about it.'

'I will leave the healing to you, and the slaughtering to my men.'

'Do we know how many Fir Bolg he has gathered to his

302

damnable army?'

'Nothing but conjecture. Anywhere between five hundred and two thousand.'

'Just one is enough,' Grainne said.

'We need our slaves to help farm our fields, but you are right—the Fir Bolg should have been slain after the Great Invasion.'

Grainne looked at the army behind her. 'You do not have any of the foreigners yourself?'

'I followed the overking's lead, as many of the northern clans did. When he refused to take any, many others did likewise. I am told you travelled with them during the invasion.'

'That is correct. I was a free captive.'

'How can one be both free and captive?'

Grainne's smile was small and came with great effort. 'I was not shackled. Their leader treated me with respect and sought my opinion in times of indecision. But I cannot forgive him for the pain he caused our lands.'

'If he kept you against your will, you were a captive, a slave. I trust he has already perished.'

'At Knockdhu.'

'I will make it my responsibility to protect you against further slavery.'

'I am grateful for your words,' she said, noticing Gallen pulling his carbad closer to them, 'but my acolyte has already proven himself a great asset in protecting me.'

'Lady,' the boy called. 'Stop the march.'

'What is it, Gallen?'

He glanced at the chieftain beside his mistress. 'Forgive me, Lord, but some of your men are sick with rashes.'

Torin Ó Neill called a halt to the line of men. He and Grainne dismounted, and the boy led them down the length of warriors. Grainne brought her pack of herbs and poultices from the carbad.

'Here,' the boy said. 'This man, and this one. And there are more at the rear. I counted twelve in total.'

'Show me,' Grainne said to the closest man. He pulled up the sleeve of his tunic and revealed a rash of angry red marks in defined strips across his flesh. The next man had the same markings on his leg, another on his back and torso.

'It itches,' one man said.

'Do not scratch it,' Grainne told him. She turned to their chieftain. 'Did your men bathe this morning?'

'Of course,' he said, indignant at her accusations that his men were unclean.

'Where?'

'In the ocean.'

The man who was trying not to scratch his itch said, 'We made camp by the shore last night.'

'Jellyfish,' Grainne said. 'The markings are clear.' She opened her pack and produced a large bottle of cloudy liquid. 'Gather all the affected men to me. We cannot continue until I have removed the stingers. Gallen, fetch me a bundle of dock leaves from the roadside.'

'What is it?' the warrior asked her when she removed the stopper from the bottle.

'Sloe vinegar. It will ease the burning, and then I can remove the needles.'

'Jellyfish are not in season,' Torin said. 'It's too early in the year.'

'The currents push them where they will. Their season begins with Beltaine.' She turned to the man whose leg was flaming red. 'You did not feel their sting when they hit you?'

'Yes, but the waters were thick with seaweed.'

'Seaweed does not burn.'

When Gallen returned with an armful of dock leaves, Grainne poured small quantities of the sloe vinegar on the smooth, upper side of the leaves, and she wrapped them around the arms, legs and torsos of the affected men, tying them in place with twine. 'We must wait now. Let the vinegar do its work.'

One of the men complained, 'It stinks.'

Torin Ó Neill said, 'Be thankful I didn't order you to piss on each other.'

'That's a fable,' Grainne said, quick to dispel the myth. 'Urine has no power over stings and burns.'

'Then I am grateful that you were here to educate us.'

'Your praise is due to Gallen, not me. Without him, it would have gone untreated.'

Later, she unwrapped the dock leaves and saw that the raised rashes had eased, and the burning redness was lessening. 'Now the hard part,' she said. She found a flat stone from the roadside and chipped at it until it was sharpened on one end.

'If you're going to cut his leg off,' one of the unaffected men said, 'you can use my sword.'

She ignored him. On her knees, she rested the warrior's ankle against her thigh, and dragged the sharpened stone down the length of his skin, scraping the small jellyfish needles from his flesh.

When she removed them all and inspected his leg, she said,

'Don't touch it. I will apply a brooklime solution to it once I have dealt with the others.'

She chipped another flat stone and handed it to Gallen, showing him how to handle it. 'Like this,' she said, scraping another man's affected arm. 'Gently; not too much pressure or you'll break the skin.' When he had cleaned one man's wound in her presence, she allowed him to do another without her supervision.

When all the men were treated, she and Gallen returned to Torin's side. 'They can march,' she said, 'but those whose legs were affected should not push themselves too hard.'

Torin checked the position of the sun. 'We can journey far enough to find a clearing and then make camp for the night.' He extended his hand to the young acolyte. 'The gods have sent you to us, young man.' To Grainne, he said, 'He has not completed his training?'

'He has only begun, my lord.'

'My tribe is without a druid. I would trade handsomely for him.'

'When he has completed his studies, we can talk. Until then, he is mine to train.'

The Ó Neill chieftain left them to assemble his men into marching formation and move out.

Grainne said, 'We will ride together again.'

As they walked to the fore of the line, Gallen said, 'How much was he willing to pay?'

'How much do you think you are worth?'

The corners of his lips curled upward. 'More than he would like.'

'But less than you deserve. You did well, spotting the rashes.

Have you studied the effects of jellyfish stings already?'

'I saw the men scratching. I thought it was something worse.'

'But now you know the striations you can treat them easily. The stings are not life-threatening, but if they go untreated and the sufferer scratches them and opens the skin, he can become infected. Sometimes, the simplest woe can become the greatest concern.'

He nodded and they mounted their carbad. He said, 'That sounds a lot like life. You start with a mild itch, and end with bleeding pustules.'

Grainne tried not to laugh. But she was too tired to suppress it.

Chapter 36

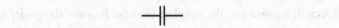

As Bromaid picked his way over the tangled thorns of the forest floor, he looked through the branches overhead, and could see a patch of sky that was darkening above the leaves. Around him, his Fir Bolg companions were cast in green shadow.

The forest was endless.

They won their latest battle three days before, spent a day scaling the shallower side of a mountain face, and entered the darkness among the trees. He had forgotten what sunlight felt like on his skin.

The shield on his arm weighed heavy and, with an increasing need, he had to rest his spear against a tree bole and flex his fingers to ease the tension in his muscles. He removed his leather war cap and shook his hair to loosen the tendrils from his sweat-dampened skull. The air was muggy beneath the dense forest where the breeze dared not stir.

'That sacrifice,' one of his companions said. 'How long does it last?'

Bromaid swished his spear at the underbrush to pick his path.

'We won the battle,' the man said, 'but will we also win the next?'

Bromaid stopped and flexed his fingers. 'You doubt your

countrymen's abilities on the battlefield?'

'I just wonder if we need to sacrifice another girl.'

Bromaid picked up his spear and moved forward. The foot-falls of his companions were noisy as they stumbled in the dim light. 'As long as the gods are pleased with us, we will do well.'

'Is it not better to overpay rather than underpay the gods?'

'The druid knows what he's doing.'

He pushed on. The man, a young lad, naïve, would no doubt question everything. Bromaid would not fold him into his circle of friends. In the days since entering the suffocating forest, he had picked his way from one man to the next, men he saw fighting on the field and who impressed him. He was formulat-ing a plan. Pushing the idea that now they were free, it was time for one of them to step up to the kingship. Most were receptive to the notion, but only because Bromaid did not state outright that it was he who should rule them. If one man's name were put forward, another warrior would slaughter him in his sleep.

It was the way of things. For the Fir Bolg, dominance was key. A ruler dominated his chief advisors, who passed that fear to their children, down to the serfs who controlled their cattle. Power was always in flux. A modest farmer could one day rule a kingdom if he had the right mindset and the right tools. The Fir Bolg were a nation of ambition.

And rightly so.

When he whispered with these warriors under the silence of the forest, he took great pains to make them believe that he favoured their rule above others. Their thoughts would turn to kingships and egos would swell. And when they squabbled among themselves about who should be the victor, he would slit their throats and take the kingseat for himself.

Rían was the prize, but like so many prizes, he was hidden from sight. He marched at the head of his army through the forest, but was surrounded by a circle of guards, kinsmen of his own kind. It was clear to Bromaid that King Rían, newly appointed Ard Rí of Éirinn, had freed the Fir Bolg slaves only to enslave them to his own will. He did not value their lives, and when they went into battle, the Fir Bolg warriors would charge first, long before King Rían took to the field.

Bromaid considered his best chance to turn on his king. He could not achieve it while the native man slept or when they marched, for he was under continual guard. His best course of action was to kill him on the battlefield, cut off his head and hold it high for all to see.

But to do so was problematic. With the slave warriors charging the field in advance of the natives, Bromaid would have to fight behind him to get close to the king. He had speed and agility over the king's broader encumbrance. And he had a Fir Bolg's spirit. It would be an easy fight.

He questioned the king's druid, the tall man with the grey hair whose name was Gorid. He saw the warrior-priest stooping to pick berries from the forest floor and Bromaid offered to help.

The druid showed him one of the berries. 'We need these ones. They must be smooth, without bumps, and they must be more green than black. If the black splotches cover more than half of the berry, discard it.'

'Your magic is powerful,' Bromaid said as he used the butt of his spear to search the ground.

'It is not magic, it is wisdom.'

'Many men believe that the cures you give and the healing you perform come directly from the gods.'

'It is true. But not how most believe it to be.'

'Wisdom is magic when those who are lesser fail to understand it.' Bromaid handed the old druid a fistful of berries. 'You know the king well?'

'The Ard Rí,' Gorid corrected him.

'Forgive me. Weren't you one of the first that he freed?'

'I was the first of his own slaves that he spoke to. I told him of our gods and of our wisdoms. It impressed him.'

'So, you follow him blindly.'

'I follow no man blindly. To do so would be to stand naked in a snake pit and scream that all snakes are cruel.'

'Are they not?'

Gorid bowed and said, 'Thank you for your kindness.' He attached the pouch to his belt before walking away.

The druid was too close to the king to be introduced to Bromaid's plans right now. And he would vie for the kingship himself given the chance.

Bromaid would continue to work on his friends and award their allegiance to him. And when he took the kingseat, all would bow to him. No indigenous man would remain alive.

He had already slaughtered one Fir Bolg warrior, last night under cover of darkness, when he introduced his idea to the man and the warrior was quick to suggest himself as an ideal candidate for kingship. They shared a meal of hardened bread and a cup of beer, and Bromaid listened with his lips flattened together while the warrior gesticulated with grandeur, outlining his desire to rule.

Bromaid, holding the last of the bread that was too tough to tear by hand, asked to borrow the warrior's dagger to section the bread so that they could share it, and when the man handed the blade over, Bromaid brought the dagger down into the warrior's neck. He would no longer desire to breathe, let alone rule.

Bromaid dragged the body into the darkness to hide him among the underbrush and, during the subsequent march, he had not been missed.

He flicked his spear through the tangle of weeds and thorns and stepped forward. He could see, ahead, King Rían's guard. When they made camp, Rían called his advisors to his tent and they discussed tactics and advancements. But when the army marched, Rían was surrounded and his guard impenetrable.

As he moved on, a greener patch among the browns and blacks of the dark forest opened before them. Bromaid stepped into the clearing. The sky was dark, and a breeze tugged at his hair. He gulped fresh air as though he were starved of it.

Rían broke from his circle of guards. 'We will camp here for the night.'

The clearing was not big enough for the entire army, and many would lie among the trees, but they welcomed the break and the cool, midnight air.

When breads and cold meats were passed around, two men came from the north of the clearing. 'My lord,' one of them said.

They were relay scouts, running between the fore and the aft.

Bromaid watched as King Rían attended the men.

'The advance scouts, my lord—they have disappeared.'

'Men do not just disappear.'

'We fear they have been killed or captured, Lord. They were to wait for us at the edge of the forest, but we saw no sign of them.'

'How close are we to the edge?'

'Close, Lord,' the second scout said. 'Four hundred rods, maybe five.'

'It is too dark to advance,' Rían said. 'Did you notice any enemy activity?'

'No, Lord, but it was already dark when we arrived there.'

'What was the lay of the land?'

'Beyond the forest is another mountain, my lord, but there is a pass that runs through it.'

Rían looked towards the darkness as though he could see the end of the forest. 'Return to the edge of the treeline but do not venture beyond it. You two are now my advance scouts. I will have a relay set up.' The two men bowed and turned into the night. To Gorid, King Rían said, 'The enemy is close. The northern tribes have had plenty of time to align themselves. If I am right, beyond this forest we will find our greatest fight in this campaign. The north is almost ours.'

The warriors who were close enough cheered when they heard this. They were sick of trudging through the forest and were itching for a fight.

They ate and slept in fits. When the treetops brightened with the morning's light, Gorid and the few other druids who served their master mixed herbs and berries to produce a blue dye. The bowls were passed among the men.

Bromaid stripped off his tunic and dipped his fingers into the dye. He made spirals on his face, neck and chest, symbols and emblems of his tribe, the straight lines of longevity and the swirls of a powerful warrior. He gave the bowl to one of his tribesmen, a man he knew for years before leaving Hellas, and he painted more symbols on Bromaid's back before Bromaid returned the favour.

When all the men were decorated in their unique tribal markings, Bromaid stood among them and raised his hands for quiet.

'You wear the favour of your ancestors,' he said, loud enough for all to hear. 'Truly you are remarkable warriors. We set sail from Hellas too long ago. Our power was interrupted. But we are free men now, and we are strong.' They cheered him and he let it continue. 'We conquer the land that was once ours, a land that will be ours again. We are fearsome, terrifying.' He paused to let the cheers subside, and King Rían stepped near him. In a grand gesture, Bromaid bowed to the man he would one day kill. 'At your command, my lord, let us slaughter every native man who stands in our path.'

Rían silenced the ovations. 'I have been informed of a clan living in the east, half a day's trek. They are a simple people, but they are rich in soil and property. They control much of the eastern coastline in trade. One of my men hails from there. If what I am told is correct, they have bartered for more than sixty of your kin since you were first enslaved. I will take one hundred men with me and free them to join our cause, and in the process, we will gain control of the shores and the trade routes. Who will come?'

Freeing additional slaves would benefit not only King Rían, but also Bromaid's aim. But they were so close to the edge of the strangling forest that a detour seemed unwise.

'And the rest of us?' he asked. 'We march north to face the

great Rónán Ó Mordha, and you abandon us?'

'The Ó Mordha king is no great threat, my friend. He is a fool with a sword in his hand, and such fools are easily rebuffed. March to the edge of the forest and await me there. If the northern overking does not stand before you by the time I return, we will face him together and I will let you take his head from his shoulders. If we control the shoreline, we will command the whole land. One hundred men is all I need; it is a minor expedition for a major reward. Step forward if you'll join me.'

Bromaid considered following the king. If he was surrounded by fewer men, he might be able to kill him and succeed to the kingseat with little effort. But he knew that if the northern tribes were to come, they would need as many able swords as was available.

Rían left with his band of men, striking out east among the dappled shadows.

Bromaid, self-appointed spokesman, looked at the remaining men. 'King or no king, we have a war to fight.'

The Fir Bolg army rose within the clearing and whooped their war cries. When they returned to the darkness of the tree cover at the far side of the clearing, it was with high spirits. Soon, blood would spill.

And a warrior is worthless if he is not spilling blood.

Chapter 37

A yellow haze broke the early morning darkness and Rónán, together with Seanach, set their armies along the narrowing of the pass, high up on either side. The rest of the men were fanned out across the rocky mountainside to ward off flanking breaches, and others were stationed beyond the path further up the foothills. If they could herd the enemy into the pass, they could kill many and cut their fighting time by half.

Last night, after he and Cormac said good night, Rónán was unable to sleep. Images of Cormac's body plagued him, and he turned on his mattress of furs, willing the thoughts to leave him. Sleep was necessary; he could not command an army with bleary eyes and heavy limbs. And yet Cormac continued to dance in his mind, the feel of his arms, the press of his naked chest, the softness of his lips. Rónán opened his eyes to the darkness, because it was easier to shake off the mental images than with his lids closed, and still he could feel the warmth of his companion's body pressed against him as though the heat lingered long after Cormac had kissed him with finality and retired to his own sleeping furs.

Rónán rose and prowled through the night, slipping from one watchman to the next, ensuring there were no further signs of the enemy following their earlier strike against the scouts.

As he stood upon the rocks where, not so long ago, his clothes had been discarded in a pile with another man's, he looked at the dark outline of the trees below and an idea struck him.

He returned to the camp and woke Seanach. 'How many spare spears do you have?'

'Spears?' Seanach asked, fogged with sleep in his eyes.

Rónán said, 'I have two a-piece for each of my men and a backup wagon filled with eighty more. You?'

Seanach sat up and looked around as though the answer lay beside him. 'Two per man, just as you do. But I have none in addition.'

'Gather ten men and fifty spears. I will collect the same.'

'Are we under attack?'

Rónán did not hear the question as he hurried away.

From the spear wagon, he took fifty of the bronze-tipped poles, and he ordered ten of his nearest men to carry them down the pass. When he joined them, Seanach and his men were standing nearby, confused by what was happening.

Rónán brought with him four lengths of rope. 'We'll tie the spears to the rope, a man's width apart, and lay them flat.'

'And when the foreign bastards come from the trees, they'll get a surprise,' Seanach said.

They lit two torches so as not to brighten the sky too much around them, and they set to work.

'Genius,' Seanach called it.

'Resourceful,' Rónán said, then added, 'If it works.'

While they were setting up the trap, two more of King Rían's scouts came to the treeline, creeping through the dense

317

foliage, adept at moving without noise, but the glint of torch-light flashed on one of their shield bosses and they were spotted.

Rónán, Seanach and the other men drew their swords and entered the trees, giving chase. The two scouts were cut down fast and their bodies were dragged back towards the road to be discarded with the previous men.

Standing among the trees, Rónán listened. There came no charge, no battle cry; they had not been heard or discovered. He nodded at the others and they returned to camp.

In the daylight, he looked down from his hidden perch and could see no outline of the spears. They were covered during the night with grasses and gorse, and the wind that stirred the area had made better use of the cover. When he strained his neck to see better, a man crouched at either side of the roped spears, clinging to the thick pullcord with both hands and hidden from view by boulders. When each man pulled on the rope, the spears would rise, and many would be staked.

Rónán spotted Cormac across the pass, his head visible over the ridge, too low to be seen from beneath. Cormac nodded at him and then returned his gaze to the road.

They shared a quiet moment at dawn while the men ate and bathed with a swiftness that was predestined only in war. They embraced, as friends would, and wished each other well.

'Let us put an end to this war,' Rónán said. 'And then we can go home.'

He looked down the path. In the dark distance of the trees, he heard a rustling of the underbrush that intensified as the enemy grew near. He gripped his bow and nocked an arrow, but he kept the string loose until he could see the army.

The sound of men stepping over twigs and dried moss increased.

The wait was interminable. When the glint of spearheads and swords approached the treeline, the Fir Bolg warriors stepped forward unaware of the ambush.

Rónán drew his bow string, waited until the men were close, and then he shot the arrow into the air as a signal. The two men in charge of the trap pulled.

The spears rose as the warriors ran into it.

Shouts and cries echoed into the morning.

Enemy swords were drawn and as they cut at the ropes between the harpooned men so that they could pass, Rónán gave a call. Slings were whipped and shots were fired.

Arrows darkened the morning and whistled down upon the enemy like a cloud of ghosts.

But the men kept coming.

After the first assault, they fanned out beyond the treeline, their shields raised against any renewed onslaught, and they broke for the pass. Rows of olive-skinned foreigners vied towards the narrow road.

As they entered the mouth of the pass, Rónán shouted, 'Now!'

His men, and those of Seanach's army, descended upon the road.

They choked the path, swords blurring, and bodies fell.

But the enemy were countless. They came in waves, and when the pass was clogged with warring men, more of the foreigners separated to tackle the rocky hillside at either end of the road.

Seanach shouted something from across the way and pointed.

Rónán saw it too. He and many of his men ran to the edge of the plateau and threw spears and rocks upon the warriors who climbed.

And as one man fell, another jumped over his body and continued the ascent.

Rónán unsheathed his sword. He cut at one of the men who breached the defence and sliced his face. He kicked him and, as the man tumbled, one of his comrades gripped the body, threw it aside, and hopped closer to the top.

There was no end to the foreigners, and more were spilling from the trees below.

As they mounted the hill and broke the edge, Rónán's men were forced back. He raised his shield to block a blow and then took the arm from his enemy, butting out to knock the man from his feet.

'Shields up,' he shouted. 'Form a wall. Do not let them pass.'

Each of his warriors pushed forward with their shields, enemy feet slipping on the uneven ground. They rammed the Fir Bolg and sliced with their blades.

They edged forward, one small step at a time. When one of Rónán's warriors fell, another took his place in the wall.

He pushed.

The enemy was hitting back against their wall.

He forced harder.

It was working. They came to the edge of the plateau and he screamed with effort. As a unit, his men swung their swords and hit forward once more. The line of foreigners tumbled from the side.

They may have been injured—some dead—but many of the

fallen enemy rose to his feet and charged the hillside again.

Rónán had no time to pause. The narrow passage between the two cliffsides was littered with bodies, both his and theirs, and yet more foreigners came to its mouth.

Below him, Fir Bolg warriors streamed from the forest as though it were a gateway from their homeland.

He was outnumbered. And there was no sign of King Rían or any native man among them.

As a new wave of men breached the top, Rónán ducked underneath the swing of a huge man whose axe was as long as a spear.

The warrior had no shield, using both hands to swing, and Rónán kicked out at his exposed knee, cracking bone, and bending the leg backwards. As the tall man slipped, Rónán pounced, his sword penetrating the leather tunic at the man's chest, and they tumbled together on the blood-drenched rocks. He brought the edge of his shield down on the man's face, blood spraying in multiple arcs, and he twisted his blade, extracted it, and rolled aside from the fray.

The morning sun dried the blood that stained the rocks, and when Rónán's men were pushed back from the edge by a barrage of enemy warriors, he knew they had lost their advantage. His men were backing up without an order and soon they would be overrun.

He looked for Cormac and did not see him, but across the way, Fionn was swinging his sword with both hands, his shield broken, the forearm strap and a small section of treated wood hanging from it. He cut down two enemy warriors with one swipe.

Their wall of shields did not work a second time. Though

they tried to form the barrier, they were attacked with vigour.

They were losing ground, and the rocky floor was giving way to hollows and crags.

'Pull back,' Rónán shouted. 'We need solid ground.'

His men let the fight come to them, and each time they blocked with their shields, it allowed them the chance to look at the ground behind them, cautious of any hole into which they might stumble.

When the ground levelled out, the men at the rear put their hands on the shoulder of a fighting man in front of them and helped to guide him back.

The enemy advanced.

As the battlefield opened out around them, away from the edge of the plateau, Rónán's and Seanach's men renewed the fight with enthusiasm. They had solid ground at their feet and though their arms were tired, their spirits were not.

But amid the battle, a giant man rose from the cliff's edge. Two heads taller than most, he stood erect and wailed against the sky.

A horn blew a long note.

The beast continued to scream. Rónán was convinced even from this distance he could see the man's spittle as it stringed between his lips.

The Fir Bolg warriors formed a shield wall of their own.

'A challenge,' the huge man shouted. 'Who will fight me? I will kill two of you at once and send you to your gods.'

Rónán gave a shout and his carnyx blower sounded three short notes.

The fighting ceased for the challenge, something that Rónán had forgotten the Fir Bolg loved so much.

At first unseen from the rank and file behind Rónán, Cormac stepped forward and clanged the flat of his sword against his shield in acceptance of the challenge. A panic overtook Rónán, but he would not speak against him. Anyone willing to accept the offer of a challenge was entitled to walk towards his fate.

But Cormac was stopped by a heavy hand on his shoulder.

'I've got this,' Fionn said. He moved towards the centre of the field, giving Cormac no option but to retreat.

Fionn nodded at one of his warriors and a new shield was thrown to him. He caught it before it skittered on the ground, strapped it to his arm, took up a spear, and marched towards the enemy challenger.

Rónán whispered a prayer to all the gods whose names he could conjure. The panic at losing Cormac was replaced by the horror of the potential loss of his tanist.

The battlefield grew silent and a breeze stirred the grasses.

'You are taller than most,' the foreign challenger said, his voice a deep baritone against the stillness of the early afternoon. 'Come closer so I can crush you.'

Fionn puffed his chest, staked his spear in the ground, and unsheathed his sword. When he was close enough, he ran.

The giant roared and came to meet him.

Their swords clashed and Fionn ducked under the enemy's swinging arm. Had the large wooden shield connected with his face, he would have been knocked from his feet.

Without taking his eyes from the challenger fight, Rónán moved around his men to Cormac's side. 'Why did you step up to the challenge?'

'Because I am half that man's size,' Cormac said.

'What kind of reasoning is that?'

'I could slip under his legs and slice his balls off before he even knew it.'

'You joke,' Rónán said, 'but it is a foolish fight.'

'You could not have stopped me.'

'I would not have tried. But I would miss you.'

When Cormac looked at the king, Rónán was smiling. 'I know exactly what you would miss.' He looked back towards Fionn and the giant. 'Will he win?'

'In battle, you only lose once. I pray that he wins.'

In the middle of the field, Fionn jumped aside of the huge man's swing and his ankle buckled against a rock, causing him to tumble to the ground. He rolled away, bouncing back to his feet, his sword arcing as he came up. The blade glanced across the tall man's forearm and, although blood wept from the wound, the foreigner did not react to it.

Using his size against him, Fionn jumped and weaved, and when he dived underneath a new attack, he rolled under the man's shield and, as he came up, his sword was not in his hand.

Rónán could see the panic on Fionn's face.

Fionn's warrior friends stepped forward in horror. Later, when Rónán had time to think about it, he would realise that every man was holding his breath.

Fionn danced aside from the giant's blade and ran around the man, back towards the spear he had planted in the ground.

As he reached it, the foreigner turned, unhooked his shield, and threw it towards Fionn. The shield glanced off the smaller man's back and Fionn fell, tumbling with the spear, a tangle of limbs as he came down on his face.

The giant advanced on him, jumping forward, wielding his massive sword in both hands, and he bore down on Fionn.

Fionn twisted on the ground, raised his knees, and slid backwards. He fumbled, gripped the spear, and when the giant man leapt upon him, he raised it as if from nowhere.

The spearhead penetrated the behemoth's throat and extruded from the back of his neck.

Pinned there, Fionn rolled to his feet. He looked for his sword but could not see it among the grasses. And when the giant's own sword slipped from his grasp, Fionn took it, raised it, and hacked at the man's head.

The head was not quick to free itself from the neck, thick flesh and bone splitting apart with difficulty. Fionn chopped at it until, with a muffled thump, it hit the ground.

Both sides were silent, one in fear, one in awe. And then, as a ripple, soft and expanding ever outward, a cheer rose from Rónán's army.

Fionn, panting, stared at the opposing warriors. He planted the giant's sword in the ground before his pinned body, retrieved his own sword, and raised his arms in victory. The cheer resounded as he strode back to his men.

During the short time it took to clear the field, Rónán found Fionn among the men who surrounded him in congratulations. They clasped arms and Rónán pulled him into an embrace. 'You old fool. You fought well. I am in your debt.'

'Let us hope that he was the biggest among them. I could not face another.'

'I do not want you accepting another challenge.'

'I understand why,' Fionn said, and they both knew he was referring to Áed who had championed himself during the Great Invasion. 'But if I think I can take him, I will do so.'

'Then I say it again—you are a fool.'

When the field was cleared, carnyx horns were blown, and the fight renewed.

Through the afternoon, they lost and gained ground, and by nightfall, they were unable to reclaim the edge of the plateau. When the sun touched the horizon, the fighting ceased. As an unspoken rule, darkness meant that a truce was called. Drums beat and carnyx horns sounded the end of the day. First one side, and then the other, took to the field to retrieve their dead before the scavengers scoured the empty field for discarded or broken weapons.

Rónán, whose tent was erected at the rear of their camp, sat outside the small temporary structure, and he ate in plain view of his people with his hound at his side. Seanach came to him and, together with their advisors, they discussed the events of the day, lauded Fionn's accomplishment against the giant foreigner, and cups of wine were passed among them. Wounds had been packed and wrapped, and the dead were carried beyond the furthest quarters of their encampment and cremated on pyres. Rónán knelt as the bodies burned and bowed his forehead to the earth to honour them.

When it was too dark to see beyond the reaches of the firelight, he called to Cormac and led him to his tent.

Inside, Rónán faced him.

'We fought well today,' Cormac said.

'Not well enough. Tomorrow we will do better.'

Cormac did not speak.

Rónán asked, 'Are you tired?'

'No, Lord.'

'Then come to me,' Rónán said. And he came.

Chapter 38

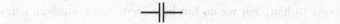

Grainne sat by the fire, away from Ó Neill's men. She closed her eyes and was praying to her most gracious lady Cáer. The Ó Neill army made camp at the northern reaches of Lough Samhaoir, surrounded by forestry and evening birdsong. The small islands that were splashed throughout the lough appeared to float and sway as the wind stirred their tall, untouched grasses.

Earlier that evening, Grainne inspected the men whose limbs had been irritated by jellyfish and she was pleased to see they were healing. The striations were fading, and skin tones were returning to normal.

Each night, when they made camp, Torin Ó Neill bid her to his council and they discussed their progress south. He worried at how much of the land before them they still had to cover and offered unreasoned estimations on how many Fir Bolg slaves King Rían had amassed.

Their aim was to reach Teamhair, pushing back the slave army and reclaiming the seat of the high king. The gods only knew how far north of Teamhair Rían had already journeyed.

'There will be a fight for Ard Rí when this is done,' Torin said.

'It should be you, Lord,' one of his advisors told him.

'There are far better men more suited to the job.' He turned to Grainne. 'Like the Overking of the North.'

'You know Rónán,' she said. 'He would take the position only with reluctance.'

'And that is why he is most suited to it. The north already bows to him, and we do not know how many southern kings are left.'

Grainne unsheathed her dagger and drew lines in the earth. 'Éirinn is vast. Teamhair is here. King Rían and his Ó Hargon clan originate here.' She drew a line to connect the two points. 'No doubt he will have ventured away from the road to free his foreign slaves, but I am hopeful that these areas were unaffected by his force.'

'If he left anyone alive, let us hope they have united to attack him from the rear. The fight may already be over.'

'That is something the omens do not show, Lord.'

As she sat by the fire, she did not feel Cáer's presence.

When Gallen spoke, she turned to him. 'Are you well, my lady?'

'Join me. How are you finding your time away from the northern druids?'

He plucked a strand of grass and placed it flat between his thumbs, blowing through the tiny gap to make a whistling sound as he considered his answer. 'I tire of the changing landscape. When this is over, I hope to sleep until the Yule.'

'These are not typical times. We do not often journey so far and so fast.'

'Why would a native king raise a foreign army? It makes no sense.'

'Personal gain at any cost. I do not believe it matters to him who fights for his cause, so long as he achieves his desire.'

Gallen said, 'Kings are so irrational.'

'Many of them, yes.'

He blew again on the blade of grass, producing a sharp warbling sound that could hardly be called a tune, and then he said, 'I have not yet seen a war.'

'With any luck, you will not see this one, either. I pray to all the gods that Rían is stopped before we reach the frontline.'

'Do you believe that your king has reached the war yet?'

'I cannot say. I am ever hopeful. He is a great warrior, but none of us can know how far into the northern territories King Rían has journeyed.' She poked at the fire with a stick, sending glowing sparks dancing into the air above the flames. The smoke that swirled there when she stirred the fire coated their robes and their faces before folding skyward again.

Grainne considered her words before speaking. 'When we were attacked, where did you go?'

'I went nowhere. I was with you.'

Grainne tapped her temple. 'In here. I could see in your eyes that something had taken over, someplace where the anger comes from?'

'I cannot explain it. A darkness comes over me and when it comes, I cannot stop it.' He looked towards the horizon as though he could see things there that no other could. 'When the foreigners came—the first time—their huge warships came to our shores on the east and my father took up his sword, like many fathers. I was a farmer's son, and I had some training with the sword, but I was not old enough to join the battle. My father and the other men of our clan marched to war. And he was not seen again.

'Eleven nights came, and the men did not return. And my mother—she milked the cattle as though nothing in her life had changed. She would wake me in the morning, and we would take to the fields. And in the evening, we returned home, and she prepared a meal. Mostly, we ate in silence. At first, I had questions. Why had the men come? When would they leave? When would Father return? But she did not have the answers.'

He fell silent for a long while, but Grainne knew he was not finished. She waited.

At length, he said, 'Then the foreigners came inland. They burned our sept, slaughtered our livestock. And I was hiding with the children; seven of us cramped together at the back of the food store. Seven little children crying and hiding and waiting for it to be over. And in my tears, I watched through a crack in the wood of the wall. I watched as they raped the women and the older girls—they did it in the open between the homes, unashamed. And I made fists with my hands,' he said, holding his fists up to demonstrate. 'I drew blood with my fingernails. When I looked at my hands, I could see the blood dripping to my wrists. I looked through the crack again and I saw one of the foreigners punching a woman in the face. Punching her and laughing. I saw the woman's blood, and when he let her fall to the ground, she was unrecognisable. Except I saw the brooch at the neck of her dress. I knew it because Father had given it to her.'

Grainne closed her eyes. She had known that the boy had lost his parents, but she did not know he had witnessed it. When she looked at him again, there were no tears on his cheeks, just a steely expression that would plague him for the

330

rest of his life.

'When the men left, we children managed to escape from the food store as it burned around us. Not one single *brú* was left standing. I ran to my mother and I shook her. I shook her but she did not wake. And I lay down beside her. I put her arm around me—so cold—and I cried into her dress. I wept until my face was numb. And when the night came, I slept there in her arms. And then it was morning. I woke when I heard someone scuffling around. I thought it was one of the children, for I did not know where they had gone. Perhaps they lay with their own mothers; I cannot say. But when I looked, I saw that it was a man, one of the foreigners. He was alone, drunk, searching through the bodies for valuables, pulling rings from fingers and brooches from dresses.

'I lay there in silence, half hidden by my mother's cold body, one hand groping the earth, hoping that a sword had been dropped near me, but all my fingers grasped was a rock. And I brought it to my chest. The man approached, and when he leaned down to pluck the brooch from my mother's dress, I swung the rock. He stumbled back but did not fall. I stood and I swung again at him. And still he did not fall. But all I could see was him; I could not see my mother on the ground, or my father dead in some unknown valley, buried where he fell as they always do in war. I saw him, his face. As though he alone was responsible for my losses, as though he alone had taken both my parents from me.'

Grainne touched his arm and he did not shy away from her.

'I kept hitting him with the rock. And when the rock was covered in blood and slipped from my hand, I punched him, just like Mother had been punched. I knelt on his chest and—I do not know how long I sat there, my rock entering the mush of his face because nothing was left. He *had* no face; not anymore. I was ten winters old. And I had killed a man.' He licked his lips, dried from talking so fast, and then he said, 'When my arms grew tired, when all I was punching was white skull, and my knuckles were torn, when I realised what I had done, I stood from him and returned to my mother's side. I lay down beside her and went to sleep, too tired to cry. And even in the brightness of daylight, I slept. When I woke, I do not know if it was the same day, or a day later, or a year. But that is how the druid, Mánús, found me, lying with my mother, asleep beneath the coldness of her embrace.'

Grainne cleared her throat. 'He took you to the archdruid?'

'I do not know why.'

'He will have seen something in you, as one day you will see something in another.'

'When I anger now, I see that man's face. I try not to break things, or lash out, but when the anger takes me, I cannot stop it.' He looked at her. 'But I would never hurt you, Lady. You have shown me a great kindness, taking me from the druids where I languished, giving me life.'

'I have not given you life,' she said. 'You already had it. But I hope, together, we can channel it.'

Gallen shuffled his feet in the dirt and he looked for the blade of grass he had dropped, could not find it, and plucked another to blow.

Grainne reached for her pack and withdrew a vial of powder. 'Pass me that cup.' The amount of water that remained in the cup was enough, and so she poured some of the powdered root into it, swilled the cup, and turned to face the boy. 'Close your eyes.' When he complied, Grainne said, 'Still your mind and drink.' He sipped from the cup and passed it back to her. She drank the remains and took his hands.

Grainne spoke in the tongue of the gods, slow and reverent. In time, when they opened their eyes, they stood in a field of snowdrops.

They recognised the drooping white flowers specked with blood and, across from them, the four stones that they laid to mark the thieves who attacked them. On the hills in the distance, a storm cut the landscape with a darkening haze, and the night sky above them shone from a million stars, casting the field in a stark white sheen.

She did not notice him at first, but when Gallen pointed, beyond the four graves, dressed in his warrior's garb, her brother stood to attention. Áed's white tunic shone bright, and upon his arm was a golden shield, a perfect circle into which had been etched the likeness of Neit, god of war. The amber pommel of the sword at his hip was incandescent, and in his right hand he gripped a spear made of silver birch. A gold circlet framed his head and his feet were bare and unblemished by the blood that soaked the field.

She wanted to go to him but could not move.

And as though her eyes were just now opening, she saw beside him her most gracious lady Cáer, standing tall and proud in a simple dress of blue, holding the hand of her father, Ethal Anbuail, his long white beard and white hair untouched by the breeze, his purple eyes bright in his face.

Walking with a slow purpose towards them, from the distance, was another man, robed in grey, and when he stood beside her brother, she saw that he was bald and blind. She recognised him at once as Mogh Roith, the druid god, Gallen's personal deity.

The ground beneath her shook, and a rumble came from the belly of the earth. The soil cracked and peeled, and the four stones of the buried thieves crumbled into dust.

And still she could not move.

The storm on the horizon was drawing near.

Four hollows in the earth parted, and the dead thieves climbed from their graves, wielding great spears and axes, their features contorted into masks of rotten death. The stench of their flesh was putrid.

The dead men charged towards them, but Grainne and Gallen were unable to flee. She reached for her dagger at her hip but found it missing, and Gallen looked for a stone or rock to lift but there were none at hand.

The corpses came closer, charging over the broken land.

And now Mogh Roith, druid-god of druids, stepped forward and his stature grew to giant proportions. His body blotted out the sky above them and when he leaned low, his face surging towards the dead thieves with his blind and milky eyes wide, he breathed upon the four men, and they turned to stone.

Four stones as tall as men.

Even the ground around the thieves, the grasses and the tiny flowers and the earth itself, solidified into basalt, and the rumbling beneath the ground ceased. At once, the storm dissipated.

Mogh Roith raised his head and he returned to the size of a man. He came forward and placed his hand on Gallen's shoulder. His eyes—unseeing; seeing all—blinked, and the god smiled a soft and gentle parting of the lips.

Gallen took to his knees and bowed to the earth at his god's feet. And Grainne released her hands from his.

By the light of the fire, Gallen looked at her. 'Did you knowingly conjure my god?'

'No.'

'The warrior, it was Áed the Executioner, am I right?' When she nodded, he said, 'And your goddess Cáer and her father. How do I know these things?'

'Because we are connected. You, me, all the druids and the gods. Through the earth we are connected, joined as one.'

'And the meaning of our vision?'

She could not answer that. 'Perhaps many reasons. Or none. I would like to think they are telling us that they are here, with us on our journey.'

'Protecting us.'

She nodded. 'We should sleep now.'

When she lay down, Gallen's back to hers, sharing the same furs for warmth, she closed her eyes and remembered her brother. She recalled every detail of his face, the mottled blue of his eyes, the fairness of his skin and hair. And as sleep took her, she smiled.

Chapter 39

When they came from the forest, they were not expecting an ambush. As he drew his sword, Bromaid cursed. Their senses were dulled from the darkness of three eternal nights among the trees.

The men at the frontline screamed as they were impaled, and Bromaid charged forward. When he saw the trap, he hacked at the rope and kicked two of the dead men aside. He was too late to shout orders; the men were rushing for the pass. He flanked left, searching the hillside for his enemy, raising his shield as a shower of stones rained on them.

He grabbed the man beside him. 'Forget the pass. Take the hills.'

The bodies of his comrades littered the narrow passage.

The order spread through his ranks and the men fanned out across the valley in either direction. Above them, the opposing army dropped rocks and spears on their heads. As Bromaid climbed, he forced one of his fallen warriors out of his way, leaping over the body as it tumbled beneath him. He needed to reach the top. If they could fight on level ground, they would have a better chance of survival.

Their enemy fought with bravery, but the Fir Bolg warriors

had determination. They pushed higher. When they crested the plateau, they charged. The natives formed a wall to drive them back and Bromaid tumbled down the hillside with the others.

He roared. He would not perish from a fall.

Bromaid scrabbled up the rocky face, his sword tight in his hand as he climbed.

When they retook the cliff's edge, he shouted, 'Advance,' and the Fir Bolg warriors pressed forward with resolve. It worked; they were driving the enemy back across the plateau. When Eolid came over the bluff behind him, Bromaid shouted his name. 'Time to do your thing, my friend.'

Eolid roared and called his challenge. 'I will kill two of you at once and send you to your gods.'

It was a lengthy fight, and twice Bromaid was sure Eolid would cleave the enemy's head from his shoulders. But when the giant beast succumbed to the smaller man on the battlefield, Bromaid spat on the ground, cursing Eolid for losing, and cursing the man who killed him. Too far to see the details of his features, he studied the man's gait as he walked back towards his camp. He would have his head.

'Regroup,' Bromaid shouted, and the battle was renewed when Eolid's body was carried by six men from the field.

By nightfall, he counted the dead. The remaining Fir Bolg outnumbered the enemy by twice their total, but to lose one man was to establish a weakness in his side.

When one of the men came to him and said, 'My lord, the dead are being burned,' Bromaid did not correct him on the title. He had been issuing orders since dawn, and his people were listening to him.

He went to the edge of the field furthest from the enemy and watched the flames engulf the dead. Rían's druid knelt before the bodies, giving praise. He had stayed behind when Rían turned east in the morning. When the hooded man stood, Bromaid said, 'You should make a sacrifice.'

'You are not my king to command me.'

'Your king is not here, but I make no commands. It was a suggestion.'

'We have taken the hilltop. The gods are on our side.'

'Gather the king's advisors,' Bromaid said. 'We should discuss plans in advance of Rían's return.'

Gorid did not hesitate; without the Ard Rí, the chief tacticians and strategists should meet to consider their actions. But the old man did not bow, and that vexed Bromaid.

When the men sat together in a circle with him, Bromaid said, 'We did well. We have secured the hilltop and driven them back.'

'But we have lost Eolid.'

'We do not need him.'

'He fought as ten men.'

Bromaid said, 'We are fourteen hundred warriors. It is of no consequence.'

'They say that the Ó Mordha overking is among their ranks,' another of the men said.

'I am glad. It means we will not have to march north to claim his seat. If we kill him here, the north is ours.'

'The north will be High King Rían's,' Gorid said.

Bromaid ignored him. 'We must push harder tomorrow. We will keep driving them back until they have no place left to go but into the ocean. We have achieved more in these few months than our friends and brothers did when we arrived on this filthy land. Toshid, you have studied drawings of these shores. Do you know how far north we have come?'

The man he addressed shook his head. 'We came through a vast forest, but the country is filled with such forests. If I could get to the top of the mountain behind the enemy, I would have a better understanding. Until I get a clearer view, the northern shore could be a day's march, or a hundred days' march.'

Gorid said, 'If the Ó Mordha king is camped beyond us, I am sure we are in the northern reaches. What king would march beyond his borders to fight a war in another man's land?'

'We will crush him. Now that we are on level ground, can we flank them?'

'They will anticipate such a manoeuvre,' Toshid said.

One of the other men said, 'We should drive through their ranks and push for the Ó Mordha stronghold.'

Bromaid shook his head. 'If we must fight back on ourselves, it will be chaos. This is not a time to penetrate their armies but to suppress them. Leave no native man standing; that is our objective. Can we chop trees to make a trebuchet?'

'We have neither the tools nor the time,' Gorid said. 'War engines are not an option.'

One of the younger advisors, a man who had impressed Rían with his sword skills if not by the sharpness of his mind, asked, 'Is the Ó Mordha king really as tall as they say?'

'If he were, we would have seen him. Éirinn's bards exaggerate everything; he will be as small as a pig and just as fat. The more impressive his title, the lazier a man becomes.'

'He was responsible for the deaths of many.'

'Two years ago, yes. He won his war. Since then, he will have sat on his backside receiving gifts for his former successes.

339

Look to the field for him tomorrow, a short man who is pregnant with food. But know this—he is mine. I will slaughter this Bare-Arsed Warrior who likes to show his shrivelled taproot to men. If he reveals it to me, I will slice it from him and feed it to his children. The Ó Mordha king's head will be a souvenir on my gatepost.'

Before the others left, Bromaid added, 'Tomorrow, we must box them in. Set your factions in a curved formation. We will rotate in from the left and right at alternate turns until they are clamped between our vice. There is not an army alive that we cannot crush.'

With the campfires lighting his path, he walked among the men. Those of Rían's tribe who had not gone east with their king assembled in a corner of the site. The Fir Bolg warriors, almost one and a half thousand men, spread across the southern end of the plateau and down the hillside to the base of the forest. They had succeeded in pushing the native army back, and the battlefield between them was vast and rocky. The ground was not ideal, but a warrior fights where he must.

A song of their homeland rippled through the camp, a thousand-year-old tale of woe. The barrels of wine they pilfered on their journey were brought through the forest on the back of narrow carts. They were opened and men were scooping their hands in the barrel tops to drink.

In the darkness, Bromaid watched the flicker of the enemy fires across the field. If the Ó Mordha overking was indeed among their ranks, he would find him and tear his head from his shoulders.

He would need to consider how best to handle King Rían when he returned from his eastern raid. If the advisors listened to him, he was in a strong position. Rían's tribesmen were outnumbered by the Fir Bolg. His brothers would fight for dominion, but while the war continued, they would not care who led them. It would be Rían, or Bromaid, or another who stepped up to the role. So long as they were driving forward with swords in their hands, they would be happy.

When he lay down for the night, he imagined his kinsmen chanting his name, saviour of his people, ruler over all things.

Only two men stood in his way—the kings, Rían Ó Hargon, and Rónán Ó Mordha.

Chapter 40

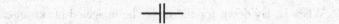

The morning broke cold and cloudless. When Rónán woke, he found Cormac still lying under the furs with him. He leaned in and kissed him awake.

Cormac stirred against him and Rónán kissed the corner of his jaw where it met his ear, his hand searching under the furs to touch him.

'They will be calling us to war soon,' Cormac said, his voice dry and arid.

'We have time,' Rónán said. He pressed his body on top of Cormac's, allowing his weight to pin him down, and he could feel Cormac's firmness beneath him.

He traced his tongue along the length of his companion's neck, tasting the dried sweat that lingered there from the night before. He kissed Cormac's broad chest, and his head disappeared under the furs. Cormac's stomach tightened when Rónán took him in his mouth.

When he moved back up Cormac's body, he kissed him with fervour, and Rónán took his arm and turned him over onto his stomach. Cormac twisted his head around to kiss him, and when Rónán broke him for the first time that morning, he inhaled and held his breath.

Rónán could feel the man's body tensing beneath him. He pressed his lips against the lobe of Cormac's ear, and he pushed his hands underneath the man's chest, clasping his fingers together below him.

As his ecstasy left him and entered Cormac, a carnyx horn blew a long, dull note outside the tent.

They had no time to bathe; the war was renewed.

The young hound rose when Rónán did and followed him into the daylight as he prepared for battle.

Rónán stood upon the back of his carbad, seven spears at his side, locked against the wall by a wooden curve that kept them in place but allowed for easy access. His shield was wedged by his feet, and the weight of his sword was comforting at his hip, a small dagger at the other side. Against Fionn's insistence, Rónán wore his torc crown, a circlet of gold that flourished at each end in a knotted symbol of eternity.

'It will reveal you as king to the enemy,' Fionn said. 'They will flock to you to kill you.'

'Let them come. They will see that a king does not stand at the rear of his army and cower like a child.'

When the Fir Bolg army came forth from the forest yesterday, King Rían was nowhere to be seen. Rónán looked for him all day, but even when the champions were fighting each other in single combat, Rían was not there to witness it, or had not revealed himself as king. Although the army was made up of Fir Bolg slaves, there were a few natives among them, members of Rían Ó Hargon's clan, men who followed him with loyalty regardless of his actions. But none of them appeared as a king or addressed the men with orders. The Fir Bolg swarmed the battlefield, scaling the cliffside and broaching the precipice as rats would a hole in the earth. They moved as one, and yet they were individuals without order. Despite hating them as the enemy, Rónán had been impressed by their tactics on the field.

And he was grateful, though he could not tell him, that Fionn championed himself against the giant and won. It was one less foreign bastard to come up against today.

From the back of his carbad, he nodded to his driver, and they moved down the line of his men who mixed with Mac Fachtna's warriors as though they were brothers. He raised his voice. 'Men of the north. We have no time for speeches. Get out there and slaughter those foreign bastards. Are you ready?'

The men cheered and clanged their swords against their shields.

Rónán's driver turned the horses and drove him back. As he passed, Rónán tipped his head to Cormac who stood among the rank of archers. And when he reached the end of the line, the carnyx blower sounded his battle cry.

The warriors ran forward, into the field, and the Fir Bolg army came likewise. In a second wave of men, those who were adept with the sling started forward, swinging their shots at their sides. When they were close enough, they let fly over the heads of their people, and the hail came down upon the foreigners. The carnyx sounded again and the archers let loose their arrows before dropping their bows and charging the field.

As Rónán's carbad rolled into battle, he passed Fionn whose long legs gave him a swift advantage, his sword drawn, and his shield arm raised for protection. All signs of his earlier weakness were gone, and he was stronger than before.

When he entered the clash of men, Rónán threw his first spear. The Fir Bolg warrior it hit was lifted from his feet and

344

thrown back, knocking another of his fellow warriors to the ground.

Rónán lobbed another, and as the driver turned the carbad, an enemy warrior mounted the back of it. Rónán ducked to avoid the swing of the man's sword and he drew his dagger, punching in close. Together, they rolled from the carbad's floor and onto the muddy ground. Rónán stabbed him in the arm, jabbed him in the chest, twisting the short blade, and turned to the carbad, but the driver was dead.

At the front of the carbad, the horses were surrounded by Fir Bolg men and they were both unfastened. As they cantered, an enemy whipped up onto each of their backs. The Fir Bolg were skilful warriors on the back of a horse during combat.

Rónán rolled onto the carbad and took his shield from the floor, but he had no time to strap it to his arm. An enemy came to him and, gripping the shield in both hands, he whipped it across the man's face. He drew his sword and swung.

When he slipped his arm through the shield straps, he turned and hacked at another warrior. 'Protect the horses,' he shouted. 'Carbads, fall back.'

Of the seven carbad's still in action, they turned and rolled to the rear. The two warriors who secured Rónán's horses were riding through the fray, swiping their swords in all directions from their elevated positions. They were too far for him to tackle.

When the Fir Bolg's challenger horn blew, Rónán's tunic was soaked in gore and his face was flushed, bright cheeks matching the colour of his stained clothing.

The man who strode forward from the Fir Bolg army was not as tall as the giant who appeared yesterday but was still a formidable size. Fionn did not have the chance to champion himself today as one of Mac Fachtna's men charged into the field without a word.

Later, when the fighting day was done and the field was cleared of bodies, Rónán counted his losses.

'We have suffered worse before and won,' Fionn said. He had gathered the men's daggers to be placed on their funeral pyres atop their chests.

'We should not suffer at all,' Rónán said.

When the dead were cremated and warrior songs sung in their honour, Rónán assembled his council and joined with Seanach's men. 'They are one army. During the invasion, we were opposed on all sides. Why is it that we have not defeated them yet?'

Seanach said, 'I swear they multiply overnight.'

'Has anyone seen their bastard king yet?' Rónán turned to Cormac. 'You're the only one who knows him. Does he fight among the men or is he hiding like a coward?'

'I have not seen him, Lord. If he fights, he does not come to the front. I have seen his druid, a fighting man, old but strong, though I have not been able to get close to him.'

'These Fir Bolg—I can no longer tell—are they fighting for their king or for their freedom?'

Seanach said, 'Perhaps they've already killed Rían and are led by another?'

Fionn shook his head. 'Rían's kinsmen would not fight alongside them if they had. He lives. He just cowers behind them like a child between his mother's legs.'

'He cannot call himself Ard Rí if he refuses to fight for the title,' Rónán said.

Seanach scratched his chin. He had not shaved in days, dark stubble flecked with silver. 'If we can get behind them, we can retake the cliff's edge and box them in.'

'Fighting uphill against them would not work; they have the numbers,' Fionn said. 'Our only chance of winning this is to kill every one of them. No slaves, no pardons. They will not stop unless we eradicate them.'

'And they have great skill,' Rónán said. 'They have conquered half of our lands already. If we do not stop them now, none of our kind will be left. Have we had word from any other northern tribes? Do they join us?'

'They will come,' Fionn said.

When the men returned to their duties, Rónán sat with Fionn and Cormac. Outside the tent, several warriors were singing the songs of Áed the Executioner. There were no bards to instruct them on any new ballads.

'I wish the Executioner was with us today,' Fionn said. 'He'd take them all out with one swing.'

'And then stomp on their bodies to fertilise the land,' Rónán agreed. They listened to the words of the song outside, and when it ended, he ate from a bowl of pale persicaria seeds so that he would not have to speak.

Fionn left in search of wine, and when the tent flap folded back against the outside darkness in his wake, Cormac cleared his throat. 'You look tired.'

'My mind will not stop; all I do is think. How can we win this war?'

'With perseverance. One Fir Bolg at a time.'

'If you are only killing one at a time, you should sharpen your blade.'

They kissed.

When they lay together, they did so with furious passion. It was fast and embarrassing, over as swift as it began, but when they were both spent, their breathing laboured, their skin moist with perspiration and hair trailing over their foreheads in wet tangles, Rónán kissed him and ran his fingers down the length of Cormac's arm. When they pressed their chests together, he could taste the salt of Cormac's neck.

Cormac turned away from him to be held firm in the king's arms, and when their eyes were no longer locked together, he said, 'If we win this war, we should stay here, the two of us.'

'We will win this war,' Rónán corrected him.

'Will things differ when we return to Ailigh?'

'Why should they change?'

'Here, we are warriors; there, you are king.'

Rónán laughed against his skin. 'If I am not your king in bed, why are we here?'

Cormac nestled his head against Rónán's cheek. 'I should go before the dawn,' he said, but he did not stray from Rónán's side.

When they made love again, it was with quiet longing. While they were joined as one, a tender and deliberate embrace, the night would never end.

And when sleep overtook them, it was deep and dreamless.

Chapter 41

Her first night outside the walls of Ailigh was a peaceful one. The sun fell and a cold air crept in, the waters of the lough rose, and she waited in the grasses for it to recede. She slept there, bundled with her child under a large fur that Achall, true to her word, had sent down with one of her cumal maids. The girl brought food, lest they starve, and she waited until Orlaith ate before returning within the walls.

Orlaith let her baby feed from her and, when he was done, she wrapped him in her arms, and they slept.

By morning, when the sun dazzled the surface of the lough and the tide returned to worship at the foot of Áed's standing stone, she secured the baby among his blankets, stretched over a small hollow in the ground so that he could not roll away, and she undressed to bathe in the cold water. It refreshed her and, for a time, she remained submerged as far as the neck, listening to the babbling of her child on the bank.

Later, when the sun dried her body and she was dressed, she strapped the child in a sling around her waist and took to the forest at the southern hills. She pulled a thin branch down from a tree, twisting and tearing until it broke loose, and with the small dagger that she wore at her hip, she chipped the end of it into a sharp point.

'Growing up by a river is not without its advantages,' she told her son.

He rested within the sling when she waded into the lough, raised the fishing spear, and stood still. Fishermen no longer used spears, but she had seen the practice done in rituals. She stilled her breathing and waited, and soon the fish returned around her feet where the waters were no longer disturbed and muddy.

She drove the spear into the water but missed her target.

When she hit a fish, she succeeded only in pushing it away with the point rather than impaling it. She would need more speed and force.

By the time the sun was overhead and shone upon the soft downy pate of her child, she had secured only one fish, a trout no bigger than both of her palms, but she was pleased. She could survive alone if she needed to.

When the cumal came the second day with bread and cold meats, Orlaith showed the girl her prize. 'I have caught a fish. But I have no way of cooking it.'

The girl looked up the hillside as though her queen could hear them, and then said, 'I will bring you a flint and striker as soon as I can. I am to wait while you eat and return the basket to the cook.'

'And if I am not yet hungry? Are you to wait all day?'

The girl did not have an answer.

Orlaith handed her the child and then sat among the grasses to tear chunks from the bread. She peered into the basket. 'No honey to dip it in? No matter.' She chewed and swallowed without feeling. The meats, cooked the night before, had been salted and packed in brine, and when she finished them, her fingers were wet and salty. She dipped the remaining bread into the brine, but it soured the taste and she left it.

When she exchanged the basket for her baby, the young girl said, 'My lady wishes to know if you were warm enough last night.'

'Your lady has a heart, it seems. Tell her I would like another fur if it is not too much trouble.'

The girl bowed and hurried up the hillside.

With the baby in her arms, Orlaith walked the length of the lough as far as she could, and she sat on the dark sand while her legs rested for the return journey. With no chores to perform, she did not know how to fill her day. The war in the south, however far from Ailigh it may be, could last until the festival of Lughnasadh or longer. Or it could already be won, and her husband would march back into her life by morning.

She was forgetting the smell of him and the sound of his voice. She remembered his eyes, wide and warm, and the braid that fell from either side of his moustache to frame his lips, but when he spoke in her mind it was not the sound of her husband she heard but her own voice.

The fire in his hearth would have gone out untended, and his floor would need swept before his return. But she would not ask Achall's maid to do that in her stead. Fionn would understand. He would see that, as his wife, she had not willingly failed in her duties.

That afternoon, she sat under the shade of Áed's standing stone and untied the neck of her dress for the child to feed. Later, when the girl came with another basket of food and an additional fur blanket, she produced from under the folds of her dress a flint stone and striker rod. She handed them over with circumspection, waited for Orlaith to eat, and curtsied.

'I am not a lady,' Orlaith said. 'Why do you bow to me as one?'

'You have been wronged, thrust out here with a baby. All the girls think it, but none dare say a word.'

'This is my punishment for disobeying her ladyship. Do not suffer the same fate. Still your mouth or you may end up down here with me.'

'I am a cumal. I would not be banished, just flogged or killed.'

'Then I have it easy. The sun warms me, and I have the company of my child. I have not been wronged so bad.'

The girl came closer to whisper. 'There is a rumour that the lady despises your man. There is no proof, but they say his sickness was at her hands.'

'Achall despises everyone, but none more so than herself, I would say. The only sickness she is capable of giving anyone is nausea at the sight of her face.'

'They say her husband gave her that scar, but no one knows. Some say she did it to herself in a fit of rage when the lord refused to give her another child. The boy is two; she should have been pregnant twice over by now. Some say she is sterile. Others say the gods deem her too stern to grant her another wain.'

'You listen to too much gossip. Whatever happened, you can be certain nobody will ever know the truth.'

When the sun was shielded from her by a bank of silver clouds and the wind swayed the grasses around Ailigh's hills, she gathered some twigs and branches from the southern forest and ringed a pit in the sand with stones. She took the flint and striker, lighting a fire to warm her, and she retrieved the fish that was wrapped in leaves, laying it on the burning wood to cook.

By nightfall, she climbed up the bank away from the tide, and wrapped herself in furs to sleep with the baby at her side.

Her third day outside the walls began with a drizzle of rain that blanketed the land. She huddled under the furs, the child nestled between her thighs, and she watched the light rain gain weight. Soon, it ran in gullies around her and broke the surface of the lough like hail. The sun was too weak to shatter the incessant downpour, and much of the morning was spent in shelter under furs that were heavy and saturated. When the rainclouds did not move away, she picked up her baby, held a fur over her head, and ran for the forest cover. She sat at the base of a thick tree and marvelled that rain only falls between tree boughs once the storm has moved on.

When the rain stopped beyond the forest and dripped among the trees, she returned to the bank of the lough and hung the furs and her wet dress over Áed's standing stone to dry.

Achall's maid did not come to her that morning and, when the hunger was too much for her to bear, she returned to the shallows of the lough to hunt for fish. But the branches were too wet for her to light another fire.

With her dress dried and the furs still airing, she watched the southern road for signs of her husband's return.

She did not hear the shuffling footsteps behind her and turned only when Achall spoke. 'You weathered the storm, I see.'

Orlaith looked over her shoulder at the queen but she did

not rise to greet her.

'I have brought you some food and a fresh fur.'

'Your cumal was not available to attend me today?'

Achall took a step closer and placed the basket on the ground. 'I had a need to see the baby well. I hope he did not suffer in the storm.'

'In my belly, he marched through thick snow. A little rain is of no concern.'

'He is made of strong stuff.'

'The girls of Ailigh; do they train without me?'

'They do not. I have forbidden it, as well you know.'

Orlaith stood but did not turn to the queen. She stared across the lough at the far side, shrouded in thick foliage. 'You're a fool, *bitseach*. The world is at war, and yet you treat the women as feebleminded.'

'A woman's place is not on the battlefield.'

She turned then. 'We have every right to defend ourselves from the wars of man.'

'A husband will shield his wife. Fionn fights now not for himself but for you.'

'And if the men do not return? If Ailigh is overrun by Fir Bolg warriors; what happens then, when they break the walls and enter with rape and murder in their minds?'

'We have guards and boys to defend the walls. It is a safe place.'

Orlaith said, 'If our husbands are defeated, no place is safe. You fail to recall the devastation of the invasion. Give the women a fighting chance. Even with a sword in their hands they can protect their bodies if not defend the walls.'

'As you protected yours?'

Orlaith made a fist with her hand, but she did not move to strike the woman. 'I would change nothing. My child was not the product of rape. If you do not allow the women to defend themselves, they will not be so lucky.'

'I have made my orders clear.'

'You ignorant fool. You play the part of a queen, but you know nothing. I hope for all our sakes that your husband and mine are successful in their campaign against the foreigners, because if Rían leads his men here, we are all ruined.'

'It is your fault he revolts against us, bringing his child to our gates. You should have given him back to his father; he is a king's son.'

'He is my son, and you will do well to remember it. I will protect him—from you, from Rían, from any foreign bastard that dares to come close. And you can talk; that child of yours is no more Rónán's than mine is.' She turned, hunkered down, and sat on the bank of the lough.

'Do not turn your back on me.'

'If you mean to stab me, do it swiftly. I have nothing left to offer you but my life. I will sit here, in rain or sun, and I will wait for my husband, a man they say you hate. And when he returns to me, we will walk away. You will never have to look at us again. You, wife of the overking; you have everything you ever desired. You are the queen you longed to be, the little brat all grown up, who lords her status over everything you see.' When Achall did not respond to her, Orlaith said, 'You may leave me now; my child is hungry.'

She heard the swish of Achall's feet in the grasses and she closed her eyes. She could no longer raise an angry word. When she opened them again, Achall held out the basket of food towards her.

'I am none of those things,' Achall said.

Orlaith took the basket without a word.

'I am queen only in name, and perhaps not for much longer. I have had to fight to maintain some semblance of status among the wives of the other kings who attend Ailigh while their husbands conduct business.' She lowered herself to the ground beside Orlaith. 'No one says it aloud, but they all think it— Achall's child is not the king's. When will he give her a child of his own?'

'Nobody thinks that.'

'You do.'

'I know the truth of it. Rónán is a friend, as was Áed. I knew the love they shared for each other before even Rónán did.'

Achall looked away from her. 'I think I also knew it, too.'

'Then why did you force him to go through with his marriage to you?'

'Because it was ordained. My uncle, his surrogate father, had planned it. We were wed before we knew that my uncle defected against us to the Fir Bolg during the invasion.' She paused. 'And, yes, I did it in spite. He was supposed to be mine, but he had no love for me. He was my husband, and I hated him for it. But I loved him, too. I still do. He will not touch me, but I love what he stands for. He is strong and wise because Áed made him so. I cannot doubt it. No one knows it, but I come here often to look upon the stone that my husband had erected in honour of his lover, and I want to punch it into the waters. But I do not. Instead, I touch its face and I am grateful that he fashioned my husband into the man he has become. But it is over now. When he returns to us, I will be nothing. I have made bad judgements. Against you. And Fionn. But mostly against my husband.'

When she stopped talking, Orlaith said, 'You have been angry since the day we met. If you have made any bad judgements, it has been against yourself. Why do you not say these things aloud?'

'I do not know. As a queen, I must present myself as a woman of grace.'

'A queen does not need to act with spite. Ask nicely and men will obey you just as much as if you threaten them.'

'I fear I cannot change a lifetime of regret, and the outcomes that I have brought upon myself.'

'You regret your marriage to Rónán?'

'I do not. But I do regret how I have treated him. It is common for boys to take to each other's beds in their younger days, I know this. But most grow up, they leave those practices behind. They go on to sire many children and have multiple wives.'

'But Rónán is not one of those men.'

'No. If not Áed, it would be another man. He has no desire for me.'

After a moment of silence, Orlaith placed her hand on top of Achall's and said, 'Treat him with kindness and your life will ease. He may never desire you, but at least give him the opportunity to love you.'

'It is too late for that. I have destroyed all hope of happiness. I would apologise to you if I thought it would cure our rift.'

'We have all done things we regret.'

Achall patted Orlaith's hand and stood. 'When you are ready, return to Ailigh and you will be let inside. I cannot undo the pain I have caused but allow me to at least alleviate your future. I am sorry we have bickered so much.'

Orlaith eased herself up, the baby asleep in the crook of her elbow, and she held out her arm in the manner that men do when saying goodbye. 'I am comfortable here. I will await my husband's return, where I can see the road clearly. It is not a disrespect to you, Lady. Our peace will not fix broken hearts.'

Achall nodded. She clasped Orlaith's extended arm and they shook.

As the queen walked up the hillside, Orlaith faced the southern road. The men would be marching home soon, she was sure of it.

Chapter 42

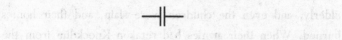

The smoke from the fires of the dead darkened the sky both north and south of the plateau. The rancid smells of war were overpowering, and Rónán's fingernails, even after bathing, were black with dried blood.

As the sun descended over the third day of war, Rónán walked among his men, ensuring they were well, joking where he could, sympathising with those who had lost close friends, and listening to the songs of legendary heroes that broke out in small groups across the camp. He was grateful that his warriors were integrating well with Mac Fachtna's men and there were no divisions of allegiance.

While a champion from either army fought in single combat in the centre of the saturated field, a tribe of northern men joined Rónán's side, arriving from the north-east. They came down the hill towards the gathered army who watched, with interest, the champions' fight. Mac Fachtna's warrior was holding strong against his opponent.

Rónán recognised their leader, King Fergal Ó Fuinseog, a man who had fought beside him at Knockdhu. 'It has been a lifetime,' Fergal said, pulling Rónán into a tight bear hug. 'You have become a man at last.'

'I grow daily. And you, you're gaining weight.'

Fergal smacked his solid stomach. 'Extra warmth for these northern nights.' During the Great Invasion, Fergal had marched his men north before the southern reaches of Éirinn were raided by the Fir Bolg and, later, when the war was won, he learned that his tribal lands had been sacked. His wives, the elderly, and even the children were slain, and their homes burned. When their armies had retaken Knockdhu from the foreigners, one of Rónán's first acts as overking was to offer those lands to Fergal. The king spent the last two years rebuilding the landscape and finding new wives for his men.

At the edge of the field, Fergal looked out at the champions as they clashed, and beyond them to the Fir Bolg army. 'I thought we were done with these sorry bastards.'

'They keep you entertained, old man.' Rónán's heart lifted with Fergal's arrival, even if he had come with only one hundred men. Any gain to the number of defenders was a bonus.

'I do not see Rían among them,' Fergal said.

'He has not shown his face since the fighting began.'

Rónán introduced Fergal Ó Fuinseog to Seanach, and when Seanach's champion cut the head from his opponent's shoulders, the northern armies cheered him as a hero.

The field was cleared and Rónán turned to Fergal. 'I hope that belly hasn't slowed you down.'

'I wear it like armour,' the older man said with a bellowing laughter, and they charged the field for the renewed battle.

When Rónán finished his walk among the men that evening, he returned to his tent and his council gathered. Fergal bowed to him when he entered, and said, 'If you have no good wine, I may defect to the foreigners.'

'You know me well enough; there is always good wine.'

Fergal and Fionn embraced, and Rónán introduced Cormac to the big man. Fergal slapped him on the back, and they sat.

Seanach said, 'Did you pass any other armies on your march south?'

'No, but others will come. How do the foreigners fight?'

'Same as before,' Rónán said. 'With a unity hard to find among our armies, and with ferocious disregard for their own lives.'

'Two years of slavery will have driven them insane. They may fight for Rían's cause, but they must have ranks among them. Can we tell who leads them?'

'It seems each man leads himself. No one commands them on the field. The occasional order is given, but not enough to suggest a leader.'

'Have you taken out their horn blowers yet?'

'Their carnyx boy is a lad no bigger than a fawn,' Seanach said. 'He does not fight.'

'The horn blower wields every single sword on the field. He calls them to battle and signals them to retreat. Kill the music and they will tire. Without their champion's cry, they will not know when to cease.'

'And when they replace the boy with another?' Rónán asked.

'Have you ever tried holding a carnyx aloft and blowing it? It is not so easy. Some might make it sputter, but their men would have no idea what the sound should signal. Do we push forward? Do we drive left? Whatever unity they have will be lost.'

'And if a man does command them, he will reveal himself and will be ripe for slaughter,' Rónán said. 'I knew there was a reason I liked you.'

'You do not get to my age without picking up a few tricks.' Fergal drained his cup and poured another. 'King Rían—is he really not among the foreigners?'

'No one has seen him yet,' Cormac said. 'If he is there, he hides.'

'Or he has already been slaughtered by the Fir Bolg,' Fionn said. 'They will not fight for him indefinitely. When they tire of him, he will end up at the bottom of a ditch with his head on a spike. The foreigners may not care about the position of high king, but they know we do; they will take the kingseat at Teamhair from Rían and aim to rule in his stead.'

Fergal said, 'While they're slaughtering their king, how can we convince them to turn on each other?' To Rónán, he said, 'Where is that beautiful druid of yours?'

'She was with her kin when all this began. I can only imagine she journeys south to meet us.'

They concluded their discussions, and before Fergal left the tent, he said, 'If my men can forge a path through their ranks, are your bow skills still sharp enough to get a shot off at their horn blower?'

'Get me close enough and I will have two arrows in him before he hits the ground.' When he was alone, he used the tip of his dagger to clean his nails, and he waited for the darkness to bring Cormac back to his side.

When he came, they did not fall straight to bed. They played a game of fidhcheall by the light of four tallow candles that burned around the edges of the tent, moving the small stone pieces over the board with deliberate precision, and as they played, they talked.

They did not say much of importance, but Rónán had long since known that it is the words unspoken that offer the greatest insights. Both Áed, before his passing, and his druid-sister, thereafter, had taught him to see stories in the things unsaid. A man does not always speak his mind, but his silences do.

When they blew out the candles and settled under deer furs, their silent exploration spoke loudly of longing. And when morning came, neither was satiated.

He met with Fergal, Seanach, Fionn and Cormac before the carnyx horns were sounded, and they discussed their plan. Fergal's men would form a wedge through the masses of Fir Bolg ranks, creating a gap for Rónán and his warriors to cut through and eliminate the enemy's horn blower. 'And while you're there,' Fergal said, 'find that bastard, Rían, and put an arrow in each eye and one up his arse.'

They filed out. When the enemy charged the field, Fergal and his men cut forward as though it had been any other day of battle. With an imperceptible swiftness, they grouped together, fanned their shields, and butted their way into the horde.

Rónán's sword was sheathed and he carried his bow in his hand, a small quiver of arrows at his hip. Around him, Fionn, Cormac, Seanach and six other men would protect him if any of the Fir Bolg broke through Fergal's ranks.

Fergal led his men from a centre point to a wide arc, pushing the foreigners back, swiping and hacking at them in a tight formation. This was a new tactic and the Fir Bolg knew it. Those who were not engaged moved towards the line of warriors who tore through their flank.

'Steady, men,' Fergal shouted. 'Push harder!'

Rónán ran, his guards surrounding him. When two men

ploughed through Fergal's wall, Cormac and the others cut them down hard.

'Keep moving,' Rónán shouted.

He could hear Fergal screaming from the fore as though the thrill was greater than the reward.

They moved closer through the ranks.

At length, his boots slick with mud, Rónán could see the carnyx lad. He could have been no older than fifteen winters, a local boy from Rían's own tribe. He nocked an arrow.

'Break!' Fergal shouted, and his one hundred warriors, fifty on either side, pushed apart. Cormac hunkered and put his hand on Rónán's back to steady him and offer protection when the swarm of Fir Bolg would crush upon them, and the other men raised their shields and swung their swords.

Rónán raised his bow and drew the string. When the sea parted before him, he took his shot. The arrow pierced the boy's throat and he was thrust off his feet.

'Regroup,' Fergal shouted. 'Fall back!'

Rónán looked for signs of Rían but saw none. Fergal's wall of warriors pulled back, but they were no longer in formation. The line was broken and the Fir Bolg fought against them.

'Lord,' Cormac said, swinging at the nearest enemy.

Rónán threw his bow over his shoulder, hooking the string under the quiver at his side to keep it in place, and unsheathed his sword.

'I'm good. Fight on.'

Cormac left his side.

Rónán hacked the arm from his nearest rival and blocked another with his shield that, even when using his bow, had been attached to his left arm. He thrust under the shield and cut through the man's leg.

He took a step back, slipped in the mud, swung his sword, and rolled as he lost his balance. A javelin sailed over his head and struck a mark behind him. Rónán could hear the deep exhale from one of his men as the javelin hit him.

He turned.

And he cried aloud.

Fionn lay on the ground, the javelin rod protruding from his chest.

Rónán pushed through the men to his tanist. 'Fergal,' he shouted. 'Cormac!'

With his shield raised in defence, Rónán knelt at Fionn's side. His friend coughed and spat thick blood that coated his chin and the braids of his moustache. He tried to speak, but Rónán hushed him.

When Cormac and Fergal came to his side, Rónán said, 'Help me carry him back to camp.'

'Don't pull the spear,' Fergal said. 'You'll release the wound and he'll bleed out before we get there.'

Rónán and Fergal picked him up while Cormac fought off the enemy around them. His body peeled away from the muddy ground and, beneath him, a pool of blood collected like rainwater on a bog. The javelin had cut straight through him.

Holding him under the knees by one arm, Fergal gripped the javelin to keep it from moving, and Rónán hitched him under the armpits. When they made it back to camp, Cormac dropped his sword at his side and turned to attend them.

'We need to patch him up,' Rónán said.

Fergal put a hand on his shoulder. 'We need a druid.'

Fionn coughed.

'Stay with me, Fionn.'

Fionn's eyes locked on Rónán's, the whites visible around the irises, and his mouth gaped but he could not draw a breath. His nostrils flared.

When his eyes left Rónán's face and wandered across the skyline, Rónán came to his knees. 'Stay with me, damn it. Fionn, don't you leave me.'

'Rónán,' Cormac said.

'He's fine. He will survive this. Why do we not have a damn druid?'

Fionn's hand groped in the earth at his side and he gripped Rónán's tunic. 'Orlaith,' he said, guttural, slow, forming the syllables with care.

But he said no more.

His chest stopped rising, and his eyes stared up as though questioning the tip of the javelin.

He was gone.

Rónán turned from him, his sword in his hand, and without a word, he ran back to the field.

His focus shifted from one Fir Bolg warrior to the next as he cut them down. Each one was responsible for Fionn's death, and each one would suffer. His sword was a blur in his hand, tearing through the enemy as though the *sidhe* rode his back. Where before he slew one man, now he took two.

War and all the scourge it brings—it would end here.

Chapter 43

When the northern army formed a wall of shields and flanked through their eastern ranks, Bromaid did not know what advantage they would gain. They did not appear to be circling them.

With Rían not yet returned to war, Bromaid shouted to his men to push back against the wall. He jumped over fallen comrades, slicing through the gut of an enemy warrior, and attacked the wall with his men. If they sought to box them in, they would be disappointed.

When one of the northern men shouted for the wall to break, Bromaid was unsure which target they sought.

And then their horn blower fell.

He understood—the enemy wanted confusion. Without the horn blower sounding his calls, the Fir Bolg army would have shorter reaction times if the tides changed.

Bromaid saw the Ó Mordha king amid the wall of men, the one who had shot the horn boy. Yesterday, the man entered the battlefield wearing a king's circlet on his head as though he challenged anyone to his side.

There were too many men between Bromaid and the northern king. He sheathed his sword, picked up a javelin that was wedged in the muddy earth, and he took aim, swinging his arm high overhead, releasing the javelin, and following through. But the Ó Mordha king had ducked or fallen. The javelin missed and hit another man. It was the man who killed Eolid in single combat on their first day on the plateau.

Bromaid was not disappointed. Rónán Ó Mordha would die at his hand. It was just a matter of time.

The wall of northern men broke and attempted to retreat, but the Fir Bolg army was strong. Bromaid lost sight of the overking while he was dragging the man's body away, and the rest of his day had been spent slaughtering man after man.

He spotted the king soon after, the one they called the Bare-Arsed Warrior, blurring through the field, cutting through any man who dared to stand before him, but again he was too far from Bromaid's position.

Rónán Ó Mordha was the last man fighting that day, even after the northern carnyx blower had sounded the day's end. Bromaid watched as the Ó Mordha king was dragged from the field by his own men, calling an end to his one-man war. The self-elected Fir Bolg leader was pleased that he had incensed the king so much. Whoever the blond man was, he had been important to the overking. Brother, friend; it did not matter.

It was a good day.

When the dead were brought in from the field, Bromaid's side had suffered many losses from the overking's zeal. They did not have the space to set a pyre for each man, and so the bodies of the dead were stacked together, the druid offered his prayers and his songs, and they were lit as one, an army of the dead travelling together to their gods.

As the stars hid from view by the smoke that rose to touch

them, Bromaid met with Rían's druid and several of the men who were respected among the others. 'If Rían has been wounded in the east, we will need a new tactic.'

The druid stood. 'Our strategy remains the same—take back these lands, slaughter every native we see, and give thanks to the gods that we have a home. Rían will return to us soon.'

One of the men said, 'You speak of slaughtering natives, and yet you defend one as your master.'

'Rían is the master of us all. Without him, none of us would be free, toiling away in fields and eating the scraps of food that even dogs leave behind.'

The man stood to face him. 'I have no master; I am slave to no one.'

'Enough,' Bromaid said. 'You are both correct—without Rían, we would still be enslaved. But I will not bow to another man, Fir Bolg or not. We do not need a leader. What we need is a commander, someone who will coordinate our battles. And when we are done and no native man is left alive, let each among us find a stake of land and grow in his independence. We will send great ships to our homeland for our women, and we can prosper here. Gorid, you defend the honour of the man who freed you, as is your right. But if it comes to it, whose side will you choose? You are Fir Bolg, like us. Where does your destiny lie?'

Gorid looked at him and then at the men who had gathered to listen. 'I align myself with the gods.'

'Our gods or theirs?'

'Ours, of course. We take the lands that were promised to us, and we live in peace at last.'

'And when Rían returns?' one of the men asked.

'He is not a native man,' Bromaid said. 'We shall leave no native man alive.'

He hunkered down and the men drew closer as they discussed a plan. He had not expected the druid to betray the man who set him free, but as he pointed out, they were Fir Bolg. And native men were not.

That night, twenty men were placed on watch around the perimeter of their camp, and a further twenty men unsheathed their daggers, crouched low, and moved from one sleeping native to another. Since Bromaid's release from captivity at Clonycavan, Rían's kinsmen had no desire to spend their downtime with the Fir Bolg. They would group together at mealtimes and at night when they slept. They might fight alongside one another, but there was no trust between them. Bromaid's plan to slit their throats—because no native man deserved to rule them—had filtered through the ranks of his kin throughout dusk, and when the moon was shrouded in thick clouds and the night was at its darkest, those twenty men he trusted most crept through the camp.

Bromaid entered a tent, crouched, and in one movement he covered the sleeping man's mouth and forced the small blade into his throat.

When only one of Rían's clansmen were left, Bromaid woke him with a slap in the face, and held the dagger to his throat. 'You can scream if you want. Your kin are dead.'

Bromaid took him by the hair and dragged him through the camp. He let the man fall at Gorid's feet.

'The last of Rían's kin,' he said, holding his dagger out, hilt-first, so that the druid could take it. 'Sacrifice him so that we know the gods are pleased with us.'

'You test my loyalties against the Ard Rí.'

'That you still call him Ard Rí gives me reason to test you.'

Gorid took the dagger and made sacrifice of the last native man to stand among them. His screams were pitiful. When he cut the heart from the man's chest and buried it in the earth, he turned back to Bromaid, blood on his beard, and said, 'It is done. I stand with my own. When Rían returns, we must be swift, or he will have his revenge.'

The Fir Bolg men cheered and celebrated with wines and beer. They would kneel for no man.

'We are each capable of great things,' Bromaid shouted so that all would hear him. 'In the morning, we will slaughter the northern armies and take their lands. This nation is ours and none of our kin will ever suffer another pain.'

He had instilled himself as commander without provocation. When Éirinn was devoid of its native inhabitants, his men would have no need for a king. Let them live lawless, and the gods would see that they were great.

He sat with Gorid and his closest kin, and they passed a wineskin among them. And when the dawn came, the usurping Ard Rí arrived with it.

He rode from the edge of the forest behind them and up the hillside to their camp. The hundred men he took with him into the east were also riding huge horses of the finest stock, and behind them came sixty-six freed slaves. They were hungry and dirty, and their beards were long, but they were sixty-six warriors ready to join a cause.

King Rían dismounted, patted the horse's neck, and looked at the men who gathered for his arrival. He did not register that each of those faces who looked upon him were Fir Bolg. Only when Bromaid stepped forward with his sword drawn, did his eyes dart from one face to another.

'What is the meaning of this?'

Bromaid said, 'Your services are no longer required. We are taking back what is ours.'

When Gorid came to Bromaid's side, Rían said, 'You, too?'

Gorid drew his sword. 'For my freedom, I am grateful to you. But my kinsmen and I came here two years ago for a reason, and we are going to finish it.'

Those of Rían's tribe that had joined him in the east were taken from their horses and slaughtered without ceremony.

Rían was trussed up in chains. 'You do not kill me like the others?' he asked, his tongue laden with menace.

'Not yet,' was all that Bromaid said.

Chapter 44

'What are they doing?' Cormac asked.

Through the night, Rónán sat in mournful vigil at Fionn's side. As tanist, he would not be cremated with the other men. Rónán insisted that he would be wrapped in a shroud and carried home to his wife, to the hillsides on which he grew. He would be buried there with great ceremony.

As the dawn sky brightened and the smoke from the fires of the night dissipated, the northern armies gathered on the edge of the field for another day of ceaseless war, but the Fir Bolg army did not rise to meet them at the appointed time.

'If they mean to surrender,' Rónán said, securing his sword belt at his hip, 'they should hurry up about it.'

Cormac touched Rónán's shoulder and the overking tried not to react under his fingers.

'Are you well?'

Rónán nodded. 'I will be glad when the smell of death no longer lingers at my nose.' He could scarcely recall the day's slaughter yesterday. When Fionn fell, Rónán knew that he had helped carry his tanist from the battlefield, but then a darkness descended over his mood and——though he knew he returned to the field and fought——he did not remember for how long or in what condition he had been when the day was done. Cormac later told him that he and Fergal had to manhandle him from the field when he refused to quit fighting.

'You almost took a swing at me, in the darkness,' Cormac said.

Rónán was quick to sleep that night, and now that the early morning sun broke the haze of high clouds, he stared across the field for signs of the enemy.

Fergal approached with some cured meat and a cup of water. 'Perhaps our plan to take out their horn blower means they sleep still. We should wake them.'

'Wait,' Seanach said from the far side of Rónán's carbad. 'Look.'

Across the open field that was churned and sticky from days of war, a line of Fir Bolg men came forward, one behind the other.

'What do they carry?' Rónán asked.

In each of their hands was a round parcel, but with the sun low in the sky and shadows stretching into the grasses, Rónán could not tell what they held.

'Boulders?' Fergal asked.

As one, the combined northern armies unsheathed their swords.

'Stand your ground,' Rónán called. The Fir Bolg men who approached were not walking as though to battle.

They came in single file and when the first man reached the centre of the field, he stepped aside until all the men were lined shoulder to shoulder. On command, they raised their arms and threw what they were holding. They did not come so close as to touch the northern armies, but Rónán and the men could see they were heads.

Rónán took a step forward.

In the field, the line of Fir Bolg men parted, and a warrior stepped in, leading a large native man on a chain whose face was bloodied and bruised. Clumps of his hair were pulled from his head so that his sweating pate shone through in patches.

Cormac came to Rónán's side. 'It's Rían.'

The Fir Bolg warrior who gripped his chain shouted, 'I am Bromaid, son of Gamid, son of Terrid. I present to you your Ard Rí.' He kicked Rían's leg and forced him to kneel in the dirt.

Seanach said, 'Can you get an arrow to him from here?'

Rónán raised his hand for silence. 'He's still too far.'

'I could reach him,' Cormac said.

'We wait.'

Bromaid shouted again. 'We have been enslaved for too long. Your high king thought that he was freeing us from our tormentors, but in truth he imprisoned us to his own will and for his own gain. We have no need of your titles and status. We are free men and we will remain as free men. The north will fall before us just as the south did. We do not seek a truce. Keep your treaties and accords. We will not take slaves or hostages. You should kill yourselves with your own blades, for if you do not, we will end your miserable lives today.'

He whispered something to Rían, close to his ear, and then he released the chain at his neck.

'Run,' Bromaid said. 'Run to your people. They cannot protect you.'

When Rían remained on his knees, Bromaid kicked him in the back, forcing him to the ground.

375

'Get up and run to the kings you sought to overthrow. Pray that they kill you before we do.'

Rían, muddied and weak, pushed himself from the ground and took a tentative step forward.

'We should kill him before he reaches us,' Fergal said.

Rónán watched as Rían took another step, his eyes darting from one army to the other.

He ran, stumbling in the greasy mud, his wrists still bound but otherwise unhindered, the chain of his neck trailing in the earth behind him.

'Run!' Bromaid shouted. And then he stepped forward, stamped his foot on the dragging chain, and Rían choked at the end of it. He fell to his back in the mud.

Bromaid flipped his sword and thrust it into the Ard Rí's chest. When he pulled it free, blood swept into the air above him.

Bromaid screamed a guttural war cry and the rest of his men who had remained in their camp charged the field, many of them riding atop the horses that Rían had brought to their camp before dawn.

Rónán drew his sword and their armies ran to join the battle.

The Ard Rí's body lay face up among the damp earth as men fought around him. When a king falls, the mourning can be heard for days. But for Rían, his life and deeds were forgotten when his blood ran from him. He had no legacy, no heir that he knew of, and his short time as high king would be overlooked in the annals of time. He who loses is never remembered; the bards sing no songs of forgotten men.

The Fir Bolg's fighting style had changed. Each man pushed forward as hard as he could. He did not care about lines, about ranks, or about how far he stood from his kin. They came with a ferocious spirit, and Rónán knew that to defeat them, they would have to work as a single unit, they would have to close ranks, or they were sure to lose.

Rónán signalled his carnyx blower and when the boy sounded his long notes, the northern armies pulled together.

Fergal, damp with Fir Bolg blood, shouted, 'My men to the left. Seanach, go right. We need to get behind them and box them in.'

Rónán said, 'My men will contain the forward lines and fan out as you gather around them.'

He swung his sword, took a blow to his shield, and then backed up, looking for his men. He made another hand motion to his carnyx boy. The men spread out, forming a line. They were trained for this. They knew what they were doing so long as they remembered the formation.

Rónán stomped forward with his shield raised. He butted against one of the Fir Bolg men who was able to thrust his sword under the block. Rónán rounded his sword over the shields and took the man's shoulder, but his leg was cut. He could feel the blood dripping from his shin.

He pushed harder, swiped again, and the man fell.

The cut was not deep, and it would clot, if only he would stop moving. But he had no time to stand motionless.

The Fir Bolg, recognising the northern armies' plan, formed their own wall against the encompassing attack. They stretched out hard in both directions to stop the northerners from ringing them like sheep.

A hail of slingshots tore down from Fergal's men, and on the right, Seanach was shouting commands to his warriors.

'Drive!' Rónán shouted. His men flipped their shields forward and pushed against the enemy, wall against wall. Feet churned in the mud and the man beside Rónán fell when he slipped. The Fir Bolg man before him thrust down with his sword into the back of the man's head.

Rónán bore his blade deep into the enemy's stomach and then moved to close the gap.

'Drive!' he shouted again.

The men pushed into the wall.

But the Fir Bolg pressed back. In spots around the arc, first one man, then two, broke through the line and turned to kill their opposition. Soon, the line was broken into pieces. They had failed to encircle them.

When the wall broke, Rónán flicked his blade across one man's face, and turned to swipe at another.

Across from him, Cormac pierced one of the foreigners and used the dying man as a buffer when he pushed forward to attack further.

Rónán raised his shield as a shower of slingshot rained on him, pocking the wood of his defence, and cracking the edge of it.

They were driven back, inch by precious inch. Their camp was not far behind them and if the foreigners could get close enough, they would burn it from a distance, or push harder to sack it and broach their lines.

Bromaid, the man who addressed them on the battlefield and killed King Rían as he fled from him, had spoken true—the Fir Bolg were not intent on taking prisoners or slaves. They would kill them all.

Rónán's carnyx player blew his horn, a long tone followed

by a two short blasts. It was not a champion's call; nor was it signalling the end of day. Rónán fought off one of the enemy and then scanned the distance. The boy lowered the long horn with its boar-shaped head and pointed.

On the horizon, an army force crested the hill, and when they saw the fighting, they charged towards it.

'Cormac,' Rónán shouted. Panting, out of breath, soaked in other men's blood, Rónán pointed and when Cormac smiled, he cut the head from his closest enemy.

'Fergal,' Cormac called, closer to the king than Rónán. 'Did you request back up?'

Swinging his sword, Fergal ducked under an attack and then impaled his rival. 'Did I not tell you they would come? I will spend six nights in prayer if they help us end this today.'

'Where is Seanach?' Rónán shouted. He could not see the chieftain among the throng of warring men.

The arriving army came down the hillside and charged onto the field. When one of the men was close enough to him, Rónán said, 'Whose men are you?'

'Ó Neill's, my lord,' the man said, his clothes fresh and free from blood, his sword gleaming, unsullied by foreign stains. He gave an overhanded swing and cleaved a Fir Bolg warrior's arm at the elbow. 'Your druid lady rides with us.'

Rónán blocked an attack and fought on. If Grainne was here, all was saved.

The afternoon advanced, and Rónán's limbs tired. When he found himself with some respite, the dead strewn at his feet, he backed out of the fray to join those men who returned to camp for a cup of water before forging back into war. No man could sustain a fight for the whole day, and regular breaks were necessary when the opportunity arose, as seldom as they came.

Grainne greeted him with a warm hug and filled a cup for him.

Rónán drank and asked for another. 'The gods bring you just in time. We can win this with Ó Neill's help.'

'The Ard Rí?' Grainne asked.

'Dead. The foreigners killed him as a spectacle.'

Gallen came to Grainne's side. He was taller in the few short weeks since Rónán had seen him.

'Give me a sword, Lord. I can fight.'

'Gallen, no,' Grainne said. 'We are healers.'

'Let me be a warrior now and a healer later.'

Rónán looked back onto the field. With the increase in strength from the Ó Neill army, he knew the fight was almost over.

'Change out of your robes, lad. Take a sword from the growing collection; too many men have perished.' To Grainne, he said, 'Let the boy fight. I will watch him.'

'Get back out there and win this, Lord. All the gods are at your back.'

Rónán embraced her and then took her hand, his face ashen. 'Fionn has fallen. I have not cremated him. We will carry him home.'

Grainne lowered her head and Rónán saw her lips move in silent prayer.

'Orlaith should see him one last time. And he should be buried with our heroes.'

'He is already on his way to Tír na nÓg,' she said. 'I will sit with him while you fight.'

'It is good you are here. We have been in desperate need of a

380

druid.'

He ran back onto the field, passing the young druid boy on his way. He slapped him on the back. 'Come, boy. Let's see what you're made of.'

Chapter 45

The blood on his shin had dried. The muscle ached but not with extreme pain. As he returned to the fight, Rónán saw the Ó Neill chieftain rolling across the field in a carbad and circling to the left, throwing spears into the clash of men.

Rónán swung, looked for Cormac among his warriors, and swung again.

He did not see him. Every man in the field was covered in blood and only their backs and sections of their faces were visible among the blackening redness. Rónán blocked and riposted.

Fergal was unmistakable among the warriors, as broad as he was tall, laughing as he tore through the gut of an enemy warrior; and Seanach, gangly and thin, was recognisable in the distance.

Rónán tumbled when a Fir Bolg fighter barrelled into him, and as he slid in the slick mud, he twisted onto his back, brought his foot up, and kicked the man in the knee. He heard the crunch of bone. Rónán raised his sword as the man fell on him.

When he dug himself out from beneath the dead man and retrieved his sword, blood arcing from the Fir Bolg's body as he tore it free, he searched again for Cormac. His panic abated when he spotted him to the right, tackling one of the taller enemies.

He fought on, searching through the foreigners for the one who called himself Bromaid. The Fir Bolg were outnumbered for the first time since the battle began, and it was evident to them as they sought to group together for protection.

Rónán took a breath and raised his shield to block another blow. He was no longer planning calculated strikes. He did not know the names or the faces of the foreigners that he slaughtered, nor did he care. He forged a path through the field, attacking one Fir Bolg warrior after another, sustaining few injuries and dealing many blows.

When he slipped in the mud, he raised his shield arm with instinct, and as he did, he saw Fergal fall. He did not see what hit him, but the man dropped, limbs splaying as he fell, and he lay unmoving in the bloodied earth.

Rónán roared. He struggled to his feet in the mud and slipped a second time. A sword came down on him and he managed to block it, but he tumbled backwards over the body of a fallen warrior. His fingers squelched through the pulp of the body as he found purchase in the claggy ground. He needed to get out of the mud. He had to drive the enemy back to the edge of the field, to the cliff face above the forest.

He bellowed from deep within his chest and he forced himself to his feet. He butted his heel against the body behind him and used it to wedge himself in place as another attacker came to him. He sidestepped and whipped his shield out to knock the man off balance. When the enemy tumbled to the ground, Rónán flipped his sword and thrust it into the man's back.

He looked for Fergal's body and saw that three of his men had lifted him. He was pleased to see they carried him back towards the camp where Grainne was treating the wounded, and not towards the dead.

Rónán picked up a discarded javelin and hurled it through the air, tearing the side of a man's face from his head. Cormac was fighting strong. And fewer of the Fir Bolg enemy were standing.

When he caught a glimpse of Bromaid, he barrelled towards him.

Bromaid saw him, too, and he jumped over his fallen companions to come towards the overking.

When they clashed, their shield bosses vibrated together. Rónán cut in with his sword and Bromaid rebuffed it.

'I will have your head,' Bromaid said, through gritted teeth.

Their shields butted again. Rónán's feet slid backwards in the sodden earth with the force. Off balance, he raised a leg and pushed forward.

Bromaid released and steadied himself. When he lashed out, Rónán swung to block, but he had not risen his arm enough and Bromaid's sword glanced off Rónán's blade, causing it to twist from his hand and tumble to the ground.

Bromaid took the opportunity and pounced.

Rónán's shield felt the brunt of the attack and he pushed back against him. When Bromaid stumbled, Rónán went to his knees, his eyes on the warrior, and he searched the ground with a hand for his sword.

He did not find it.

Bromaid twisted his blade overhead and came down on the king. The sword shattered Rónán's shield, the wood tearing from his arm, and he rolled aside. He found his sword, scrabbled to grip the hilt, and as he came up, he blocked a renewed effort from the foreigner.

He found his feet, feigned a swipe with his sword, and as Bromaid raised his shield to block it, Rónán gripped the edge of the wood, twisted, and broke the man's arm.

Bromaid fell to his knees but as Rónán swung for his neck, he rolled under the attack and came up headfirst into the king's stomach.

They tumbled together.

When they stopped rolling, both men were without their swords, Rónán's shield was shattered, and Bromaid's shield-arm was useless. But he punched Rónán's face with his free hand. Rónán tried to claw back through the mud to stand, but Bromaid pinned him down. He punched him again, gripped his hair and knocked his head into the spraying mud. Rónán took a fistful of the dirt and thrust it into Bromaid's face.

His fingers locked around Bromaid's broken forearm and he twisted. The foreigner cried out in pain, but he punched the king until Rónán's fingers released him.

Rónán's face was bloodied, his left eye swollen and his nose broken. He felt his limbs pinned to the mud as though he were growing roots.

Bromaid knelt back, reached for his sword, shrugged his shield off. He tried to lift his broken arm to two-hand the hilt, but he could not. Spitting in the earth, he forced himself to his feet, using the point of the sword in the ground for support. Rónán could not move. His face was a mess, his left eye closed, his right one barely open. His fingers twitched in the dirt. He was being sucked into the earth to be swallowed and forgotten.

Standing over him, Bromaid raised the sword and brought it down on the king.

A shadow swooped over him. Rónán sensed the man disappear from above him but he was unable to raise his head. He felt as though all the blood from the field had thickened underneath him and pinned him in place.

He could see the sun, high in the sky, tearing through a dark cloud that brightened only at its edges.

He swallowed and forced his head from the mud. Bromaid was on the ground, Gallen kneeling over him. He was without a sword, but he held a shield between his hands, and he brought it down upon the foreigner's face.

Rónán coughed and spat blood in the dirt. He rolled to his side, eased himself to an elbow, and then got to his knees. He groped blindly for a sword among the mud, and he stood.

He stumbled forward.

Gallen thrust the shield's edge down upon Bromaid's face and Rónán could hear a crack.

Rónán gripped his shoulder. 'Enough,' he said.

The boy did not listen. He raised the shield again and Rónán caught it in his hand, stopping its descent.

'Enough.'

The boy looked up at him, his face caked in blood, his eyes wide and wild. His lips moved, but no sound came. Rónán tore the shield from the boy's hands.

'Easy,' he said.

When the boy stood, Rónán looked down at Bromaid. Though his face was a bloodied pulp, one eye roved with maddening jerks, a white speck among the gore. He coughed and blood gurgled in his throat.

Rónán put his hand on the boy's shoulder, using him for support, and he raised his sword, crunching it into Bromaid's chest with force.

Cormac was quick to the king's side, taking his arm. 'You need tended to, Lord.'

'We must fight on.'

'We have them. There are few of them left.'

Rónán did not have the strength to lift his head and see the carnage across the field. He let Cormac and the boy limp him towards the camp.

The fighting did not stop with nightfall. Torches were lit and the field shone yellow and red. The final Fir Bolg warriors, Rían's druid among them, did not kneel and beg for mercy when they knew they were outnumbered. They threw themselves into the fight, knowing it was their last moments, calling out the names of their gods as they fell.

When the moon had tracked across the sky and the horizon brightened in the east, the Fir Bolg army was dead, a thousand bodies littering the ground.

And Rónán's men were too tired to cheer.

Chapter 46

The sky was black, not just from the billowing smoke that fogged the air above them, but from the birds that circled over the field in hunger, screeching their delight into the evening darkness.

For a long time, Rónán lay on a pallet bed in a haze of herbal fumes as Grainne applied fresh salves to his face and arms. The wound in his leg had reopened, and the druid heated a bronze needle and threaded the skin closed. It would heal, but it would scar.

Men came and went from him, but he recalled none of them. He lay in silence, listening to the sounds of activity outside the tent and smelling the rich herbs that dried on his face. When the numb feeling in his chest subsided enough that pain crept back into his limbs, he raised himself onto one elbow and reached for the cup of water that Grainne had left for him. But he was weak, and he tumbled from the bed.

He fell asleep where he lay and was woken later, in the gathering darkness, by Cormac who knelt at his side.

Rónán looked up through his undamaged eye and said, 'I dreamt that I lost you, that the foreigners had cut you in half before my eyes.'

Cormac nudged his hands under Rónán's arms and lifted him. 'I am alive and well. You, however, should not be out of bed.'

'I needed water,' Rónán said. A coughing fit pained his chest. Cormac brought the cup to his lips. When he had drank enough, Cormac mopped his chin with the edge of his hand.

'Do you ache?'

'I ache for the dead. Fergal—does he live?'

'He does. He has lost an arm, but Grainne has tended him. He screams like a banshee—but not in pain; all he wants is wine.'

Rónán tried not to laugh. His chest sent pains throughout his body.

'Lie with me.'

'You are too sore for company.'

'I mean for you to hold me. Lie with me for a time.'

Cormac shuffled onto the small mattress beside the king and eased his hand down onto Rónán's sweat-damp chest. 'You fought well.'

'I was saved by the druid boy. Where is he?'

'Gallen tends the injured with Grainne.'

'I should thank him,' Rónán said, twisting his neck so that Cormac could slip his arm underneath his head.

Cormac kissed his brow. The blood had been cleaned from him, but his face was swollen and bruised. 'Do not think on it now, Lord. You should rest.'

In the morning, when Rónán was well enough to stand and the sting from his leg wound reminded him that he was alive, Cormac helped him out of the tent and led him to the fires of the dead that continued to smoulder.

'The smells of war have been sickening me since childhood,' Rónán said.

'They are not easy to forget.'

Rónán, with great care, knelt in the grasses and bowed his forehead to the ground before the fires. 'How many were lost?'

Cormac did not answer him. The number of the dead would sting him.

When they rose, Cormac helped him to the body of Fionn, who was laid in a tent. He had been shrouded, wrapped tight in white linens, and his sword rested upon his chest. It was not often that a king's tanist, heir to the kingseat, was dead before the king himself. He would be taken home and buried with his kin.

'My friend,' Rónán said, touching the binding at Fionn's feet.

Grainne and Gallen stood at either side of him in vigil, and during the morning, the men who had fought alongside him came and bowed before him and touched his feet.

Seanach came to pay his respects, and he bowed to Rónán. 'I am sorry for your losses, my lord.'

'And I yours.' They clasped arms. 'I would know the names of each of the fallen when our clans are back in order.'

Seanach bowed and left.

A stool was brought for the king and he sat by the head of his departed friend.

'You should rest,' Grainne told him.

'He has seen me through many lonely times. I will see him through his last.'

As the sun journeyed across the sky, lighting Fionn's way towards the Otherworld, Rónán bowed his head and stilled his breathing. Since the loss of Áed during the Great Invasion, Fionn was his one constant, a friend in a time of immense need. Rónán would remain at his side for as long as he could, and when Cormac joined him, he stood behind the king in silence.

When Fergal entered the tent, his left arm missing from the elbow, a blackened bandage wrapped around the stub of the limb, Rónán rose to greet him.

'I would hug you,' Fergal said, 'but I seem to have misplaced an arm.'

'Are you in pain?'

'I am full of wine, Lord. It will hurt more tomorrow.' He turned and bowed to Fionn, touching his feet with reverence. He said, 'The kings, chieftains and their councils meet, Lord.'

'Where is Cormac?'

'I am here,' Cormac said, from the shadows at the rear of the tent.

Fergal led them to the gathering of chieftains. Rónán stood before each of them and thanked them for their efforts in the war, and he offered his comforts in a time of loss. 'I would give my life to have our men return.'

They settled in a circle on stools or stumps of wood and wine was brought to them. With Grainne at his side, Rónán felt the peace of her presence, but he could not shake the grief from his mind.

Torin Ó Neill said, 'Other clans will have Fir Bolg slaves.'

'Can we issue a kill order?' Seanach asked.

Fergal nursed his shorn arm, easing a pain in his shoulder. 'Who would listen? What is more important is the need for a new Ard Rí, someone who can unite us all against any threat.'

Seanach said, 'I would bow to Rónán as high king.'

'No.'

'As would I,' Torin said.

Rónán shook his head. 'I cannot.'

'My lord,' Fergal said. 'You are overking of the north. You have more clout than any of us.'

'As overking, I offer you the role.'

Fergal raised his stump. 'I am blemished and no longer fit to govern. I have handed Knockdhu over to my tanist.' The man, who stood outside the circle, bowed to the overking.

'Rónán,' Seanach said. 'You continue to unite the northern clans. Extend your reach and you can unite the whole land if you try.'

'I scarcely have a mind to lead the Ó Mordha. I do not have the will to rule a nation.' He paused, breathed, and said, 'There are other kings or chieftains. We are too few to make such a decision. All the kings of Éirinn should be gathered.'

Torin said, 'We have no way of knowing how many kings remain in the south.'

'Then we should employ runners to check. No tribe should be left out of the decision-making.' Rónán stood. 'High King Cillian—he had sons, am I right?'

'Four,' Fergal said.

'If they have not been slaughtered, award his eldest the kingseat in the interim. When the kings gather, only then should a new Ard Rí be chosen.'

He bowed to them and returned to Fionn's side.

When the field had been cleared of the Fir Bolg warriors and all the dead were burned and their ashes buried in unmarked pits, the kings gathered their remaining men and prayers were said by Grainne and her acolyte.

Cormac mounted the carbad beside his king and touched his shoulder. 'We go home, at last.'

Rónán whipped the reins. 'There is something I must do, first.'

When he entered the gates of the Ó Nallon settlement, Emer rushed to his side. She wept even before he spoke.

'I am sorry, my lady.'

She stilled herself and nodded. 'We saw the fires burning just south of us. I knew that my husband had already journeyed west to the Otherworld. I am grateful for your kindness in returning to inform me.'

'I wish I had better news, my lady.'

'Tell me the war is done, that my husband's death was not without merit.'

'It is over,' Rónán said.

Emer nodded. 'The pup—he is well?'

'The hound is in the care of a druid boy as we journey home. He is well. I would repay you in some way if I can.'

'You cannot. You have brought me most grievous news and I will mourn my husband for all the days of my life. But I am in your debt. It is all the clans of Éirinn who should repay you.'

'I did not do it alone, my lady. There are far greater warriors than I.' He offered his hand to her. 'You are always welcome in my lands. May we finally see peace for years uncountable.'

She did not take his hand, but instead embraced him. And when the gate was closed behind him and he returned to the road, he could hear the widow sobbing in her grief.

He offered Cormac the reins of the carbad. 'Home,' he said. 'I have not yet finished giving dire news to widows.'

Chapter 47

By the time Rónán's men marched north, they had spent twelve nights on the road. The journey was slow, as it always was after war when thoughts are thick with memories of the dead. They had stopped often along the way, watching the summer sun haul itself into its nightly mourning, hanging on the western ridges of the world in forlorn moments of worship. The wind bowed the tall grasses into sombre genuflection in their wake.

Gallen walked alongside Grainne's carbad with the young wolfhound, and Rónán heard him answering Grainne's questions as she called the names of gods to him, asking the purpose of their herbs and taproots.

In the days since leaving the valley beyond the Ó Nallon tribe, Rónán's swollen eye had subsided, and the purple bruising turned yellow and green. His nose, broken and bloodied by the Fir Bolg warrior, Bromaid, was healing and at last he could breathe through it. The stitching on his leg itched its incessant irritation, but he could walk unhindered and without limp.

Each night on the road, when his tent was erected, he lay to sleep with Cormac, but both were too tired to do more than talk. Their words were soft, languid, true meanings shrouded in inconsequential expressions. They held each other and Rónán slept in Cormac's arms. He thought of another time, of another man, in whose arms he had also slept, but he made no comparison between them. Áed was his first love, and first loves are eternally special. Cormac understood this, and in their quiet conversations, he told Rónán that a future is nothing without a past. That a man is the combination of all that he has been before. The gods knew that; man still had to learn.

When they came from among the trees at the foothills of Ailigh, Orlaith was waiting for them with her baby in her arms. From across the wide, twisted path, she waved. Behind her, Achall, young Áed and Grainne's niece ran towards the approaching army. The younger boys of Ailigh and the guards who were tasked with protecting the walls followed at the rear.

Rónán called a halt the marching army and he dismounted the carbad.

'Do you wish me to come with you?' Cormac asked.

Rónán shook his head. He stepped forward.

When Orlaith stopped running and her eyes widened, Rónán caught her as she went to her knees. He wrapped his arms around her and the baby. He did not speak.

For a long time, she wept in his arms on the side of the road.

At length, Rónán said, 'We will mourn him together, you and I.'

Orlaith touched the yellow bruising of his cheek. 'Did he die a hero?'

'The bravest.'

They mourned him for seven nights inside the walls of Ailigh. Orlaith did not leave his side and she slept by him and cried upon his shroud. On the final day of mourning, when Orlaith's tears were dried in streaks upon her cheeks, and

Rónán was certain that she could cry no more, when she sat by his covered form and stared at the fabric that shielded his face from view, unmoving, Rónán came to her and said it was time.

She did not move until he touched her arm.

A pyre was erected on the edge of the lough, in view of Áed's standing stone, and only when Orlaith was ready did Rónán allow his men to carry Fionn down to the water. She did not cry as she walked behind the procession with her child in her arms, her face frozen in grief, and tears did not fall when Cormac, her brother, embraced her and kissed her hair. She did not cry when Rónán spoke of Fionn's deeds, of the many currencies he had to offer Manandán for his passage to the Otherworld.

And when Rónán bowed to her and lifted the torch that would light Fionn's pyre, he knew that she may never cry again. He felt similar pains and knew such agonies were never forgotten.

When the flames caught, Grainne sang a song of valour, a song for the gods. She was accompanied by Gallen, and their voices rose with the smoke that flowed towards the solemn sky, the wind carrying it west in the direction of Tír na nÓg.

And when the morning came, Orlaith, Rónán, Cormac and Grainne were still sitting among the grasses, silent and waiting. Fionn's ashes were collected into a decorated pot, its lid secured in place, and he was buried at the foothills of Ailigh where he had spent his life.

In the days since their return from war, Rónán learned that Achall had banished Orlaith from his walls. That she later repented was of no concern. He entered the home in which she now resided and said, 'It was Fionn who spared your life. For his sake, I will honour that. But when Grainne decrees our divorce, you are stripped of your title. You are no longer a king's wife.'

'I have wronged you, husband. I am deserving of your punishment. But do not reprimand your son. I accept our divorce without argument; it is your right to disown me. But your child is faultless.'

'You may remain within these walls. This home is yours. But I cannot forgive your actions.'

He walked away from her and did not look back.

'Will you stay?' Rónán asked Orlaith when he visited her as she sat with her brother by Fionn's grave.

'I cannot,' she said. 'Not now.'

'Where will you go?' Cormac asked.

'Rían is dead, so I could return south. But I may go east, back towards our father's clan. Though our parents are no longer there, I miss the smells of the east.'

'I cannot convince you to stay?' Rónán asked.

Orlaith looked at the stone that marked where her husband's ashes lay. She shook her head.

In the morning, they held a naming ceremony for the baby, and all the men and boys of Ailigh queued to kiss the mother and greet the baby, calling him by his name—Fionn.

'A strong name for a strong child,' Grainne said.

Rónán and Cormac offered her gifts for her journey, and Rónán embraced her. 'Send word when you reach your destination. I will miss you.'

Grainne gave her a collection of vials and pouches, instructing her on which to use for any given situation, and then Orlaith and Cormac walked down the hillside.

From the gate, Rónán watched them. When they reached the valley below, they embraced for a long time, and words were exchanged. And then Cormac waved as Orlaith strode forward into the forest path, leading a pack horse behind her.

When he came up the hill, he joined Rónán on the walls, looking out into the immensity of the world around them.

'I fear I will never see her again.'

Rónán put his hand on the man's shoulder, but he had no words to console him; he had the same worry.

That evening, when the boys and the tired warriors had retired to bed, Rónán sat in his hall with Cormac and Grainne.

They drank in silence, each one taken to his own thoughts.

When Rónán closed his eyes, he could see the faces of the dead. Ailigh was a quiet and sombre place without them.

In time, he said, 'War tears families apart.'

Cormac nodded, staring into his cup.

Grainne said, 'War tears everyone apart.'

'But in the fullness of time, sorrow can bring people back together, yes?' said Rónán.

As he said it, there was a knock on the door of the great hall. Gallen entered, the wolfhound in his shadow, and he bowed to the king.

'My lord,' the boy said. 'You asked to see me?'

Rónán clasped the boy's arm. 'I am indebted to you for saving me on the battlefield, Gallen.'

'I saw a vision during the battle, my lord. A light shining down upon you. The light led me to you, not chance. It is the gods' will that you live, not mine.'

'I am grateful all the same,' Rónán said.

The boy sat beside Grainne.

'You are not tired?' she asked him.

'I had another dream.'

'The snowdrops?'

'No,' the boy said. 'I fear it is something yet to pass.'

Rónán sat forward on his kingseat and they listened to the boy recite his dream of death and destruction. Standing in the centre of it all, he said, was a woman, tall and with hair of flame.

A woman with darkness eating at the ground beneath her feet.

A new omen.

The *Ailigh Wars Saga* continues!

STONE SOUL

Book 3 in the *Ailigh Wars Saga*
will be released soon.

Keep up to date at
www.peterjmerrigan.co.uk

**Love it or hate it? Don't forget to leave a review
on your favourite online bookstore! Authors
appreciate it more than you know.**